Invaders

Book One

John Fitzgerald

Invaders

Book One

© 2023 John Fitzgerald

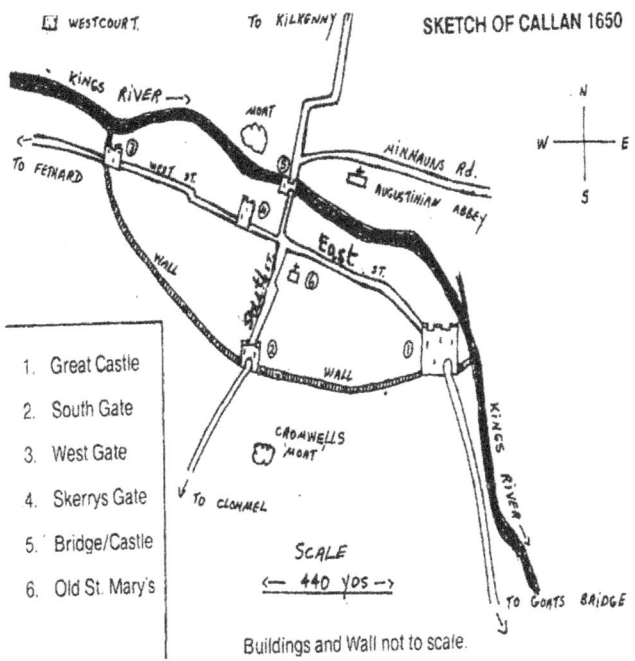

Callan, County Kilkenny: 1650

3

Prologue

Westmeath, Ireland. 1632.

"Press harder, child!"

Marianne squeezed forcefully with three fingers on the smooth sliver of iron. Father called it *the trigger*.

Her fingers began to hurt but she persisted. The trigger was attached to that bulky polished tube with its curved hand-grip. The hunk of wood and metal was so heavy she could barely hold it, let alone make it "speak", by which Father meant to cause that loud noise that hurt your ears almost as much as the trigger hurt your fingers.

He'd made the noise many times, showing her how to do it, and she'd gotten used to the loudness that at first she thought deafening. But she couldn't press the trigger hard enough to achieve the mighty bang he longed to hear.

She relaxed her fingers, got a firmer grip on the contraption, and aimed as instructed at the sack of stones propped upon a mound of straw at the rear of the barn.

She took a deep breath. If it didn't work this time she'd tell him she just couldn't do it and ask to be let play with the other girls in the village.

She'd prefer if they could have this stupid grown-ups' game outside in the sunshine but Father said Mother didn't want her "playing with guns."

"Silly Mother", he'd whispered, with a wink, because Mother was standing right behind him ironing a dress.

She shut her eyes, summoning all her strength. She could do this. After all, she'd turned seven today and a girl of seven was capable of so much more than a baby, as Father had insisted, and now she wasn't a baby anymore, even if Mother called her "a delicate child."

Groaning with the supreme painful effort of pressing the trigger her whole body quaked and, *oh... God be praised*, the iron tube spoke loudly in her hands. Even as the force of it flung her backwards into a bed of straw she was dazzled by the bluish- orange flame that spat towards that silly sack of stones.

The dusty old building lit up for a glorious moment, but her vision was then just as abruptly clouded by a fug of black-grey smoke that swirled all around her. It made her cough and it tasted

awful when some of it wafted up her
smelled like rust...or maybe rotten egg

She shook her head vigorously t mist.

Rising dizzily from the straw, she felt the iron tube being eased gently out of her grasp, and basked in the hearty compliments of her father.

"Well done. You're the best girl in County Westmeath, a warrior of Ireland." Stones were dropping out of a big gash in the sack, clinking into the straw.

Her mind adjusting quickly to his sudden change of mood, she asked "Can I go and play now, Father?"

"Of course my dear, and tomorrow we'll have more practice. I'll show you how to prepare the firearm for shooting. There's a lot to learn but you'll find it easier as you progress, and, who knows... you might even try your hand at the old matchlock."

"The other girls don't play with such things, Father."

"That's what makes you special, child. You'll be able to shoot when they're still picking flowers...or helping their mothers to bake griddle cake."

Exiting the barn, he ruffled her head of auburn hair. She beheld the purple crocuses that were beginning to wilt and the sparkling daffodils that had appeared, Marianne thought, out of nowhere in the past week to brighten and beguile. A red squirrel, spotting the two of them, bounded away in just three springy leaps.

Marianne waded into the daffodil patch. She loved the way those golden yellow trumpets swayed and quivered on their green stalks. Somehow they seemed to look brighter than earlier, but she reckoned that was only because she'd emerged from that pokey old barn where the sun never shone, with its silky lattice of cobwebs, dark shadowy straw and hen feathers.

So benign and welcoming was the flower patch that she cried out: "I love you all!" and bent to embrace a clutch of daffodils, fondly kissing one of them.

Father gave her a cold look, or she thought it cold. He laid a hand on her shoulder.

"The world might look like a grand, lovely place, child. Especially when you see those flowers...or a smiling face...or taste something you fancy...or when you see how deeply Mother cares for you. But there's evil in it too. Never forget that, child....bad people in the world, a lot of them, and you need to be a match for those."

"What kind of bad people, Father, who are they?"

"Enemies…child, people who'd deny us our freedom, or who'd dearly like to, who would rob or kill us, or steal our land, our culture, the very language we speak...if we let them."

"There are no enemies around here, Father, are there?"

He hesitated before answering. Ruffling her hair again he said merrily "You'll get to know them child, and you'll surprise them. Tomorrow, and every other day this month, I'll show you how to defend your honour and your precious life. Our enemies have weapons, but so will you, my dear, and you'll be the best little warrior in Ireland if I can help it.

"Can I get my toy now, Father and play with my friends?"

"Of course; and from that too you'll learn…something new every day. Off you go and oh…whatever you do, don't tell Mother about this. She'll be harping on about playing with guns. That'll be our secret, eh?"

She laughed and scampered to the end of the garden, the voice of Mother ringing in her ears, calling her inside. "Later, Mama, I must fetch my toy!"

She ran to where she'd left it when Father had summoned her for "weapons practice."

For a moment she feared someone might have snatched it, one of those enemies perhaps that Father spoke of.

Relieved, she saw it resting against a head of cabbage.

Marianne picked up her crossbow.

***

1

Callan, County Kilkenny, July 1649

Friar Malcolm waved at his two colleagues as they set off on their quests, their grey habits shuffling as they headed towards the exit unto Goose Lane from the abbey meadow. He envied them today, though he knew he shouldn't as envy was a sin.

Maybe it wasn't envy. He felt entitled to a little grumpiness; for a few minutes anyway, after getting up so early in the morning. He had, as he did every day, risen at midnight to recite Divine Office; then slept for a few hours before rising again at dawn for prayer and Morning Mass.

A weak sun cast wispy shadows across the gently rolling meadow. The stone casing of the Blessed Well, between the abbey and the river, glistened in a shaft of burnished gold.

The magnificent oblong abbey church itself looked especially imposing today. Glancing back at it as he prepared to open the gate into Goose Lane he fancied that it had a halo of divine radiance around it. A raven had alighted on one of the crenellations of the central tower, fluttering and shifting its head restlessly, as if uncertain of its pose. It then flapped its wings and flew off.

Malcolm closed his eyes and uttered a prayer. Not that he hadn't prayed enough already, but another invocation wouldn't go astray, this one in thanksgiving for the way of life he'd chosen. Life at the abbey had seemed unbearably tough when he entered the Order, but once he'd settled in it was as natural to him as breathing, or the passage of the seasons.

His work in the herb and vegetable gardens he found especially satisfying. Food resulted from his daily labours, and he derived sustenance of a different kind from his daily half-hour of service and reading in the library. Work and pleasure combined. There was arranging and indexing to be done, but then, time and duties permitting, an opportunity to dip into the works of Cicero, Aristotle, Horace, and those other great writers of antiquity.

They weren't Christians but they had much of interest to say about the world and man's place in it. *They had their own ways of making sense of what we're doing here.* They might be way off the mark, unaware of the true faith, but he found their cogitations captivating.

He yawned, excusing himself, forgetting that his two Brothers-in-Christ were already out of sight and earshot. Their quests would be a great deal more comfortable, less demanding, than his own, today. They'd be calling for offerings to homes inside the Town Wall: the ones with sturdy stone or wooden walls and chimneys. Some would even have gardens.

His own quest this morning took him to the less affluent homes outside the wall. Not that the people in them were less generous in their offerings. Some of them gave more than a typical Inner town resident. Instead of money they'd present a friar with freshly baked bread, a block of tobacco, or maybe offer a measure of whiskey. Whatever the offering it was gratefully accepted.

Malcolm approached the first house, a mud cabin with two small glassless windows on either side of the front door. He knocked lightly. The door squeaked open, and he almost choked from the sudden outrush of smoke.

"Sorry about that, Father. Come in", the raggedly little man greeted, coughing as he spoke, and swatting away the puffs of smoke.

Inside, Malcolm perceived three human forms, all with clay pipes in their mouths. But he couldn't see their faces in the murkiness. After a few seconds his eyes adjusted and he beheld a table laid out with cakes and loaves of bread.

The woman of the house, laying aside her pipe, lit two candles on the table. The room filled up with a dazzling luminescence, diluting the smoke like a morning mist.

The man of the house rasped: "You'll have an oaten cake Father, and there's enough tobacco to keep yerself and the good friars puffing for a week. By God ye deserve it, and all that ye do for us. My family has been going to Mass at the abbey for a hundred-and-fifty years. My grandfather was the last man to kneel down in that church in the meadow for Sunday Mass back in 1540 before that auld fucker; I mean that awful man, King Henry, closed it down. None of us has missed Mass there since it opened again and auld Henry was sent packing off to the fires of Hell."

Malcolm winced but responded graciously: "Thank you so much. However, we mustn't presume that Henry or anyone else is in

Hell. Only God in his wisdom knows the status of King Henry in the afterlife. For all we know he may have repented and gone straight to Heaven..."

The man nodded grumpily. "Anyway Father, will ya have a drink before ya leave?"

"No I must be getting along. I'll take that oaten loaf... and thanks again, Patrick."

Exiting, he fell into a fit of coughing. *God, you'd think he'd punch a hole in the roof to let the smoke out. How on earth do they endure that day and night?*

The next five homes he visited were less smoky but no less generous. He declined a donation of a half-crown from a woman who was clearly not in a position to donate. He could feel her relief when he opted instead to accept a bag of apples.

Another ten visits and he'd call it a day for this month's quest. The poor donkey would be weighed down with the people's generosity.

He felt good as he headed back to the abbey. But then his anxiety returned. That stab of trepidation he'd felt a week ago when the Prior, Fr. Kearney had prayed at Morning Mass for the safety of the Callan friars.

Ireland faced a mighty challenge from across the sea, the Prior had hinted, almost in a whisper. With God's help and providence, he prayed, they'd survive whatever the enemies of the faith were plotting.

What was he referring to? Fr. Kearney knew or suspected something, but he didn't elaborate when another friar asked him at breakfast, saying only that he awaited further news of events in England that could have dire consequences for this island.

*

From the diary and letters of Mathias Blunt, soldier of the Commonwealth

July 1649

Dear Meg,

I write this in a state of euphoria. I find it difficult to collect my thoughts. Firstly, I must apologise to you. I promised you, darling, that I'd call you to me here in London after I'd settled into my new position as bookkeeper with the sugar importing company. We would then wed, assuming that your father confirmed his decision to allow you to marry me. That's all changed, Meg. In fact, I'm scarcely the same Mathias who left you back in the village and took the long journey to the capital.

I'm not one to make rash decisions. You know how painstakingly cautious I was throughout our lengthy courtship, how scrupulous in facilitating supervision of our every meeting by people I'd prefer had been elsewhere...anywhere but prying into our love like gawkers at a cockfight.

You'll recall how aghast I was when I first met you in the midst of that riotous band of milkmaids, how I winced at their silly pranks and outlandish frivolity that tested my Puritan principles to the utmost. You'll surely agree that I took that most challenging human virtue of patience to new levels in all my dealings. My life, I believe, has been a veritable lesson in prudence and circumspection.

Here's what happened to your true love: Yesterday, the man who would have been my boss-well, I suppose he was that for a few hours- asked me to accompany him to Charing Cross to witness a special event, a "festive occasion" he called it. I didn't bother to ask him what it was, my priority being not to discommode him on my first day at the office. So I went along.

Now, you know me Meg. I said to you a thousand times, right from the day we first met in that scorching summer hayfield, that politics meant nothing to me.

My only concern was making my way in life...becoming a prosperous merchant like my uncle, and not, with due respect to him, a humble farm labourer as my poor father was, right up till his death. I didn't join either side in the Civil War; I steadfastly refused to get involved in leafleting or agitation for any of the factions. I really did think I could avoid all that ghastly and often incomprehensible politicking and militaristic nonsense.

Well, today my eyes were opened, all my senses awakened. Upon arrival at Charing Cross my head quaked. I felt the ground shake under my feet.

The air was riven by deafening roars and the blare of trumpets.Pennants and banners bedecked the streets, displaying the colours of our glorious British Commonwealth. Thousands of men, women and even the smallest of children had lined up, shuffling and jostling on the footpaths. My boss had to speak aloud to be heard above the clamour: "It's the man who's been assigned the task of sorting out the Irish rebels and routing the remnants of the Royalist opposition over there. This is the official launch of his mission."

The crowd swelled by the second. Soldiers with pikes stood to attention at spatial intervals, keeping the surging mass of humanity lining the pavements from spilling onto the streets.

I never saw so many red George's Crosses, all fluttering gaily on that July morning against an indigo sky. The streets wobbled as a cavalcade of carriages and wagons appeared to my left, churning up dust in billowing little mushroom clouds, as they trundled towards us. Deafening cheers and applause sent rooks and pigeons hurtling skyward, in frantic search of refuge from this unearthly commotion.

The lead coach drew near, pulled by six whitish-grey Flanders mares. It slowly came to a halt. Behind it rested scores of other conveyances and endless lines of horsemen. The coach stood less than ten feet from me, partly obscured by flag-wavers and a wary pikeman.

"Oliver Cromwell", the boss whispered reverently, "that's him."

A shudder of anticipation ran through me. The commander stood in his coach. It was quickly encircled by musketeers and pikemen, who he ushered away with a quiet signal. Stewards who'd fanned out along the streets in front of the onlookers called for silence.

Then, pistol and sword wielding troops quickly formed a shield around the commander. An armed cluster of brightly attired uniforms moved through the parting sea of people to my left.

I joined the frenzied rush to see and hear his address. I gazed at a high wooden rostrum, obviously prepared for the occasion, up which he ascended.

He stood alone, regally surveying the multitude.

For the first time I saw him clearly in the flesh, and not as an engraved image in a newssheet or woodcut. He was tall and straight, and physically robust; dressed in black, apart from a

11

ceremonial breastplate. His thick brown hair flowed over and around his collar. His nose was prominent and he had a slim moustache.

But it was his eyes that captivated me. The greyish green orbs flamed with passion; windows into a world beyond.

And then, Meg, this unsurpassed leader of men held up both hands, one of which held a marshal's baton. His head rotated slowly, as if he wished to draw the whole assembly to him.

His armour mirrored the rays of the sun that seemed to single him out for God's favour. Only birdsong could be heard amid the blanket of reverent silence.

When he started to speak he sounded grave, almost melancholic. He didn't strike me at all as your typical politician and even less a military man. His demeanour, despite the pomp and splendour that surrounded him, was that of a humble servant.

He introduced himself as the man whom Parliament had appointed to undertake a special mission, one upon which the future of England depended. He thanked all of us who'd turned out to see him off in his departure to the port from which he'd leave for Ireland a few weeks hence. Today marked only the symbolic launch of the great enterprise.

Then, his face brightening with zeal, his voice rose as he addressed the importance of his assignment. He recalled the great victories of Parliament over the Royalists, reciting the names of battlefields and honouring heroes who had fought for the liberties of English men and women against a corrupt monarchy. Applause greeted his words as he pronounced with solemnity places like Marston Moor, and Naseby. He called for quiet again.

The crowd changed from civic deference to sheer jubilation when he pledged vengeance for the massacre of all those defenceless Protestants in Ireland by rebels, funded and cosseted by the papists and continental enemies of England. Casting his gaze to Heaven, he called upon God to ensure that justice would be done for the thousands of women, including expectant mothers, who were forced at gunpoint into the freezing waters of the River Bann by Irish rebels in 1641.

His grip on the baton tightened. His eyes shone like two earthly suns, blazing with a divine righteousness. He appealed to all true Englishmen who valued their liberty and treasured way of life to *enlist in Parliament's army. Others had, he thundered, gone to the Holy Land in another time to vanquish the heathen. He asked us to join him in a new crusade... to crush England's Royalist enemies in Ireland and restore that land to the godly faith.*

He spoke then of how God had changed his own life, how he'd turned away from sin to follow the Puritan path, eschewing the temptations that the Devil had laid before him. He'd been born again in Christ. He was now, not just a servant of the nation, but a servant of God as he sought to protect the Commonwealth. Its enemies had risen, he thundered, from the bowels of Hell to grind England into the dust.

And, my God Meg, he looked straight at me, as if reaching out to me, mind to mind, on behalf of our imperilled settlers in Ireland, and our English homesteads to which those Irish savages might soon lay siege.

He spoke again but at this point Meg, I swear I was entranced, only half aware of my boss's presence beside me- he was gently pressing his hand on my shoulder- as I listened to the most compelling, charismatic human being that ever entered into my field of hearing or vision. Such piety; and selfless devotion to his people: Such unwavering self-assurance. This was no mere politician or common soldier. He was Heaven-sent. I'm sure of it.

Throughout my life I've weighed up situations, carefully gauging the relative merits of what I'd heard or seen, uncertain of where the truth or solution lay. But here was certainty.

From this man there was no dissimulation, no mincing of words: only strength and resolute devotion.

Gone were any notions of a safe profitable career with the sugar importing company, of sailing along blithely as if political events that rocked this nation to its foundations had nothing to do with me.

The speaker had undergone a conversion, and so had I. A thunderbolt struck me. The Lord was calling me to fight.

I queued with hundreds of other men to enlist for the Irish campaign. Had my boss not caught my arm and shaken me I fancied I would have swooned like a feeble woman, in the presence of this colossus of our age.

I disagree with my boss's comparison of this messianic Englishman to an ancient Roman emperor. A more apt contrast I think would be with Christ himself, giving the Sermon on the Mount, or performing the Miracle of the Loaves and the Fishes...for this light of our lives walks in the footsteps of the one and only Divine Lord. I'm sure of it.

I must finish writing, Meg. What a day this has been. I'm to be fitted for a uniform this evening. Soon, I'll become more than your ever-loving future husband. I'll be a soldier of England.

I'll return to you, God willing, when our mission is accomplished.

-Your adoring Mathias.

*

Mathias Blunt's diary: Late July 1649

My life has changed so much in just a week. It's as if I got caught up in a whirlwind. I can barely register how far I've come since I enlisted for the great crusade. The training camp here in Bristol has men from every conceivable background and walk of life, some volunteers like me, many others pressed into service.

That measure was necessary to ensure that the expeditionary force was sufficiently strong numerically, for the great venture awaiting us. I had my hair close-cropped within half an hour of arrival at the camp. I have to say it improves my appearance.

Long hair is unbecoming, the training officer told us, except in the singular case of Mr. Cromwell, for whom it is a noble and distinguishing characteristic. His hair is long in a Christ-like way, and aptly so as the man walks in the footsteps of the Divine Lord.

I'm undecided as to whether to opt for musketry or to be a pike-man, or again to try the cavalry. Maybe not that. My horsemanship is mediocre. I've been thrown from those creatures more times than I like to think about. If tackling them on the farm was challenging, I daresay I wouldn't last long in the fires of battle on a less than sympathetic mount as ill-disposed towards me as I to him.

Meg would be proud to see me in uniform. It's quite striking and I can see there won't be any confusion on the field as to which side I'm on. Unlike the rather dull leather "buff" coat worn by the cavalry, I've been decked out in a large coat that reminds me of a cassock. It's a visually pleasing and instantly recognizable Venetian red; a kind of jacket and overcoat fused together, with long sleeves and buttons. The garment reaches almost to my knees.

My new grey breeches fit nicely, and I've a choice of headgear. I can have the basin-shaped helmet that the lads liken to a lobster pot, or a broad-brimmed felt hat that musketeers favour but also, increasingly, the pike-men.

The helmet offers more protection in battle, the trainer advised, but the hat has the advantage of lightness. Take your pick, he teased.

I'm undecided about what exactly to put on my newly-cropped head. The trainer tells us we'll be introduced to the different weapons briefly and he'll help us decide in which capacity we can best serve, depending on how we perform in training.

I relished the thought of my first taste of real military life via training. We need to learn quickly because we'll be crossing the Irish Sea in less than a month. Before adjourning for a bite to eat, the trainer gave way to a chaplain, who fixed us with a look of reproach as if we'd already erred in our new careers as soldiers of the Commonwealth.

With him were two severe looking young men, holding boxes. The chaplain reminded us of the great responsibility placed on our shoulders. We must uphold the Gospel of Christ at all times in the course of our military service. There will be no room, he declared, for swearing or blasphemy, and any man who uttered the Lord's name in vain, even in the heat of battle, might find himself facing a firing squad or the gibbet.

My heart sank a little, for, although I considered myself a loyal Puritan and upholder of true Christian values, we faced a daunting task, and here was this man already threatening us with punishment for infractions we hadn't committed yet.

He warned us to be on our guard in Ireland against the Devil's work. The Irish papists were worse than English witches, he informed us. They didn't cast spells or consort with the Evil one around bonfires, but they conspired to overthrow the rightful rulers of the Commonwealth and worshipped graven images in breach of God's Commandment.

His face reddened like a strawberry. His mouth frothed. "Worse of all are their priests. You have a bounden duty before God to *dispatch any of these lucifarian confessors you encounter. Smite them down wherever you find them. Let none escape."*

The trainer looked ill-at-ease as the chaplain spoke; through I'm sure he concurred with his rousing spiff.

Concluding his talk, the chaplain nodded to his acolytes, who promptly opened their boxes. From these they produced pocket bibles to distribute among us. I accepted mine gratefully.

Though slightly taken aback at the idea of killing priests, I like the beautifully bound bible. Flicking through its pages I'm sure it will provide me with the spiritual sustenance I'll need to see me through the upcoming mission.

But as we broke up for a meal of cheese and biscuits, I doubted that I would have the strength of purpose required to kill unarmed clerics, even hopelessly misguided Catholic ones. If God willed it, I would find the strength, I presumed, so I'd leave it to him. He'd know what to do, or more precisely, what I should do...when the time came.

While my devotion to this great cause remains steadfast I fear I volunteered for the wrong arm of the infantry. I opted to be a pike-man, having been swayed by the trainer's spiff about this weapon being an honourable one, dating back to the mists of time when war was a primitive but gallant affair.

Oh yes, he pouted, cannon and musket had revolutionized warfare. They cut down enemies in their droves, turned human flesh into raw meat with their fiery discharges. Then he raised a pike that had been leaning against the table in the middle of the field where he was lecturing us.

"Behold what the manliest of us take into battle" he crooned, his face screwed up into painful delight at the sight and thought of this weapon.

Ideally, he said, a pike-man should be the tallest and strongest infantryman, and I could see why: the implement he held was, he informed us, sixteen feet long with an eight-inch sword-pointed head.

The pike-man would also be equipped with a three-foot sword. Primitive it might seem, but the pike could be crucial in stopping a cavalry charge. You'd aim at the horse to throw the rider, and at the rider when he falls, or, if possible, at the rider when he's in full flight. And I was surprised to hear that pike-men had the job of protecting musketeers. The latter needed protection because of the time lapse between each shot. Reloading a musket was a cumbersome process, until you got used to it, but even the fastest re-loaders would be at a severe disadvantage once they'd fired a shot. An enemy would be upon them before they'd reloaded. But a covering pike-man would see to it that the enemy soldier or cavalryman wouldn't get through.

The trainer adopted a jovial bearing. "So, lads, don't think that if you wield a pike you're an out of date warrior like the fellows depicted on old vases and sepulchers. You'd be playing a vital part in winning this war."

I was smitten by this alluring talk and before the day was out I had a pike my hands, learning how to hold it, and the various standing positions on the battlefield.

But while the trainer commended my speedy grasp of combative tactics and postures, he thought I struggled to move the pike with sufficient dexterity, and had doubts about me being tall enough. I thought I'd get around this quibble, and persevered over the next four days of my training.

The sun bore down on us. I normally like sunny weather and the warmth God gives us in July but not when it made me sweat buckets.

The stronger men had an easier time. I should have known. It made sense that they'd handle the pikes better. They were heavy. Tactics one could learn, but the pike wasn't going to get any lighter for me.

I hated the idea of showing weakness but at the end of the fourth day I approached the trainer. He was resting on a rick of hay, smoking his pipe. He didn't seem in the least surprised when I asked if I could switch to musketry.

It was as if he'd expected me to buckle. He clapped me on the back, removed his pipe, and quipped "That stint won't go astray young man. Every experience has value. You've an insight into how a pike is used...Next time you meet a pike-man he won't be a stranger to you. Tomorrow you'll handle a musket."

And so I did.

2

Friar Malcolm removed the treasured instrument from its leather case and attached the tripod. The two-foot long telescope had been a gift from an Italian Bishop five years earlier. The prelate had called to the abbey in Callan during the memorable visit of Archbishop Rinuccini to Kilkenny.

What a week that was. The Callan abbey had celebrated along with the rest of Catholic Ireland, or at least the parts of it under the protection of the Confederacy, as the Papal Nuncio offered spiritual, political and military support to Ireland's Provisional Government.

The telescope had generated curiosity and a little excitement at the abbey, though for the others the novelty had worn off within a week. Being able to observe faraway objects with this device, and see them up close, was a new experience for them, but the relentless daily routines and the cycle of their devotional lives quickly pushed aside any attraction this wonderful spyglass, as the Prior called it, might have for them.

Except for Malcolm. At least once a week, sometimes twice or three times, he'd ascend the stairway of the central tower of the abbey church and reach for the leather case that was tucked into a wooden box to shelter it from the elements.

His favourite time was after Midnight Prayer. Tonight looked ideal. The sky was a vault studded with twinkling lights. Malcolm started with the moon. Not that he expected it to look any different from on other nights. But it never failed to enchant.

Until he'd got the telescope, Malcolm had thought of that celestial object as just a bright shining disc in the heavens. Apart from legends associated with it, he'd known only that it mirrored the light of the life-giving and life-preserving sun.

But through the circular lens he'd perceived another world, with craters, valleys, slopes and mountains. Oceans? Maybe. He wasn't sure about that.

Inhabitants? That was a touchy subject. The Prior had cautioned him that even to contemplate such an ideal might be sinful, since the Bible had made no reference to lunar life-forms. If there were any entities dwelling up there, scripture would surely have factored in such a momentous truth.

Slowly he scanned the strange features that pockmarked the lunar surface, his heartrate increasing as the thought occurred to him that at any moment some living creature might become visible. He longed for and yet dreaded any such revelation, but each time he viewed the moon those conflicting emotions vied with each other.

Tiring of the moon he diverted his attention to a galaxy that resembled a splash of milk across the heavens. Magnification revealed a seemingly limitless spread of yet more stars. He lowered the telescope and sat back in his star-gazing chair.

He shared the Prior's feeling that the immensity of the universe as revealed by the telescope was further proof of God's greatness. How could that unfathomable vast cosmos have come about by itself, as some crazy heretics had postulated? How foolish those men were. He'd read that some of them clung to their delusions even as the flames consumed them at the stake.

Malcolm disagreed strongly with punishing them in that way. Confinement in a lunatic asylum would have been a more apt response by the clerical authorities in Spain and whatever other countries the heretics had come up with those erroneous ideas.

No, this modern invention only served to bolster his faith in a supreme being that ruled over all. Those same stars, that same moon would be there tomorrow night, and on every other night till the end of time. God would see to that. Without his divine will, everything up there would disappear, or fall from its position in space.

Taking a last look before retiring to his cell, his heart missed a beat as something fluttered across his field of vision. Quickly he lowered the telescope to spot a bat circling the Blessed Well before flying out over the King's River.

The momentary fear that he'd detected an alien species up there gave way to relief. *Everything is as it should be.*

He yawned as he put away the telescope and replaced the case in the wooden box. He stepped softly down the stairs and headed back to the Priory, careful not to disturb the other friars who'd settled in for a short sleep in their cells.

He'd soon be joining them for another round of prayers and recitations.

*

Mathias Blunt's diary: Mid August, 1649.

The sea's calmer now and that awful feeling is gone. I can reach for the quill to record my experience aboard the Blue Fox, the converted merchant vessel taking some of us to Ireland... to reclaim that land for the Commonwealth.

I'm here in a stuffy cabin, squeezed in along with fourteen other men, our muskets, bandoleers and assorted baggage laid out in what little space remains. Thank God, our equipment isn't rattling, falling, or rolling around the cabin so much now. One lad got a nasty cut earlier when his head crashed into the barrel of a gun held by the man sitting opposite him.

And our stomachs are beginning to settle. The storm is abating after raging for at least three hours. The thunder crashed relentlessly above us like a heavenly cannonade and the ship was tossed about by the surging waves. I'd been told about sea-sickness but had shrugged it off as just silly talk.

Nobody ever died of it, so how bad could it be? And the seasoned sea-travelers laughed at us land lubbers who succumbed. I'd thought my youthful outings in a fishing boat on a lake had given me an edge. But the sea is different. From almost the minute the ship set sail from Bristol I had that nauseous feeling in the pit of my stomach.

My mistake, I think, was to scoff down my ration of cheese and salted beef so soon after boarding. I was hungry, I hadn't eaten for hours, and all that waiting about on the docks prior to boarding had whetted my appetite. I was thirsty too, so I went through a third of my allocated gallon of beer.

I'd no sooner laid back; thinking I could settle down to a rest in this cramped cabin, when my stomach started heaving. I threw up on the floor in front of me, narrowly avoiding the man hunched opposite. He cringed at the sight of vomit, with the bits of half-digested beef and cheese in it. I reached for a rag to mop it away, feeling sick all over again as I did so.

A soldier squatting to my right didn't seem bothered, I noticed. I envied him. He nodded at me, letting out a hearty laugh. "Better to be rid of it here than on deck. When I served in the king's navy I went to vomit over the side and didn't the wind blow the puke right into the face of an officer who was lounging about. I still have the lash marks on my back."

His words elicited a few grunts, titters, and moans of annoyance. Other men started vomiting, swearing and shouting as they heaved forth the contents of the bellies. I must have disgorged everything I had inside me, because when I felt a renewed urge to vomit nothing came out. It still felt bad, but at least I wasn't going to soil the poor fellow opposite, who was regarding me with a look that was half pity, half extreme annoyance.

I sat clinging to my stomach with both hands, as if that would make me well. Someone to my left was singing, and then a few lads laughed. Others swigged their beer or attempted to play cards. The cards were a bad idea. The ship was rocking and swaying, its timbers stretching, creaking and whistling as if about to break into pieces and let the water in to engulf us.

But that awful sensation passed and then the ship was sailing along nicely. A few of the lads opted to go up on deck for a breath of fresh air, which one of them opined was a cure for sea sickness. I joined them, trusting that nobody would steal my musket or bandolier while I was up there.

The light momentarily blinded me when I climbed out of my little wooden dungeon, for that's how it feels below deck in this vessel. My eyes quickly adjusted to the welcome sight of a sky that was a pleasant pale blue. Just the remnants of wispy cloud and those were fading.

Then I beheld a wondrous spectacle: to my left and right, and behind me... a host of other ships appeared in my field of vision. A soldier who'd served in the King's navy before converting to our side helpfully identified the vessels, rattling off a succession of fancy names: He pointed to what he called the three-masted barques and, with a dramatic flourish, indicated the gigantic multi-decked galleons that carried far more troops than the vessel I was in.

The chaplain had come up on deck. He too was quickly invigorated by the salt sea air that refreshed us all. He beheld the vast fleet of ships, their billowing sails putting me in mind of the proud puffed up crests of exotic birds

Someone else gave voice to his feeling that this "Armada" was mightier than anything that even Spain at the height of her glory

21

had ever cobbled together. It projected the power of the Commonwealth.

Though the storm had gone, our faces were lashed intermittently by the briny surf. The chaplain had removed his broad-brimmed hat. Looking towards the sun, he quipped: "It is God that has put the wind in our sails, brethren. He's assuredly on the side of this great mission."

"Land!" someone shouted. The sun was brighter and I had to shield my eyes. I perceived a distant shore. Others pointed excitedly towards it. "Not long now, lads", an unsteady fellow hollered; a naggin of rum in his fist, his voice barely audible above the roar of the sea.

That thin stretch of emerald green on the horizon had a benign aura. How deceptive, considering the task that lies ahead of us in delivering that stricken land from the clutches of Catholicism and its Royalist allies.

Sergeant Blunden, who had said nothing thus far after coming on deck, made a sweeping gesture with his right hand at the ships. "If those barbarous wretches knew what was coming, they'd hang themselves right now and save us the trouble."

Most of the lads laughed. Some cheered. I shared the sentiment, but didn't feel like being too cocky...just yet. I suspect that the Irish may not take kindly to our mission.

*

Shane Dennehy had almost forgotten that he was on a school assignment. Master Counihan had asked the class to return after the weekend with samples of foliage from the countryside around Callan demonstrating the "arrival of autumn."

It wasn't the usual boring home exercise that nobody wanted and that could earn you a severe beating if it didn't measure up to expectations. He'd visited the same terrain many times, but without bothering to notice which birds were about, or how the leaves had changed colour, or what berries were to be found in the ditches and hedgerows.

He'd asked his friend Luke to join him in his search for evidence of autumn. He felt a little guilty about this because Luke had never been to school. He helped at his father's forge, and would, some

22

day, be a blacksmith himself. But he'd never be able to read or write, according to Shane's mother, who lamented the lack of education for so many boys in this tough and unforgiving world, or so she often reminded him whenever he complained of schoolwork.

Shane passed unchallenged through the wide-open Bridge Gate in North Street. The two helmeted guards had set aside their fearsome pikes and were playing cards on the footpath. Up ahead he prepared to step aside for old Patsy Daly and his donkey. Patsy, with his long grey cloak flapping, always managed to block the footpath, his ass striding alongside him on the dusty street.

Two wicker baskets hung from the donkey, each containing his usual consignment of fish from the river, destined for the market in East Street. Drawing nearer to Shane Patsy squinted, removed the clay pipe from his mouth and spat on the street.

"Would your mother fancy a few nice eels for supper, young Shane? I'll give 'em to you at half the price they'll cost above."

"No thanks Mister Daly, I'm off in the other direction. Can't take them now. I hope you do well at the market."

"Aw, pity…there's great value in these little wrigglers. Have a peek…"

Patsy stopped and opened a basket, causing the tired donkey's head to turn inquiringly. He leaned the basket forward to reveal the squirming oily creatures. Their eyes shone, pleadingly.

Shane felt queasy. He hated eels. He'd seen one wriggling on the table at home one evening, right in front of Mother as she readied a knife to slice it. It wasn't really alive, she assured him, teasingly. Eels just seemed to be alive owing to something weird messing with their insides. But that didn't assuage his distaste, and he'd refused to eat any part of an eel, whether definitely dead or pretending to be alive.

Patsy clapped the lid back on the eels and resumed his journey, blood dripping from the bottoms of both baskets. He shouted back "That river is alive with fish today…eels and trout and pike…more plentiful than Manna from Heaven…"

Beyond the bridge and the swelling waters of the mighty King's River Shane turned right into Goose Lane. He passed the picturesque abbey meadow where the friars were busily gardening or pacing back and forth through the grass, engrossed in their prayer-books.

He took the narrow dirt-road leading to the Kilbricken forge where Luke awaited him. Under a balmy blue sky they headed off on the nature quest, grateful that the road wasn't muddy or rain-soaked as it had been a week ago. Shane felt beads of sweat breaking out on his brow. It was pleasantly warm, but unlike a summer's day, when those awful midges swarmed around you.

They entered a country lane that twisted like a corkscrew. Thinking of the class awaiting him, Shane focused on familiar surroundings as if he'd arrived in a strange new land. Looking to his right over a stone wall, he took in the sight of farmers forking hay on a rolling stretch of ground. A feeble wooden barrier divided them from a longer patch of land, where men harvested barley. It was Luke who informed him that it was barley, not oats as he'd thought.

"Oh thanks" he mumbled, ashamed that his friend who had no schooling knew more about the countryside.

T o his left more labouring; endless heaving, forking and scything, and men dropping sheaves of oats or barley- he wasn't sure which- into carts.

The aroma of newly-cut hay reached them and Shane inhaled it deeply, closing his eyes. "I love that smell", he quipped.

Luke gave him a funny look. "That's just hay, silly."

Walking on, Shane saw the sun brighten, dispelling the leftover clouds like melting snow. He felt warmer, and a mild sensation of giddiness. He beheld in the distance a whitish green landscape tinged with gold.

They climbed a stile into a field where nobody laboured. Shane wanted to collect a few samples of the season, as the Master had called them. Approaching a bramble bush that sagged with blackberries, they picked greedily and began stuffing themselves.

Shane savoured the sweet pulp dissolving in his mouth. Delicious! He'd brought blackberries home to Mother last year to bake tarts, but they tasted better this way. He wiped the juice from his lips with a sleeve. Pulling the little cloth bag from his pocket he dropped in some ripe berries, his first "evidence of autumn" for the Master.

They turned their attention from the ditch to a giant oak tree that stood in the centre of the field: He'd circled that tree before, whooping like an ancient warrior. Now he was on a mission, one that the Master promised would expand his understanding of the world.

He already knew that the oak was a strong timber from which great castles were built, and the ships of the mightiest navies.

He scooped up a handful of acorns, the green and shiny seeds of a tree dubbed the "King of the Woods."

"Those should satisfy your teacher", Luke said chirpily.

"I reckon".

"There are ashes and beeches over there", Luke added.

They set off in that direction and Shane halted before a tall and seemingly old ash tree with its grooved grey bark and thick twigs. He stood on his tippy-toes and snapped off a twig for his bag, reaching his other hand out to grip a dangling cluster of tiny purple flowers.

Crossing to the Beech, he noticed immediately that it had changed since their last visit, when the leaves had a greenish tinge.

Now they were golden-brown. He took some leaves and then bent to pick up a few of the brown triangular nuts that had fallen to earth.

Rising to his feet he spotted a wispy cobweb. Suspended between two twigs it was shaking slightly in a light breeze.

Luke urged him not to damage it. "The spider needs that to catch a fly for his meal. Did you know a spider has eight eyes and that he doesn't eat the fly? He paralyses it with a single savage bite and then turns its insides into a nice drink. He throws away what's left. Not very nice but they say it's bad luck to break his web."

"Eight eyes. If I had that many I'd be able to doze off in class with most eyes closed and one or two open to make sure the Master didn't see me."

"Forget spiders…there's a squirrel!"

Shane looked just in time to catch a glimpse of the reddish bushy tailed animal darting to cover behind the Beech trunk.

"It's easily frightened", Luke whispered, as they crept closer. They stopped and waited. Seconds passed and the squirrel peeped around the trunk. They laughed, startling it. It sprang from its position, disappearing in a flash.

Luke prompted him to seek out the Horse Chestnut tree they'd called to in the past in search of nuts to play conkers. Shane loved that tree, but not the obstacles that separated them from it. It stood forlorn in a small meadow, encircled by weeds.

Seeing the tangle of high thistles and thorn bushes, Shane wanted to turn back but Luke pressed him on. Avoiding the nettles that threatened to sting his bare shins and ankles, Shane collected the glistening brown nuts in their spiky green cases.

Luke tittered. "You remember …I beat you at conkers last time we played?"

Shane had hoped Luke wouldn't remember, "Yeah...but these are just to please the Master. Won't be any conkers this time."

Changing the subject, Luke looked up at the sky, "What about the birds? They act differently in this season. Do you have to bring him in birds to show you went to the trouble of catching them?"

"No, but he might ask about them..."

"There" Luke pointed at a jet black bird with a yellow beak sitting on a bush. "Listen. Can you hear it sing?"

Shane cocked his ears. "It doesn't sound like a song."

Luke seemed to enjoy knowing more about this bird than Shane did. Preening himself he announced "It's birdsong. Others birds must think it sounds nice. And what about those?" He pointed upwards.

Shane saw the flock of brownish grey sparrows flutter above them, zigzagging crazily. "I know those birds. I've seen them outside our window."

Feeling the weight of the cloth bag, Shane reckoned he'd gathered enough seasonal samples to avoid a telling-off. But he didn't feel like going home just yet. "What was that?" he asked. He'd heard somebody holler.

"There's a hurling match on in Mattie Hanrahan's field, will we have a look?"

The voices grew louder as they approached the hurling field. Shane heard the whacking of the wooden sticks they used. The Master had told them about the ancient sport of the Irish and how it all started when a boy called Setanta had inadvertently killed the watchdog of a powerful lord with a ball propelled by a stick. To compensate its owner, he became the man's human watchdog.

The killing of that dog back in the mists of time had led to the invention of hurling, Counihan told them. The Master had a faraway wistful look when he enlarged upon how every boy in the class would one day wield a hurley. And some boys would excel at the sport. The whole class should be grateful, he said, that Setanta had sent a ball hurtling down the gullet of that salivating hound. The Master had likened the ill-fated hound to the English trying to kill or enslave the Irish and Setanta to a brave soldier fighting for Ireland.

Entering the field, Shane stepped onto the shortest grass he'd ever seen. It was as if the bare earth had been dyed green. Loud cheering assailed his ears, along with cursing, jeering and astringent name-calling. But the whacking of the ball against the sticks could be heard above even the loudest voice.

He and Luke, the newcomers; were stared at for a few seconds by the cluster of fans, but they quickly forget the boys and resumed shouting encouragement or its opposite to the players.

Shane was awestruck by the spectacle of so many grown lads running and jumping about wildly; all wielding those sturdy wooden sticks. Stripped to the waist they wore only soiled raggedy loin-cloths and soft leather boots. Most of them were smeared with mud and bits of grass from head to foot, but their eyes, noses and mouths had none of it. Just as well, Shane thought, as they'd need to breathe properly and see clearly...

Some lads had patches of dried or wet blood on their legs or torsos, which didn't bother them. These players ran or pranced or dived as nimbly as the ones with only the mud-covering.

The fast-moving interplay confused him at first. But the apparent mayhem soon resolved itself into a pattern.

He recalled what he'd learned at school. Those were two sets of rival hurlers, each vying to get the ball that was flying around the field either over or under the goalpost defended by a rival team member. The action went back and forth as players fought to breach their rivals' defences and reach the "enemy" goal to score.

Luke filled him in on a few vital details, including that the hurleys were made from the wood of the Ash tree, like the one he'd taken the twig and the clump of flowers from. Other features of the game came back to him. Hearing about it in class though wasn't the same as seeing these athletic, passionate lads in action. The competition was fierce, as if their lives depended on it.

Shane winced when a hurler belted a rival across the head, knocking him down, and then kicking him on the ground. A burley fellow wearing a bright yellow loin-cloth that was cleaner than the others, and sturdy rawhide boots, ran to him. Wagging his finger, he urged the assailant not to kick the man. "This is hurling", he shouted "not football!" He yelled at the man on the ground to get up and stop whining.

They carried on. More belting and kicking and punching ensued, and bouts of fighting broke out at a corner of the field. Two players were dragging a third along the grass, uttering insults at him. Shane couldn't hear what they said. The burly man who seemed to be in charge ran to them, dispersing the quarrelers and roaring at them to "hurl like civilized men."

"That's the referee", Luke informed Shane. "He keeps the game fair for everyone."

A hurler had got the ball bouncing on his stick, running straight for the goal. Deafening cheers arose. He was about to strike the ball when another man swiped it from him as if by magic. It happened so fast that Shane wished he could see it again.

The second hurler ran towards the opposite goal, losing the ball several times but recovering it. Close to the goal, it was knocked from his hurley upon which he'd been bouncing it with astonishing skill but he outwitted three rivals to regain it, performing a breathtaking pirouetting movement that confused his rivals.

Then, this man whose sweat leaked through layers of mud; pucked the ball. It sailed gracefully past faces warped by pain, rage, and disbelief and went crashing into the goal. Wild elation ensued.

Meanwhile another fracas had flared up in a different part of the field. A hurler was wrestling an angry spectator who'd run onto the pitch.

The referee ran to quell the disorder, urging them to think of their honour and act like true Irishmen. Tempers cooled and the action continued.

Shane found it difficult to keep track of who was winning or losing, continually consulting Luke for updates and explanations. But he reckoned that in time he'd get the hang of it. He was disappointed with himself when the match ended and the team he thought had won was declared the loser.

As the players put their clothes back on, or wiped away the mud and the blood, further rows and fighting broke out across the field. This time some of the fans took sides, exacerbating the disturbance, and drawing in more participants by the second. The referee let them at it. His job was done and he was happily drinking from a long glass bottle that someone had given him.

Fans began to exit the field, and Shane heard, or thought he heard, a grumpy older man say in a half whisper "Enough war without us fighting over a match…" to which a younger fan replied out loud "thousands of them landed yesterday…"

Shane strained to catch more of this exchange, but the two men walked on and their voices faded. Turning to Luke, he asked "did you hear that? Something about a war and a landing…"

Luke shrugged: "Just hurling talk. They get carried away…did you know about the ball?"

"What about it?"

He informed Shane that they made the ball from hair scraped off a cow's back and compressed tightly until it was as hard as a stone.

Shane said he'd seen enough hurling but would love to watch it again and maybe join in the fun some day.

"Fun… They don't think of it as fun…You saw how serious they are and it's definitely not fun if you lose. Dad says hurling is not a game at all. It's a religion, he says."

Shane reflected on that as they headed back into town. He couldn't imagine anyone worshipping a hurling ball. Or could it be that the referee was their God? He certainly worked hard to keep the players in line.

Father Brannigan wouldn't take kindly to anyone worshipping a false god, as the second Commandment called it, though he'd heard that the PP was a hurling fan himself.

***

3

Mathias Blunt's diary: late August, 1649.

Dear Meg, I hope this finds you in good health. I have arrived safely in Ireland, one soldier among so many assigned by God, under the command of a Heaven-sent General, to restore this land to its rightful place in the Commonwealth.

After so many weeks of hanging about in the taverns and hostrlries of Bristol it was a relief to board the vessel that bore us hence. I should say that it was but one of more than a hundred. I heard mumbings about the possibility of us being attacked by that Royalist upstart Prince Rupert. His raiding ships loiter off the Irish coast, intent on harrying us.

He may have taken flight at the sight of our mighty fleet. If he has an ioto of sense in his traiter's head he'll turn his back on the papists and either surrender or hi-tail it to the continent like so manyof his cowardly Royalist colleagues.

My dear Meg, I wish you could have beheld the scene: It was a nautical extravaganza, dearest, a picture painted by the hand of the almighty on the choppy sea: our ships stretching to the far horizons and all headed this way, to fulfil the destiny of our great nation.

And then we reached that country that, from afar, looked like a long misty sliver of green under a tranquil sky.

"Don't let the scenery fool you, enemies skulk yonder , waiting to rip our gizzards out"", a corporal cautioned me, and I must admit that I and many of the lads expected a dismal, if nor overtly hostile reception when we set foot on Irish soil. I mean, given what we know of this race.

But not a bit of it. You see, the natives who turned out to greet us were all stout-hearted godly folk. The territory, including the docks where we came ashore, had- thank the Lord! - been cleansed of Catholics and other heathen riffraff prior to the disembarking of our expeditionary force.

The roars of adulation that echoed around Dublin when the Lord General appeared lifted our hearts. Celebratory bunting in the bright colours of the Commonwealth festooned the docks. Drums rolled and cannons fired in tribute.

And then...oh what sweet sounds to our ears. The Lord animated him and his voice sent shudders of pride and elation through us. Deafening cheers when he reminded us, and the assembled native throng; of his divinely ordained mission to chastise the barbarous Irish and the Royalist conspirators colluding with them.

He pledged to restore Ireland to its former status as a peaceful island under the protection of England's Parliament. He would not rest, he said, until this backward, savage land was again a sweet and tranquil domain.

I thought of you Meg as he spoke, of your dream of acquiring land here once we have wrested it from our enemies. I've heard of the Lord General's master plan and I can assure you, dearest, that your dream will become a reality before twelve months have passed. That's how long our leaders estimate it will take to tame the Irish and mop up Royalist resistance.

In the meantime, please be patient and pray for me. When this land is cleansed, you will join me here to take what is ours.

Remember the garden and the orchard you wished you had, with apple and cherry trees...and our very own farm, with labourers and servants to do our bidding as we bask in the glow of married life? That's all going to happen. Our wedding will be the happiest ever seen or heardof on these islands. Ireland purged of savages will be as close to our hearts as the tiny village that both of us grew up in...No, even more so, I imagine, since neither your family or mine ever owned more than a puny patch of soil.

Over here, I'm reliably told, is some of the most fertile land in the world, and the landscapes are a wonder to behold. If it weren't for the vile inhabitats, (excepting the godly folk who've converted and the noble settlers) it would be an earthly paradise.

I know you'll be fretting about me back in England. But don't fear. I will, I'm convinced, emerge from this trial of fire as a man worthy of your hand. Until then, I'll keep your image in my heart and, whenever I'm disheartened I'll think of you...your freckled face, your golden tresses and that silken dress with the Commonwealth broach you receved as an engagement gift from your esteemed mother, for whose soul I will pray later, though I'm sure she's in Heaven with the legion of godly Englishmen and women who have served the Commonwealth.

I must go now, dear Meg. The Sergeant calls us to attention.
Farewell, apple of my eye. I'll write again when time permits,
  Your adoring Mathias.

*

Upper South Street, Callan, third week of August, 1649

Tom Brennan stood outside the *Fiery Spirit,* arms folded. He was almost hoarse from greeting everyone who passed the two-storey alehouse: Must be on the best of terms with as many people as you possibly could.

That was, he believed the key to success in the vintner's trade. There were those who repelled him, or that he dearly wished didn't behave in the outlandish way they did on his premises, but he couldn't afford to lose a customer. He'd learned that lesson in the first week of running the *Fiery Spirit* after inheriting it from his ailing father.

You could throw an unruly fellow out on the street, but then, in addition to him not returning, and imbibing elsewhere, he'd be sure to take several other customers...friends... relatives, workmates, with him. In exceptional circumstance, he'd get Mags the barmaid to eject a troublemaker. But that didn't happen too often. So, best keep that "welcome to all" smile intact and exude goodwill every day- not just at Christmas.

Today, though, it wasn't to win new customers or cling on to old ones that he was beaming outside his alehouse. He was positioned strategically in front of the window because this was Fair Day, and the driving of cattle through the town to the fairground at the upper end of South Street, beynd the Town Wall, was a big part of it. The only part he didn't like.

Earlier, he'd taken a stroll around town to savour the convivial atmosphere that always accompanied this flurry of buying and selling. The event transformed Callan into a carnival of joy, with old friends meeting, money being made hand over fist; and the taverns and cookhouses packed to the rafters.

Schoolgirls played and danced "rosy" around the big wooden cross in the Town Square. His ears still rang with the pealing of bells, the clattering of carts and hooves on the cobblestones, the cries of traders offering fruit, vegetables, ballad sheets, or alleged cures for every known aliment; and the shrill howling of dogs that ran among the throng,

He loved how the delicious aromas wafting from the fresh bread and cake stalls and the booming coffee houses offset the stink of drainage , the odd rotten fish, and the fumes from coal fires that burned day and night, venting into an otherwise bright and clear autumn sky. Yes, Fair Day gladdened his heart...apart from these damned oxen being ushered, prodded, and occasionally beaten along the street. Since he started serving ale and spirits his front window had been broken more than a dozen times by them.

Perhaps they saw their reflections in the glass and couldn't resist poking their horns into it. Or maybe the drovers just couldn't control them. Understandable that, given the numbers involved and the unpredictability of any beast: But he wasn't letting it happen this month. He kept his composure as some of the animals brushed against him, mooing and spluttering and almost knocking him backwards.

On they came, hundreds of them. They streamed up from North Street, and from around the corners of East and West Streets; cloudlets of breath hovering above them as their hooves pressed on dung-carpeted South Street. Relief lightened his heart as the last steaming bovine heaved passed him, now safely removed from the danger zone. *My window's in one piece for another Fair Day.* He headed back inside, where Mags was rushing about with two mugs of ale in each hand and the sweat oozing out of her.

Tom was quickly in demand too, with calls from all sides of the big stone-walled alehouse calling for service. No rest, he muttered, pouring ale into a pewter mug and whisky into a cup for two lads in workmen's clothes standing at the counter. A line of thirsty drinkers gathered and he soon had them all happily sipping or slurping at their tables.

He prided himself on the speed of his pouring. He had won a competition for the fastest pourer of beer and spirits organised by the Brewer's Association, and the award of a brass statue of a jolly drinker was displayed prominently on a shelf overlooking the counter.

"Tom."

He instantly recognised the voice of Alderman Pat Vance, seated beside the wide-open fire with its blazing sods of turf and hefty logs. Now there was a prestigious customer, one to hold onto at any cost. Vance owned twenty-nine properties in Callan, and was the second richest man in the district after the Mayor himself.

"Yes Pat", he crooned, leaving down a tankard he was washing in the basin under the counter.

"Can you sit down for a minute, Tom?"

"Of course." Tom pulled over a stool to the fire and faced the alderman, who was dressed in his usual yellow and purple silks, and elegantly wigged; a snuff-box clutched in his left hand. He sneezed gently and dabbed his nose with a satin handkerchief.

"Well Pat. Any interesting developments on the civic scene? There's a Corporation meeting on Tuesday night, isn't there?"

"Yes, Tom, that's what I wanted to mention to you. You may have heard about that suspected case of Bubonic Plague in Kilkenny?"

"I heard something...was it a false alarm, or is someone in the City afflicted?"

Pat nodded gravely, his face horror-stricken, "It's been confirmed, and other cases are possible, which is why the Corporation is likely to vote on Tuesday for a temporary ban on any but the most essential- as in life or death- journeys to Kilkenny...while this health scare persists."

"Temporary, how long will that be?"

"Who knows, as long as necessary; could be weeks...or months. So, Tom, if you have any business in Kilkenny I'd suggest you get it done before Tuesday...as soon as you can."

Tom shrugged. He didn't need to travel to the City...but wait: His supply of beer was running low. "How about travel from Kilkenny to Callan?"

Pat shrugged. "That could be affected too. It's up to the City Corporation. I know that several prominent business people have already left the City to stay with relatives in other towns or in the country to escape a potential epidemic."

"I'll need a consignment from the brewery. I wonder if that's going to be a problem..."

Pat pursed his lips. "I can tell you it is. The two men who deliver to Callan and other towns have left the City. I reckon you'll have to pick up that consignment yourself, or hire someone else to do it for you. The proprietors of the *Dragon's Tooth* in West Street and *The Sign of the Helmet* in North Street left this morning for Kilkenny with wagons to stock up, and I hear the *Heartbreak Tavern* has someone going tomorrow."

Tom's mind raced. He couldn't afford to be out of beer. Not even for one day. There was too much competition, with thirty-five other watering holes in town. Customers wouldn't wait around for him to replenish his stocks. They'd desert him and drink elsewhere. He must make that journey, and fast. He'd need the loan of a wagon and a pair of horses.

Luckily the blacksmith gladly lent him these. Next norning he prepared the covered wagon, after feeding and watering the horses. No time to lose, bearing in mind the general panic that might sweep the City. God only knew how things might have progressed in Kilkenny since the alderman heard the news. Then again, maybe the scare had ended. The physicians might find that the supposed victim or victims had contracted a minor illness, mistaken for the plague: A harmless cough maybe, or a bellyache. *People get excited over anything nowadays. Imaginations run wild.*

But he couldn't take a chance on it. Running out of beer would spell disaster for him, plague or no plague. He checked the two chestnut brown horses. They seemed to be in fine fettle, ready to go. And the capacious wagon was ideal to carry merchandise of any kind, beer included.

It could accommodate ten passengers, maybe more if the need arose. That was enough space to fill with the necessary quota of barrels and kegs at the brewery. Broad sturdy wheels too; and they needed to be, given the sorry state of the road to Kilkenny. Bumpy and pot-holed, it had tested the patience, and sanity, of many a traveller.

He knew far too many merchants whose conveyances had broken down while journeying to or from the City, and since Kilkenny had become the supposed capital of the Great Catholic Confederacy; the traffic both ways had increased several-fold. It was mainly carriages and coaches though that had succumbed to the poorly maintained road.

The roads in the county just weren't suited to long journeys. For those a pack-horse was speedier and more comfortable, but there was a limit to what one horse could carry. Having the wagon covered was vital in this instance too: The sight of all that beer wheeling past could prove tempting to thirsty tipplers or brigands.

He planned to stop and rest at an inn halfway to Kilkenny, and resume the journey after a few hours so that he'd reach the City good and early next morning. He'd stay with his friend, Doctor Holohan, at the *Smulken Inn* and leave the City again after dark, hoping to avoid prying eyes or infringing any unexpected new rules aimed at quelling the Plague... if indeed an outbreak had occurred.

Waves and shouted greetings came at him from all sides as the wagon trundled down South Street, rattling on the cobblestones. It was quieter at the Square, with only Mrs. Lanigan fingering a rosary at the Cross. Tom guided the horses around the great wooden crucifix, which had partly shielded his eyes from the dazzling orb peeping out from behind a cloud.

Now it dazzled him again. He hoped the horses weren't similarly affected. A group of youths lazily moseyed out of his path as he continued down North Street. At the Bridge, the friendly unhelmeted guard waved him through, the Bridge Gate being, as always, open to traffic and amblers. The yawning soldier's pike rested to one side against a gate railing. Why did he even bother with a pike? Who did he expect would need to be barred from passing up and down the street?

Seeing a carriage edging towards him from the end of North Street, and a line of horseman following that, he avoided these by entering Goose Lane, which would also take him onto the Kilkenny Road. Nobody about on the lane, but he spotted to his right a grey-habited figure leading a donkey across the sun-drenched abbey meadow.

It was Fr. Malcolm, known as the friendly friar, because he was more sociable than any of his colleagues at the abbey who tended to keep to themselves. He had even dropped into the *Fiery Spirit* one day for a tipple, unusual for a friar.

Tom thought the sunshine made Malcolm look saintly against the gently rolling backdrop. The friar exited the meadow and, seeing the wagon, greeted Tom, who returned the salute. "Off on the quest again, Fr. Malcolm. Hope you get a nice response. Weather's not looking too bad for it."

The friar had a grumpy look, and the donkey eyed him with apparent sympathy. "Yes, Tom. Thank you, but the smoke gets to me every time."

" Haw! You should try running an alehouse. You'd get soon get used to it. I'm off to Kilkenny."

Malcolm whistled softly in admiration, regarding Tom with a look that he thought betrayed a hint of envy. "Lucky man! The heart of Catholic Ireland. I received the personal blessing of Archbishop Rinuccini himself there. When was it? 1646 I think. Kilkenny belonged to God that day. It was a Holy City. Some swore they heard angels sing.

" Others perceived the face of the Almighty in the sky and over the River Nore. The Papal Nuncio no less, here in this county to convey the backing of the Pope himself for a Catholic Ireland. I pray for him every day, you know, and for the people of Callan, including those who live outside the wall in houses without chimneys."

"Oh, and why not? They're all human. Well, I'd better keep going Father. My own journey today is only to stock up on beer, no spiritual purpose to it I'm afraid. Fair play to you and the others at the abbey, you keep God on our side. I hope all your prayers are answered!"

He tugged at the reins and the horses pressed on towards what Tom found it difficult to think of as a Holy City. But he admired the friar's simple faith as the Man of God headed off with his donkey to beg for alms.

**

4

Callan Town Hall: Third week of August 1649.

Edward Comerford, Mayor of Callan, pushed aside the sheaf of papers he'd been examining. Proposals for the repair of the numerous long neglected potholes in East Street...letters of complaint about the quality of food in a South Street tavern, where, it seemed a local wool merchant almost died after consuming an undercooked chicken caked in green mould; complaints about drainage in parts of the town and the stench of human waste on Woodcock Lane.

And there was a cluster of minor legal issues to be dealt with, since, as Mayor, he had also to adjudicate in the local Court of Justice. Nothing of any great consequence: a dispute between locals over a faulty garden fence; a chamber pot allegedly emptied from a window onto somebody's head; the alleged theft of a piglet and two roosters at the Town Fair; inter-communal spats (Every town had them)...repairs needed to the whipping post in North Street, which had fallen into disuse since being knocked over by a rampaging ass-and-cart.

He'd return to all that later. But first he'd savour a glass or two of that exquisite Italian wine he'd reserved for a special occasion, if not exactly this one. When the aide to Archbishop Rinuccini, the Papal Nuncio, gave him the bottle, he promised himself not to open it until he had cause to mark an event of surpassing importance in his life. Well, that time had arrived, even if it wasn't an event to celebrate.

Far from it. Taking a generous sip, he stood and went to the window of Callan Town Hall overlooking South Street. Life was getting along as normal outside: Good-humored women chatting loudly and men leaning against the walls, puffing thoughtfully on their clay pipes.

Snotty-nosed children darted about, playing their silly games, distracted now and then by a shout or reprimand from a shrill, cloaked mother. The door of the *Crab's Claw* tavern was ajar, and, even through the half-open window of his office, he could hear the hearty laughter inside.

Not too troubled down there. But then, they haven't seen nor heard what I've learned. He drained the glass and returned to his desk for a refill. *The Archbishop knows his wines. I'll say that for him. Whatever about his grasp of political and military affairs.*

He drained the second helping like a mug of water or buttermilk. Closing his eyes, he wished he was dreaming and that on waking the news relayed to him less than an hour ago would vanish into the realm of nightmares. But he knew it wouldn't go away.

Rising again, with a third glass to fortify him, he stepped over to the large map of Ireland on the wall opposite the street window. The enemy hadn't made much headway in the past year. Just a few little patches marked in on the map in Dublin and a tiny portion of Munster. The Royalist/Confederate Alliance had kept the small numbers of Parliamentary troops on Irish soil at bay.

Edward believed, like so many others, that Ireland would never succumb to the vile regicide regime that had triumphed in England, Scotland and Wales.

Ireland was different. The forces loyal to King Charles I, and now to his exiled son following the king's execution, had put aside their quarrel with the rebel Catholic Confederacy and made common cause with their once deadly Irish foes to take on whatever forces the regicide English Parliament might send against them. Fighting together, the Old English, native Irish, and royalist English troops would, he'd hoped, prevail. But doubts had been gnawing at him for months, ever since the rumours began, and the succession of warnings from sympathetic sources…all pointing to a massive military build-up along the West Coast of England.

Troops had been pouring into towns and villages for weeks and there was little doubt as to what their ultimate destination would be. It was more a question of *when* they'd embark for Ireland.

The messenger this morning had been effusive with apologies for being the bearer of bad tidings before informing the Mayor that a Confederate spy had witnessed large numbers of troops disembarking at Ringsend in Dublin. Their uniforms were of a colour and design he'd never seen before.

Ship after ship had appeared, and the stream of men, horses and military hardware seemed endless. Ringsend was within the small swathe of territory occupied by Parliamentary forces and by God they'd made damned good use of its capture. From there, they'd move across the country, until, hopefully, the Irish defenders stopped them in their tracks.

He resumed his seat at the desk, and realized that he was breathing rapidly. *Calm down. Panicking won't help.*

Ormonde! What will Ormonde do? He'll know how best to counter this threat. He must.

Outside on the street it had started to rain: A heavy shower…people dashing for cover. He heard the clatter of boots and brogues on the cobbles, and the softer footfalls of shoeless urchins. There hadn't been a cloud in the sky, so nobody had expected that. Though they should have allowed for it, like he should have anticipated the forthcoming storm that threatened to destroy everything he held dear.

His own position would certainly be vulnerable, but so too would the town he had served intermittently since he was first elected Mayor in 1632. Not because Callan was a town of any special political or military significance in its own right. Callan's problem would be its proximity to Ireland's rebel Seat of Government: Kilkenny. All the more reason for James Butler, the Marquis of Ormond and supreme commander of the Confederate/Royalist alliance, to prioritize Callan's defence.

The room was getting dark, and, almost on cue, he heard the door-knock. In stepped the caretaker, Shawn Holden. He had a flaming torch in his hand. "I suppose you'll need the lamp yer honour?" he asked.

"Oh thanks Shawn. The weather's taken a turn for the worst. We'll be lucky to see two or three more hours of daylight."

Shawn removed the globe from the lamp and lit the wick. He placed the lamp on the desk, taking care to avoid the documents. He was about to leave when Edward called him back. "Shawn…the Council chamber might need a bit of tidying and see that the seating is in order. I'll be calling a special meeting. Something's brewing."

Shawn's face lit up with curiosity. "Anything I should know about, yer honour?"

"Nothing to concern yourself with…for now…political affairs and forthcoming, ah…challenges to the wellbeing of our lovely town, Shawn."

"I see, I'll tell Alice and Scutty to scrub the floor and I'll lay out the chairs. When's the meeting?"

40

"Two days from now. I must contact the aldermen. Can you leave now, Shawn, and attend to that? It's…you know…somewhat urgent."

Despite the urgency, Edward helped himself to another glass. It would be weeks, maybe months, before the invaders reached Callan. And maybe they'd never get there if the Irish forces and their gallant allies managed to repel them early on.

He had confidence in Ormonde as an administrator and shrewd businessman. In the years he had served as a legal agent for the Marquis the man had struck him as an organizational wizard driven by a fierce ambition, someone who let nothing stand in his way.

Edward's own wealth he owed to his lucrative dealings with Ormonde. The Mayor owned half the properties in Callan and many more throughout Ireland. Without the Marquis' patronage and the numerous commissions he'd received from him he might never have risen to be Mayor of a thriving market town, someone respected by every man and woman in the district.

Nor indeed might he have landed that influential position on the Supreme Council of the Confederation. Pushing aside the bottle, he forced himself to attend to the tedious but still pressing matters contained in the pile of vellum papers on his desk. If nothing else it would get his mind off the sickening prospect of what might lie in store for him, and the town he was honored to serve.

***

5

Tom Brennan whistled to himself as the horses cantered along jauntily on the road to Kilkenny. Just a mile now to the *Halfway Inn*, he estimated, so-called because it was located halfway between Callan and the City.

He and his horses would rest for a few hours there before resuming the journey. No hurry. He'd have plenty time to lounge about at the inn, after a meal, before resuming his trek to the City.

What was that? A splash of water across his face. And another.

The sky had abruptly turned grey. *Oh damn.* From out of nowhere the rain pelted down. He reined in the horses and stopped the wagon, promptly crawling under the canvass wrapper.

The temperature had dropped too. He shivered. Just an hour earlier the sun had been a molten ball of warmth and reassurance.

Bloody weather: Sometimes he thought that the crazy *End of the World* fellow who went around Kilkenny with the placard predicting the demise of humanity might be right, at least about the climate changing. It was certainly behaving oddly in recent years.

In his childhood, if he remembered correctly, the summers were all bright and sunny, the winters the exact opposite, and the autumns, well...they weren't as changeable as this, surely.

The clatter of rain on the canvass abated and then stopped, as abruptly as it had begun. He stuck his head out. The sky was clear again, and the sun was back to its normal function at this time of year, keeping things nice and warm.

Birds chirped in the ditches on both sides of the road, but less salubrious were the puddles that overflowed from the potholes that pockmarked the highway. They were a curse of all travelers, but especially anyone in a coach or wagon.

Climbing back onto the driving board, he signaled the horses to get moving. But he hadn't progressed more than a few yards when a loud cry assailed his ears. "Stop...Stop... or you're a dead man!"

Alarmed, he halted the wagon, the horses neighing loudly; incensed probably at being interrupted so soon after the last cantering break.

The masked horseman had appeared from somewhere behind him. He hadn't noticed anyone on the road, so the rider must have followed him at a distance.

Tom's heart raced when the man raised a pistol and pointed it directly at his chest. "Put your hands in the air and, very slowly, give me your money. And don't pretend to be poor. Nobody with a pair of horses like those can be a vagabond."

Hands trembling, Tom reached inside his coat for his purse. His heart sank at the thought of having to call off the journey because, without money to pay for the beer, he'd have to return home. Then something occurred to him. *That voice.* He'd heard it somewhere. It hit him like a brick in the forehead:

"Martin Conway! Is that you...?"

The man shuddered, let out a gasp of air, and holstered his pistol. He moved closer to the wagon, his hands firmly on the reins of his horse.

"Oh, it's you, Tom...I didn't recognize you. Look, forget about the money...where are you off to? I've never seen you in a wagon."

"It's not mine. I'm heading to Kilkenny to stock up on beer before that bloody plague has the whole City closed down."

"You'd want to be sure to wear a mask if you set foot in there."

"A mask?"

"It's a rule they've brought in. To stop the plague from spreading. You'd better have one. A piece of Hesian cloth will do the trick."

"But surely it's not that bad...I heard there's been a case or two..."

"That was three days ago. It's rampant now."

"I'll wear a mask so. God, Martin; are you still at that caper? You'll end up on a scaffold one of these days if you get caught. Can't you pack it in and do a decent day's work?"

"I'm just taking back what's mine. My family was dispossessed of all our lands. Yes, I know that was a hundred years ago, but they wererobbed of what was theirs."

"That doesn't entitle you to rob innocent travelers, does It? "

Conway laughed. "No, I suppose not, but I don't feel too bad about robbing tax-collectors and greedy landlords, even if they claim to be patriotic native Irish ones who love their country and all that blather. It doesn't matter who rules s Ireland, King,

Confederation, power-mad chieftains...you'll always have the exploiters and the people they exploit- or dispossess- like what happened to my family. I'll redress the balance a little by lightening the heavy coffers of the ones who lord it over us."

"I'd better be going, Martin. Thanks for not robbing me, anyway. I'm certainly no big knob who's exploited anyone. I'm just trying to make a living. Mind you don't make a wrong move one of these days. You'll end up being offered the joys of the Next Life... at the end of a rope!"

"I don't propose to make an appointment with the hangman for a while yet, Tom. Be seeing you!"

Doffing his cap, the highwayman wheeled around and his horse galloped at high speed down a narrow lane that branched off from the road.

So that's where he came from. Probably knows all sorts of handy nooks and crannies of the county to facilitate his getaways.

Martin had been a regular customer until a few years before, when he left Callan to live in a shack in the countryside and embark on his life of crime. It was the worst-kept secret in Callan that he'd taken to the roads to pursue the highwayman's illicit career. Everyone knew about Martin's double life but nobody would testify against him in court, so the bailiffs didn't bother hauling him in for questioning.

Locals sympathized with his plight. Cases of dispossessed families, or their descendents, turning to crime abounded. It wasn't viewed the same way as ordinary crime, the kind perpetrated by the dregs of society that all decent people shunned.

They'd heard, at the *Fiery Spirit* and other alehouses and on the streets, about the injustices endured by Conway's family at the hands of past monarchs. He saw his robbing and pilfering as payback for those wrongs but, while the man in the street might turn a blind eye to his activity, the authorities took a different view. Even in the New Ireland run by the Catholic Confederates and their allies, highway robbery was still a capital offence, regardless of what grievances motivated the culprit. If caught red-handed Martin would swing for sure.

Tom patted both horses, thanking them wordlessly for their patience. He urged them on, guiding them to one side to allow a coach to pass. It was moving at breakneck speed, like a chariot of old, as though fleeing some large predator intent on devouring it. Not very wise: the wheels could come off at that rate. The coachman's eyes blazed with urgency. Tom waved at him but the frenzied driver ignored him, lashing his horses to move faster.

Another coach appeared within seconds, followed by three carts and a covered wagon like his own. After these came men riding pack-horses, the animals weighed down with bags and accessories; also seemingly in a mad rush. The horses looked anguished, their eyes pleading: and no wonder: they were too heavily laden.

Tom figured that the scene of an accident might lie up ahead. He could do without that. He wasn't too pressed for time, but that kind of hold-up could delay him for hours. He opted to holler at the next horseman.

As the man drew alongside him, about to pass, Tom noticed that he was wearing a mask, though he didn't look like a highwayman. "What's up, do you mind me asking? Was there a mishap on the road up ahead?"

The man roared through his mask, his voice muffled but audible: "No. No accident... worse. Didn't you hear? The City's walking with the plague. I won't be going back there for a while!"

Tom had forgotten about the need for a mask to which Martin had alluded. He'd better concoct some sort of face-covering before he arrived at the City gates.

Another coach rushed past, almost striking the side of his wagon. *"Jesus"*, he rasped. *They're leaving Kilkenny as if their lives depended on it, and here am I, heading right into the bloody place. God help me. The things I do to keep drinkers merry and myself in business."*

*

Tom had to squint to make out the stately, magnificent form of Kilkenny Castle. He'd left the *Halfway Inn* just two hours earlier and had made good progress, allowing for coaches and wagons slowing him down.

As he drew nearer the City walls the castle came into sharp focus, defying the fusty greyish fog that swirled about it like an angry wraith, turning day into a dusty twilight.

45

He'd heard there were twenty-five rooms inside the castle, and its capacious grounds accommodated a lovely park, gently rolling meadows, a lavish flower garden, and a meticulously kept dove cote.

He'd been inside the castle once, but strictly in his capacity as a tradesman delivering crates of wine. That was in his youth. It was known as the jewel in the crown of the City, with its jaw-dropping three towers that rose proudly up into the heavens and dominated the skyline for miles around.

He wondered, though, why anyone would wish to own a castle like this one, given the expense and responsibility of running such a colossal enterprise. Managing an alehouse occupied most of his time, and the building was just a speck compared to that masterpiece of architecture and human ingenuity.

Then again, the Marquis of Ormonde didn't reside in Kilkenny most of the time. He was in Dublin a lot and let others manage the day-to-day affairs of the castle. *I'm sure he's not there now, with this plague rampant.*

He halted the wagon at the main City Gate, which, though open, was guarded by four musketeers. Normally it was lightly secured. One of the guards approached the wagon.

"What's your business, sir?"

Tom didn't like the way he held his musket cocked, as if expecting trouble. "I've to collect a consignment of beer from the brewery."

The man nodded, lowering his weapon. "There's a curfew in half-an-hour. Keep your mask on and avoid touching anyone!" He waved Tom through the gate.

He was no sooner inside the walls when he heard a loud sobbing, followed by a piercing shriek from further up the street. People shouting...the noise of angry exchanges reached him but the fog obscured the speakers. Then, a man darted out onto the street in front of him, mouth agape and eyes bulging.

Tom reined in the horses, but the wagon struck the man as he crossed to the opposite footpath, limping and screeching. He stood on the pavement shaking his fist at Tom, who wanted to apologize but urged the horses on.

He could see only to within a few feet ahead, but as he knew the street he pressed on. To his right the sight of prostrate people- or were they corpses? - materialized. Others were stooped over them. The guard at the gate had advised him to avoid contact.

Approaching the City centre the fog seemed to have thickened rather than abated. He strained his eyes but couldn't see anyone about, though that could be owing to the veil established by the all-pervading haze. Street-lamps shone eerily, piercing the murk but not shedding much light on his surroundings. He detected movement ahead... on the pavement to his left. One or more people moving: The fog rendered them invisible for a few seconds. Then they reappeared.

Tom shuddered. From out of the vapours emerged three ghostly figures. They moved in a cautious and creepy manner. They didn't seem human. Were they emissaries of Heaven...or Hell?

Shivers ran though him as the phantoms took shape in the half-light and he perceived them to be men in long flowing black- or no, *dark brown*-robes with a waxy sheen, each man wielding a long white rod in his right hand.

But most startling of all were their heads. Under broad drooping hats they wore bird-like masks, with ugly beaks protruding from them.

It occurred to Tom they might be blind, with those rods they were swishing about as they edged towards him. But they didn't seem unsure of their steps... *must be a theatrical caper of some kind: Ill-timed pageantry, with a disease prevalent in the City.*

Or were they criminals; intent on robbing unsuspecting citizens in the fog? The weird trio stopped as his wagon approached them. They stepped off the street to let him pass. The horses grew nervous. Tom feared they'd bolt at the sight of these apparitions.

He calmed them, as the bird-men casually turned to regard him. He raised his hat and greeted them. "Good...good morning gentlemen", he muttered, instantly regretting having said anything. One of them returned his nod, wordlessly, and the three of them continued past him, conferring silently as they went, their rods moving to convey gestures as they communicated in the deathly quiet of the street.

Within seconds they had disappeared into the fog, leaving Tom scratching his head with a mixture of nervousness and puzzlement. *Not brigands then. Must be actors.* He'd seen an open-air pageant in Kilkenny a few years before in which a figure symbolizing Death played a fiddle supposedly made of bones. It was part of a semi-religious drama harping back to the City's last plague. Perhaps these fellows were enacting a similar display.

You'd think they'd wait for the emergency to end. Kilkenny was renowned for its theatrics, amateur and professional, and he supposed the present occasion struck some of the more avid thespians as an opportunity to exhibit their acting talents. If so, they were even dafter than he thought they were. *Never mind. I must get to the brewery.*

Turning into the next street he heard wailing. *Just keep going, whatever it is, it's no concern of mine.* On the sidewalk to his left he made out the shadowy forms of men dragging what looked like a corpse, or grievously ill person, out of a house. They dropped this poor wretch in the street: *Could be a plague victim.*

The men were masked, but not decked out in that silly bird costume. When they spotted Tom they shouted at him, gesturing frantically: "keep going, you don't want to catch it, or have you got it already? Keep going!"

He gladly followed the advice.

Entering High Street he was partly relieved to find the fog had dispersed somewhat: Only partly, because its dissipation only served to reveal scenes of chaos and panic. Men and women, most of them masked or holding cloths to their faces, ran to the left and right as his wagon rolled towards them.

They hopped and sprinted, even the older ones, as if their lives depended on it, avoiding each other as they dodged the wagon. Above the babble of giddy voices one shrieked "keep your distance!"

Tom caught sight of the frenzied man who'd shouted. He was waving a pistol about. Suddenly a shot pieced the air. Smoke mingled with the dregs of the fog around the man's head. He started coughing and wheezing.

Whether he'd intended to discharge the weapon this added to the frenzy. He remained standing, as if lost, or frozen to the spot. The crisscrossing runners on the street ran faster to avoid him.

Tom noticed that some of the house and shop doors on both sides of the street had large red crosses painted on them, presumably notices or warnings connected with the plague. People darted about crazily and, when they passed close to the wagon, some cast hostile glances in his direction. He feared someone might try to seize the wagon or the horses to make an escape from the disease-stricken City.

Further down the street, he had to tighten his mask and hold another piece of cloth to his face to ward off smoke that blew on a strong breeze from a house to his left. The building was ablaze and a small masked group was huddled together on the opposite side of the street, a woman among them wailing pitifully as flames consumed the thatched roof. Shards of blackened glass peppered the footpath fronting the house.

Tom urged the horses to move faster. A few houses further on flames belched from another doomed edifice, with onlookers again sadly beholding the misfortune, but strangely doing nothing to quench the fire.

Had the City gone completely mad? Men with bird beaks, shots fired in the street, and fires being allowed to engulf homes. Another excited man emerged from a laneway, wielding a firearm, this one a blunderbuss. He dashed onto the street and stopped in Tom's path, pointing the weapon straight at him.

Not waiting to discover what the man wanted, Tom urged the horses to giddy-up. The man nimbly hopped out of the way, shouting something Tom couldn't hear as the wagon went speeding past. A shot rang out behind him. Tom felt nothing so he assumed the fellow had either missed, or maybe hadn't fired at him.

Not looking back, he urged the horses on towards the brewery, praying that the bloody place wouldn't be boarded up or burned down when he got there. He didn't blame the brewers for abandoning deliveries to taverns and alehouses. And he wouldn't have bothered making the journey to Kilkenny if he'd realized how desperate the situation was. He recalled a phrase often used by a customer of his in Callan; who complained that the world these days was "upside down." Well, this part of it seemed to be...

Entering Parliament Street, he was relieved to find a calmer atmosphere, with just a few masked people walking, respectfully keeping their distance from each other and not exhibiting any signs of panic. A priest in full clerical garb was administering Communion, or was it the Last Rites, to a woman who lay crumpled at the entrance to an apothecary.

Another woman stood beside her, shaking her head frantically and gesturing with her hands: a heart-rending scene. As he drew closer Tom saw the anguish in the woman's face as she grasped the cleric's arm and he quickly pushed it away, returning to whatever sacramental duty occupied him. Tom had slowed down but accelerated again to banish this calamity from his field of vision.

Thank God, he lisped, seeing the brewery just a few hundred yards ahead. *Please God, let it be open, or I'll throw myself into the Nore!*

As the high and broad wooden gates of the brewery loomed, he felt a surge of relief at the sight of the open entrance, guarded by three pike-men.

He caught the pungent whiff of the place; the spicy herbal aroma of the hops and the sweet toasty malt. He knew many men and women who found these scents repellent. He'd acquired a love of them, much as he had developed a liking for the taste of beer, and its effects, as well as a healthy respect for the profitable living it provided.

His brief reverie was shattered by the appearance, seemingly from nowhere, of another man sporting one of those weird bird beaks and long cloaks or coats, and this fellow was chasing a second man, who had no mask and appeared to be heading towards the brewery.

The bird-man was using his white rod to beat the unmasked fellow, landing several strokes that elicited loud yelps from him. Tom guessed the man's offence was not wearing a mask, or maybe not "keeping his distance."

He guessed the pursuer was probably acting on behalf of the civic authorities to enforce the covering of the nose and mouth to prevent the spread of the disease...if indeed that was how the disease was spread.

*

Mathias Blunt's diary

We, six of us including the Sergeant, are billeted in the home of a godly Dublin Protestant who's sympathetic to the Parliamentary cause. He and his wife have given us a break from the daily diet of

50

bread and cheese and the odd biscuit that we'd accepted as our lot: Roast beef, chicken, floury potatoes, bacon, cabbage... and goblets of wine to wash it down.

The Sergeant told the housewife that she's spoiling us, but she answered with gushing praise for Master Cromwell. She'd originally lived in Ulster, she told us, but the family was forced to leave after the papist uprising of 1641. Her three sisters and her parents were stripped naked by the rebels and pushed at musket point into the freezing waters of the Bann.

Her neighbours were hacked to pieces by a rabble shouting "Long Live the Pope!" Even as we savoured her hospitality, all of us resolved to cleanse this fair land of the filth who had committed that unspeakable crime against innocent Protestants, and the Royalist idiots who now shamefully collaborated with them against us. A soldier from Leicester swore he'd make every Irish rebel pay for what this poor family had endured. The householders cheered him.

As we caroused after another helping of the finest food, a small child toddled into the dining chamber. She gurgled and handed me a tiny yellow and white flower. I took it and she gabbled away in that strange alien tongue.

All the lads, even the tough and slightly crazy one with the head of a bulldog and the big scar down his left cheek, were touched by her innocence. I can't get it out of my mind that if this child had been present when the rebels took her kin, she too would've been dispatched.

Yes, this is no ordinary war. The enemy is not human as we understand the concept. They must be expunged from the land of the living. God will reward any man who strikes down these vermin, as the Lord General said last week in Ringsend.

*

Tom felt relief when the heavy oak door of the *Smulken Inn* creaked open to reveal the elegant form of Dr Holohan. With the City gripped by panic and suspicion he feared his knock would go unanswered.

"Ah Tom, you're welcome. If you don't mind, before you come into the sitting room, would you kindly douse your hands in that basin there?"

Tom thanked him and sighed. This was the fifth time he'd been asked to wash his hands in vinegar, to comply with the City's anti-plague clampdown.

They had vinegar ready for him at the brewery when he got inside. After leaving the brewery, where his wagon would remain until the following morning when he'd return to collect his beer supply, he'd been directed to wash his hands in what he first took to be holy water fonts positioned at the corners of several streets.

They were in fact receptacles of vinegar, in which he had to cleanse his money also. As he followed the doctor's instruction his friend crooned, "I'm not quite sure if it makes a blind bit of difference, but even if it doesn't, it won't hurt either. Vinegar has some curative value. It wards off certain ailments. Whether it protects against plague is far from certain though."

Having dried his hands, Tom asked if he could remove the mask. Underneath it, his face was lathered in sweat.

"Of course...it's uncertain too what value, if any, that has..." He pointed doubtfully at the mask.

"Thanks, Lawrence. My God, the City has been upended by this damn thing. Do you think it'll be brought under control? I should have come sooner..."

"You'll have something to warm you up and relax you after your journey, Tom?"

The doctor handed him a steaming mug of hot whiskey. He had prepared one for himself too. Reclining in the ornate ebony armchair opposite, he regarded Tom with a look of reassurance, mingled, Tom thought, with pity.

He accepted the drink with gratitude, and gasped."Between dodging men seemingly intent on murder and being scared half to death by monstrous bird-like creatures, I'm lucky to have got here at all. The nicest person I met since leaving Callan was a highwayman who kindly decided not to rob me!"

"It's a frightful time, right enough. Those bird men, though...they're doctors, like me. The costume might raise a few eyebrows, but there's a purpose to it. It's protective clothing. That beak you saw covering the nose of the birdman holds specially selected aromatic substances. They serve, in theory anyway, as a sort of filter against the deadly odours issuing from plague victims, or people suspected of carrying the disease.

"The mask can also emit a little cloud of plague repellent smoke. Again, that's the intention. I wouldn't swear on the Bible that it actually works..."

"And the white sticks they carried?"

"Just to keep away unwanted folk, like the rod used to drive a herd of cattle."

Tom felt better after downing half of the whiskey. The warmth suffused his entire being. The plague seemed less of a threat now.

"Are you not bothered by this, Lawrence? You don't look overly concerned?"

The doctor shrugged. "Panicking won't help. If I don't seem perturbed it's because I'll be out of the City two days from now. You were lucky to find me here at all. I plan to stay with my sister in South Kilkenny, though I suspect I'll be on the move again before too long, even if the plague dies out.

"Move...where?"

"I mean out of Ireland, Tom. You mightn't have heard yet, especially with your mind on your present journey...keeping your business afloat. I heard this morning from a merchant who paid me a fleeting visit- he was on his way to Waterford to exit the country- that a large invasion force has landed in Dublin. He caught sight of soldiers disembarking from ships... thousands of them."

"Invasion? Is he sure they weren't our own troops?"

"Not with the uniforms...and the guns they had. I'm afraid it's started Tom. Parliament has beaten all its enemies over there and now they're coming here... *An armada*, that's what the merchant called it. Ships arriving for two days, and more still that he saw... stretching out to the far horizon, all disgorging troops, horses, artillery. It's not for a picnic they're coming Tom. Our side might beat them of course...but I wouldn't wager my life on that prospect."

He fell silent, and refilled his glass.

He continued: "God, the Confederacy was riven by internal squabbles and rivalries even before it linked up with the Royalists in the great alliance that was supposed to be invincible. Imagine the tensions between fiercely independent-minded native Irish... and

Royalists whose loyalty is to the exiled Prince of Wales who's waiting to return and be crowned Chares the Second?

"Yes, I know they've united against a common enemy, but will that unity of purpose be enough to put it up to the Roundheads? As I say, I'm not waiting around to find out. France is lovely at this timeof year. I expect to renew some old friendships there."

Tom sank back in his chair. "And there was I, worrying about running out of beer. Invasion? As if a plague weren't bad enough. Jesus. Could you manage another mug of that stuff?"

*

Next morning, Tom felt a weight lift from his shoulders once he'd passed out through the City gates and was heading for the Callan road. In another day or two he might have been prevented from leaving, with all sorts of new rules planned to restrict movement due to the plague.

His splitting headache from having overindulged in the hard stuff into the early hours had abated, thanks mainly to the doctor's own remedy, the recipe for which the wily medic refused to share. But his relief at getting out of Kilkenny was short-lived, as his mind began to revisit the doctor's lengthy and sometimes difficult to grasp spiff about the evolving military situation.

The doctor was a trusty old friend, and he appreciated very much his hospitality under the present challenging circumstances, but he tended to be a bit long-winded when he stared rabbiting on about politics and modern history, subjects that Tom didn't especially care for, except in suitably small doses, like when he was batting the breeze with customers in the *Fiery Spirit*.

Lawrence had grown misty-eyed as he spoke of the glory that was Kilkenny since becoming Confederate capital of Ireland in '42, a magnet for the rich and the powerful. Before its dissolution in January of '49, the doctor recalled, the Confederation's constituent bodies had met in various parts of the City, turning every venue into a renowned centre of civic pride and excellence: The Supreme Council met at the Castle, aptly enough given its regal splendour at the heart of the City.

The General Assembly convened in Market Street, and the Ecclesiastic dignitaries attached to the Confederation gathered in solemn conclave at Rothe House. Tom knew his way around the three-storeyed Late Tudor building with its luxurious accommodation and breathtaking courtyards.

He'd worked briefly in its sumptuous garden that could have been modelled on the original Garden of Eden itself, with its abundance of floral and herbaceous attractions.

The hope, according to the doctor, was that, once the king had triumphed over Parliament, the Confederacy could reassemble and then, naturally, Kilkenny would recover its status as de facto capital of a semi- independent Catholic Ireland loyal to the monarchy.

"But now, well..." The doctor's tone had changed. A deep sadness overcame him as he lapsed into a string of doom-laden prophesies that had Tom seeking refuge in further helpings of whiskey...or whatever it was that the doctor had added to the large beaker from an even larger one. It could be that much sought after illicit stuff that Tom was finding it harder to acquire.

"If the Parliamentary army can't be stopped by our lot, Tom, it won't be long before it comes to batter down this City's walls. And frankly I don't see us coming out on top. No, not even with a castle that's the pride of Europe.

"Serving as the Confederate capital could prove to have been a mixed blessing. It makes us a bigger target; they'll reckon that the City has great symbolic value after its seven years of cultural grandeur."

Tom had interrupted. "Wait just a second. I'm thinking...will it really make such a difference if the Parliamentary side wins? I mean, say they take Kilkenny. Instead of its being the capital of a rebel arrangement, a Confederacy, or whatever you like to call it, won't the City continue as before under whatever new arrangements the English parliament decides to impose on it? For centuries we had a King or queen ruling over us. And it wasn't exactly plain sailing, and that includes Charles, God rest him. Surely to God having a bunch of politicians in London calling the shots in Ireland, including here in Kilkenny, wouldn't be any worse than what we've put up with here since Adam picked apples?"

The doctor said nothing for several seconds, then left down the mug he'd been about to rise to his lips.

"You'd be forgiven for thinking that, Tom, for trying to see some prospect of things just continuing as before. But I've been following events closely. I've known for the past seven mouths that an invasion was likely. More recently I was sure it would happen; only I didn't know the actual date. I've read the newssheets from England...about the decision to commission a top general to lead an expedition... to bring us rebellious Irish back into line.

"For the past month there was a heck of a lot of activity on the West coast, especially Bristol, and rumours abounded about something big. But what bothered me most was a transcript of a parliamentary exchange in the House of Commons. Tom, they've decided that if and when they succeed in reconquering Ireland, the natives will be robbed of their lands and properties. They plan to eliminate the educated classes...suppress the Catholic Church, and well, destroy our culture. Everything we hold dear."

Tom had listened to these cogitations with deep unease and growing horror, but he was less concerned about the uprooting of landowners and the chastisement of the educated classes than with his own domain back in Callan. If Kilkenny was high on the list of cities to be captured, would the invaders also take a shine to Callan, which was only ten miles from the city?

The Doctors shrugged. "If you're lucky, Callan might be by-passed, but as a significant market town, with a wall and garrison, I can't see them sparing it. Look, if they get as far as this part of the country, we'll already have lost the war, and so, if I were you, I'd consider getting the hell out of Ireland, as I'll be doing."

Tom was grateful for the soothing effect of the alcohol when he flopped into the fine feather bed at the inn. It blocked some of the panicky thoughts prickling at the edge of his consciousness. They threatened to invade his head as surely as the Roundheads had embarked on their crusade.

Now, as the two horses pulled the large consignment of beer back to Callan, worries ganged up on him. What future had the *Fiery Spirit?* Would life ever be thesame again?

***

6

Fr. Malcolm stretched himself after rising from his straw couch, his straw-filled pillow having fallen onto to the cold stone floor of his dormitory cell. He heard the other friars shuffling about in their cells. The balm of sleep quickly gave way to a buzz of expectation and suspense.

He heard loud whispers outside his cell. Speculation was rife. Just what did the Prior want to talk to them about that merited the skipping of Morning Prayer in the chapel? Fr. Kearney had told them to be in the refectory at the time normally reserved for Mass. Breakfast would commence following the Prior's spiff.

One theory doing the rounds since the Prior's intriguing announcement was that they were all in for a telling-off over the quest. Maybe the takings weren't adequate, or not to the Prior's liking. Was he going to reprimand them, encourage them to try harder next time?

Another possibility, one that bothered Malcolm, was that the Prior wasn't happy with the degree of religious observance at the abbey. He had alluded more than once in the past six months to the need for a deepening of commitment to the faith: Less worldly concerns and more prayer, fasting and abstinence.

Malcolm hoped that flagellation wouldn't be introduced to the Callan settlement. He honestly believed they were doing enough to please God and uphold the values promulgated by the Gospel without tormenting themselves with whips or blades.

Or maybe a transfer was in the offing for one or more of them. He hoped he wouldn't be moved on. This was his home. He loved the town and the austere life of the community. Working in the garden uplifted his spirits, as did his cherished forays into the bookish treasures of the library.

Lugging heavy buckets of water from the Blessed Well was a laborious chore, but one he'd grown to like. He loved the chorus of birds chirruping around him as he filled the bucket. And it kept him fit.

A posting elsewhere might deprive him of these routines that he had integrated into his life so that they were as vital to him as breathing God's clean air. He'd known a friar in his first year here who'd been abruptly re-appointed to an abbey on an offshore island.

He shuddered to think of what that might entail: A barren existence in a glorified cave setting, with barely enough food to survive on and nothing but the seagulls for company, apart from maybe one or two other equally bereft friars, all languishing together in an earthly purgatory.

He would of course accept such a posting without question, as a manifestation of God's will. The Prior's word on the matter would be final, not open to dispute. He'd prayed repeatedly to be spared from re-assignment elsewhere, but if God chose not to listen, he'd accept that, though with a heavy heart.

Having washed himself and dried off, he donned his grey habit and exited the cell. The others were clustered in the corridor, their hushed, conspiratorial voices creating little worried echoes as they conferred like gossiping women. They fretted about a feared dressing-down over their progress as true servants of God.

The oldest friar, Fr. Jeremy, was the only one seemingly not bothered. Malcolm found this unusual "You don't seem so worried, Jeremy", he jibed. "Do you know something we don't? Is the Prior planning to give us all a bottle of the finest wine, do you think, to celebrate his birthday...it's this month, isn't it?"

Jeremy smiled. "No, but I like your jest. No, no. I've had my life. I long only for God to take me to the next world where joys beyond measure await. If he sends me to languish on Rathlin Island, or Inish Boffin, or to some desolate windswept mountainside it won't bother me in the slightest. I'm not long for this Vale of Tears. I'm thinking that a tougher schedule might well be what I need to hasten my passage to that...to that place we can only dream of down here."

Fr. Ambrose, who had gained at least half a stone in weight in the past year, wasn't so sanguine. Head bowed, he covered his face with his hands, and rasped "I know what this is about. He's going to give me a right tongue-lashing over my fondness for apple pie. You all know how I can't resist it. Those townsfolk have a lot to answer for. Generosity is fine, but it's turned me into a glutton. I just hope he doesn't take in out on the rest of you." His voiced cracked as he spoke.

Fr. Timothy, the abbey's joker, clapped him on the back. "Cheer up Ambrose. We won't hold it against you if your ...ah...obesity...gets you into some hot water." Winking at the others, he added: "we'll miss you though when you're sitting in your cell far from Callan, with the broad Atlantic beating against the sides of your new home on the edge of a cliff."

Ambrose laughed nervously, seeing the pointlessness, Malcolm guessed, of his concern, given that God's will would be done in any event. "Will we get this over with, then, colleagues?" he asked, leading the way down the wooden stairs, along the next stony corridor, and into the refectory.

The light streaming through the windows dazzled Malcolm. A bright sun shone outside. The Prior was already seated at the head of the long oak table, and Alice the cook was laying the porridge dishes for later.

Fr. Kearney didn't give anything away. He retained his usual impassive demeanour. He didn't look angry. That might be a good omen, Malcolm thought. Then again, it mightn't mean anything. He wasn't known for allowing scrutiny of his thoughts. He could be a veritable statue, blank and unreadable.

When all were seated and Alice had left the hall, the Prior stood and paced about the room, serving only to increase the tension.

God, something really is up.

"I called you in here, brothers in Christ, to share weighty news..." He paused, turning to look each of them in the eye.

They all shrank in their chairs. The Prior seemed to have aged a few years since the previous day. Or was it the effect of the light...how it emphasised the creases in his perpetually intense face?

In grave tones Fr. Kearney continued: "Dear colleagues; what I have to say grieves me more than tongue can tell." He paused again, as if lost for words. Closing his eyes tightly he extended both hands like a priest at the Eucharist.

"Our work here, at this great monastic settlement, is under threat", he went on, opening his eyes but now avoiding eye contact with any of them. His attention seemed to be fixed on a spot above the window opposite.

Malcolm wondered for a second if he had spotted something unusual outside. He looked around. Nothing, apart from a sparrow pecking at crumbs on the window sill.

The Prior continued haltingly: "Our way of life, our Augustinian mission; our service to the poor of the district, all the precious

59

elements that make up this community of friars, may soon be at an end."

Malcolm stood and raised a hand, the suspense too much for him: "What's the matter, Fr. Kearney? Have we failed in our work? How is our work here under threat?"

The Prior motioned him to be seated and he continued pacing, hands now clasped behind his back. He spoke gratingly. "Events in England have conspired against us. You know that in the war between King and Parliament over there the monarchy lost and the King was executed...murdered...last January. And you'll be aware that the new government is even less favourable to our Catholic faith than the monarchy was?

"Well, the victors in that bloody conflict have now turned their attention to Ireland. Up to last week, the Parliamentary army held only a small parcel of territory in Dublin and was struggling to gain ground in Munster. The Catholic Confederates and Royalist forces assisting them proved more than capable of keeping them at bay."

He stopped in front of the window, his back turned to them. Facing them, he again made an abrupt gesture of resignation. "Yesterday, shortly after morning Mass, a messenger arrived here at my study. He had ridden for more than four days with barely a break for food or water to bring me the news that he'd seen troops disembarking from ships at Ringsend in Dublin: Thousands of them. As soon as one ship had emptied another one began disgorging soldiers. The uniforms were of a colour and design he'd never seen before.

"They were singing hymns as they fanned out along the docks. Another witness told my messenger that this was the start of the reckoning. When he inquired as to what that meant, the witness told him that the greatest expeditionary force ever to land in Ireland had been sent to avenge the massacre of 1641, to crush Royalists still holding out on Irish soil against parliament, and to uproot the Catholic Church from this land."

He fell silent. Malcolm wanted to speak, but his lips refused to part. Words stuck in his throat. He felt numb. He could see the others were similarly affected. He forced himself to ask: "But, Prior, won't this invading army be resisted by the Confederate/Royalist alliance? Might not...our side...eject these invaders...before they can establish a firm foothold?"

The Prior gave him pitying look. "I'm not a military man. None of us are. We're doing the Lord's work. Any decisions about battlefield engagements will not be our concern. And in fact we must stay well out of the deadly if inevitable business of war. We'll pray today, and beseech the Lord to safeguard our community from harm. But we must prepare for the truly awful consequences should these invaders succeed."

Ambrose had his hand up. "Prior, if I may. This has echoes of what happened here back in 1540, when King Henry suppressed the monasteries. The abbey was closed, the friars dispersed or forced into hiding, the buildings here damaged. It took decades for the community to recover, but it did. We're still here, despite Henry's best efforts to be rid of us..."

The Prior nodded. "Yes. This could be a repeat of what happened back then. Except that the enemy this time is a great deal more hostile to our faith than Henry was. A vein of searing hatred of the Irish runs through the whole Puritan ethnicity. And the leader of the Parliamentary faction, the man who it seems is leading this...crusade...against us, hates the Irish almost as much as he abhors the Catholic faith. A fellow called Cromwell."

"So, do you think we'll have to close the community for a while like the abbey had to do in 1540, wait for things to blow over, and then re-establish the settlement?" Timothy asked.

"It may be. But let's not get ahead of ourselves. The invaders may be routed. They've just arrived. Or at least they had a few days ago when the messenger saw them. Who knows how the situation will develop, apart from God himself, and I suppose the commanders on both sides. For now, we must carry on with our work, our devotions; our service to the poor. Take each day as it comes and pray for deliverance from this evil that now stalks the land... like a wolf in search of the lamb."

Fr. Jeremy drew open-mouthed stares from the friars. Malcolm couldn't believe that the man had a cheery smile and was nodding joyfully, as if humming a tune to himself.

The Prior addressed him "This frightful news doesn't appear to trouble you, Jeremy."

"I expected different tidings, Fr. Kearney. We all did. We were under the impression that some of us might be for the chop... I mean transferral. It turns out it's just the prospect...a possibility...that we might have to go to ground, as our predecessors did, as indeed members of our Order have to do on the Continent and across parts of Asia, at various junctures, to avoid persecution. I'd much prefer to be taking a temporary break from my vocation than trying to exist on the side of a mountain or on a barren island in the middle of a lake...no offence to your judgement in these matters and not implying that you'd ever pack us off to such inhospitable places."

"All the same", said the Prior, "it would be difficult for you, Jeremy, at your advanced age, to go into hiding, or exile abroad... as we'll have to consider doing if Callan is captured."

"I agree, Prior. That's why I'm already resolved not to leave...whatever happens. Unless of course I'm instructed by your good self to so act, in which case I shall obey my superior. I'm not long for this sad old world. I'd prefer to end my earthly journey here than live like a hunted animal, as I believe the friars did when Henry turfed them out."

The Prior relaxed his tense features and regarded Jeremy with compassion. "See if you feel the same if and when we have to make that decision about leaving our beloved Callan...and this abbey that has endured for centuries.

"But enough for now. Malcolm, please tell Alice to serve breakfast in twenty minutes. We mustn't allow this Mr. Cromwell to dictate the pace or quality of our daily calling as Augustinians. Until further notice, we carry on as normal. Let the military people handle affairs of war. We must do what we can to preserve this little oasis of peace."

He promptly exited the hall, leaving the friars speechless.

Malcolm broke the silence, "I'd better ask Alice to serve..."

"I'm not hungry," Ambrose lisped. Malcolm nodded sympathetically and left the hall.

*

Tom Brennan joined the larger than usual crowd streaming into St. Mary's Parish Church in Callan. Word had got round via the town crier, and newssheets for those who could read, that the PP had some terrible news he wished to share with the congregation.

No hint of what the news related to, but Tom knew, and it gave him a sinking feeling again as he dipped his hand in the holy water font: the business he'd built up and worked so hard to advance faced ruin if Callan fell.

Apart from the havoc that any battle would cause, there was the additional prospect of alehouses countrywide being shut down if this Cromwell fellow had his way. The doctor had informed him that Puritans disapproved of alcohol, and that a new regime might close any premises serving drink.

He'd considered leaving Callan, but what would be the point? The new laws would apply equally throughout Ireland.

The church was thronged, as he'd expected. No better plan to fill the seats than to keep people on tenterhooks, wondering what big revelation was coming. Gossip had been rife for the past three days, but none of it, as far as Tom could deduce, got even close to what the PP had in mind.

Fr. Brannigan emerged from the sacristy to take up his position at the altar, his two white-clad servers dutifully flanking him, clasping lighted candles. Sunbeams filtering through the stained glass fashioned little dancing patterns of light on the ceiling above the priest and across the ancient stonework behind him.

Tom noticed with a twinge of discomfort that the brilliant blues, reds and yellows of the window depicting the murder of Thomas Becket had an eerie glow. The sword poised over the saint's neck glinted ominously, and translucent spears pierced the vibrant artwork.

The PP looked more solemn than on other Mass days. He didn't have that warm, welcoming smile at the commencement of mass that was his hallmark. He looked less confident or in command than usual, and his thick bushy eyebrows seemed to sag under theweight of what he had to say.

He went straight into the mysterious Latin routine that nobody understood, except maybe the odd schoolboy with a smattering of that quaint foreign language.

Tom always found it unsettling that the priest spent most of his time with his back turned to the congregation, intoning all those undoubtedly sacred but fathomless words and formulas as mass-goers tried to keep focused, though he knew most of them, like himself, were distracted by thoughts of the Sunday Dinner, and counting the minutes to when it would appear on a table in front of

63

them. But today even the Sunday Roast did nothing to lighten his heart.

At last, Fr. Brannigan turned around, eliciting the customary sigh of relief from his flock. Little bells tingled. A brief silence followed; and echoing coughs from the altar.

"My dear people", he began, haltingly. "I'll read some notices before addressing you on an issue of the greatest urgency. Ah...yes...thirteen petty offenders due to be punished in the stocks in East Street on Friday next will be spared chastisement as the bailiff has discovered that the stocks have fallen into disrepair. Punishments will resume a fortnight from now by which time the stocks will hopefully have been mended.

"On that subject...(he looked up from the parchment) I'd appeal to you not to engage in the obnoxious and all too common practise of pelting people displayed in the stocks with rotten fruit or vegetables, or indeed, foul-spelling liquids. The miscreants suffer punishment enough through the public humiliation they must bear. Think of the Lord's admonition: Let him without sin cast the first stone.

"Ah...The banns of marriage are announced between Michael Doherty and Mary Tierney. A collection for renovations to the Town Cross will be taken up after Mass."

He removed his spectacle, puffed up his mouth with air, and rotated his head, scrutinizing the faithful, scanning the pews, up and down, to left and right, as if he wanted to ensure nobody was omitted from his all-seeing gaze.

His voice took on a sharper tang when he resumed: "My dear people, since I came to Callan fifteen years ago you and I have got to know each other. I have endeavoured as best I could to serve you, and you have come here to pray and uphold the faith of our fathers, week in, week out. We celebrate the birth of the Saviour at Christmas, his death and resurrection at Easter, and the other feasts of our church throughout the year.

"Going to Mass is to some extent a routine, and for me I must admit that saying Mass can seem a chore, a duty I attend to as I would wind my clock or have my breakfast or go to sleep every night. That's not as it should be. We are human, and prone to error and distraction."

He scanned the pews again before resuming: "But there may come a time when our faith can no longer be taken for granted, when indeed we may have to suffer for it...perhaps just a little, but maybe a lot. Such a time draws nearer by the day."

He paused again, blinking and rotating his head. Tom felt he was looking at him, quickly banishing the thought.

"As you may or may not have heard, a powerful English army has landed in Ireland. This force was sent by the Parliament of England to reconquer our land, to subdue us. But it won't be just a case of one governing authority replacing another if this invading force prevails. The commander of this force, a Mr Oliver Cromwell, has pledged to obliterate the Catholic Church in Ireland. It is his belief that we are unworthy of being alive, let alone of having the right to our beliefs.

"We know that we belong to the one, true, and apostolic church; that God is and always has been on the side of this great institution that Christ himself founded. Be in no doubt but that it is this Cromwell and his followers who are the heretics, not you and I. I do not know what the future holds for us... whether our own armies can stem the tide of evil.

"What I do believe is that you, my good people, will stand firm against these enemies of the faith. I have spoken to the Mayor. He has promised me that everything will be done to defend this town if we should comer under attack. I implore you: If the invaders threaten Callan...Do not leave it to the soldiers assigned to protect us. Let every citizen rise to this challenge. You must *all* become defenders of the faith.

"The coming weeks and months will test us to the utmost. We must be strong. In the meantime, as we await developments, I appeal to you: pray for deliverance, pray for your church and, my dear people; pray for me."

His voice cracked with emotion as he ended the Mass; completely out of character for him. In fact, the whole Mass had a different tone this Sunday. He was usually pokerfaced, apart from a hearty smile at the outset, speaking calmly and dispassionately, and rarely making eye contact with anyone.

The congregation was struck dumb. Understandably: Callan folk didn't like change. Set in their ways, they treated outsiders with caution, suspicion, or downright hostility. Now their whole world had been turned topsy-turvey by what they'd heard from the pulpit.

A forlorn murmur swept the pews. Men gaped...women held hands to their faces. Heads shook with bafflement. Some whispered frantically, others just stood transfixed. The oldest woman in Callan, sitting alone in the front pew to Tom's right, tightened her scarf and blessed herself, staring up at the plaster statue of St. Anthony.

Communion relieved the tension somewhat, though worshippers whispered and gestured frantically as they queued to receive the Body of Christ. Reaching the altar rails Tom inhaled smoke from burning incense and felt invigorated. He loved its woody smell with a hint of flowers, even if it also hinted vaguely at death.

After Communion the priest seemed in a hurry to finish. Tom thought he rushed the final blessing before he and the two servers genuflected and re-entered the vestry.

It took several stunned seconds before the congregation began its slow exit. Outside, animated exchanges followed. Prophesies of doom rang in Tom's ears, though he wasn't as fazed as most of his fellow worshippers obviously were.

He left the church feeling slightly better. He hadn't expected that, but somehow it seemed easier to cope with this unfolding ghastliness now that everyone knew about it. Maybe things wouldn't be so bad. The Irish might rout the invaders.

He whistled a patriotic song to himself as he quickstepped up South Street. Casting a backward glance at St. Mary's, he noticed that the upper half of the stately gothic building was bathed in sunlight...a sign of hope, perhaps?

He'd open the alehouse next day as normal, and serve his customers as if he'd never heard of Oliver Cromwell.

*

Mathias Blunt's diary: early September 1649

Our waiting about, carousing, and daily drilling ended rather abruptly. Orders came from the top. It wasn't towards Kilkenny we were headed, as many of us expected, given its status as the self-styled capital of the rebel papist entity. That will come later.

We learned that Drogheda, in County Louth to the north of Dublin, was the objective. Twelve thousand of us, between infantry, cavalry and cannon crews headed towards the large town. We foot soldiers envied the cavalry and the dragoons, and the men riding on wagons or carts who didn't have to slog it out through this miserable countryside. I and two colleagues spent half an hour extricating a soldier from a bog-hole that nearly swallowed him up.

On Sept 3rd we arrived on the outskirts of Drogheda and encamped. Two days later the powerful artillery train disembarked from vessels on the River Boyne. I didn't get to see that, as it happened downstream from my position. But I was promptly roused from my musings- I was about to make another entry in this diary- by the Sergeant who informed me that I was required to guard an artillery crew.

That seemed straightforward enough and I readily agreed. But the Sergeant eyed me closely. "Are you a fast learner, lad, eh?" he asked.

"Fast enough", I replied hesitantly. He got to the point. Guarding artillery necessitated use of a slightly different weapon. My matchlock musket wouldn't be ideal, because it wasn't wise to have lengths of smoldering match, which were necessary to ignite the priming powder in a matchlock, in the immediate vicinity of so much gunpowder. A spark could detonate the stuff.

So, I was to be issued with a flintlock, which dispensed with the need for match. It was also easier to load, he assured me. But I'd have to get used to it quickly, as the bombardment would likely begin within a day or two, depending on whether the town garrison agreed to surrender.

While I honed my musketry skills with a flintlock, two siege batteries were being painstakingly moved into position. Their purpose was to unleash their deadly fire against the southern and eastern walls of the town.

It took me less than three hours, I estimate, to become a proficient marksman with the new weapon. I was quite proud of this achievement, a sin for which I chide myself. The flintlock is not as heavy as the matchlock either, a considerable asset.

The Sergeant lined us up on a hillside overlooking the town and gave us a rundown on what to expect. The town's defences had been built long before our modern weaponry was heard of, but still posed

67

a formidable challenge. Its circuit of stonewalls was about three yards thick, and the town was bisected by the River Boyne.

Spies had relayed to us that the defenders might be short of ammunition but seemed to be well stocked with food and other provisions. There was also a curious misconception on the part of the defenders that advantaged us: they believed that our presence here was just a clever diversion, that Kilkenny or another city or major town was the real objective. An understandable error: We'd have thought the same in their stead.

When we'd dug in, and the artillery had lined up, our hearts fluttered to hear that the Lord General had issued a formal summons to the Town Governor to surrender.

More waiting followed as we prayed that those foolish rebels and their Royalist allies of convenience would run up the white flag. Men around me played cards or dice, and some swigged mouthfuls of rum or ale, which were supposedly forbidden at this point, with the countdown to possible combat underway.

I availed of every chance I got to record my impressions, all the while trying not to brood on the fact that if I fall in battle this diary will die with me and my musings and observations will have counted for nothing.

Then the call came: "They've refused, prepare for battle!"

We all tensed. Cards and dice disappeared. We reached for our weapons. I headed off to guard the five men who hovered around their artillery piece, a culverin, they call it. My job, and that of the other flintlock bearers assigned to this duty, was simply to protect the gunners if the enemy got near us.

That didn't seem likely just then, with the town almost completely encircled by us. The first cannon boomed and spat fire to my left; then another pounded to my right. Within seconds a cacophony of ear-splitting roars shook us. My bones rattled. I clenched my teeth and my grip tightened on the musket. I steeled myself against this new experience.

The weapon vibrated in my hands as the earth itself quivered. It was one thing to hear a cannon from afar, quite another to be in the midst of the firing.

Four or five minutes into the bombardment, I heard a voice cry out above the clamour: "Rebels!"

The man shouting fell to earth, and stepping over his body was a wild looking fellow in a tattered uniform. He was fumbling with a matchlock, working furiously to reload it. As he hastened to push the ramrod down the barrel a rapier plunged into his back. He shrieked and collapsed unto the man he'd killed.

"They've sent out small bands to harry us" the Sergeant warned. Apparently, the Irish had been prepared for us and had posted fighters outside the walls. Another warning cry rang out.

I half turned to spot three rebels rushing towards me. My arms shaking, I somehow managed to squeeze the trigger, but missed the man I aimed at. They drew close enough for me to perceive the rage in their faces, their eyes flaming orbs of hatred.

All three fell to musket fire. I praised the Lord. A soldier rushed to finish them off, slashing them repeatedly with a sabre until the Sergeant gently nudged him away. An artillery man gave me the thumbs-up, though my bullet hadn't struck home.

All day the cannons spat their load unto the heads of the savage Irish, and towards evening the nuisance attacks on our ranks diminished. We breathed easier, and I availed of the respite to chronicle this fortuitous day...

***

7

Edward Comerford wasn't in his usual upbeat mood for his daily stroll around Callan. Setting out from his palatial mansion at Westcourt he opted to take in all of the local sights and landmarks. He felt a need to reassure himself of his position, which remained intact and unassailable. But for how long?

Up to the moment the town passed into the hands of the rabble sent here by England's parliament, a gang of regicides with the blood of an anointed king on their hands, he would be its Mayor. His vast portfolio of properties in Callan and elsewhere were still his…not yet in enemy hands.

Climbing the little moss-encrusted stile he stepped into the Motte field. The grass; thankfully, had been cut and the quietly grazing cattle barely registered his presence. The mighty Motte hill had a peaceful look to it. The scotch pines and beeches towered like giants of old in a semi-circle around the hilltop, fiery autumnal hues contrasting with the green mound of earth hosting them.

Callan prided itself on having reintroduced these trees that had, if folk history was to be credited, disappeared from the landscape in remote antiquity. He knew of no other town in Ireland that shared this honour.

He enjoyed climbing to the hilltop where, back in the 13th century, a castle or fort built by the Norman invaders stood: a symbol of lordly dominance.

Long gone, of course. And the invaders? They hadn't departed exactly…just intermarried and intermingled with the natives as they had elsewhere in Ireland. They became Irish, in effect, which made their invasion seem rather pointless with the benefit of historical hindsight.

Reaching the hilltop, he paused for breath. He'd forgotten how high it was. Or maybe he needed more exercise, to go easy on the feasting and drinking. Mopping his brow, he surveyed Callan from the Motte hill, or as much of it as he could perceive from this vantage point.

There was St. Mary's to his right, and Fr. Brannigan confabbing with locals outside the church entrance on South Street. He'd love to hear that exchange. Was he alerting them to the situation up north, and what it meant for Callan…or maybe just chatting about the harvest or the price of spuds.

And the good friars were tending to their garden in the Augustinian abbey meadow. From this distance they resembled ants scurrying about on their little patch of earth. The abbey…what a jewel on the landscape: And there. The bell in the central tower was tolling.

Must be for ten o' clock mass. I see a few people heading across the meadow. A pity that the friars and their spiritual powerhouse are located outside the Town Wall. But they live humble lives devoted to God and I suppose they prefer it that way. It brings them closer to the common folk.

An attitude I'd like to cultivate, if it were possible to thrive while at the same time retaining that rapport with the…all those folk who haven't quite made it up the ladder of achievement. Or weren't allowed to? That too. I've been fortunate.

From the age of twenty-one Edward had been blessed with riches: the best of food, clothing, and a home that most of those people down there could only dream of. Yes, so much to be grateful for.

Being outside the wall wouldn't be a good place for the friars to be in the event of attack. They'd have no protection, and, from what Edward had heard they'd need it more than most.

He watched people passing up and down North Street along the bridge, some stopping to exchange greetings or to chat.

Something darted out of a bush behind him. Startled, he quickly turned, in time to see a pair of scuttling rabbits. They misapprehended his presence.

He wondered if Callan folk had the opposite problem. They seemed to be in a general state of denial or delusion about what might be coming. People still didn't think of events further north as concerning them. Perhaps it was time to prepare them.

But first he would convene another Corporation meeting; *we must ensure that Callan has the best defence if and when the regicides come knocking at our door.*

He took a deep breath of the cool fresh air. It was how God intended it be: So much healthier than the smoky taverns and the stench of street stalls when the fish had gone off.

How many more times would he stand on this ancient site? He had learned as a child of its mystical bond with another Ireland, as far removed from the one he lived in as the Land of unspeakable horrors that would surely follow if the parliamentary army triumphed in their assault on everything Irish...*our religious liberties, our culture, our right to any kind of life worth living, would disappear.*

He had to tread carefully descending the hill, and found himself breaking into a run as he reached the bottom. A crow watched him bemusedly, and birds shrieked from a hawthorn bush as he made his way to the field exit on to Motte Lane, from where he strolled up North Street.

He was happy to be stopped by two soldiers at the Bridge Gate. It showed they were alert, a little more than usual. Recognizing him they let him pass. At the Town Square some venders were peddling pots, pans, and fishing gear from their stalls, all of them keeping a respectful distance from the revered wooden cross. Today it was adorned with flowers honouring a Christian saint.

 Sauntering down East Street he passed shops teeming with customers and produce: Vegetables abounded: carrots, potatoes, onions, cabbages. Fish-mongers sweated in the unseasonal heat of this September morning as they served those loud fesity women.

Horses and donkeys, some pulling carts filled with more vegetable en route to or from the shops, passed him on the street, salutes or friendly acknowledgement greeting him along the way. He was satisfied to see the schoolyard, with the lads playing wildly, and Master Counihan pacing up and down supervising them.

And, towering over the school, that symbol of military power and prestige, and of Callan's supposed invincibility to attackers: the magnificent Butler Castle. Now there was a fortress that no enemy could subdue. He must enquire again about its military assets, but he was sure he'd heard that the walls were several yards thick, and no artillery weapon on earth could penetrate them.

Today though, there was no sign of military goings-on. The Confederate flag fluttered defiantly from over its wide-open entrance gates and inside, he noticed, when he passed by the castle, three half- uniformed men in straw hats lay back on wicker chairs, drinking beer and soaking up the sun. "For now, lads, for now", he mumbled, shaking his head.

Further on, he passed the slate-roofed and thatched houses that were his own properties. Would the tenants still be there a year hence? Who would own those fine buildings then?

*

Mathias Blunt's diary, second week of September 1649

I don't know how long I've been in this place. It's a kind of hospital. Not like the one I stayed in when I was sick as a child. Another patient tells me it's a farm building that the army has converted for its own use. It's on the outskirts of that accursed town of Drogheda that we've encircled. My handwriting I think has been affected by whatever affliction I suffered when I fell, so early in the battle.

A kindly nurse assured me I'd be fine, given a few days rest; that I just got knocked unconscious after striking my head forcibly against the barrel of the cannon I was helping to guard. There had, apparently, been a small explosion when a barrel of gunpowder was hit by enemy fire.

I hadn't been hit directly by shrapnel or flying bits of metal, as other soldiers had, but the blast had propelled me towards that unfortunate impact with the cannon.

There was also a slight wound to my left thigh; the nurse told me, that I see is covered with a bandage. What an unexpected way to be laid low. We'd all prepared for the possibility of being shot, stabbed, blown to pieces, or decapitated by a ball flying at breakneck speed... any of the usual ways one exits this world honourably in war. I'd prayed with the others, our minds fixed on eternity.

I'd read and reread my pocket Bible furiously, not daring to take my mind off the sacrifices that lay ahead. I was ready to meet my God on the battlefield. I still am, but naturally I hope to survive and take my share of the fertile land to be distributed to us in lieu of pay at the conclusion of this campaign.

But here I am, still in the land of the living; not mortally wounded; with just a bang on the head and a flesh wound; exempted by the grace of God, or my own good fortune, from the hazards

73

being endured by hundreds of my fellow countrymen, as I inscribe these words, albeit with an unsteady hand.

Perhaps I'm wounded within, as something causes my hand to write shakily. Ah well. I'm probably the only one who'll ever read this, unless God wills it otherwise.

When I've finished writing I must pray again. Thanksgiving is in order. My temporary absence from the fray has spared me a host of horrors, if I can trust what the surgeon's been telling me. He'd taken a break from tending to the scores of wounded men. Sitting on a little wooden stool by my bedside, he sipped brandy from a tankard, a small balding man with about a week's growth of beard...delicate spectacles perched on his slightly turned-up nose

After hearing that I kept a diary and intended to record my narrow escape, he offered to give me "something to bloody write about." He indicated a man lying on the floor next to me, snoring softly and covered by two Hessian sacks stitched together. He'd been asleep since at least last night.

The surgeon whistled pitifully. "When he wakes up, which he will soon, he'll wish he hadn't. While you were in slumber land, I amputated his left leg and dressed wounds to both his shoulders. He'll walk, but he won't fight again. That missing leg will be his ticket home, but to what kind of life?"

I told him I knew one-legged men back in Liverpool who got by without too much difficulty.

He cast me a sceptical look, shaking his head "It's the other wound I'd worry about. You see, I removed some of the splinters, but not all. The remaining bits can still cause infection and that's what could kill him. Could be next week, could a year from now. Or maybe never. Wounds don't heal well if not thoroughly cleaned. Infection can finish what the musket ball starts. Those damn things are designed to kill, remember, or mess up your insides. They punch big holes in you. They're not made to give you a chance to recover. I'm the one who has to help you do that if one of them has your name on it."

He fixed me with a steady gaze. "Speaking of wounds, your own scratch to the thigh mightn't have seemed like much but even that could have become infected and given you grief, so I treated it yesterday while you were out for the count. Applied a lotion comprised of egg yolk, oil of roses and turpentine. Always does the job I find, unless of course it's a deep wound packed with lead fragments, bits of splintered bone, or other nasty stuff that I can't fully extract.

"You'll be up and about in no time, lad. Oh, and yes, I removed the leeches earlier, shortly before you woke. Luckily for you, you were in dreamland, blissfully unaware they were sucking some of that bad blood from you. I deemed that treatment necessary to banish the high fever you had when you arrived here: Nothing like a leech to give that old fever the heave-ho."

I felt almost guilty to be doing so well, surrounded by others afflicted by life-threatening wounds and constant pain. Their moans reminded me of Gregorian chant, sung out of tune.

The surgeon droned on about his healing of the wounded, his daily snatching of precious life from the jaws of death. As he spoke a soldier was being led by two others into the building. His bloodied uniform hung in tatters and smoke frizzled from him, as if he'd caught fire. He cried, and whined, a low eerie sound.

Then I saw his face. Part of it was missing, like in an incomplete painting where the artist hasn't gotten around to adding the requisite features. No left eye; and his nose had disappeared. His right eye dangled from its socket, a meaty blood-soaked pendulum. And his lips... two slivers of burning flesh scarcely recognisable as such.

Seeing a corpse is one thing. This was a living being. I felt nauseous, though not in that sea-sick way I'd experienced back on the ship.

"Look away" the surgeon advised, talking a long swallow from his tankard, "I'll be attending to him later, though I can see he hasn't got a future in the army, or anywhere else. Bloody war! When will men see that it solves nothing? Just creates a world of sorrows!" He raised the brandy again to his quivering lips

Despite what I'd just seen, this remark stung me and I reprimanded him. "That's defeatist talk", I fumed; "We're doing the Lord's work here. We must be strong in the face of adversity. That's what the chaplain has been saying all week. We defy the divine will if we relent in our commitment to final victory."

I wanted to say more, to remind him of the massacres of innocent Protestants by Irish rebels back in 1641; how the settlers in Portadown were herded naked unto the bridge over the Bann and *thrown, shivering and pleading, into the freezing waters. Those that didn't drown were shot or hacked to pieces. Or the other reports that reached us from Ireland of entire settler families being dragged from their homes and killed. Some were roasted alive on spits and eaten by the native savages, egged on by popish clerics.*

I'd read the newssheets at the time and, like all godly Englishmen, was sickened to the core. And I'd seen the woodcuts depicting atrocities. This present campaign initiated by Parliament, with a magnificent commander at its head, would avenge the papist uprising, and the wounds sustained by that man I'd just seen. We'd bring justice to a barbarous race and security to our new, thriving Commonwealth.

I wanted to tell this man sitting at my bedside all this, but something stopped me: A combination of sleepiness, depleted energy, and a feeling that there would be no point anyway arguing with this man whose position possibly entitled him to be dismissive of the non-medical folk around him. His importance as a healer, I supposed, trumped any foolish talk from him, even if it verged on the treasonous.

He turned and regarded me with a quizzical look. I suspect he partly read my mind, and knew I detested his remarks. He shook his head sadly and then took to reminiscing about his work: "I treated wounded and dying men all over England, Wales and Scotland, and the result of war is always the same.

"I started my career as a surgeon with the King's army, you know, but switched sides...I can't remember exactly when...or rather I didn't have a choice because I was among a group captured by this Cromwell fellow and his Roundheads- no offence meant - and when they invited me to apply my surgical skills in the service of the Parliamentary army, which was clearly winning the Civil War at that point, I jumped at the chance. Why wouldn't I? I'm a surgeon, not a soldier or a politician. Human flesh is the same whatever clothing, or uniform, covers it."

A door swung open and the sudden burst of daylight startled me. A man with a long shabby brown coat smudged with blood and excrement came running in. His coat flapped around him, though none of the gore and filth on it seemed to be his. He looked the picture of health

Panting and holding his chest he rasped: "You're needed in the other field hospital...quickly!"

Sighing and stretching, the surgeon arose and gave me a friendly nod as he swigged the last of his brandy. Wiping his mouth he quipped "Duty calls, I'm afraid. I'm off, but you lad, don't worry your godly little head. You'll be back playing soldiers before the week is out. In the meantime, stop fretting about being here and thank your lucky stars. The war's getting along just fine without you."

*

Later, the same day...

The surgeon was right about the war getting along fine without me. While I was lying in the field hospital, which thankfully I've just been discharged from; our glorious army by God's grace had subdued the town of Drogheda.

I was still reclining in that stuffy room that reeked of sweat and blood, and human smells too numerous and revolting to recount when the wonderful news was brought to me. Its bearer was an officer who'd come to check up on recovering soldiers.

He quickly decided who was sufficiently recovered to resume the fight. I'd beckoned him to my side even before he got around to assessing my state of health, along with the surgeon who accompanied him. "Are we winning?" I asked.

The surgeon, standing a little behind him, winked at me, which I found irksome, because I didn't wish to be part of any silly conspiratorial notions he might have. His treasonous proclivity was already known to me.

The officer was in high spirits. "Listen up everyone", he hollered, "Our friend here wishes to know where we stand."

Men fell silent: One-legged ones, lads with cloth or bandage-covered faces; pain-racked soldiers. Men stifled their groans, some covering their mouths to aid the process. The officer went on: "I can tell you that our brave troops have vanquished the foe at Drogheda."

A feeble cheer erupted, some voices heartier than others among the prostrate soldiery.

"Yes. It wasn't easy. Repulsed twice with heavy losses, but once the breaches appeared in the wall the defenders bore the brunt of our righteous fury. So, Drogheda is ours, gentlemen; the first town to fall to us since our great expeditionary force landed last month. This triumph comes with God's divine blessing and the leadership of a commander the likes of whom walks among us only once in a millennium."

He was about to say more when a man somewhere behind me in a corner of the room emitted a piercing screech. The surgeon rushed to him, examined him briefly and pronounced him dead.

"What a pity", the officer said, in a more subdued tone, "He hasn't survived to savour our victory, but rest assured, all of you, that his death will be avenged...is being avenged as I speak. The papists are at this moment paying for what they did in 1641. And let me tell you...they did scream louder than that valiant soldier there. Their cries will reach to the very floor of Heaven... but no further, for the lord has already cast them down into the depths of Hell!"

With that he turned on his heels, replaced his hat, and exited; the trailing surgeon audibly out of breath.

*

Shane hadn't liked the look of Master Counihan from the moment the teacher pushed in the door that morning. It had been raining heavily. Shane barely avoided a ducking by running to school when he felt the first droplets.

Other boys were soaked, the water running down their ankles, creating little puddles on the flagstones. The Master had almost crashed into the classroom, his saturated hat and cloak sagging under the weight. He hadn't hung it on a hook outside in the pokey corridor, which was unusual.

It was as if he was in a hurry, had something big on his mind, which it turned out he had. His announcement that he was suspending Latin class and singing practice was greeted with an initial sigh of relief. Nobody liked Latin, and singing suited only the boys who had a note in their heads, which was less than a third of them, according to the Master.

But then, as the Master dried his sodden hair and face with a cloth, the boys learned that their lucky escape came at a price. The

Master informed the class that he wished to speak about matters of the gravest importance. So important, he declared, that the morning recreational break was cancelled to accord this new subject due priority.

He produced a piece of white chalk and sketched a rough likeness of the island of Ireland. He then reached for a stick of red chalk and inscribed the name of a town: *Drogheda*. He drew a circle around it.

Further down the map he wrote *Kilkenny* and circled that too. Shane found himself yawning as the Master droned on about the invaders who'd dared to threaten the great political arrangement that had brought liberty, and the glory of the one true faith, to most of Ireland.

They'd captured the proud town of Drogheda; he intoned, but would not succeed in conquering "our devout nation."

Shane had heard it all in the playground and in the streets. The grown-ups talked endlessly about those fierce warriors who'd crossed the Irish Sea to convert all decent Catholics into crazy heretics like themselves.

He could see the other boys were bored too. Shane was seated beside the window in the second last row. His disappointment at having no play-time to look forward to gave way to annoyance and anger when he felt the rays of a warm September sun on his cheeks.

The rain had gone, but he was stuck in that stuffy classroom, made even stuffier by the clouds of white and pink chalk dust swirling about in the wake of the Master's vigorous scratching on the blackboard. The Master had gone from updating the class on the progress of the dastardly invaders to the fundamentals of the Catholic religion, to which he'd devoted at least an hour the previous day and he'd had asked the class to learn what he'd told them off by heart.

Shane hadn't bothered to listen carefully the day before and now he was distracted too, this time by the thought of no play-time. His attention wandered to the window, through which he noticed carts passing by on East Street, locals engaged in lively banter, and two cats fighting over a discarded lump of raw meat.

He felt sleepy...then. *Wham!* A clenched fist crashed on his desk, shaking every bone in his body and causing him to cry out in fright.

"Dennehy...you seem to find what's happening out on that street more to your liking than the faith that, at this very second, thousands of our countrymen are fighting with their lives to save. Did you hear a word I sad, you little fool?"

"I did, sir… I did…" he spluttered.

"Up to the board with you, up!"

Shane was shaking with fright. He hadn't been beaten for several weeks. He'd been careful not to do anything to draw punishment or even a telling-off in class. But now he'd been caught out badly. The Master hated boys not paying attention more than any other failing on their part.

He felt a hand push him gruffly from behind, almost stumbling before he reached the blackboard which he pressed against to restore his balance and avoid falling.

"Now" the Master bellowed, "write on the board exactly what is the difference between a saint and an angel. It's a very basic question that any boy who'd been listening to my religious instruction would know."

Shane hesitated; then jumped as the Master roared in his ear: "The answer, boy!"

In a blind panic and rigid with fear, Shane raised his trembling hand to inscribe the only answer that came to mind. He'd completely forgotten the correct one, or maybe he'd never properly heard it, day-dreaming as he was by the window.

His stomach heaving, he scrawled the words on the blackboard, not a sound to be heard as he wrote apart from the squeaking of the chalk and the wheezing breath of the Master behind him.

He stood back to let the Master and the class see what he'd written. The Master read the words aloud, pausing after each word as if it merited special attention.

"Angels can fly anywhere they want to go and have great time up the sky, while saints go around blessing people and animals, saying their holy prayers day and night."

After reading it out, the Master roared: "Has my class has come to this? Boys can't even pay heed when I speak to them of God's own messengers from Heaven and the most blessed of his subjects. Again, boys, and remember this time, all of you...A saint has a halo and an angel has wings. That's the essential difference, as I've told you more than once. An example is required here. Bend over...that desk!" the Master roared, pointing to an empty desk at the top of the classroom.

Shane heard the hushed collective intake of breath in the room. All eyes were on him. He couldn't hold back the tears. Despite his best efforts they broke through and he quickly wiped them away with his sleeve. "I'll remember next time, sir, I promise I will."

"Oh you will. That I can guarantee. Bend over...and...O' Brien...get me my blackthorn."

His face pressed to the desk, Shane waited, each second like a little eternity as he heard the crunch of boot leather on the flagstones.

"Let every boy learn from this" the Master rasped, and the first blow came. Shane howled as the stick with its thorns still intact whacked his bottom. And then, after a brief pause, the stick came down faster and, it seemed to Shane, harder. He couldn't see the desk that was just an inch from his face, or any other part of the classroom from the corners of his eyes, both of which were streaming.

Then it stopped.He felt himself being pulled up from the desk and flung to the floor. He narrowly avoided striking his head on the flagstones at the last moment, shielding himself with his hand.

"Back to your desk Dennehy and, listen, the rest of you, you'll get the same... and worse... if you think that what's outside on the street is more to your fancy than what you're here to learn. Understood?"

"Yes sir" the class confirmed, and Shane even managed to join in the zealous response. But deep within he was raging, fear replaced by a searing hatred of the Master and the school. He hated them, he told himself, far more than he loathed those invaders who might be coming to Callan and that the Master was so fond of talking about.

They hadn't done anything to him, but that...bollocks... up there; had. He wished with all his heart that the Master would *drop dead* that instant.

When it didn't happen he felt guilty for wishing it, but only a little. He had to force himself to stay attentive for the remainder of the class, as the Master continued his mixture of religious instruction and lamentations onthe plight of Dear Old Ireland.

Callan: late September 1649

Malcolm collected the satchel containing the curative herbs from the friary garden. He'd be taking them to the three apothecaries in town. They were much in demand locally and the physicians thoroughly recommended them for their efficacy in relieving pain, aiding digestion, and banishing various ailments.

Apart from helping to keep the locals fit and healthy, the herb garden contributed to the abbey's financial upkeep, a vital consideration that couldn't be overlooked in the unrelenting daily preoccupation with the spiritual side of life. God would provide, Malcolm knew, but man must facilitate that divine process.

As he prepared to leave the abbey field he noticed that Jeremy was busily raking leaves around the yew trees. The elderly friar had a tranquil air about him as he made little heaps of the dying red, yellow and brown foliage. He worried about Jeremy. The octogenarian had raised eyebrows that morning in the refectory, when he dared to signal that he might disobey a direct order from his superior.

At that fraught breakfast address, the sixth in three weeks, Fr. Kearney had again warned that the war might impinge on the future of the settlement, but this time he'd gone further. He'd raised the prospect of closing the abbey and leaving, *before* the invaders arrived.

Disturbing reports reaching him from Drogheda had persuaded him that, while their work was of the utmost importance, and blessed by the Almighty, a most painful and truly heartbreaking choice would present itself should it be confirmed that the Roundhead army intended to capture Callan.

To remain would be to place the lives of all the local friars at the abbey in mortal danger. No purpose would be served by sacrificing their lives, he stressed, given their greater value as servants of God in the land of the living.

Martyrdom was commendable, but throwing one's life away simply to defy an enemy was not to be encouraged. Even if Callan was not directly targeted by the invaders, an enemy victory would in any event inevitably lead to the Augustinians in Callan, as elsewhere in Ireland, having to go to ground...for a while...until the cruel regime in London was replaced with a moderate one, or perhaps by the return of the monarchy.

The Prior seemed to have aged ten years in a few weeks. He ended his spiff with a long sigh and some words of solace. "It may not come to any of this. The invaders may yet be halted. In the meantime we'll carry on with our duties here as normal: fulfilling our vows of poverty, chastity and obedience, our daily devotions, the masses, our reception of the local community, and all our work in the kitchen and the gardens..."

It was at this point that Jeremy had raised a quivering hand. His voice also trembling, he stood and looked his Superior straight in the eye. "With the greatest respect, Prior, I cannot leave this abbey unless I am transferred elsewhere. I will not leave for fear of what this... Cromwell...might do to us. Like the season that's in it, I have reached the autumn of my life, and winter is closing in. I have no fear of death. Why should I fear the transition to a better world that we all look forward to? That we know awaits us if we obey the commandments and live a good life?

"Maybe we'll be left alone if we remain...if we make it clear that we pose no threat to whatever new arrangement is planned for this country?"

The Prior interrupted. "Your commitment to your vocation is an example to us all, Jeremy, but I'm afraid that we're not dealing with reasonable people. If what I've heard from Drogheda is correct, Cromwell is hell-bent on the destruction of all Catholic religious orders...of the church itself. He wants rid of us. Please Jeremy...Reflect on this. If you opt to stay, I won't compel you to accompany us into hiding. But I implore you to reconsider..."

Malcolm felt a surge of pity, mingled with admiration and a deep respect, for this old man. If only there was a way to allow him to live out his days here.

But Malcolm couldn't bear the thought of leaving him behind if they had to flee. The outline of an idea began to form in his mind. He'd have to think it over, and pray for guidance, but somehow he must offer support to Jeremy.

***

8

Shane had started to walk home from school, but he'd been so hyped up by the war game in the playground that he broke into a run, dodging his way around grumpy adults, pack-horses, wagons, and bemused mongrels as he raced along East Street and on up to his house in Lower South Street where he knew dinner awaited him.

The forty boys, from three classes, had all participated in the mock battles that saw them divided into groups that fought each other with "weapons" that were, unusually, supplied by Master Counihan.

That was odd, because the Master had never shown the remotest interest in play-time. But today he had given them a spiff about the need to be aware of their duty to fight for Ireland when they grew to be men. That wouldn't be for a while yet, but the day would come and they'd better be ready! Shane wasn't sure if he was being serious or just teasing them.

Sometimes he did that. Not very often, but occasionally he might not be in his normal foul humour. He'd surprise them with a light-hearted tone in the classroom that was as welcome as a bag of apples.

Whether he was serious or not, the boys loved squaring up to "pretend" opponents in the game devised by the Master. He'd explained that, in a war, different weapons would be utilized by the combatants, so the boys would have to use their imaginations, which he emphasised he knew they had, if they'd only put them to correct use.

So, one group of boys armed themselves with long sticks that served as pikes. Another group had stick "muskets" and would handle them accordingly, taking aim, and "firing." The groups had great fun miming the sound of gunfire and the battle-cries of pike-men, and the Master, moving among them, made sporadic booming noises to replicate the roar of cannon. It all lasted for half-an-hour...longer than play-time.

And the bell for the end of lessons rang as soon as they returned to the classroom. What a joy! This was better than boring school work any day, not to mention better than being whacked, whether for failure at lessons or inattention. The pain and humiliation of his recent beating still stirred a rage within him whenever he called it to mind.

Shane arrived, gasping for breath, at his house. The door, as always, was ajar. His mother closed it only at night. In he went, to find Mother repairing the hem of her cloak.

Behind her the cauldron simmered on the big open fire, radiating heat. The aroma of beef and mutton stew wafted over to him, and the euphoric afterglow of the war game quickly gave way to a mad hunger. "It's not cooked yet" she hissed before he could raise the heavy iron lid to have a look.

She'd spoken without raising her head, her attention focused on her sewing and darning. "You're all excited. I don't suppose it's because the teacher was happy with your progress at school, so what is it?

"We had a break from that, Mother. Longer play-time. We played at being soldiers. I killed five times. I was better than anyone else. And my group won the battle!"

Shane's spirits drooped a little when his mother dropped the cloak at her feet, frowning. She shook her head and he thought he detected a tear in her left eye.

"It's time enough you'll be soldiering. That's no game. Did your father ever tell you how he came to have only the one leg? Did he?"

"No, I never asked him. I mean...he always had only one…"

"Not always. He was born with two legs, like you, and the boys you were playing with. He had two legs when he went up to Ulster to fight for some cracked auld Chieftain. I can't remember what the fight or skirmish was about. Anyway, when he came back in that door he was hobbling and limping, with a smirk on his face as if he'd done something marvelous. He was proud, he said, proud to able to say that he gave a leg for the cause.

"What cause, I asked him. I forgot what it was. I didn't care. All I cared about was that he had only one leg instead of the two that he should have. He got the wooden leg then, but it was never the same. They buried it with him last year. Must have thought he'd need it in the next world. I'm sure Jesus will give him a new one."

She took up the cloak and resumed sewing.

"I want to be a soldier when I'm a man, Mother, but I'd rather die than have only one leg. I'd never walk with one leg."

She fixed him with an icy stare and laughed silently. "Your father did." she lisped.

Shane slumped into his wicker chair beside the fire and watched the cauldron's contents frothing and bubbling. It would be ready soon. *I'll be sure to keep both legs, whatever happens.*

He craved a plate of that stew. When he scooped it into his mouth it would drown those irksome images of hobbling about on one leg and the thought of the Master beating him.

Father must have been careless, to lose his leg when other soldiers, like Henry's uncle's father, returned to a hero's welcome and no need for a crutch. Henry said his uncle's father was a brave warrior who never got a scratch.

*

Edward Comerford sat back in his cushioned Mayoral seat in the Council Chamber. He'd opted not to avail of the two-hour recess to take a breather outside, or in the tavern on the opposite side of South Street where most of the aldermen had retired for the duration of the break.

The military situation was worsening by the day, and the minds of the Corporation members altered accordingly. At the first meeting, following confirmation of the landing of an invasion force at Ringsend, there was unanimous support for a motion tabled by Alderman Crotty, an ardent advocate of complete Indepedence of Ireland from English dominion in any form.

Following a strident speech that set pulses racing and patriotic hearts throbbing, the Corporation backed his motion calling for a robust defence of Callan from any attempt by the Roundheads to capture the town. The motion also declared that under no circumstances should the town even contemplate surrender.

Though a little hesitant at the time, Edward added his name to the others endorsing the motion. But the military landscape had changed for the worse since that meeting. Today's meeting reflected that change.

The fall of Drogheda had shaken the Confederate/Royalist Alliance on every part of the island where it held sway, but far more ominous than its capture had been the fate of the garrison and thousands of innocent civilians who'd been put to the sword.

The invaders had cleverly summoned other towns, threatening a further "effusion of blood" if they dared to resist. Now, the Roundheads were advancing down along the coast towards Wexford.

Today's meeting was much more subdued. There was no jingoistic clamour about taking the fight to the enemy. Five of the eighteen aldermen declared themselves open to the idea of negotiating with the Roundheads if they came knocking on Callan's door.

Four were adamant that surrender must always be "off the table" as an option. The remainder were noncommittal, their grim reluctance to speak their minds a statement in itself. There was, however, unanimous approval of the pledge by Ormonde to reinforce the Callan garrison with a further three hundred soldiers, bringing the total to five hundred, but the more militant members wanted more, given the likelihood of an attack on Kilkenny and Callan's unfortunate proximity to what the Puritan enemy had dubbed the Inner Circle of Popish Hell.

Edward suspected that as the invaders drew nearer to Callan the Corporation might edge correspondingly closer to a decision to surrender, if the conditions were reasonable. But there would be a complicating factor: Ormonde had indicated to him in his recent correspondence that he would be appointing a Military Governor to Callan. While the Corporation's views on all issues of civic, political, and military importance would still be considered and respected by this Governor, he would not be bound by the Corporation's decisions.

So, the Corporation would become a mere talking-shop. Dipping his quill in the inkwell, Edward added to the draft of a presentation he planned to make after the recess, explaining the new reality that the aldermen, and indeed Callan, would have to accept in the coming weeks.

Their fate would rest on the shoulders of one man. He didn't know yet who'd be appointed as Town Governor. Would he be a moderate, a radical...soft in his religious views, or extreme and uncompromising like Archbishop Rinuccini, the well-meaning Papal Nuncio whose refusal to support the alliance of Confederate and Royalist forces had dealt the Irish cause a severe blow?

As for himself, he'd await further developments. Cromwell might yet be stopped, before reaching Callan or Kilkenny. But whether Callan surrendered or resisted, he knew his own political career and indeed his vast suite of properties would be history if the Roundheads triumphed in Ireland.

*

Malcolm knocked at the door of the Prior's study.

"Enter." Just one word but he thought there was sadness and a hint of exasperation in it that he hadn't heard before on the few occasions he had cause for a private chat with Fr. Kearney. God knew he had reason to be unhappy, with an army heading his way that hated everything Catholic.

The Prior had his back to Malcolm, hunched over his escritoire, quill busily scratching out whatever communications to others in the Order he had yet to make before the inevitable heart-breaking departure. Turning his head around brusquely, he motioned Malcolm to sit.

He thanked him and pulled out a stool that looked as if nobody had sat on it for decades. He brushed a cobweb from it and sat.

The Prior wheeled around to face him. "Well, Malcolm...is the upcoming parting of the ways preying on your mind...rest assured that you are not alone in lamenting this truly dreadful decision that has proved necessary...we..."

Malcolm tentatively stopped him. "It's a different predicament I'm dealing with. It's Jeremy. He's adamant that he's going to stay. As you know, he doesn't fear the invader. Death means nothing to him, except maybe as a positive rather than a negative development. He sees it as a release from a long and, from his point of view, devout and now fulfilled life. Of course we all hope to meet death, when it comes, with equal fortitude and faith in God's divine mercy, but..."

The Prior finished it for him. "...but we should avoid crossing the great divide before our time. Quite. Yes. And he shows no signs of revising this...hankering after martyrdom?"

He sat back, twiddling his thumbs and gazing at the low stone ceiling of his study. "I think, Malcolm; that Jeremy needs to reflect on the implications of his decision. To stand up for the faith is one thing. But what he contemplates might be construed as amounting to...well...a form of suicide. That, as we know, is a grave sin. For anyone to take that route would be unfortunate, and unforgivable, but when an anointed friar of our order indulges in such forbidden contemplation the very saints in Heaven must despair..."

Malcolm had expected this. He'd already tried that approach with Jeremy but the man still wouldn't listen. He'd made his peace with God and he didn't think of staying on as a suicidal act, but more as a calculated risk. Malcolm shared this information with the Prior, who shook his head forlornly.

"When we breakfast tomorrow, I'll address all of you and lay down the law on this. I'm still not prepared to bind any of you to obedience on this specific matter. Whether you choose to leave or to remain has to be your own decision. But I'll argue as strongly as I can within the limits of my authority against the utterly irresponsible idea of hanging about here... anywhere in Callan... when the invaders arrive, let alone at this consecrated abbey that we know Cromwell is sworn to destroy..."

Malcolm felt the weight of the Prior's ecclesiastical authority, but forced himself to hold his composure.

"I appreciate very much your efforts to cater for the safety of the Callan friars, Fr. Kearney, but the reason I came here was to inform you that, after a lot of prayerful reflection, scrupulous consulting of the Gospels and the works of our blessed founder, Augustine, and agonizing introspective analysis, I have decided that I will remain here at the abbey if Jeremy refuses to leave. I feel I cannot in conscience abandon him to face...whatever is coming...alone. I will, of course, continue to press him, up to the last possible moment, to take the sensible course, but..."

The Prior sighed, smoothing the thinning hair back over his head. "I can see why you would do that...and I won't prevent you, any more than I will bind anyone to leave as I've said...but you are a valued member of our Order, Malcolm. From everything we know about this new enemy, we have to be prepared for the worst. I commend your sense of Christian duty and sacrifice. But I implore you to rethink, Malcolm. Will you do that?"

His mind was made up, but he made a show of acceptance, out of respect for his Superior.

The Prior dismissed him, and Malcolm left the study feeling unexpectedly relieved that he'd gotten that onerous obligation out of the way. Yes, he'd pray that the stubborn, damnably awkward Jeremy would change his mind. He'd try a few new approaches to talk him into leaving.

But he was resigned to the prospect of a bleak and possibly hideous future, at least on this earth, whatever about being rewarded elsewhere for...for what? For linking his own fate to that of Jeremy, whose ominous decision could well owe more to dotage or to him losing his wits than to any inclination towards martyrdom.

Malcolm hoped God would help him on this one. The Almighty didn't intervene too much in human affairs, not directly anyway, these days, but he might make an exception, given the pointlessness of deliberately putting oneself in harm's way...

***

9

Frevanagh, County Westmeath: early October 1649

Captain Mark Gegan sat back in his favourite armchair. A fire blazed in his stonewalled Westmeath home. Winter wasn't far away and the place needed warming up.

He was relaxed, despite the news borne to him by a messenger that morning. The youth had come to his door, breathless, bearing orders from the Supreme Command of the Confederate/Royalist alliance. The messenger had been under orders himself to get the message to the Captain within a few hours.

Sipping his glass of brandy, Mark read the terse communiqué again. It informed him that he was to take command of a small castle in the town of Callan, County Kilkenny, two days hence. The town garrison had been reinforced considerably since the enemy's arrival at the outskirts of Wexford on the South Eastern coast.

Mark put away the parchment with its broken seal and yawned. He'd never heard of Callan till now. He'd looked it up on the map. He presumed its importance lay in its proximity to the seat of the provisional government in Kilkenny. It certainly didn't appear to have any strategic value as had, for example, Drogheda at the mouth of the Boyne, or the vital seaport of Wexford that was now under siege.

Therefore, it must be that Ormonde believed Callan would play an important role in any upcoming showdown in that part of Ireland if Cromwell's advance wasn't stopped. Thus far, the Irish hadn't succeeded in stemming the enemy tide, so he could well end up seeing some action in Callan.

After five years of respite from war, he steeled himself for more of it. The prospect of again leading men in the fires of battle didn't bother him too much. Everyone had to die sometime and to be killed fighting was infinitely preferable to either a painful death from illness or to survive and endure a living death from wounds that didn't heal properly or deprived you of the will to live.

What he'd seen in Spain and Austria, where he'd fought alongside other Irish mercenaries, made him sanguine about his new orders. He'd witnessed the worst of man's inhumanity: men literally ripping each other to pieces with swords, knives, and hatchets...human beings starved into submission, or decapitated by cannon fire.

On all sides of him men had fallen, or been blown to perdition, while he emerged from every encounter almost unscathed, apart from the odd flesh wound. His dreams had never been sweet since his days of service to foreign kings and emperors, but that was a small price to pay.

Nothing awaiting him in Callan could compare remotely to those horrors beyond description that he'd already experienced -and survived.

In fact, he relished the opportunity of getting back to what he'd been trained to do, and yes, what he was damned good at: bearing arms.

Refilling his glass, he raised a silent toast to the Irish who fought to preserve the fragile semi-independent status they'd won from England. Having fought for a price for a cocktail of foreign causes that meant nothing to him, he would now be putting his fighting skills at the service of a cause close to his heart: that of his own native land.

Thinking of his one-hundred acre farm that nestled in some of Ireland's richest agricultural land, and his herds of prized beef cattle, he felt privileged. But many were not so fortunate. And if Cromwell prevailed, that division between the classes would be greater still, maybe worse than anything previously endured by this long-suffering race.

No, combat didn't faze him, but something else did. Was that her now? The rustle of leaves outside betokened her return from her friend's house down the road. How on earth was he going to tell her?

Marianne was a loving wife, but loyal only up to a point. She'd repeatedly warned him that if and when he was assigned to a potential battlefield post she'd be joining him. He'd argued with her on that point, explaining that it didn't work that way. War was men's business. She'd look after the house if he was called away, and with help, the farm. Knowing what war entailed, he abhorred the thought of her being put in harm's way.

In Austria, he'd watched helplessly as men attached to his own regiment slaughtered civilian captives. He didn't want that scenario replicated on his watch, and certainly not for Marianne to be among the victims.

But Marianne persisted. She'd filled her head with romantic notions about female warriors who'd distinguished themselves down through the ages. That was fine, but nicely written stories didn't reflect the reality of war. Not the blood-drenched images that had burned themselves into his brain and kept him awake at night.

Then, of course, she had that perfect excuse, as she saw it. They had no children, so he couldn't hold forth on the motherly duty she owed to their offspring to remain on the farm. What a powerful impediment that woud have been to her following him into war. To leave a young family behind and risk her life needlessly in those circumstances would have been unthinkable.

The thought of their childless marriage pained him. Every other officer he knew had a family, big broods most of them. They'd dutifully acted on the Biblical exhortation to increase and multiply. He longed for that extra presence in the house, the pattering of tiny feet, the gurgling of an infant. *God knows we tried, but God has not blessed us with the joy...*

A door creaked. He finished the brandy and steeled himself, not for battle, but for a worthy opponent, one he feared would bend him to her indomitable will. Before the sitting room door opened he heard her voice call out: "Mark; was that a messenger I saw riding off earlier? What news?"

The door burst in and their two Irish wolfhounds playfully accosted him, licking and slobbering all over his jacket, and wrestling him to the floor. Pleading for rescue, he laughed and feigned a struggle as he tried to shush them away, "Marianne, call them off!"

"Thor, Apollo...down. Sit!" Instantly they obeyed, as if an inner mechanism had kicked in at the sound of her voice. The dogs never obeyed him: it was Marianne they responded to. They settled in their allotted corner, tongues lolling and tails wagging happily.

Marianne held out a hand to pull him up off the floor, her face alive with curiosity and just a hint of suspicion: So pretty, with her auburn hair hanging loose and those glistening sea-blue eyes. The powder had, he noticed, been rubbed off the blemish. It showed again, but that didn't matter. The scar from the deadly pox that had almost killed her never diminished her loveliness in his eyes.

93

He embraced and kissed her, crooning; "My little warrior. Let's have dinner first, and then we have something to discuss..."

"Ah, it *was* a messenger. Tell me now. Is it anything I should know about? Speak, or I'll set the chaps on you!" She went to the table and uncovered the plates of cold meat and potato slices she'd prepared earlier, humming to herself as she reached for the jug of buttermilk on the nearby cupboard.

Sitting at the table Mark tried to brazen it out, pretending to have forgotten her request. But she glared teasingly at him, the jug in her hand. "Well, what's happened? Have you been promoted again? Or have those awful taxes been raised? God knows they're high enough as it is...."

He motioned her to sit. She filled his mug and then her own. "Marianne, I'll be going away for a while. A new posting and it's not something I can avoid or procrastinate about. Not sure for how long it'll be. Duty calls, as they say."

"Oh, right...to Athlone...or is it Mullingar? Surely you'll be able to travel back here some days?"

"No pet. It's quite a distance. It's in County Kilkenny, a place called Callan. With all that's happening on the war front, I've been assigned command of a castle down there. I imagine it'll be some time before I return."

He avoided her eyes. Silence followed, apart from the tick-tock of the big grandfather clock and the fervent shuffling of the dogs in the corner.

"I see, well, there's only thing for it then..."

His heart sank. "And that would be?" He already knew.

"No arguments, Mark. I'm coming with you. You remember our marriage vows? We promised to support each other through thick and thin. Sickness and in health, remember?"

"No Marianne. Look, I'd do anything to oblige you...anything on earth, but not this. Callan is one of those towns that could be in the firing line...because of its location. I can't let you put your life at risk. Please... can you be reasonable? I'm the soldier here. I will arrange for help in managing the farm. You practically run it anyway as it is and damned efficiently too, I might add!"

"When do you leave?" she asked, icily.

"Two days hence."

"We have to move quickly so, to ensure that everything's in order here...I'll.."

" Darling, no, please, you mustn't, ah, get involved...this is not like any other enterprise, you can't just..."

She stood up, almost knocking over her plate, and spitting a piece of half-chewed mutton towards the dogs. "I'm coming...no debates or arguments!"

He raised both hands in pleading "Look, Marianne, I'll tell you what. Will you take a week to think it over? Talk to Cathy about it, she'll have an opinion and I know she'll be adamant that you remain where you belong, in your home, until I return..."

She sat down, smiled and nodded "Fine. I'll do that. But if I still feel the same way about it a week from now, I can join you?" She went around to him and pecked him on the cheek.

God, she was getting her way again...

"Agreed?" She rubbed a hand through his thinning blonde hair, playfully pulling at it.

With a sigh that drained him of energy in an instant, he acquiesced. "Yes...but, I can assure you. When you've had time to consider you'll see how absolutely inappropriate it would be for you to accompany me to what might become a damned battle zone. Oh God, Marianne, I'm just concerned for your safety..."

"I know Mark, but how do you think I feel about you putting yourself in harm's way while I skulk around the house or the farm, fretting about you, possibly never to see you again? But yes, I'll think it over as you ask. More buttermilk?"

He knew she'd be like this. She'd probably made her mind up already. He wasn't great for praying, but he'd implore the Almighty to knock some sense into her; into that unbelievably stubborn, adorable little head.

His mind raced. He must get to Cathy before she did; persuade her to talk Marianne out of her insane notion. *Must make it worthwhile for Cathy. A nice gold sovereign should do it, maybe a pig on a spit too. Cathy and her old crippled brother would like that. God, this woman hasn't a clue about war... what it means. I've got to keep her away from Callan.*

*

Marianne Gegan sat disconsolately on the stool in the outhouse, the stink of dung a welcome distraction from the tension-filled house. With winter drawing near she must wrap herself up a bit better, she thought. She was sitting on the milking stool though all the cows were long since milked and were out grazing in the field. The clucking of hens only slightly intruded on her brooding.

It was because he loved and cared for her, she knew. That's why he was adamant that she oughtn't to accompany him to Callan. But he was wrong...his thinking flawed. He just couldn't see how unjust and cruel it was to exclude her from this journey...into what? A splendid victory? Wounds that would disable him or make him less than a man? Or might death await him?

Besides, she had no familial ties to bind her to the farmstead, or to Westrmeath. Every day since she married five years before she'd awoken to the expectation of possible news...a sign, the merest hint... that the child they craved might be on the way. She'd consulted with midwives, doctors, and herbalists at the first indication of any change in her body that just might herald an event that she knew would change her life...take it on to a new level.

There was that day when she imagined she felt a strange unnaccountable stirring within. Could it be the long awited sign? She'd rushed to the doctor, who cautioned her on raising her hopes. He said he couldn't be sure. A possibility... but there could be a hundred other causes for what and how she felt.

The local "piss prophet" examined a sample of her waters and said, after a lot of tinkering about with phials and bottles, that the evidence was inconclusive. There could be something happening...but then again the colours might mean that a simple change of diet was advisable. She'd almost struck him.

She'd prayed and prayed...all to no avail. She tried potions, every known conoction deemd by wise folk to be an aid to pregnancy. Nothing worked. She succumbed to the dark oppressive thought that maybe Mark was the problem, that his body was at fault, not her own, or that God had opted to deny him the great privilage of children. She'd disimissed that latter notion, chiding herself for having entertained it for an instant. At twenty-five she was still young and maybe, some day...

Anyway, their childless status now made it easy for her to pack up and leave home. The thriving farm, for all its value, held no great sway over her. It would still be there when they returned...if they returned.

Duty called Mark, and perhaps her falure to give birth was a signal from God that she was free to fight for Ireland.Whatever awaited him in that faraway town that neither of them had heard of until today, she wanted to be there when it happened.

So typical of men, he couldn't see beyond his preconceived notions of masculinity and femininity. Her own father, though, had coached her in the use of arms from childhood. She was only four years old when he showed her how to shoot an arrow from a bow. At seven she was fencing, albeit in a less than professional arena, with boys that he'd arranged to challenge her. Then she'd learned to use firearms.

His reasoning was that every native Irish person, male or female, should be able to fight, in readiness for Ireland's call.

Her mother chided him on his obsession with militarism. Marianne should be knitting or picking flowers, not playing with a silly bow and arrow, she scolded, as they supped at the dinner table. Will you ever stop encouraging the girl to be a tomboy? she'd howled. Marianne loved the way Father would wink at her when Mother turned her back during those exchanges.

He countered that knitting wouldn't be much use when the "big day" arrived. Father had died the year before, and Marianne had been commended, if in a jocose way, at the funeral by an assortment of chieftains and warriors who'd turned up. Mark, she knew, didn't like her fondness for archery and what he dismissed as her "dabbling" in musketry. Mention of it had him reaching vexatiously for the whiskey bottle.

She loved Mark as much as he loved her, but he needed to get over his belief, however popular and established it might be; that this was a man's world. It wasn't. Men might have most of the power, but without women they wouldn't have been born in the first place. *We have minds, even if we apply them differently in some spheres of life.*

And as for leaving war to men, Marianne had whispered stories of female heroics into the ear of her half-asleep and occasionally incensed husband, eliciting groans of acknowledgment to shut her up. But never an endorsement of a woman's role in wielding the

97

sword of equality in a world ruled by men. Her female role models, she knew, were anathema to him.

But she persisted, not just at bedtime, but at breakfast, dinner, supper, and in fireside chats. Sometimes she relished his discomfort at any mention of Grace O' Malley: how the 16th century pirate queen with her three galleys and two-hundred fighters had ruled the seas around Ireland.

Now there was a woman who wasn't held back by the supposed weakness of her sex. In one sea battle, though heavily pregnant, Grace climbed unto the deck of her ship to shoot the captain of a Turkish pirate raider who'd boarded the vessel.

And then there was Joan of Arc, Marianne's revered martyr; the Maid of Orleans who'd led the French to victory over the English in the 1400s. Many believed she was divinely inspired, and the young warrior paid the ultimate price for her bravery when she was burned at the stake. Joan showed the men of her time how a woman could fight.

Marianne stood up abruptly and threw open the cow-house door. The sun was setting but it still shone brightly if not warmly on the extensive Gegan farm.

Yes. She'd give him his week of reflection, but then she'd travel to Callan to join her husband.

It might prove to be a one-way trip, but that doesn't bother me. Now I know what my father meant... the big day he spoke about is almost here. It's time to fight...

***

10

It seems that the Lord truly wishes to keep me off the battlefield. First I missed out on the splendid victory at Drogheda, restricted as I was to a minor engagement during which I couldn't aim straight. Some marksman I proved to be

Now, I'm again recovering, but not from any visible wounds this time, nor indeed from any action of the foe: I have fallen victim to an accursed illness, possibly marsh fever or something brought on by insect bites.

Whatever it is, I've endured two days of hellish torment that has withheld me from an eagerly awaited settling of accounts with the town of Wexford on the River Slaney.

This port has long served as a base for those damned pirates that have stalked and attacked Commonwealth vessels off the Irish coast. It also shelters a nest of papist clergy known for their backing of the satanic confederacy.

The town's defenders had rejected reasonable surrender terms, and our commander accordingly ordered the commencement of hostilities. I and twenty others assigned to guard our artillery train, as at Drogheda, had been devouring cheese and biscuits at the edge of a wood, near marshland, when several men complained of nausea and muscle aches.

Some vomited; others held their stomachs as if in agony. I made the mistake of trying to comfort one of those; an action that the doctor tells me probably resulted in my catching the illness or disease, whatever it was; from him. Or maybe I'd have caught it anyway.

I have never been as sick in my life. First, I started to feel dizzy. I had to sit down on a tangled tree trunk, the world whirling around me. I became delirious, drifting into unconsciousness. Next thing I knew I was in a tent along with five more patents, all of them groaning, grunting and complaining.

One cursed loudly when he wasn't groaning. No sooner had I come to when I was overcome by a raging fever. I thought my head would split in two. Could being wounded in battle be any worse than this? I asked a soldier who observed me from a safe distance.

The doctor said there was nothing he could do as he didn't know exactly what the ailment was, but from past experience he advised me to stay in the tent and rest, let it run its course. It didn't make me feel any better when he showed me my reflection in a glass which he did to drive home his warning for me to stay put until I'd healed. My face had turned almost completely yellow, as had the whites of my eyes.

Today, I feel much better, but though the fever has abated and my features seem to have regained their normal flush of health, I'm crestfallen at the news that I've missed another great milestone in our campaign.

I've just learned from an excited corporal of the drubbing our lads gave the Irish rebels and the treacherous Royalists. God was indeed watching over us in Wexford. Our soldiers made a clean sweep of the town.

Having routed the garrison, all papist clergy were hunted down like vermin and put to the sword. The corporal described a chaotic scene...papists attempting to flee in boats that buckled under the excessive weight. Our musketeers marked them well, picking off the foul rabble, and then, in what he believed must have been God's judgment, their boats sank.

Those who didn't drown were either shot or clubbed or hacked by our ever vigilant warriors. It was a dreadful spectacle, and I'm glad I didn't witness it, but I thank God for showing us whose side he's on.

The wrongs perpetrated by the papists have drawn down the wrath of Heaven...Blessed be the name of the Lord.

Once the shaking in my hands had ceased I reached for my pocket bible. It's proving a great comfort to me. I find that whatever page I open has a message for me. There's always a line that seems to address me personally, as if God wishes through his own Holy Book to let me know where I stand and what he wants from me.

I pray that final victory is not far off, so that our army's harsh but justifiable actions will no longer be necessary and I can return to my dear Meg.

Oh Meg, it's for you, and all those godly folk back home that we wield the Sword of Christ in this savage and disease-ridden land. How I yearn for the day you and I are married.

When I close my eyes I can hear the musket volley and the cheering...the chaplain pronouncing, the simple but elegant ceremony that will make us one.

And I can visualize the land that will be ours, my sweetheart, once we have seized it in the name of the Commonwealth.

*

Shane threw his satchel of school books on the wainscot bench beneath the front window and slumped into the backless bench by the fireside that he'd made his own. Mother had been stooped over the big cauldron that frothed and sizzled under the flaming logs, making way for him when he barged in without saying a word.

It had been another bad day in class. The Master beat him again, this time for alleged daydreaming. He felt hard done by, because the Master had accused him in the wrong. He might have looked a bit distracted, but his full attention was assuredly on the blackboard.

He'd tried to explain, but before he could speak the Master was dragging him by an ear to the top of the classroom. He lashed him across the knees and the bottom, finishing with an order, delivered in a frenzy of spitting and fuming, to stand in the corner.

"And wear this", Counihan howled, tossing him a dunce's cap made of damp rushes. He felt like a witch when he put it on. His minutes standing in that humiliating posture, staring at his classmates as they listened to the Master, seemed endless.

Shame convulsed him. He wanted to die, but death wouldn't oblige. He didn't expect it to. It only took sick folk or soldiers in battle, and he didn't qualify on either count.

When class did end, his burden of embarrassment lifted. He walked free from the Place of Horrors, which is what the school had become for him in recent weeks.

Now, brooding at home by the fireside, he inhaled the mouth-watering fumes of the beef and mutton stew.

His mother spoke: "What's gotten into you...not a word from you since you walked though that door."

He hadn't intended telling her, but anger got the better of him. "That cruel teacher...he made me feel such a fool...he..."

She stopped him with a quick reproving finger: "You'll not speak ill of that man. He's helping to make you a decent young fellow..."

"He's a monster!" Shane felt a teary rage rising from the pit of his stomach.

She shook her head, her eyes lighting up with annoyance. "Listen here, you need to learn everything you can at that school. Do you want to end up like all those men hanging around smoking pipes all day, waiting for someone to give them an errand...or in the madhouse for lads that go to pieces...or the folk that can't read a single line...or the ones who are blown to and fro in life, at everyone's beck and call, slaves to ignorance and illiteracy?"

He wasn't listening, but he made a show of respect. Dinner was only minutes away, so this was no time to fall foul of her.

Avoiding her eyes, he blubbered: "I don't want to be ignorant..."

*

Frevanagh, County Westmeth

Marianne wiped her feet outside the entrance to Cathy's little cabin. It looked tiny compared to her own capacious abode, though it could be that Cathy was in the better position as she wouldn't be facing dangers of the kind possibly awaiting Mark and herself.

The door creaked open and Cathy's small delicate face lit up with delight. They'd been friends for the past three years. Cathy had done some housework and helped on the farm before she had to quit. She needed to care for her brother who had lost an arm and leg when a cart rolled over him. Though of slight build like herself, Cathy had brawny biceps from working and was stronger than she looked.

Marianne looked forward to her chats with Cathy. They talked about everything, shared worries and joys, and Marianne took special pleasure in giving her eggs. It wasn't a huge gesture. The hens laid hundreds of them, and the farm supplied stalls and shops in nearby villages.

Cathy would occasionally produce a loaf of sourdough bread, though Marianne was reluctant to accept food from her, aware of the pressures Cathy and her brother were coping with.

Marianne sat at the little table as her friend boiled a pot of water for coffee. Their two mugs planted on the table, they went through the usual list of topics...the weather, the brother's misfortune, and his long absences at the tavern- he got around despite his handicaps- and how close the war might come to their homes.

It was Cathy who broached the subject of the invasion. Marianne seized the opening: "As you mention it...I'll be leaving here soon..."

Cathy stopped her, but the expression wasn't one of total surprise, or shock, as Marianne expected.

"I feel awful about this Marianne, but your husband was here yesterday evening. It was out of concern for you, Marianne, and I don't blame him. But I shouldn't have taken this from him."

She took a gold sovereign from her petticoat and laid it on the fractured wooden table.

"Mark is so worried about you...I mean about you possibly going with him to this town in County Kilkenny, that he asked me to help talk you out of it."

Marianne was gobsmacked. "He what?" she blurted.

"Don't be angry with him, Marianne. He was so worked up. I could see he'd do anything to protect you...but, well, I'm no good at this kind of...conspiring and conniving."

She pushed the coin towards Marianne's hand that clasped the coffee mug. "No. keep it...I'll say you bent over backwards, begged me not to go to Callan..."

But Mark's devious tactic upset her. "Look, Cathy, you'd have been wasting your time if you had tried to argue with me. I'm going, and that's it."

Cathy said nothing for a few seconds, then her eyes glistened, and she took a deep breath. "I was thinking, Marianne...could I come with you?"

"What, are you completely mad?"

"I knew you'd say that, but Tim is moving in with his brother in Mullingar so, well, I have nothing to keep me here now. And if you're not around I won't have anyone to, you know, confide in.

You've been more important to me than I can say, Marianne. Please, let me come too!"

Marianne hesitated, unsure of what to say. Having stood her ground against Mark's opposition to her joining him at his new post, she felt hopelessly inadequate rebuffing her friend's request to make the same journey into an unknown but potentially lethal situation.

"Mark asked me to reconsider my request, and, at the risk of sounding like a total hypocrite, Cathy. I'm afraid I have to ask you to do likewise. I want to be with Mark because he's my husband. I'm prepared to share in his risk. But you have no cause to make that journey…"

A tear streaked down Cathy's face. She rubbed it off quickly, sniffling. Looking away she sobbed "I do have a reason…life without your friendship wouldn't just be less…interesting. It would be unbearable. There's nothing for me here anyway. I can do some work maybe in this town you're heading off to. I'll serve in a tavern or alehouse…anything. And we can meet like always…"

Marianne's heart grew heavy. Sighing, she stroked Cathy's shining jet black hair and kissed her on the cheek. "If you still feel the same about it in a day or two, you can come with me next week. But don't say afterwards that I didn't warn you…the invading army that's marching through the land, intent on turning us into slaves, will not be nice people to have to deal with. I know they could come here too, to Westmeath, at some point, but Mark says Kilkenny's their big objective. Think of that Cathy, and the dangers you may face, before you…"

But Cathy had stopped listening. She was already in the other room, informing her half-awake brother that she'd soon be moving to another part of Ireland.

Marianne left the cabin with a sinking feeling that she was responsible for this trusting, dear friend making a truly atrocious decision.

***

11

Mark relaxed in the alehouse. He'd dropped in for a tipple after a hearty meal of mutton stew washed down with buttermilk. He'd arrived in Callan in the late evening. The swinging wooden sign above the door said "The Grim Reaper" and already he felt it was living up to its name.

Unlike the table in the cookhouse earlier this establishment didn't have a single table that wasn't falling to pieces with woodworm, the ale reminded him of horse's piss, and the proprietor had a look of misery mingled with a hostility that was completely out of place. *Maybe he'd be a bit friendlier if I introduced myself, explained that I've come to help defend his town and his way of life...*

He'd wait until the grumpy man came around to his table. The powerfully built vintner, his bushy eyebrows like miniature haystacks over his large watery orbs, was hovering about the candle-lit room, passing disconsolately from one creaky table to another, casting suspicious glances at customers, none of whom seemed to find anything remotely amiss with this uncalled for frostiness.

Mark was worn-out after his long journey from Westmeath. He'd had only one break along the way, and that was only to get two hours rest for himself, the coachman, and the horses before resuming. And the journey was made longer by a diversion. He'd been advised by his military superiors to avoid Kilkenny City and to approach Callan via a normally disused road.

The reason for the detour was that the Black Death was ravaging the City. As if the threat of attack and occupation by the Parliamentary forces wasn't direful enough, City folk had to contend with an invisible foe that could lurk anywhere and strike down anyone without warning. The plague was spreading panic and mistrust at a ferocious rate, he'd learned. Most worryingly, from the point of view of Ormonde, the Supreme Commander of the Irish forces, Kilkenny's garrison had already been depleted by the deadly disease.

While he appreciated the advice to stay clear of Kilkenny, given the obvious dangers, he was almost hoarse from cursing the roads he had to travel to reach Callan. Roads? More like ill-defined dirt-tracks, and with so many potholes you'd swear someone *wanted* to wreck every passing coach or wagon.

But here he was, in one piece, safely ensconced in the place to which his superiors were confident he'd apply his "considerable military insights and know-how" as the Colonel in Mullingar had called it, in defence of the town.

He winced as he drained the tankard, relieved to have gotten that obnoxious concoction down his gullet. The proprietor caught his eye and Mark signalled for service. This time he ordered a whiskey. *Can't be as bad as the bloody ale.*

When the vintner brought it round to him, he coughed politely and asked "Ah, if you don't mind. I've just arrived here from Westmeath. I'm Captain Mark Gegan. I'll be in charge of a castle here. I'm wondering if you might fill me in on, you know, the town... who's who, what's what...if you can spare a minute or two."

The man took a step back, staring wildly, his eyes bulging and his mouth opening a little more by the second. Mark instinctively recoiled, thinking the man was about to hit him. Then, the frown disappeared, replaced by a beaming smile. The grumpiness fell away.

The man thrust a mighty hand out to clasp Mark's. He shook it until Mark had to gently extricate his hand to avoid having bones crushed.

"By God, you're welcome, sir. Here, that's on the house. No, I won't hear of you parting with a single penny. Jesus, I'm still trying to get my head around what that other fellow did. The whole town was raging over it. But you're not like him. I can tell by the look of you..."

Mark motioned him to stop, and took a sip of the whiskey. "Thank you so much, but before you go any further, what do you mean by the *other fellow*?"

"The fellow you're replacing, surely you know...Captain Williams. That demented halfwit! Didn't he go and fight a duel last month with another officer. Got his face blown off. Imagine: He was sent here to protect us...to save this town, and he does something that damned stupid. A silly duelling stunt, as if we can afford to have our own lads killing each other. Now... of all times!"

Mark was perplexed. He'd been told nothing of this incident, only that he was being assigned to a garrison in Callan. Clearly, he was taking over from this duellist who'd gotten himself shot.

"Let me sit down there with you", the big man grunted, "Callan is a town worth defending. I'll tell you anything you wish to know about it..."

*

Mark's lodgings were in West Street, close to the castle into which he'd be moving once living quarters had been prepared for him. Though he'd asked Marianne not to join him, he was so resigned to her stubborn ways that he'd requested his superiors to allow for her presence too.

He'd do anything to change her mind, but he had to be realistic. It was quiet outside the *Grim Reaper*, with just a few fellows ambling about: smoking pipes or chatting on the pavement. They barely noticed him as he passed. He wondered would they pay him more attention if he was in uniform. He'd find out next day when he he'd be formally installed as Captain of the Skerries Castle garrison: A misnomer really, because no soldiers had been billeted there yet and mightn't be for weeks, he'd been informed prior to departing for Callan.

The temperature had dropped since he'd entered the tavern. He shivered and wrapped his cloak tightly around him, feeling the weight of the satchel containing his uniform and encased flintlock pistol.

A lustrous full moon relieved the darkness. Its beams traced silvery lines across the cobblestones and the greasy windows of houses, shops and another two alehouses.

Reaching the top of North Street he caught his first sight of the famous wooden cross he'd been told about. And it *was* impressive. Forty feet high, it towered over the large Town Square, the four streets radiating from it. A lantern blazed above the image of the crucified Christ, its light bathing the street entrances. A fitting homage to the Christian faith, he thought, apart altogether from its function in banishing darkness from the Square.

The landlady of the *Goat's Head* cookhouse and hostelry in West Street greeted him cordially, a candle in her hand as she ushered him inside. His room was small, with just enough space for one person, and not high enough to stand without knocking your head off the ceiling. Well, it was only for one or two nights. Undressing he regretted not writing down some of what the alehouse keeper had told him about the town. But he reckoned that he'd be hearing it all again next day anyway in his first briefing from a local army man.

*

Next morning, standing beside the wooden cross in the Town Square, Mark received his briefing from Corporal Molloy, former officer of the Confederate army and now a dutiful if lower-ranking member of Ormonde's Confederate/Royalist allied force.

Much of what he told Mark was a repeat of what the tavern-keeper had told him: Callan was a thriving market town with eight castles, its own Corporation and Court of Justice. Militarily it was in reasonably good nick, the Corporal crowed, though, he added, almost in a whisper, "a few improvements wouldn't go astray." The town was defended jointly by the waters of the King's River and the town's historic wall.

The wall and river offered protection to the eight hectares that comprised the well-to do Inner Town, with its stone and timber houses, shops, and administrative buildings. The castle Mark would be moving into was, the Corporal inform him, eminently defensible. He'd show him around it later.

The most powerful of the eight castles was Butler's at the East Street gate. That's where the bulk of the troops would be garrisoned, the Corporal reckoned, once the promised reinforcements arrived. Butler Castle had walls so thick that the Mayor and the Corporation believed it to be impregnable.

Mark thanked the man for his briefing, and expressed confidence that Callan could repulse any attack. Privately he had his doubts. He feigned a breezy assurance as the Corporal saluted and left him, heading for a nearby tavern.

Mark leaned against the wooden cross facing North Street, hoping he wouldn't be proverbially nailed to it if Cromwell came to town.

The Town Wall, like all other similar defensive structures countrywide had been built in a different age, when besieging armies were armed with spears, bows and arrows, and swords...but no firearms.

The invention of gunpowder had rendered walls virtually obsolete, as no wall could hold out against a sustained bombardment. On the continent he'd seen the sturdiest of walls crumble to dust or blasted to rubble in one town after another when he'd fought in both offensive and defensive capacities for half-a-dozen different armies

The same applied to castles. They'd been built to resist attacks by lightly-armed men and maybe giant catapults and battering rams, but they lacked the lethal advantage that cannon fire provided. Even Kilkenny Castle, once deemed safe from any besieging force on earth, was now vulnerable to the awesome firepower of modern warfare. This was 1649, not 1249, and Irish military thinking had some catching up to do.

Of course, a wall circling the town was still better than none at all. Though vulnerable to artillery it had the merit of at least delaying the entry of an invading force. It gave the defenders time to prepare, or to await help.

Callan was relying on the wall and river to keep it safe. He would have to make it clear to the Town Governor, when he met him; that the garrison would need to be well-armed and equipped and, if necessary, to call upon locals to augment the professional forces.

And he wondered just how robust the wall was. To have any chance of even holding off an attack for a reasonable length of time it would need to be strong and in good repair. Many town walls he'd seen across the country were in a state of decay and neglect, mostly because they'd been deemed unnecessary due to misguided feelings of security; or obsolete anyway as defensive measures.

The river would need to be laid with stakes and traps if it became clear that Cromwell had his eye on Callan. That would give the defenders some breathing space. He looked forward to hearing what the Town Governor had in mind for this small but perhaps strategically significant part of Ireland that had come under his command.

*

Corporal Molloy wasn't at the castle to show his Captain around, as the landady at the Inn had predicted he wouldn't be. He was probably sleeping off his hangover, she suggested, after a long night of carousing in the Callan taverns. Mark wouldn't hold that against him. And anyway he hardly needed a guided tour of a structure he was familiar with. He'd seen castles of all shapes and dimensions elsewhere in Ireland and in Europe.

But still, this one was had his name on it, for better or worse, so he'd better check it out. The landlady had given him the key, which had been entrusted to her by the Corporation. Approaching the castle he stepped across the street to view it from the other side. As castles went it was impressive, if not impervious to gunpowder. The stone fortification rose to three floors, including ground level.

It pleased him to see musket loops at intervals from top to bottom. These narrow openings in lieu of windows must be recent enough modifications, he thought, as most castles dated to before the advent of gunpowder. Some arrow slits too, which were pointless, unless any of the defenders happened to be armed with those outdated weapons.

And the arched iron-grilled entrance would help in a siege. It permitted negotiations or parleys with those inside, but not entry unless the defenders willed it. He crossed to the entrance and inserted the key in the grill. It creaked open and he stepped into a dark, dusty spacious chamber. Thin slivers of daylight, filtered through the narrow slits, granted only a weak illumination. Ideally the interior should have candles or braziers burning even by day.

The castle hadn't been occupied for some time, it seemed. The furniture consisted of broken desks and tables, and a rusting musket lay on a heavily cobwebbed chair. A musty smell pervaded the chamber, but no hint of recent human habitation.

A little tidying would sort that out. He ascended the narrow stone stairway up to the second storey. In the middle of the wooden floor he spied a murder hole; as some called it; a useful convenience that allowed defenders to fire downwards or drop rocks, pitch or boiling water on the enemy.

Adjusting his sight to the gloom his heart lifted a little to see a large Confederate Banner draped on the wall to his left. It was out

110

of date since January and the dissolution of the Confederacy but continued to fly in many towns and cities across the land, the hope being that it would be restored to its former high status once the Confederate/Royalist alliance had beaten Cromwell.

He moved closer to the banner, his feet disturbing lattices of dust and bird-droppings. The lavishly embroidered multi-coloured design encapsulated Irish aspirations rather than the grim reality now facing Ireland.

The banner incorporated the inherent contradictions that had bedevilled the Confederacy from the outset: At the centre of a circle a cross stood proudly, resting on a flaming heart and above this the wings of a dove.

That was fine. It denoted the Roman Catholic ethos of both the native Irish and the Old English. But then there was what Mark deemed a conflict of loyalties: To the left of the cross a golden harp glowed, but to its right stood the crown. The banner's motto seemed equally at odds with itself: "For God, King, and Fatherland, Ireland is United."

The idea of being loyal to an English King- any English king- while claiming to be an Irish patriot, stuck in his craw, but he, like so many Irishmen and women accepted that the Confederates had no option but to join forces with the remnants of the Royalist army to stand any chance of beating Cromwell.

Turning away from the banner he stepped to his right where he perceived the beginning of another stairway. He ascended slowly, the steps barley visible. He pushed open a timber door to the third floor.

Much the same as below: In a state of neglect, with empty crates and a ladder, but the walls were robust. And two additional murder holes. *Good.* Before exiting he kicked something that jingled and rolled in front of him. It glinted in the half-light.

He picked it up. A coin: Confederate currency, minted in Kilkenny in 1648. Just a year old and already defunct, or at least until after the invaders were repulsed. It had the familiar motif, a cross enclosed within a circle, and the motto of a semi-independent Ireland.

He pocketed it, offering up a silent prayer that, a few weeks, or months, hence, this might again be the unit of exchange in Ireland. He had a moderate faith in the divine, and did his best to be a decent

Catholic, but the rational side of him didn't hold out much hope of a return even to the limited form of self-rule that the murdered King Charles had permitted.

This top storey, which he presumed would serve as temporary living quarters, was no more attractive than the rest of the caste, but then it wasn't built for comfort or to be a pretty sight. A mouse scampered across the floor, squeaking in protest at the intrusion.

Another spiral stairway opened out onto the roof and the battlements. Yes, Skerry's Castle was a decent enough defensive arrangement, but he hoped the town's seven other castles would be well-defended if the fighting reached Callan. A ferocious resistance would need to be mounted to have any chance of repulsing a determined attack.

He'd fought many battles across Europe, seen many castles fall, and a smaller number hold out, and had survived to reminisce on those engagements. This present assignment didn't seem any moredaunting than previous ones, but that assessment could change. He'd been luckly thus far, narrowly dodging death. He'd seen other officers whose luck, however elongated, eventually ran out.

Exiting the castle the sudden burst of sunlight dazzled him. Then something blocked his vision. The Corporal had appeared in front of him. He looked more dishevelled than he did the day before, dressed in a sleeveless buff-coat, and a shaggy green woollen pullover. His baggy breeches were tucked in at the knees into a pair of rawhide boots that stank of pig-dung.

Pushing back his threadbare woollen cap and saluting shabbily, a barrage of shrill words escaped his foul- smelling mouth. "Apologies Captain. I met some important people last night. Had to talk about the big decisions we'll soon be facing. You see, everyone knows I'm military. Since the last Captain got shot and the Sergeant absconded I'm the one they all come running to.

He sniffled and coughed. "They want to know what's going to happen...will they have to leave town, should they stay and fight, or what? And when will the Roundheads be coming, and, well, you know how it is... I couldn't say no when they pushed all that drink on me. By the time I left the fifth alehouse I was absolutely stocious. Won't happen again, sir, now that you've arrived!"

He belched loudly and discharged a globule of phlegm onto the street. Wiping his mouth with a sleeve he pulled out a parchment from inside his coat, and blurted "Oh yes, and Captain, I'm to give you this. It's from the Governor, Sir Robert Talbot. He wants to see you. I imagine it's just an introductory meeting. To have a chat about the military situation and how we're going to stop that mad English bollocks if he shows up here..."

Mark motioned him to stop. "Alright Corporal, I've had a look around the castle here. You might accompany me on a quick tour of the other castles later, and the gate defences.

The Corporal snickered, "Begging your pardon sir. Most of them are only fit to be demolished, apart from Butler Castle. That's a hell of a set-up. No cannon in England could batter its walls down...Oh and there's another thing. The Governor decided last week to have all the troops in town garrisoned at Butler Castle until further notice. It's certainly got the space for them. I'm sure he'll be releasing some to your own command at Skerry's once things are bit more organised."

"Thank you Corporal. Perhaps when I go to see the Governor I can have a look at Butler Castle. Sounds like a formidable place."

*

"Missed again", Cathy moaned, regaining her balance after being almost thrown to the ground by the recoil.

She regarded the pistol with a seething dislike, dusting off its varnished ebony stock and gleaming metallic barrel as smoke billowed around her and the smell of powder wafted up her nose. "I hate this...silly contraption", she whined.

This was her fifth attempt at hitting the target ten feet away. Marianne wasn't too put out. She'd expected Cathy to struggle with the six-inch long flintlock.

Though not heavy or large as pistols went, the weapon was still a challenge to someone who was, Marianne, knew, squeamish about the idea of firing any kind of weapon: A natural and even commendable attitude, but not one conducive to staying alive in this treacherous age.

"Can we try just once more?"

Cathy gave her an exasperated look, but nodded.

Marianne reloaded the pistol for her, asking Cathy to observe the procedure closely so that she could do it next time.

113

She handed the pistol to her friend and then, standing closely behind her, directed Cathy's clenched hand to a position where she might stand a slightly better chance of success.

Cathy pressed the trigger, the flint sparked and again Cathy shook, but less than previously.

The smoke made her cough, the hand holding the pistol went limp, but Cathy was delighted.

"You did it! Look." Marianne went over to the tree trunk and pointed to shards of glass and splintered wood where the three dilapidated offal jars had stood.

Cathy's dour expression turned to radiance. She emitted a little squeak of joy and ran to see the result of her marksmanship, smoke still piping from the barrel of her pistol.

Cathy balked at the size of Marianne's own pistol. It was sixteen inches long.

"This wouldn't suit you Cathy. It's a cavalryman's pistol; they have them holstered as they ride. Mark brought this back from Spain I think. It took me ages to get used to it. It's damned heavy too, so I find it best to use both hands when firing. You hold on to your own. Practice again tomorrow…keep at it till you hit the target every time. But remember… the range isn't great. Don't use it unless your enemy is close, and the closer the better. I hope we'll never have to use these, but things are looking bleak."

Cathy sat down beside the tree trunk, and set about laboriously reloading the weapon. "That's another thing", Marianne quipped; "You'll need to be as fast as you can reloading. If two fellows are coming at you, you won't have time to be fiddling about with that. I'll give you this too. Keep it safe"

She handed Cathy a short dagger. Cathy tipped the point of it delicately. "Nasty" she cringed, feigning horror.

Marianne loaded her own weapon, as quickly as she could to let Cathy see. Swiveling about she fired at a wooden gate that she thought might be just out of range. Unable to see the result she went to the gate and was happy to find that the ball had struck, even if not with great force. It had made a small impact in the wood and fallen into the grass. But that might still have wounded a man within similar range

Cathy made coffee at the house and the conversation swung to their forthcoming journey.

"Are you absolutely sure you want to come to Callan, Cathy. You see what a gun can do. We could be on the receiving end of those awful things. Or worse: Cannon balls that can take your head off, or an arm or a leg…and God knows what they'll do to us if we're captured alive."

Cathy brooded for a few seconds and put the mug down. She brushed aside a strand of hair from her left eye and gave Marianne a fierce look. "There's nothing for me here, with my brother leaving. And this war…surely as the country has been invaded the invaders will come here to Westmeath too… eventually? If I have to die, what's the difference if it happens in some town down the country or up here? And down there…well…I'd be with my best friend!"

Marianne nodded and put a hand on Cathy's shoulder. Avoiding Marianne's gaze, Cathy gently removed the hand, adding with a grin "Besides, I'm sure I'd get the same welcome in Heaven if I can't load this pistol fast enough in Callan as if I snuffed it up here in Westmeath!"

*

Next morning, on the Gegan farm, Cathy scowled at Marianne, throwing up her arms in exasperation. Marianne knew she was eager to travel, if only to get away from her humdrum life.

"I thought you said he'd given you a week?" Cathy moaned

"Yes, but that was just to decide whether I would join him at all. It doesn't mean we have to leave tomorrow."

"So, when?"

"When we're ready, or at least readier than we are now. I'm worried about you, Cathy. I want you to be prepared for what may be ahead of us, insofar as we can be *ever* ready. Both of us need to be fit. Mark is always on about the harsh training that can make the difference between life and death. I know that all that lugging of water pails from the well and working in the fields has made you strong, as you said, but you need proper exercise too. I suggest we both run a few miles every day for the next seven says, in addition to practicing with the weapons."

"A week? Running for miles? You can't be serious!"

"Oh I am", Marianne cooed; the crossbow under her arm as they headed for the improvised training venue on the farm.

115

She'd retrieved it from the disused barn where it had lain under layers of dust for more than a century. She'd spent hours cleaning it off, to Mark's annoyance as he'd always ridiculed her interest in archery.

He'd decried the use of bows and arrows as hopelessly outdated, since they'd been overtaken by the invention of musketry and cannon, but having seen muskets being tested, she in turn had chided him on how awkward the supposedly modern, state-of-the-art weapon was, with its long length of matchcord that needed to be lit and inserted into the musket, and the unwieldy process of emptying powder down the gun barrel.

And then, having spent several minutes loading and priming the gun, the match might fizzle out and not ignite the powder. Or some unexpected glitch might cause the weapon to malfunction.

By contrast, she'd pointed out to him; she could fire off several shafts from a bow in the time it took to reload the "superior" 17th century killing rod.

It was a long bow she'd been using in her hobby- she'd never seen actual combat- and she'd acquired an uncanny skill that even Mark, for all his belittling of archery, commended. "My little warrior" he proclaimed jovially when she arrived in from her makeshift targeting arena behind the haybarn.

The crossbow required a different approach, but she'd quickly adjusted to its use. As a child she had a scaled-down version of the weapon that her father had gifted to her. He'd certainly been thinking ahead. She doubted whether Cathy would take to it, but she'd give her a try.

"What on earth is that?" her friend asked, eyeing the unfamiliar device. Marianne explained that it was, basically, a bow mounted on a stick. The bow had allegedly been fashioned from a yew tree in Mullingar cemetery, but its origin was irrelevant, so long as it worked.

The string, according to Mark, was made of twisted mulberry berry that was resistant to wet weather. Some crossbows required a mechanism to operate them, but this one could be drawn by hand. The projectiles were shorter than arrows and called bolts. These were heavier than the arrows used with a long bow, a slight disadvantage, but could do more damage if a target was within range.

Weeks earlier, long before Mark got his orders to leave, Marianne had pestered the local blacksmith to make her some bolts, believing she'd need these and other weapons to defend the farm from intruders in the event of a nationwide descent into chaos following Cromwell's arrival. Now, it wouldn't be the farm she'd be defending, she told Cathy, but possibly a town elsewhere in Ireland.

They entered the field from which sheep had been removed a week earlier. Motioning Cathy to stand back, Marianne placed a bolt in the crossbow and took aim at a decaying sheep carcass dangling from the branch of a beech tree.

She unleashed the blot and with a breezy whoosh it sailed over the grass, piercing the dead creature between its blank staring eyes. Crows shrieked and scattered from the tree. The carcass swayed and then grew still again.

Cathy looked startled. "God, that's drastic!" she gulped.

"Mark says the big problem with this is that it won't bring down an enemy as easily as a musket or penetrate as deep…but I'd rather have my crossbow than be unarmed if it came to a fight!"

Cathy looked at her quizzically and frowned. "Marianne, do you mind me asking…why are you so…you know… involved in this stuff. I know you say it's about looking after ourselves, but I mean…you are the only woman I know that plays with, I mean, that goes in for all this soldierly carry-on."

Marianne laughed. "Mark blames my father. He made a little soldier out of me when I was barely able to walk or talk. I had a toy crossbow back then, before I knew that weapons were made to kill. Mark says it's not womanly to bear arms. And maybe he's right. But I believe that we women need to be a bit more like men, better even, to survive what's coming."

"I suppose", Cathy mumbled, taking the crossbow from Marianne and attempting but failing to pull the string.

Marianne took it back from her. "You hold it like this", she instructed, and set about the arduous task of imparting a skill that she'd honed over several weeks of trial and error, loud swearing, and daily discouragement from Mark who pleaded with her to give up trying to master "that primitive contraption!"

***

12

Edward Comerford found himself reciting the background to Ireland's political turmoil quite a lot lately. Visiting dignitaries were referred to him for his by now routine explanatory spiff. Today it was the turn of the Spanish wine merchant Senor Sanchez. He wanted to know why Edward's beloved Motherland was possibly staring into the abyss.

When the man removed his broad-brimmed purple hat, Edward thought he looked past middle-age and must be close to retirement. Eyeing his delicate hands and bronzed features, he visualised him basking in the Iberian heat. Senor Sanchez exuded affluence, and flaunted it. His rich black fabrics decorated with gold threads set him apart from locals, as did that oversized stone-studded necklace. Callan had welcomed many such business folk, but Edward wondered if its days as a bustling market town might be coming to an end.

He poured himself a generous helping of brandy and filled the merchant's pewter cup. Senor Sanchez had expressed admiration for his host's choice of dining venue. Because it was a relatively warm day, they availed of the rooftop alfresco arrangement at the *King's River Tavern,* which stood eloquently just inside the official town boundary beside the bridge in Upper North Street and within two or three yards of the Bridge Gate and watch-tower.

It was a favoured haunt of wealthy passers-through, and Edward had in recent weeks established a routine for his state- of-the-nation tutorials. First a drink, and then he sought to complete his run-down of Ireland's increasingly invidious predicament before the meal arrived from downstairs.

Their padded chairs on the florally decorated rooftop afforded them a pleasant view of the river flowing under the three arches. To their left beyond the bridge the old Norman Motte rose serenely from the vast rolling field encompassing it and to their right they'd noticed the humble friars in their grey habits; some at prayer, others tending to the gardens in the picturesque abbey meadow.

Senor Sanchez was especially taken by the heavenly vista that the towering 15th century abbey and its environs presented.

Screening his eyes from the sun, he blessed himself and uttered a reverential word in Spanish that escaped Edward, despite his reasonable grasp of the language.

Stealing a quick glance at his pocket watch, Edward quipped: "Shall we start? I give the waiter...ah... twenty minutes, possibly a little longer today. It's unusually busy below..."

Settling himself, he began. The words came to him easily as he'd fine-tuned his presentation to near perfection, or so he hoped.

In October 1641, he recalled, the native Irish, who'd been uprooted and displaced from their lands to make way for outsiders, rose up in revolt. The Irish Chiefs decided the time had come to take a stand against a century or more of oppressive and deeply unjust British policy in Ireland: In particular the effective robbing of Irish lands under the hated plantation policy, and the King's failure to keep his promise of fairer treatment of Catholics.

The rising was supposed to be a countrywide affair but, as had so often happened in our troubled history, he lamented, someone, a treacherous drunkard apparently, blabbered about the planned action to the authorities and it was a complete flop in Dublin, where the patriots failed to take the castle, which had been one of their main objectives.

Some of the leaders were caught and hanged, but the raising proceeded, if not exactly according to plan, elsewhere in the country. It was most successful in Ulster, in the sense that the rebels quickly got the upper hand militarily.

Unfortunately, and very much against the wishes of the Irish chiefs, some of the foot-soldiers and civilian volunteers went a bit overboard and, well, took out their longstanding grievances on Protestant families, not all of them landowners or the descendents of planters.

"A bad business, that", he crooned. Apart from being militarily pointless and morally reprehensible, it played directly into the hands of the Puritan faction in the British Parliament who already hated the Irish. It was a gift to them, and over the past decade, it had become a rallying cry for the Parliamentary voices that grew louder by the week in their demands for a re-conquest of Ireland, and a reassertion of control over what they perceived to be an upstart rebellious colony.

119

But the one truly heaven-sent consequence of the uprising, despite its disagreeable elements, was the establishment of the Irish Catholic Confederacy, a kind of provisional government in all but name. Up to January of 1649 its assembly and supreme council, of which Edward had been a member; met in Kilkenny.

The Confederacy's membership wasn't confined to the native Irish, though they were its most fervent backers. It had the Old English on board too. They'd been equally wronged by the cruel plantations that a succession of monarchs had inflicted on Ireland. Their ancestors were English, but they intermarried with the Irish, as the Norman invaders had done before them, and here they were...as Irish in their own way as Edward was, "or the man out there on the street rolling that barrow of beer kegs."

Sanchez tut-tutted: "The anti-protestant pogrom: I'd heard of that, and like you say it was an unfortunate aberration...not to be condoned...but I'd rejoice in any weakening of English domination of Ireland, and the easing of that country's unrelenting suppression of the one true faith. Yes, that was a singular achievement; would to God that you Irish could win complete independence from the *Sceptred Isle*, as Shakespeare miscalled that nest of heretics!"

Edward waved aside the interjection. "Oh, let me tell you. 1642 heralded an era of liberty and renewal for most of Ireland, but for Kilkenny it ushered in a veritable Golden Age. Just think: For almost a decade it served as Ireland's de facto Capital. European powers recognised the Confederacy as amounting to an independent state. They assigned ambassadors and diplomats to Kilkenny.

"The Papacy recognised us, sending money and arms. The Papal Nuncio's arrival in the City was an occasion of unprecedented pomp and splendour. The hopes of the people soared, their faith vindicated and their belief in the path to an ultimately free Ireland strengthened as never before. Kilkenny became a thriving cosmopolitan city; a jewel on the edge of Europe...a cultural, political, and intellectual hub for a fledging nation.

"Before Forty-Two, you'd hear Irish and English spoken in the City but now you had French, Spanish and the diplomat's language of choice, Latin. I was in KIlkenny in 1646 when the captured standards of the army that the Confederates defeated at the Battle of Benburb were borne through the streets, with drums rolling and trumpets blaring. My God, it was like a scene from ancient Rome..."

Senor Sanchez interrupted again, raising a finger. Confusion wrinkled his leathery features. "But wait...wasn't Charles Stuart one of the monarchs who treated the Irish badly? Even if he didn't start the plantations he didn't try to stop them; did he? And his administration in Ireland, I understand, pushed the population to the brink of direst poverty and enslavement in the thirties...

"So why is it that those Royalist soldiers are happily hobnobbing with Irish patriots? I saw scores of those elegantly attired fellows drilling in Kilkenny outside the castle last month, alongside men decked out in Lincoln green uniforms and civilian garb. I presume they were Irish. How can they breathe the same air as the English troopers?"

"I was coming to that. The forty-one uprising occurred when Charles was still on the throne, but then the political scene changed dramatically: Those dreadful civil wars between King and Parliament erupted. As Parliament began to get the upper hand on the battlefields of England and Scotland, the King decided that maybe we Irish weren't such a bad lot after all, so he sent instructions to his people over here to arrange for a cessation of hostilities between his Royalist Army in Ireland and the Catholic Confederacy.

"Not from any love of us, you understand. He needed all the support he could get with the Parliamentary armies edging towards victory. It was only as a last resort, and after a hell of a lot of soul-searching, that Charles agreed, first to a truce with the Confederates and then, what would have been unthinkable if he wasn't in an absolutely desperate fix, an actual pact with his former enemies... in a bid to turn the tide of war in his favour.

"Of course, the Confederacy's pact with the Royalists came at a price, though not as big as it might seem on paper. The Confederation of Irish Catholics was to be dissolved and replaced by a less Catholic sounding body called the Commissioners of Trust, and this would oversee all the previous governmental responsibilities of the Confederation and, most urgently, direct the war effort against the Parliamentary forces, which, until Cromwell's arrival in August, weren't making any serious headway in Ireland.

"In return for the backing of the former Confederacy for the Royalist cause, the King promised all sorts of concessions and reforms for Ireland once he'd beaten Cromwell and his cohorts.

Would he have kept his promises? We'll never know, because those ghastly Puritans chopped his head off.

"That shocked even the most ardent Irish nationalists who wanted no truck with the Royalists. To murder an anointed king was unthinkable, beyond imagining: The crime of crimes. Most decent people on this island, I can tell you, are now of the view that any ally we can win to our cause is welcome, given the nature of the invader who stands poised to destroy us.

"The Marquis of Ormonde, who had led the fight against the Confederates on the King's behalf before the cessation, is now the Supreme Commander of the Royalist/Confederate military alliance. I pray that he has the skill and ingenuity required to defend our fledgling nation."

Senor Sanchez raised his cup in a toast to the Irish cause. After draining it, he shook his head, perplexity darkening his already sun-tanned countenance. "Yes, Edward, I think I'll be taking my leave of Ireland, and not returning...at least until your side has triumphed or maybe a change of regime in London has eased your sad plight. In the meantime I shall have to peddle my wines elsewhere in Europe. Ah! Here comes the meal."

The waiter laid the plates of beef, mutton, bacon, mushrooms and potatoes on the table. He laboured under the weight of the collation, sweat trickling down his cheeks. When he asked if they wished to order a wine, Senor Sanchez waved him away.

When he'd departed, the merchant produced a bottle of wine from his satchel under the table. "Twenty years old. Seville's best...for this special occasion, Edward!"

He uncorked the bottle and filled the two empty cups. "I propose a toast...to Ireland's victory!"

*

Mathias Blunt's diary: October 1649

Following Wexford's capitulation and chastisement, we're on the move again. The effusion of blood at Drogheda and Wexford, as the Lord General called it, has proved to be a great mercy to the savages. Without it, their resistance might have been stronger. I daresay the fright saved a multitude of their pathetic lives. A string of towns and castles have since capitulated. Without a sword being unsheathed or a gun discharged the defenders ran up the white flag. We've been spared the task of routing them.

We're advancing steadily down along the eastern coast of Ireland, encountering none but the measliest and half-hearted resistance as we march, rest; and march again, singing hymns in praise of the Lord who has blessed our campaign. God be praised I have been spared any further brushes with death from fever, though we must be constantly on our guard against that invisible foe. I was glad to leave Wexford behind, even allowing for our army's splendid victory there: I didn't voluteer for service only to be struck down by a common disease.

Aside from formal military engagements, the nature of the opposition- or defiance I should call it- that we've met in some odd backwaters of this strange land is worth a mention. I didn't get to fire a single shot in any of these tussles, but witnessed one disagreeable episode on the outskirts of New Ross.

The town itself, having being summoned by the Commander, had readily surrendered but it seems that a papist rabble outside its walls weren't aware of that decision, or perhaps they'd chosen to ignore it.

Whatever the reason, we came upon a small settlement, not quite a village; more a scattering of campfires, with groups of raggedy fellows, a few shabbily attired females and some youngsters, all lounging about. Some were singing around the campfires

We called upon them to accept the dominion of the Parliament of England. They stared at us, pretending not to understand. Corporal Venebles produced a white flag that he waved above his head, raising his eyebrows in a respectful plea to them to accept their new status as subjects of the Commonwealth.

Then, from out of a cluster of these ragamuffins emerged a tall strongly-built fellow bearing a pike. His breeches were torn and filthy and his white shirt, open wide at the neck, was scarcely recognisable as linen. Three infantrymen and a mounted cavalry officer simultaneously warned him that his life would be forfeit if he didn't drop the weapon instantly.

This reprobate dropped the pike, turned around, and lowered his breeches to expose his bare bottom, from which emitted a rush of foul air. Then, having readjusted his breeches, he picked up the pike. His cohorts, men, women, and half-dressed children, howled with laugher.

The obscene fellow stepped towards the mounted officer, still holding his pike, and muttered something in that devilish native tongue of theirs. He then lunged at the horse with his pike. The officer was thrown from his mount, collapsing into a puddle of blackened rainwater.

More derision followed: A woman threw a sod of grass at a soldier and the children stuck their tongues out, making unintelligible sounds. A musket discharged from close behind me, almost bursting my eardrums.

A big red stain appeared in the centre of the man's grimy shirt, his mouth wide open in apparent surprise. He fell to the ground just inches from where the cavalryman had landed seconds earlier. His cohorts had stopped laughing.

"All of them...all of them!" shrieked Sergeant Jennings. A dozen or so of our men chased the savages, cutting them down as they darted towards nearby woodland. As I reached for my flintlock, thinking it my duty to assist the men, I felt a hand on my shoulder. A member of the artillery train to which I was assigned motioned me to leave the punishment action to the swordsmen. Balls and powder were not to be wasted on non-combatants, he chided.

I watched as the grisly chase continued. A few of our soldiers blocked the savages from eluding justice, and within a minute or two all had been either been dispatched or captured.

The ones still alive were mainly older men and children. Sergeant Jennings ordered that they be dispatched, not just as punishment for their insolence but as a warning to other local would-be enemies of the Commonwealth.

As I make this entry I must admit I'm glad I didn't participate directly in the punishment: The man who wielded the pike and performed that grievous act deserved to die, of course, but the others, it seemed to me, were just ignorant and uncivilised natives who, with appropriate guidance, might have been diverted from their savage ways, and maybe even converted to the true Christian faith which we espouse.

But it wasn't my decision to make, and it may be that God ordained this latest effusion of blood to smite our foes. I'm running out of ink. I hope to procure a new bottle before the end of the week.

For now, I'll just say that, though my conscience is clear, I would not, were it up to me, rip open the lily-white neck of a little girl with a blade, even if the evidence was clear that she was the progeny of papists.

Her eyes accused me as I passed her; or so I fancied. Blood trickled from her body, mingling with rainwater on the sodden black earth.

Not a sight, or a deed, to exult in. Yet, had the God who rules over all not wished this punishment to go ahead he'd have sent a sign, surely.

Yes. In the same way that he spared my own life at Drogheda by granting me just a knock on the head instead of a wound that would have snatched me from this world.

Blessed are the ways of the Lord.

***

13

Captain Gegan was getting used to his grey mare, and the animal, to be fair to her, was not as skittish as she'd been at first. She'd adapted quickly to her new master, and after a little coaxing and a helping of oats and a pail of fresh water from the abbey well, Mark might have been riding his own black gelding back in Westmeath.

Corporal Molloy, riding alongside him down East Street, looked more presentable than earlier. He'd cleaned himself up a bit. His stubble was gone, and his clothes, while still not quite amounting to a proper uniform, at least conferred a hint of authority, especially the rawhide boots and the harp emblem he wore on his jacket.

The harp had become a potent symbol of Irish culture and more importantly, Ireland's craving for religious liberties and self-government, since 1642. Now it appeared everywhere, with civilians and soldiers alike displaying it, mostly via harmless wooden likenesses of the instrument, but the Corporal had a nice shining bronze one that caught the eye and added to his cachet.

They were riding towards Butler Castle at the end of East Street, Mark conceding that the Corporal had been right about the castles. Apart from Skerry's, the other defensive structures were hardly worthy of the name castle. Two were semi-fortified town houses close to dereliction; another one a disintegrating heap of stones. Three more had potential, but only with essential repairs, and quickly, because one couldn't underestimate the speed of an enemy noted for its forced marches.

The Town Wall's condition was even worse. The section around the southern end of town was fully intact and quite robust, if not impervious to artillery fire. Still, it was as defensible as any wall could be; allowing for advances in weaponry.

The northern end of town was protected to a limited extent by the King's River and the fortified gatehouse at the bridge that could be defended by musketeers availing of its loop windows.

But the western wall could scarcely be called such. Soldiers and townsfolk were busily engaged in filling in huge gaps in the masonry with earth and timber, and adding shallow ditches to patch up other breaches.

He turned to the Corporal: "Can we get the wall properly reinforced and repaired, I mean with stonework, to restore it to its former strength?"

The Corporal shrugged. "Maybe...You'd have to ask the Governor, and he'd have to get on to the Mayor and the Corporation. I heard there's a shortage of building materials."

"Then they need to get those materials. It's not the strolling players who might be heading this way, Corporal!"

He was about to ask the Corporal something else when the line of stalls and pedlars on the wide stretch of pavement to his left distracted him. People had congregated on the street, blocking traffic. A carriage driver was growling at the throng to get out of his way. As the two riders tried to manoeuvre around the buyers Mark caught the whiff of rotting fish and winced, to the Corporal's amusement.

"It's the big market, sir. There's fresh fish from the King's River, most of it netted today or yesterday, but then there's the bargains. Most of it left over from the Clonmel market three days ago. Poor folk go for that. They don't notice the stink after they've fried or boiled it."

The smell worsened as they diverted around the goods carriage whose driver was now standing and gesturing with his whip at a shabby little man who was trying to sell him a pair of wriggling eels. Mark had a strong sense of smell, which didn't help when fish was in an advanced state of decay. He'd always avoided the fish market in Mullingar for that reason.

The stalls bustled, customers making off with coveted sacks of salted fish or spitted pikes. Men in tattered shirts and threadbare breeches wrestled in the disorderly queues to get the best offers as the vendors deferred to better-dressed men. Women filled baskets with dead eels and silvery trout at the bargain stalls.

Mark's stomach churned as the foulest of odours threatened to overpower him, but he tried not to show his distaste as he passed by the market. He didn't wish to disrespect the locals so soon after his arrival in town.

Leaving the fish market behind them, Mark was startled to see a man covered from head to foot in soot shuffling along the pavement to his left, a loudly protesting swan under his arm. It was as blackened as the man who carried it and recognisable as a swan only by its long wriggling neck and two spindly flailing legs.

"Corporal, please tell me the locals aren't eating the swans too? Can't they get their hands on enough fish?"

The Corporal snickered. "No, that's just Swanky Hartigan, sir, the chimney sweep. He pulls a swan off the King's River to clean his chimneys. He forces the bird up to catch the soot and when the job is done Swanky returns him to the river. The swan is none the worse apart from having to wash his old feathers. There's an old story about swans avoiding Callan so they don't get chimney work! I don't believe it though. You'll always have swans on the river."

A low moan to his right distracted Mark. He saw the town stocks perched on elevated ground between an apothecary and a cookhouse. Steam from the latter wafted along the row of six prisoners whose heads and hands protruded from wooden restraints. One of the men, his face caked with grease and fruit peelings, used his fingers to wave feebly. Mark nodded back. A pitiable sight, but Mullingar had its stocks too so it wasn't just a Callan custom.

They rode on. Mark was relieved to put some distance between himself and the fish. The receding clamour of the fish market was quickly dwarfed by the strident cackling of schoolchildren. Giddy boys came running and tumbling down both sides of the street, engaged it seemed to Mark in mock battle as they mimed shooting and swordfights.

Catching sight of the riders, some of them stopped, clustering together on the pavements to watch reverently. One shouted across at the men: "Are ye going to save Callan?"

Mark raised his hat to the boys, calling out: "if we can, we will. Will ye help us?"

"Yeah, yeah!" the boys shrieked, and they started clapping.

"The school is overlooked by the castle, so they're aware of military comings and goings", the Corporal explained.

Three boys had broken off from the rest, running and skipping alongside Mark's horse. One stroked the animal under its neck, his eyes raised awestruck and a head of curly hair standing on end. "He's lovely, Mister. Is he a war horse?" he blurted.

Mark laughed "Not yet, but he might be...if the war comes to Callan!"

The animal whistled softy as if to acknowledge the compliment. The boys rejoined their schoolmates. Their applause had cheered Mark, and his brooding over the state of the Town Wall now gave way to hope: a faint but warm feeling in the pit of his stomach to counteract his increasing feelings of despair.

First he saw the rectangular shape of the flag, to his left, high up in the sky over East Street, being worried by a light breeze. Then he spied its magnificent golden harp and the slogan: "For Ireland and the King!"

Then, drawing nearer, the finely carved battlements of Butler Castle materialised. The dimensions of the castle and its encircling protective wall - it towered over every building on the street and was as wide as ten common dwellings- surprised him.

He'd heard it was a more impressive building than the other castles, but that was a gross understatement. The others were as pebbles in the dust compared to this...*colossus.*

Even his horse seemed captivated. She became slightly agitated and wanted to stop in her tracks at the sight of this veritable fortress, and he didn't blame her.

The protective wall surrounding the castle incorporated a gatehouse building and several towers. In some of these he detected movement. He knew keen eyes watched his approach.

As they dismounted, half a dozen musketeers and three pikemen emerged from the gatehouse, one of them hollering: "state your business!" They encircled the Corporal and himself.

The Corporal waved them away good humouredly. "No need for that, soldier. Captain Gegan here has an appointment with the Governor."

"We'll have to verify that. Wait there. Don't move a muscle until I say so."

A musketeer barked an order and a pikeman hurried inside. Half a minute later he returned and motioned them to enter. The soldiers lowered their weapons and assumed a friendly demeanour. Two of them offered to take their horses as they were ushered through the capacious entrance, from which a creaking iron grill slid back to allow them access.

They entered a gargantuan courtyard, large enough Mark thought to encompass a little village. A small group of soldiers, some in light greenish uniforms and caps; others in ragtag outfits blending military and civilian garb, were performing vigorous press-ups.

Men squatted on the ground cleaning muskets, testing them, or offering tips on their proper use. A hundred or more soldiers sat about in bands of three or four nursing platters of steaming broth. A cook was serving it from a huge cauldron that trundled noisily around the courtyard on iron wheels.

"Keeping fit lads?" The Corporal shouted at the men exercising. One of them took a break, mopped the sweat from his brow and saluted the Corporal. "Must be fighting fit when the time comes, sir!"

Mark complimented the men on their exertions and followed the Corporal to the castle entrance. Like the wall portal it consisted of an iron grille. This began to open as they neared, and a small man in elegant white hosiery stepped out to greet them, flanked by two deadly serious pikemen.

The Corporal introduced him to Mark: "This is Sir Robert's personal servant, Captain." The servant said curtly "The Governor will see you in ten minutes. I'll take you to his banquet room. This way..."

They passed through a long shadowy hall and up a stone stairway, onto a landing and up two more flights of stairs. The servant opened a high polished Oakwood door and ushered them in.

The banquet room was large enough to host a full parliament. A table extended from where Mark stood just inside the entrance to within a few feet of the opposite wall, the longest table Mark had ever seen; and he'd spotted extravagant ones on the continent. But why have a meeting in a room meant for dining?

The servant motioned them to sit at the bottom end of the table. Two chairs had been laid for them. "Now gentlemen, just to remind you: Sir Robert does not wish either of you to draw near to him, under any circumstances. There can be no handshakes. Nothing like that. If you attempt to approach him he will immediately leave the room. He may even be impelled to kill both of you. He carries two loaded, half-cocked pistols most days...for his personal security. Understood?"

Mark nodded, and the Corporal just smiled, as if he'd heard it all before. The servant exited and the door shut with a sharp triple echo that pierced the deathly quiet of the room.

Mark took in his surroundings. To his left a marble fireplace caught bars of flickering sunlight filtered in by the musket loops and grilled windows. He whistled softly at the lovely upholstered chairs spaced along either side of the fireplace.

"The owner of this place is fabulously rich", the Corporal muttered, "but he's left Callan until he deems it safe to return." He shook his head sadly. "I wonder what state his castle will be in by then!"

The wall above the fireplace had portraits of Queen Elizabeth I and the murdered Charles Stuart. Oddly, Mark thought, no pictures of Irish heroes or chieftains, which he might have expected given the castle's place in the grand political scheme of things.

Lower down the wall a stretch of panelling depicted biblical scenes: Samson demolishing the temple in a final burst of strength, brave David casting his stone at Goliath, Moses crossing the Red Sea with Egyptian chariots in hot pursuit, and the entry of Christ into Jerusalem on Palm Sunday.

The wall to his right had more portraits...knights, lords, ladies, aristocratic figures, none of which he recognised. Hanging above these, from close to where the wall joined the ceiling, were lines of luxurious tapestries with Arcadian landscapes, pagan gods, and choirs of angels fluttering around the throne.

They sat at the end of the table in the chairs provided for them. Strange, Mark thought, that no battle tapestries or paintings adorned the walls, as you'd normally find in the residence of a military governor. The Corporal nudged him. "Sir Robert is petrified of catching the plague. That's what the servant was on about. He lets nobody within ten feet of him, day or night, apart from his wife and her poodle, and his servant, and the servant has to bathe in vinegar three times a day as a precaution against the plague breaching Butler Castle."

Their whispered confab was ended by the click of the opening door. Into the room stepped a man who might have emerged from one of the fine portraits on the wall.

Mark's jaw dropped: It was as if the King of France had entered, or Charles Stuart; raised from the dead, his head back on his shoulders.

Sir Robert's pinkish-blue periwig had a soft luminescence that reminded Mark of a saint's halo. His silken clothes, dappled with

131

gold, exuded majesty and opulence, and those shining high-heeled crimson boots were fit for a prince.

"Gentlemen" their host pouted eloquently, as he pulled out two pistols, raised them demonstratively above his head and placed them on the table in front of him. The servant adjusted the position of his chair and the Governor sat, dismissing his man with a rapid finger gesture.

"Don't fret, gentlemen, I won't shoot you, unless of course you decide to make any hasty or provocative move to this end of the table..."

They both nodded and Mark was suddenly knocked back by an aromatic surge. From across the glistening oaken barrier between him and the Governor a cocktail of delicate fragrances reached his nostrils. Flowers and spices vied with olive oil soaps and a plethora of unfamiliar womanly scents that sent his brain back in time to exotic places.

These contrasted sharply with the stale smell of tobacco from his own body and the whiff of rancid sweat emanating from the Corporal, hearty and more normal odours for fighting men. God, he thought, Marianne gave off the merest hint of perfume even on special occasions.

"And you, I presume, are Captain Gegan?"

"Yes, Sir Robert", he mumbled, and repeated himself to take account of the distance separating him from the Governor. Sir Robert tapped the sides of his wig delicately and beamed, his emerald green eyes fixing them with a steady but vacant gaze.

"You've come to me highly recommended, Captain: Service with the armies of three European powers, numerous battlefield honours under your belt. Impressive. I hope you'll find your accommodation at Skerry's Castle to your liking, when you move into the living quarters. It's not as grand as this magisterial dwelling but should be adequate for your needs. Now, as to the crisis we face..."

He rubbed his hands together gently, fidgeting uneasily, his face screwed up with apparent concern.

"Well, Captain, you've had a look at the town defences. What do you think? Please speak your mind. I value candour."

Mark relaxed a bit. This made it easier for him. "To be honest, sir, not much. Skerry's is the only small castle I've seen here worthy of the name, and only two of the others are worth defending. They are essentially piles of rock barely held together by mud and mortar. The King's River defensive tower might be useful. A handful of musketeers could pin down an enemy, until of course cannon was brought to bear on their position. It wouldn't withstand that, any more than, I'm afraid, Skerry's would either, though it would take longer to penetrate Skerry's judging by the thickness of its walls.

"The Town Wall, with the greatest respect, sir, is a joke. In its present condition a bunch of schoolboys with slingshots could walk straight through it, unopposed. Even one gap is fatal, but it's riddled with them, and the intact parts of it are so ancient I reckon artillery would breach them in a few hours...less maybe. The river offers some protection at the northern end of town, but the enemy could cross in boats. I suggest urgent repairs to the wall and the placing of obstacles in the river.

"Those adjustments wouldn't, of themselves, be enough to prevent an enemy breakthrough. The defenders will play a big part, civilians as well as soldiers. Vital to put up a fierce resistance, involving everyone who can hold a gun, a sword, a pike...anything capable of taking down an enemy. It's their town. They have a greater commitment to it, naturally, than any of the soldiers who've come from outside the district. I include myself in that category, though I believe I'm no less committed to fighting for Ireland's cause, sir, regardless of what part of the country I happen to be quartered in..."

Sir Robert threw up his hands. "I admire your courage and your patriotism, Captain, but despite your resolve to defend Callan I have to say that you make an equally strong case, however unwittingly, for *not* fighting...in this instance, by your quite accurate if somewhat scathing assessment of the town defences..."

"I didn't mean to denigrate the town, sir, or its corporate leaders. I merely draw attention to weaknesses that need to be addressed. There are strong points too. I mentioned the dilapidated state of the other castles, but this one, Butler Castle, more than makes up for the others. Even allowing for the firepower that enemy artillery can muster, I reckon that this place could hold out for weeks, months possibly.

"I've never seen walls so thick, and I mean both the protective outer wall and the castle wall itself. With hundreds of musketeers firing from excellent cover behind the loops and grilled windows we could give Cromwell a hell of a reception in Callan. And if our forces could then relieve the siege here and attack the enemy, I can foresee possible victory for us..."

The Governor sat forward and looked down at his pistols. It occurred to Mark that their host really might shoot them.

He twirled a pistol around on the table and raised his head. His expression had changed to one of gloominess. "It is certainly a worthy dwelling, Captain...and potentially a powerful defensive position. But whether it would be strong enough to thwart an attack on this town is another matter. No castle is unassailable these days.

"Cromwell's army has some of the most formidable artillery in the world. You know what it did at Drogheda. Maybe Butler Castle is impregnable, as it was designed to be I'm told, but I'm a born sceptic I'm afraid when it comes to claims of invincibility. The King thought he was invincible, and see where he ended up.

"We'll have big decisions to make in the coming weeks, Captain. The regicides are advancing, in spite of the best efforts of our gallant armies, and we expect them to arrive here in late January or February, allowing for an expected withdrawal to winter quarters.

"Assuming that they haven't been halted by then, and continue to press towards Kilkenny in the New Year...we have to decide on a course that is in the best interests of this town... to which I've been appointed Governor.

"As I'm sure you know, I had a long association with His Majesty's loyal administration in Ireland, prior to his foul murder, and equally with the Confederation that has sadly passed into a kind of political Limbo...for the foreseeable future...and I have always done what I deemed...most advantageous...from the point of view of promoting Ireland's wellbeing, and, what is closest to my heart, gentlemen, avoiding unnecessary bloodshed."

He lay back and spread his arms out in a conciliatory gesture.

"For indeed, Captain, what would be the point of engaging in hostilities if and when we had reached a juncture when to draw a sword or cock a musket would produce no result other than our own untimely, and I should think, quite tortuous and ghastly, demise. As our dear Catholic Gospel says, there is a time for war and a time for peace...

"Well, Captain, do you have an opinion to venture...at this stage of the proceedings? Are you a man to whom compromise, a word that some find unpalatable, with one's foes, whether in politics or on the battlefield, can ever be entertained? Speak candidly. I won't hold it against you if I happen to disagree with your analysis!"

Mark shuffled uncomfortably in his chair. "In my foreign military service I was never faced with a situation where surrender was deemed either a necessity or an option. What I would have done in such a predicament I'm honestly not sure. Possibly I might have willingly agreed to yield on good terms. Not just to save my life or those of my comrades, but because...because I was a hired soldier back then, fighting for causes, other people's causes, that meant nothing to me.

"Here, I find myself entrusted with the defence of an Irish town in the middle of what is shaping up to be a war of annihilation. It's my homeland this time, not some patch of foreign soil that I'm paid handsomely to defend. Back then, I would gladly have switched sides any day if the price was right. This is different. .."

"Your patriotism is commendable, Captain, but I'm sure you've heard of what happened at Drogheda and Wexford when surrender terms were rejected. Wholesale massacre, men, women and children put to the sword. And what happened to the towns that *did* surrender...Cromwell's army just marched on, walked away...well maybe leaving the odd garrison behind as a small occupying force..."

Mark stiffened. "You say they left in peace, sir. But haven't you also heard that Cromwell has made an exception to his pledge of clemency to towns that yield? Irish people are devoted to their Church. They treasure their religious faith as they would their lives. And these invaders have already kept the promise their leaders made before the Roundhead army set sail for Ireland. They are killing all captured clergy on the spot...priests, friars, nuns...they've sworn openly to suppress the faith of the Irish whenever and wherever they find evidence of its practice.

"In Wexford, I heard, priests were butchered like cattle in the town square. Others hunted down like vermin. A so-called surrender that allowed a crime such as that against innocent clergy doesn't sound like one I would ever agree to, sir. But then of course the decision won't be mine..."

135

The Governor blushed. Even his periwig seemed to have changed to a brighter shade of bluish pink. "I appreciate your candour, Captain...I won't detain you any longer. We'll consult further on this and related matters in the coming weeks. Who knows? The war may end soon and we can both return to our homes ..."

Mark and the Corporal rose, and the servant, responding to his master's bell-tingle, promptly returned to escort them from the castle.

*

Two days later...

Mark tried to put a brave face on the day's tidings. The heartening news he'd received earlier was now quickly overshadowed by Marianne's letter.

The Governor had given the go-ahead to all of Mark's proposals for strengthening the town's defences: An excellent development. Apart from paving the way for urgent wall repairs the Governor's decision seemed to indicate that he was thinking in terms of defending the town, and not toying with the idea of capitulation as he'd shown every sign of doing when he'd met him at Butler Castle.

But Marianne... because a fortnight had passed since his departure from Westmeath, he thought she'd put that crazy notion out of her head. But she hadn't, and to cap it all she intended to take her inseparable friend to Callan with her.

Mark and Corporal Molloy stood on the footpath outside Skerry's Castle smoking their pipes, as local chambermaids worked to transform part of the top storey into suitable living and sleeping quarters. The sleeping section would be screened, they told him, by a curtain from the remainder of the top floor, with a small space available for a third person to sleep.

It wasn't a palace, but it would serve them well, and, in any event, comfort and accommodation standards would be the least of their troubles if war came to town.

Two men shuffling about on the battlements had been assigned to repair a crumbling chimney. And a mason was hammering away at a patch of damaged stonework over the entrance.

"Imagine, Corporal, she wants to be by my side even if the worst happens? Her father made a soldier of her and I'm the one who has to suffer for it!"

"You were telling me she's good with weapons, Captain. That could prove useful when we open the armoury. Most people here haven't a clue about guns, apart from a few wildfowlers, and not too many I'd say have handled a sword either. If we want civilians to help us defend this town your wife might help to show them a few tricks. Not ideal, I know, having a woman playing with guns... but these are desperate times..."

"I'm sure she'd do that. In her letter she tells me she's shared her pistoling and musketry skills with Cathy...that's her friend. I'm afraid Marianne won't be happy until she has women acting like men. I'll have to be careful she doesn't replace me as Captain. Regulations don't allow that, of course, but Marianne has a way of getting around such trifling impediments!"

The Corporal sneered and shook his head. "Begging your pardon, sir, but I'd never allow a woman to order me about, or get above herself. They'd rule us though if they could. Be sure of it."

Mark resigned himself to Marianne's impending arrival. He took a long pull from his pipe, blowing wisps of smoke across the street towards a group of gawking boys who seemed entranced by Skerry's Castle and the activity around it.

*

Shane shielded his face with his hands from the sudden blast of heat from the forge. How did Luke stand it? Luke's father, Jimmy Dooley the blacksmith, was hammering a horseshoe on his anvil. Turning his head aside he shouted "Luke, Shane is here..."

Luke appeared from somewhere in the depths of the dingy forge, not bothered by the sparks or the red hot fumes. His hair was tossed and his face partly blackened with soot. "You'd want to clean some of that off before we go to the church" Shane urged.

Rubbing his cheeks with a sleeve Luke tittered and started running towards the grassy lane leading into town. "It's not Mass we're serving today, Shane, just going upstairs to have a gawk."

"I suppose" Shane agreed. Shane couldn't wait to see Callan from the tower of St. Mary's. As a reward for their altar boy duties

Fr. Brannigan had given them permission to go unto the battlements of the church to enjoy what the PP called "a panoramic view of our native town."

Luke had already been in the tower so it wasn't a big deal for him, but Shane had thought of nothing else since he was informed of the" special privilege" the PP had bestowed. Very few locals had the good fortune to be let mount that stairway, the PP had confided, after the boys completed their Sunday serving the day before.

They scampered up North Street, and the Bridge guard waved then though the lofty iron gateway. Shane noticed that the river beneath was swelling again, probably about to flood the Motte field as it did nearly every year.

Running past the Cross in the Town Square, they broke into a race to see which of them could reach the church first. Out of breath, Shane conceded to Luke, who was far quicker on his feet. He could run faster, and was better in a fight too, Shane knew, which possibly made up for his lack of schooling.

Mother had warned Shane not to make fun of Luke's inability to read or write. His family hadn't sent him to school so it wasn't the boy's fault, she'd reminded him. Boys who did get educated were the lucky ones and should thank God every day and night for the gift of learning.

Shane took her advice to heart, but it hadn't occurred to him to belittle Luke's absence from school. He envied him, since he hated school himself, and only went to please his mother, who he knew would be terribly upset if he didn't go. In the vestry on Sunday Fr. Brannigan had asked him to help Luke with any task that required reading. This request was made when Luke was out of earshot, so the PP didn't want his friend to know about it.

Luke led the way into the churchyard in South Street. St. Mary's towered above them: a magical sight. Shane never failed to be over-awed by it. From the entrance gate it resembled a witch, he imagined, with its two long narrow windows near the top for eyes, a slit window in the middle for a nose, and a double oblong window near the bottom that could be a mouth formed into an "O" expressing surprise or consternation at something on the street.

And at either side of the central tower the roofs of the attached stone buildings were shaped like witch's hats. It was a daft notion, he knew, because this was a church and no witch in the country would be bothered with it.

Inside the church, Luke gently nudged open the door of the tower. It was unlocked, as the PP had promised, for their benefit. They ascended the wooden steps, which creaked under them.

"Skip the next step", Luke cautioned. Shane did that, as Luke added that they'd have fallen through if they'd stepped on that one as it had cracked and splintered under the weight of an exceptionally heavy man.

As they neared the top Shane became nervous. "Being up so high, I hope I won't get dizzy. I nearly fainted once when I looked out a high window."

"You can't fall out, come on, I'll show you."

They emerged through an opening onto the roof. Nervously, Shane followed Luke to the nearest wall, with its crenallations.

"See..." Luke indicated the scene below.

Shane's head spun. He drew back, frightened of the heart-stopping vista that greeted him. His eyes registered the unfamiliar sight but his head took a few seconds to make sense of it.

"We're looking down on South Street", Luke said.

Shane forced himself to look. Yes, it was South Street, but not as he'd seen it before. From here it was a long narrow stripe, dusty and grey, with roofs and the fronts of buildings running along either side of it. To his right he beheld the lofty wooden cross in the Town Square, and beyond that North Street, another grey stripe stretching down towards the bridge over the King's River.

People were moving about below on South Street like small creatures, and traffic was stirring too: carts and wagons trundling along, their drivers greeting each other. The nods were just about perceptible. A horseman passed the slower moving traffic, nimbly cantering off down North Street and out of sight over the bridge.

The horse gone, Shane followed Luke to another vantage point in the tower and saw the high wall spanning the top of South Street (though it wasn't quite so high from up here) marking the town boundary at that point. He noticed that the mighty towers of the South Gate guard post weren't half as high as this one on St. Mary's.

The guards at the South Gate were leaning against the Town Wall, smoking pipes, their pikes resting beside them. Beyond the wall and the gate he spotted the fairground, dotted with cows, white fluffy little sheep, and ant-like people moving about.

A coach was approaching the South Gate. Shane watched as a guard lazily rose and waved it on through the gate. "What about the school...?" he asked, instantly regretting this as he remembered how Luke might feel put out by mention of schooling. Luke indicated the crenallations behind them. Shane, no longer afraid of heights, eagerly sought out the building where he spent so much time being miserable as he learned all that boring stuff against his will.

"See", Luke pointed, "Butler Castle, and the school right next to it."

Yes, the castle was huge compared to the school...the tallest and widest structure on East Street. The school looked puny from up here, he thought, the playground no bigger than a tiny pebble. Wouldn't it be great, he fantasised, to be able to sprout wings and fly up here like a bird whenever Master Counihan came at him with the blackthorn?

Now he knew what a bird's-eyes view was. East Street bustled with activity. Street traders plied their wares, if not as busily as on Fair Day.

Then he turned to admire West Street. Skerry's Castle loomed down there, a mere fraction of the size of Butler Castle which he reckoned to be the largest building visible from St. Mary's. They spent the next quarter of an hour darting from one vantage point to another, savouring the sights and assorted if scarcely audible sounds of the town.

His eyes straying from the streets and the traffic Shane marvelled at the gardens, orchards, and numerus backyards that he'd never seen, until now. It was indeed a privileged place, as the PP had called it, Shane decided, and he looked forward to coming up here again. "I can't wait to tell the lads at school", he blurted, again forgetting his mother's advice.

Luke, descending the stairway ahead of him, stopped and turned. "Why, don't they know far more at the school than us ignoramuses who can't read?" he asked, resuming his descent. Shane felt as if Luke had struck him in the face.

"Oh no...There's a lot we don't know. Hey, what's the big deal about reading? You've shown me the sights. If you like, I can show you how to read...well...to read a bit..."

Luke didn't answer, just hastened his progress down the steps of St. Mary's.

***

14

Tom Brennan whistled softy as he dried the washed tankards and passed them to Mags who was run off her feet serving customers. The Tuesday night music session always drew them in, and tonight the *Fiery Spirit* could barely contain the throng.

He'd expected a bigger than usual attendance after persuading the legendary one-eyed harpist, Edmond McDonagh to play. McDonagh had given an eye for Ireland in one or other of the Confederate wars of the early 40s, possibly at Benburb in Ulster under the great O'Neill.

Tom found the politics of conflict perplexing, and the Confederate wars especially so. He'd found the Kilkenny doctor's explanation helpful, but he still struggled to follow the ever-changing national scene.

If he understood correctly the Confederates had fought against the Crown, against the Scots, against each other when they fell out at some point, and were now allied with their former sworn enemies, the Royalists, against Cromwell. If they won this latest war God knows who or what they'd end up fighting next, though Ireland desperately wanted to win *this* war.

Tom marvelled at McDonagh's patriotism. The man was so proud of the life-changing wound he received on the battlefield that he famously refused to wear a patch over the empty eye socket, preferring everyone to see his treasured sacrifice.

Tom glanced at the clock that ticked behind him over the shelf with its wood carvings of Gaelic chieftains. The lads would be here soon...

And here they come...

The alehouse door squeaked in, and two younger men preceded the harpist, carrying between them the extra large triangular instrument for the war hero.

Then, in the doorway, appeared the tall, mildly menacing form of McDonagh. His head of bushy gnarled hair and a fierce glare gave him a wild look, adding to his dashing rebel status.

The babble and riotous laugher in the house abated. Heads turned, all attention focused on him. Men lowered their mugs and tankards, and others stood reverentially, to nod their greeting to the illustrious musician.

More customers flowed in behind him, shuffling among the ones sitting at tables and standing about, in an effort to find space. Tom thanked God he'd allowed for a crowd tonight. He'd thrown open the trapdoor to the large beer cellar, which he'd furnished with stool s and tables, to accommodate the extra revellers. The ones down below wouldn't see the musicians, but they'd hear them well enough.

Then the fiddlers came, and the tin-whistle players. Customers surrendered chairs to them.

Tom called for silence, giving a brief rundown on the night's schedule. The session would open with a piece from the harpist, only fitting, he added sombrely, with that ancient symbol of everything Irish again under threat from "bloody foreigners."

A loud cheer shook the alehouse. Hats and caps hit the ceiling, pipe ash flew, and drinks spilled, but no one complained.

The harpist strummed a haunting lament, accompanied by local singer Densy McCormack who always kicked off the music sessions. The alehouse was congested, with barely room for Tom or Mags to get around with drinks, and the cellar overflowed too.

After the harpist the fiddles came to life, and a few men tried unsuccessfully to dance, a natural urge but an impossible task tonight with scarcely enough floor space to move an inch in any direction.

As the night wore on, customers began to drift out, and a more manageable routine settled in. Tom responded to a call from a man holding up an empty tankard. He recognised him as the Englishman nicknamed *The Atheist*. In his early thirties, he had a permanent surprised but not frightened expression, his mouth dropping open even when he had nothing to say. He'd come to Callan after escaping from England following the King's execution.

He'd been on the run due to his beliefs, and while nobody in Callan shared his unpalatable non-belief in God, they grudgingly forgave that error after hearing he'd pissed off the king-killing anti-Irish, anti-Catholic shower who'd seized control of England. Tom was wary of him because he'd been barred from five Callan taverns and three alehouses following rows over his atheism. If he caused trouble here he'd have to bar him too, but he hoped it wouldn't come to that. So long as he didn't start a rumpus he'd be fine.

143

"Well, Peter, enjoying the fiddles and the harp? Better than facing the music back in dear old England I'll bet, hah?"

"You can sing that", Peter crooned, accepting a generous refill from Tom's frothing jug.

Tom spotted Captain Gegan at another table, deep in conversation with two aldermen. The women must mad after him, with those finely chiseled features: So handsome and finely-tuned from head to foot. Eyes blazed fearlessly in his noble head. You'd think his skull was hewn out of marble or stone, like those busts of great emperors and military folk of the past. So different from the man he replaced-that unfortunate fellow killed in a duel, who'd been a habitual drunkard and brawler. This Captain was a credit to the soldiers of Ireland.

His voice, though commanding and authoritative, wasn't remotely menacing, as Tom thought a military man's might be. But he radiated strength and purpose in his every word and gesture, and Tom wouldn't fancy getting into a tussle with him.

He'd informed the Captain earlier that the gentlemen from the Corporation wished to see him. He went around to his table. "Well Captain, alright for a drink there?"

The Captain eyed his mug and said, after a moment's reflection, "I'll have something stronger...a whiskey, Tom, if you don't mind."

"And yourselves, gentlemen? "

"The same, if you please", they answered in unison. The Captain quickly offered to pay for theirs, producing a handful of silver.

*

Mark Gegan had balked at the prospect of discussing the war in an alehouse, where he'd come to get away from talk and thoughts of what might be in store for the town. But it seemed he'd have to oblige-or at least humour these fellows that the proprietor said wanted to meet him.

He'd lost himself in the rousing music session in this, the fifth alehouse he'd visited in town. The *Fiery Spirit* was easily the liveliest establishment he'd called to since arriving in Callan.

He loved the fiddles and the soulful ballads, but the harp-playing especially lifted his spirits. He'd heard of McDonagh back in

Westmeath. His fame knew no county or provincial boundaries, and he was renowned almost equally for his military exploits.

Patriotic music was one thing, but he'd hoped to get a break from contemplating, let alone discussing, the war. He presumed these fellows would be anxious for news of the war, gossip basically; thinking he knew more than they did about what the future held. A notion prevailed that people in uniforms had all the answers.

But when Tom Brennan added that the patrons in question were aldermen, Mark saw immediate advantage. These men could be helpful to his quest to persuade the insipid Governor to further strengthen Callan's defences and put the town on a proper war footing, ready to take on the Roundheads.

They approached him, eyeing him up and down studiously. One was tall and unnaturally thin, as if on the verge of starvation, decked out in formal silky garb more suited to the council chamber than an alehouse. He introduced himself as Jack Ryan.

The second man had the look of a schemer. Small and slightly overweight he had a cape wrapped around him that he pulled tighter as he swaggered towards the table, his polished suntanned rawhide boots standing out among the modest footwear in the alehouse. His jacket exhibited the ubiquitous golden harp, fast becoming the symbol of national pride.

Before sitting down at the table he glanced around him conspiratorially and then extended his hand to Mark. His grip was fierce and confident. "Josiah Crotty, Captain."

They'd taken their drinks with them. Ryan held a little pewter chalice of wine while Crotty clasped a hearty tankard of bubbling ale. They got down to business instantly, Crotty explaining that the Corporation was divided on the question of whether the town should consider surrender if the enemy's terms were reasonable.

A majority was against any such move, but that position could change at the next meeting.

Crotty pushed aside his drink and leaned over to Mark, his hands clasped in front of him. "My colleague and I here were wondering if you might help us to make the best possible case for not running up the white flag, come what may..."

Mark stopped him, "but...hold on a second...you know the Governor has absolute power and discretion in these matters. His

145

decisions supersede and override anything the Corporation might like to see happen. It's the downside, I'm afraid, of having a military governor."

Crotty's face broke into a big grin. "True, but he's told the Mayor that he'll take the Corporation's views and recommendations into account. Now, whatever about his powers, he can't very well throw in the towel if the Corporation delivers a clear message that the people of this town will have no part in such a cowardly surrender...."

Mark reflected for a moment and then spoke slowly, a singer lamenting a lost love somewhere behind him. "I've met him. The enemy is nowhere near Callan yet and Sir Robert is already toying with the idea of surrender. He sees it as a possible necessity to save the town from destruction..."

Ryan spoke, his feeble voice adding to the perception that he was unwell. "Talbot isn't really a military man. Yes, he was on the Supreme Council of the Confederation like our own Mayor, but he belonged to the moderate wing, and was always wringing his hands about avoiding anything that looked remotely like a clash of arms. He'd do anything to avoid bloodshed, which might seem a noble sentiment, but we're not up against a noble enemy, Captain.

"Talbot is a skilled and experienced administrator, a landlord, and a lawyer. He's wearing his lawyer's hat instead of his ill-fitting military one when he talks of theoretical deals and so-called decent surrender terms. He's not thinking of what awaits our clergy if Cromwell prevails, whether we surrender or opt to fight.

"But if the town roars at him from the rooftops, metaphorically speaking, that it's wiling to resist the tyrant...then I believe he'll have to listen. Being a craven coward works both ways, Captain. Talbot is also a narcissist. He's obsessed with his appearance- you've met him so you'll know I mean- and what people think of him. He won't want to be cast in an unfavourable light...as the blubbing conniver that he is."

Mark drew back, a little discomfited. "Now gentlemen, we mustn't judge him too harshly. He hasn't made any decision yet. Before it comes to that, you in the Corporation might also push for the reinforcing of defences. Some work has started but I fear it won't be enough. The Town Wall right now wouldn't hold off an angry dog, and sand-castles would be as effective as the ones you've got, with three possible exceptions..."

Crotty nodded. "Thank you, Captain. Butler Castle is the key. You've seen it? ...but Talbot has command of it, and its large garrison..."

Mark agreed. "His disposition doesn't help those of us who want to mount a spirited defence of this town, but even he must see that he has at his disposal the means by which we can deal Cromwell a major setback if he comes our way...I wish you well with your meeting. I hope you get the necessary support. Sir Robert is a problem. I only wish I could swap roles with him, that he was in Skerry's and I had command of Butler Castle."

Mark caught the proprietor's eye and ordered drinks. *I'm among friends.*

*

Tom Brennan was worried. The house had fallen silent apart from the odd outburst of laughter and the few feeble attempts to revive the music session by fellows who couldn't sing. But the raised voices from one table bothered him. Earlier he'd responded to a call from McDonagh for drinks and to his surprise the harpist had bought a tankard of ale for Peter the Atheist.

Now, McDonagh was banging the table and his voice grew louder each time he spoke. He was glaring wildly at his new drinking partner. Peter hadn't raised his voice at all, but he didn't have to. His views spurred others to raise theirs. Tom could see why he'd been thrown out of the other establishments.

He went to the table to quell whatever dispute had arisen. "Gentlemen, is everything alright here, you know my rule. I try to calm tempers and avoid any unpleasantness. If you have any serious quarrels please take them outside."

McDonagh switched his angry glare from Peter to Tom. "This fellow here needs to have some sense knocked into him. Can you believe? He says there's no God? I thought I'd seen every class of a dangerous mad bastard that ever saw the light of day, but this..." He indicated Peter with a sneer that sounded almost as fierce as it looked.

"Change the subject", Tom suggested, "just talk about something else."

"But I only bought him the drink because I heard the new crowd in England had given him bother. Any enemy of Cromwell and his gang is a friend of mine, or so I thought. But a man who doesn't believe in God and goes around saying there's no God. That's too much. And he gets worse by the minute. How could anyone ever say such a thing?"

Tom sat down beside Peter, eliciting a grunt of disapproval from McDonagh. "Whatever differences ye have, keep it cool. And Peter..."

"Yes" the Englishman said, his look of permanent surprise deepening into an intense quizzical one.

"Tell us...how did you come to be here...so far from your home? Did you announce you didn't believe in God and get thrown of England for that?"

Peter assumed a thoughtful dermeanor, his eyes glazing. "That was only part of it. And I didn't get thrown out of England. That would have been fine. I was lucky to escape with my life. I never called myself an atheist. That's a label attached to me by people who don't understand my position." He finished his ale in three gulps and laid the mug aside.

"I was a big supporter of this man you're all so fearful of; who's cutting his way through your country like a scythe. Oh yes. When I met him a few years ago I thought, now here's a man after my own heart. He wanted England to be a land where every citizen had rights, freedom of conscience, and no King should ever again be an oppressor. Parliament should not be at the beck and call of a monarch. A ruler should be fair and just..."

He went silent and shrugged. "It all sounded great to me. For the first weeks after the old king got the chop, things went as I wanted them to go. Something like democracy, if not exactly as the ancient Greeks envisaged it, started to make an appearance. It was like a big breath of fresh air...across the land.

"There were several groups with ideas that wouldn't have been tolerated by the king. Now it seemed they might flourish under wise and tolerant rule. But our new rulers who'd crowed about ending tyranny... who'd held up the severed head of Charles Stuart and declared *England is free*...didn't take long to replace the old tyranny with one of their own.

"The group I was with- it had around a thousand members- believed in forging a new path in life, where we'd build up little communities that aimed at self-sufficiency and steered clear of religion...of any kind. Some in the group believed in a deity, others, like myself, didn't, but all of us were adamant that we'd said goodbye to organised religion and church-going..."

Tom gasped: "But why...why turn away from a faith in God?"

"We didn't really do that. We were free to believe or disbelieve, so long as it didn't involve bothering other people and forcing anyone to join this or that religious faction...Naturally, some of us, including myself, asked if we could, you know, dispense with the main ingredient of religion too, the deity that all the religions profess to believe in, and that every religious faction believed was on its side and against all the others.

"To me, God didn't belong in a rational world. I've never seen miracles, such as changing water into wine or turning a fish into thousands of fishes. Life doesn't work that way. And science is slowly chipping away at the old beliefs. The earth isn't the shape the churches long believed it was. That's why I wanted to proclaim that view...we left it open to members to accept or reject God- but held fast to our stand against organised religion."

"So you had to leave England..."

"Yes. At first our group was tolerated. And we honestly believed the new government would usher in an era of tolerance, a system that would brake down barriers, and allow freedom of thought..."

"But it didn't work out..."

Peter gave a cynical titter. "We were naive. Within weeks of inheriting the trappings of power our new rulers were clamping down on people who didn't conform to their Puritan order. First we got warnings, then visits. Then threats: Some of the groups advocating new ideas disbanded quickly. They saw the signs and didn't fancy a flogging, being locked up, or worse. Most of them were small bands of people fired up with hope and idealism, like the one that wanted equality for women, so they'd have the same rights as men...they felt that all men and women should have the right to vote in parliamentary elections..."

McDonagh banged the table and almost exploded with laughter. "Votes for women...that's the best I've heard all week. They must have been off their heads!"

"Oliver Cromwmell and others thought the same. So maybe you have some common ground. Anyway, our group was stubborn and refused to disband, despite several warnings.

"We still believed that the future looked...bright...once misunderstandings were ironed out. We got ourselves a printing press. We had a house in Coventry where we printed booklets and tracts setting out our beliefs. The Roundheads banned the group and put a price on our heads. I saw that as a challenge, instead of accepting we were finished. I encouraged the others to keep going no matter what.

"Eventually, after months of distributing our material, someone betrayed us. I was in the top storey of the house and saw the soldiers from a fair distance. I knew they were heading straight for our place. There were fifteen of us, twelve men and three women. The women were stitching the pages of booklets together. The ink was drying on hundreds of other pages spread out on a big desk.

"All hell broke loose. I roared: *Drop everything Forget it. Out of here. We haven't a minute to spare!* There was a hectic rush. The little stairway almost shattered under the impact of all those feet pounding on it. I foolishly tried to set a fire to destroy the stuff but I couldn't get it started.

"But being the last in the room saved me. I looked out the window. I couldn't see the Roundheads. That meant they were already in the house. I heard the footsteps, heard shrill voices. The only exit faced me. I climbed out through the window onto a ledge and on to the roof of another building and managed to get clear of the area.

"So you escaped?"

"I did, but none of the others made it. The soldiers were waiting outside the house for them. I was lucky. They were all hanged, including the women. One woman I think was disembowelled as well. They believed she was a witch. Not a nice death. They chased me across England like a pack of hounds after a deer. I heard from a man in a safe-house I stayed in that I was sentenced to death in my absence."

McDonagh scowled. "And were all your friends who got caught non-believers...in God?"

"No, as it happens, just unbelievers in religion as I mentioned earlier. I was the only one in that printing house who didn't believe in God. The others prayed every day, turned their heads to the sky for solace. That's another thing, and you fellows might think about this...they prayed for their safety. They asked God to protect them from harm."

Peter sighed. "God didn't seem to hear them, though, or if he did he didn't think them worth saving. But I escaped... I who didn't believe...another reason why I'm more convinced now than ever that your all-seeing creator just isn't up there. Could I have another drink?"

Tom rose slowly and went to the sink to fill another mug. What a strange fellow, he thought. Before he could refill the mug McDonagh was calling for two more drinks, his anger towards Peter having seemingly abated.

*

The house was at peace now, with only the buzz of jovial banter as the last drinkers began to exit. Closing time wasn't far off. Taking a well-earned rest, Mags slumped into the tattered old armchair inside the entrance that many a customer fancied.

She looked ready to drop from exhaustion. Tom was tired too, but delighted that another music night had gone nicely, apart from that minor spat between McDonagh and the Atheist. The two of them were still talking down there, respectfully now. He hoped that Peter would keep his oddball views to himself. Callan was a staunch Catholic town, and fellows who went around denying the existence of the All-Mighty were asking for trouble.

Maybe not the kind of trouble Peter could expect back in Puritan England, or that his pals found themselves in when the Roundheads caught up with them. People didn't get hanged in Callan for saying silly or offensive things, no matter how annoyed people found them, but Peter risked being assaulted or waylaid if he wasn't careful.

He seemed a decent type despite his unbelief. As Tom wiped the counter clean of ale splashes and paw marks, he shuddered at the thought of what No God would mean: No point to anything. Life, however thorny or terrifying it already was, would be downright unbearable: All hope gone.

He regarded Peter with pity as the man sipped his ale, McDonagh tolerating his sad nonsense. *Fair play to the harpist for not clobbering him.*

No God? We'd be taking all the hurts, all the knocks and then, when we'd been rightly battered and bruised and tossed about, we'd end up being lowered into a hole in the ground to rot, with no afterlife... for the cold earth to finish what disease and aging and hard times started.

No Thanks Peter. You can keep your No God delusion. Fr. Brannigan might have a word with him. I'm no religious expert. The PP might shine a little light into that befuddled head of his.

*

The long journey was nearing its end. Marianne's heart lightened at the driver's assurance that Callan was only a mile ahead. Several miles had been added to the journey owing to the need to avoid plague-stricken Kilkenny. "Had to do the same for your husband, Madam" he'd added.

Cathy was asleep again. She'd been dropping off every two or three hours over the past day of travelling. Conversation seemed to weary her as much as the endless clip-clopping of the horses' hooves on the roads, dirt-tracks and other stretches of ground that couldn't be called either and were pockmarked with holes and other obstructions.

Interesting, she thought, that being cooped up together in a small space made for longer and more exploratory chat. Cathy had spent the first half-hour of the drive voicing her shock at Marianne's decision to cut her hair as short as a monk's. "You'll be mistaken for a man," she'd blurted when she arrived outside the Gegan household to board the coach, quickly adding: "God, you *do* look like a man...why are you dressed...?"

Climbing inside the coach after Cathy she laughed, patting Cathy on the head as if she were a simpleton. "I *want* to resemble a man." she soothed, conscious of how her knee-length breeches and threadbare jacket had also nonplussed the coach driver, whose mouth had gaped, but shut quickly when she fixed him with an enquiring, and slighting menacing glare.

"If we're stopped by highwaymen who also fancy a bit of rapine they'll think twice when they see you accompanied by a man. I think it's better that one of us looks mannish. I can change into my own clothes when I get to Callan."

Opening the case resting on her lap she took out the pistol, to Cathy's immediate discomfort.

"That thing won't go off, will it? I don't want to get shot before we even get to that place that could be invaded."

"No, I'm just checking that's in working order. It was yesterday. Everything seems fine. I'll load it at the first sign of trouble...if the coach screeches to a halt, for example, and I hear the driver answering a challenge."   Closing an eye she aimed at the window beside her.

Fortunately, they didn't encounter any highwaymen. But Cathy had availed of their prolonged confinement to probe further into Marianne's motives for making the journey, repeating the concern she'd voiced two weeks earlier. "You're just putting your life in danger. Two of you could end up dying instead of one!"

"Or three, if your time has come", Marianne retorted.

"But why are you...acting like a man? I mean, you're dressing that way too. I know you say it's to fool robbers and aspiring rapists, but, well..."

Marianne turned to her, feeling sorry for what she saw as her friend's naiveté.

Unlike Marianne, Cathy had accentuated her femininity, rather than concealing it. Her glistening black hair hung loose around her shoulders, and her soft green eyes exuded trust and bafflement in equal measure.

Marianne said nothing for half a minute, sizing up whether to change the subject or oblige with an answer. *What the Hell,* she decided. *Cathy's a friend.*

"I can't remember a time in my life when I'd be happy with just being a girl doing girlish things. When other girls were picking flowers or playing with kittens I'd be fighting the boys, or throwing stones at them, or wrestling them to the ground, and often winning those silly fights. I lost count of the number of bruises and black eyes I gave the little brats."

Cathy tittered, holding a hand over her mouth."I'd love to have seen that...but then you grew out of all that tomboy behaviour surely. I mean, you found love, didn't you? You met Mark and married..."

Marianne didn't wish to continue this exchange. It was going to a place she'd rather avoid.

She answered curtly," I didn't find love, as you put it. Or rather, I didn't love Mark at first...when we met. The marriage was arranged, as most marriages are. I didn't have a choice. I was indifferent to Mark when my father introduced us. But over the following days we got to know each other, and yes, love blossomed...eventually. I was glad of that because I'd hate to think of what married life would be like if you hated your husband, or had no feelings for him.

"My father picked Mark specifically because he was an army officer. He had this strange notion that if I married a military man I'd be better able to defend myself, and I'd be protected by a strongman at my side. And he reckoned that Mark would be delighted with the military training I'd received."

"And was he...I mean... was Mark happy with you being into guns and swords?"

Marianne laughed. "The opposite: he begged me to forget about war and weapons...to be a normal wife and a woman and let him look after military affairs. But I persisted. I've never stopped practising: with guns, knives, swords and the crossbow...and keeping fit. And now.... now I'm glad I did, because I may need to handle a weapon, before I'm much older."

She saw the puzzlement on Cathy's face. "And you, Cathy, you haven't found love, and I presume nobody has arranged a wedding for you yet. And you're so beautiful..."

Cathy blushed and turned away. "I've avoided men. Looking after my brother took up my time so I didn't wish anything to interfere with that. But now...maybe I'll meet someone in Callan."

Marianne shrugged. "You'd better do it fast then, before we're all dead!"

"Oh, it mightn't come to that. We must hope for the best."

"I suppose..." Marianne tried to banish thoughts of disaster from her mind.

The coach was slowing down, at last. The driver rapped at the window and called out: "We're approaching Callan, ladies...the South Gate. Prepare to dismount."

Marianne shook Cathy awake and pulled back the curtain to see the high Town Wall. The gate with its two stone watchtowers loomed ahead. Alert soldiers had muskets at the ready, suspicious eyes glowering at the coach, but they relaxed as the gate below them swung open to let the conveyance through.

The coach continued down South Street. Through the window Marianne took in her first sight of this town that her husband had been appointed to defend. Along both street footpaths people chatted, smoked, laughed, or strolled along unhurriedly and unworriedly. Children ran about, whooping and shrieking. It didn't strike her as a place under threat.

The coach slowed to a crawl as it neared a giant wooden cross, at which women knelt, scrubbing the ground around its base. They dipped cloths in buckets and were turning their attention to the Cross itself as the coach turned left, wheeling around the Cross to enter West Street.

Marianne waved through the window at the women. One, catching her eye, stood and waved back with a hearty smile, before quickly kneeling again.

The coach stopped about halfway down West Street in front of a castle. Marianne unboarded, helping Cathy out before reaching back to fetch her pistols and crossbow.

***

15

Mark couldn't complain that Cathy wasn't earning her keep. Within minutes of arriving at Skerry's Castle she'd rekindled the fire, carefully positioning beech logs and pivots of turf and fanning it lovingly back to life. He'd let it fizzle out, as he had a habit of doing when alone. He chided himself on not having it blazing heartily for Marianne after her long journey.

Turning from the big open hearth Cathy lit the candles ensconced in brackets on the wall, remarking that the single oil lamp on the dining table barely illuminated the stone-walled room. He hadn't bothered with the candles either.

She rearranged the rushes on the floor, which needed tidying, Mark admitted, not having been attended to since he moved into the castle. Then she had the broom, swiping away at dust and cobwebs in all kinds of spots that the renovation team appointed by the Governor had clearly missed.

He feared she might go too far, seeking to turn this temporary military outpost into an ideal home, which it could never be. It was built to ward off attackers, not offer comfort, although he'd found it to his complete satisfaction even before Cathy had set to work.

"Can you stand up a second, Captain Gegan? Thank you."

There she goes again. Sweeping under my chair. Oh God...how women love cleaning.

"Marianne should be up soon with the meal, Captain...I caught the smell of it down there a while ago, Gorgeous. The mutton ought to be boiled within half an hour and the spuds are the flouriest I've ever seen. The Corporal called to drop in a jar of butter milk. A very nice man. He said you'd like that."

"Yes, thank you Cathy. No need to kill yourself. Take a rest now. I'll be fine."

She exited the room. He closed his eyes, wishing that God would take this Chalice from him, as Christ had asked his divine father in Heaven to remove his ahead of the crucifixion.

Not the looming showdown with Cromwell, but the prospect of Marianne making trouble for him in Callan. He was still reeling from the shock of seeing her in that unladylike raiment... wearing breeches and leather boots instead of a decent skirt or dress. He might have taken her for a highwayman if she hadn't removed that silly hat from her pretty little head.

Her hair was the worst. She'd sheared it off till her head could have lodged on the shoulders of a medieval monk bound to silence. Not that Marianne could stay quiet for two minutes.

And her smallpox scar un-powdered: *It's as if she wanted to be unsightly. God, how awkward...*

And that was just her appearance. Before he could offer her a helping of cold meat and a mug of coffee-he'd made modest allowances for her arrival- she had him pinned to his rickety chair beside the fireplace, standing over him like a reproachful parent.

From her rapidly moving lips came a torrent of drivel about "shaking things up" in Callan, getting involved in the military preparations, sharing her gunnery and fencing skills with townspeople, if not necessarily her knowledge of archery since, she tut-tutted, there mightn't be any crossbows in town.

He'd let her ramble on for several minutes, Cathy standing at her shoulder like a bashful chambermaid awaiting orders, and then he set about dismantling her offbeat delusions.

"Now Marianne, you've only got here, and you know nothing about this town. People here are set in their ways, as they are everywhere I suppose, but you'll be a stranger to them too. Naturally, they expect men to do the fighting, and women to... you know...maybe cook the meals, clean the house, feed small farm livestock such as hens and piglets...but, as I've told you a thousand times, soldiering is a man's profession or calling...."

She peered at him sideways, alluringly. "But you know how good I am with a pistol...and a bow...and I can use a musket too. Since you left Westmeath I've practiced a lot and I've shown Cathy here how to defend herself. Haven't I Cathy? She can hit a target as niftily as any man...!"

"Yes, I appreciate that you have an uncanny feel for weapons of various kinds, Marianne, but the fact remains that women don't belong in the ranks of our defending army, or of any army for that matter. You might consider...possibly helping out in other ways. Do a bit of nursing, tending to wounded men, that sort of thing.

"Let us do the fighting dearest, if you don't mind, and please....at least while you're here, try to be a wife...a normal wife. I know you admire that heroic French woman who trounced the English, but I

157

didn't marry her, I married you, and I don't want to see you burned at a stake, which, incidentally, Mr. Cromwell is perfectly capable of doing, especially if he captures a woman who he'll see as usurping the time-honoured function of a man in battle..."

She'd glared at him, falling eerily silent, before averting her gaze and calling Cathy to accompany her down to the kitchen where she'd prepare a nice meal for the three of them.

He was relieved when Cathy came back up after a brief spell in the kitchen to perform her clean-up ritual, having half expected Marianne to return and try his patience, if not his sanity, with another round of crackpot ramblings.

He supposed it might be too much to hope that she'd develop a flair for cooking and other domestic preoccupations and forget about soldiering. That aroma from the kitchen augured well... for a decent meal today at least. Apart from the mutton he thought he caught the tang of mushrooms and oxtail soup.

Lovely... he'd make a point of complimenting her on the meal, however it tasted. Butter her up, praise her culinary prowess and maybe bring out her feminine side, which she had an annoying habit of pushing aside like an unwanted guest just when he most wanted her to be a woman.

He loved her, deeply and despairingly. But he feared she'd drive him to the madhouse with her ambition to be a latter-day Joan of Arc.

*

November 1649

Marianne dressed more to Mark's preferment than her own before embarking on her walk to the East Street market. He looked reassured when she presented herself to him in a blue hooded cloak and black skirt. He irked her though by suggesting that she wear a wig until her hair grew back to its normal length.

For his sake, he chided, as well as that of others who might find her manly coiffure distasteful. She laughingly shrugged him off, ushering Cathy, attired in a bright red mantle and sky-blue dress, out of the castle ahead of her.

Cathy was anxious to see the stalls. As they approached the wooden cross in the Square, Cathy nudged Marianne, giggling into her hand. "I never thought I'd actually enjoy…you know…relieving myself…but that privy chamber is a godsend. I found myself singing. Can you believe that? I can tell you I wouldn't have been in the mood for singing back in Westmeath when I had to go!"

Marianne agreed. It made a welcome change from the more common practice of seeking out a suitable corner of a field or garden, or using a chamber pot that you then had to empty somewhere.

The memory of her introduction to the state-of-the-art toilet in the castle brought a flush of pleasure to Cathy's cheeks. "It was lovely" she gushed, "that smooth wooden bench, and the nice aromatic herbs strewn on the floor of that little room. You'd forget you were…it was more like sitting down to breakfast or to a picnic. And then you have a choice of hay or moss to wipe…they've thought of everything."

Marianne pulled her cloak tighter against the November chill. Mark thought it augured snow, but there hadn't been snow since last winter, the locals told him. Cathy's focus on silly mundane things at this time of national crisis baffled her. Sometimes people made no sense.

Cathy wasn't finished: "What I don't understand, or maybe I haven't thought about it enough, is …what happens to the…stuff…when we discharge it?"

Marianne had to force an answer. She wished Cathy would change the subject. "It goes down a kind of chute and plops into a field at the back of the castle."

"Oh, but doesn't it just pile up then. Does nobody mind?"

"Mark says the local farmers collect it and use it to fertilize their land. He says nothing goes to waste in Callan and that's why it's a thriving market town. He mentioned too that a woman employed by the garrison calls in once a week to clean the chamber. She throws a bucket of water down the chute to keep it nice and fresh."

Cathy winced and laughed. "Anyway, I like it. Only thing is… I don't know how I'll go back to the old-fashioned way…after sitting on that lovely bench and inhaling those herbal aromas…"

The clinking of pots, pans, and other merchandise distracted Cathy. To Marianne it sounded like a band playing wildly out of tune…metal colliding, scraping and banging, interspersed with a babble of voices.

Beyond the Cross, around which a circle of kneeling women were fingering rosaries, Marianne beheld the peddlers and their wares on East Street. Entrance to the street had been barred to horse or donkey- drawn traffic by temporary barriers. There was barely standing room along the street. The footpaths and street were equally congested. Prospective customers streamed in from North and South streets to swell the multitude. The prospect of a bargain or a quick profit seemed to trump the fear of Cromwell.

Marianne took Cathy's arm: "Want to have a look? Might be something for us…"

They shuffled through the crowd that jostled and haggled and pushed. A glittering array of wares vied for their attention. A line of stalls displayed silk cloth, skirts, dresses, linen jackets, stylishly embroidered petticoats, and selections of hats, caps, scarves, kerchiefs and kitchen aprons.

A dazzling range of garments beguiled, with damask designs shining forth from huge bundles of otherwise bleak hues and textures. Marianne winced at the sight of a garish tunic that could have been the Biblical coat of many colours. You'd only wear it if you wanted everyone to notice you, she thought.

Footwear abounded, mostly at ground level so prospective buyers could try it for size: Brogues and leather boots mainly, for men and boys and some nice women's sandals. Stacks of knee-length breeches for men nestled alongside arrangements of clay pipes and stacks of tobacco cubes. Firewood stalls traded briskly, as you'd expect in November. Marianne savored the forest fragrances.

Cathy had immersed herself in a heap of clothing, raising and dropping cloaks, caps, shifts, and underwear items as she burrowed greedily into the fabrics. Marianne liked the hectic atmosphere of the market, the distraction it afforded from the drumbeats of war. But she felt no urge to buy anything.

She passed the butchers' stalls, offering a bigger meat selection that you'd find in the shops on a normal weekday: Scores of headless rabbits hanging upside down, their legs bound, blood dripping on to the street.

Butchers hacked at big sheep and ox carcasses as customers pointed to the pieces they wanted. Hooks and knives sliced into

160

flesh, hacking chunks away to be pushed across to men and women who grabbed the bleeding portions so quickly you'd think they feared the butchers might snatch them back.

Women had hessian bags ready to receive pig's heads and feet, veins sagging gorily from the freshly dismembered body parts. One angry lady, pointing her thorny stick at a butcher, was demanding two heads for the price of one, shouting that they were smaller this month. The butcher was sulkily pulling out a second head for her, his denials weakening by the second.

Poultry stalls had freshly strangled feathered chickens, heads still attached, and headless plucked ones, all laid out for hungry locals to examine. Bags filled quickly. Fowl was cheaper than red meat. Cheapest of all were the pigeons, impaled on a board leaning against the front of a thatched house.

Envious eyes beheld a brace of pheasants, their multi-plumed carcasses elegant and repulsive at the same time, bloodstains peppering their breasts.

Another butcher rubbed his big flabby hands in a blood-soaked apron before pulling a string of gizzards from a box. Coins appeared from inside a lively woman's shabby garment and a miniature tug-of -war commenced as she sought to maneuver the glistening gut-blob from the vendor's slippery grip into her bag.

At stalls further on, hatchets, shovels, billhooks, slingshots, and slightly damaged but usable cauldrons and other cooking paraphernalia changed ownership at a fast pace. Coins jingled in recognition of profit and satisfied customers.

Leaving Cathy at the clothes stalls, Marianne progressed slowly along East Street. The stalls began to thin out. A pair of women sat behind a stall that sold religious accessories. Marianne bid them good-day but declined their invitation to consider their dizzying assortment of rosary beads and brand new plaster statues of the Blessed Virgin and Saint Anthony.

An unkempt young man holding aloft a clump of vellum pamphlets caught her eye. Positioned between two stalls that sold plaited rush-carpets, he waved the pamphlets and hollered: "News of the war, the latest…"

He wasn't making much headway, unsurprisingly Marianne thought as most Callan folk couldn't read. Literacy was a rare enough privilege in any part of Ireland.

His pained bony face broke into a thin smile when she held up a coin. She took the newssheet and walked on till she reached the end of the line of stalls where the street was almost empty of people.

Unfurling the newssheet she was struck by the stark bold headline: "Ireland and the Faith will win!" It went on to say: "The invaders will drown in the Irish Sea, like Pharaoh's charioteers when the waters engulfed them before they could catch the fleeing Israelites…"

It boasted of successful counterattacks against Cromwell's army, and claimed that the enemy had faltered in his bid to re-conquer Ireland… "We will prevail!" it pledged.

But from what Mark had said the war wasn't going well at all, and he still wanted her to leave Callan and return to the relative safety of Westmeath.

Cathy came running after her, carrying a little bag of offal and a rolled-up garment under her arm. Marianne ignored her entreaties to have a look at the displays, continuing down East Street. She took the garment from Cathy, offering to carry it for her.

The flags and pennants of Butler Castle scarcely twitched today in the absence of even a slight breeze. They seemed stiffened by the winter freeze. But the sheer size of the castle had Cathy agape. "God, I wouldn't like to have to clean that place on my own every day…"

Marianne was impressed by its dimensions too but more intrigued by a group of women in soiled working garb emerging from the castle, hauling heavy bucket s of water. Pike-men and a musketeer standing guard at the entrance cheered them for their efforts.

The women waddled in twos to a section of the wall that stretched to the right from the castle, and that extended, Mark said, all the way to the South Street Gate.

She saw teams of men at work, hammering, chiseling, passing bricks or stones to each other, and mixing some concoction in half-a-dozen barrels. The wall clearly needed mending. It looked decrepit and ancient, holes gaping where stones had fallen out or come loose.

She'd have to investigate. She called Cathy to join her, knowing her friend's inquisitive nature.

As she neared the water-bearers, a woman whose face was lathered in sweat squinted at her, nodding a silent greeting. Marianne handed the garment back to Cathy and quick-stepped to the woman. "I'll carry that the rest of the way if you like…"

The grateful woman gave her the bucket. Marianne needed both hands to hold it. She swayed and almost fell from the unexpected weight but found her balance and followed the other women to the wall, gritting her teeth as she tried to avoid spilling water. Men immediately grabbed the buckets and began watering the mixture in the barrels.

She asked them about the work and a burley fellow who spat a long thread of phlegm before speaking informed her that Callan would soon have the best Town Wall in Ireland.

The woman she'd taken the bucket from tapped her on the shoulder, thanked Marianne for helping and said she must head back to the castle yard for more water. She was the wife of a garrison soldier, she said, and she felt it was the least she could do to help.

Women, she explained, also assisted at other sections of the wall that had fallen into disrepair. Mostly small chores that didn't require strenuous activity: The men could do that, though the buckets were heavy enough and they might have to carry them for longer when the water source was further away.

Marianne decided she'd help too. She asked the woman about the work routine and told her she'd be there next day to assist in any way she could. She felt her heart racing. She couldn't wait to tell Mark. He couldn't argue, because women were already involved in the town's defence, even if in this limited capacity. It was a start. She could talk to the women; maybe take things a bit further…

Cathy echoed her. "I'll come too. I fetched water several times a day back in Westmeath…"

*

Malcolm and Jeremy exited the abbey dining hall to see what all was the noise was about, leaving their colleagues breakfasting inside.

The meadow buzzed with the clamour and energy of human enterprise. Soldiers and civilians lined the riverbank, armed with shovels, long slivers of wood and a variety of metallic instruments.

They faced squads of similarly equipped workers on the opposite bank. These were also; Malcolm learned, engaged in the task of making life difficult for any invader who sought to cross the river.

Two army officers on horseback, a captain and a corporal, supervised the activity on the meadow side of the river. They greeted him heartily; both raising their hats to him when he enquired about thedisturbance.

Work had commenced early that morning, before even the friars were up and they rose earlier than most people in Callan or anywhere else. The Captain apologised for any inconvenience to the abbey or disruption of its prayerful routine, explaining that the planned spiking of the river to thwart the enemy would continue for two more days.

Deadly sharp stakes and other obstacles were being positioned and later, if an attack was deemed probable as distinct from a possibility, the river might also be dammed at selected points to cause deliberate flooding.

Malcolm had never seen such bustle and excitement in the normally quiet meadow where nothing louder than the tweeting of birds or the low voices of the friars in the herb or vegetable gardens might be heard, or the clanging of buckets at the well.

Now he heard loud swearing, and the clatter and splash of wood in the water, boots crunching in the hallowed grassy domain in place of the soft footfalls of sandals and bare feet, or the whisperings of Divine Office. He'd blessed himself at least a dozen times, as had Jeremy, at the sound of curses and the taking of the Lord's name. They weren't used to this kind of secular intrusion.

But Malcolm saw an upside. Shocking though such necessary defensive measures were, he was happy that Jeremy was within earshot of the Captain. He hoped that the early morning ructions at the river would prompt the stubborn old man to re-think his crazy insistence on staying at the abbey if Callan were attacked.

To drive home the message, Malcolm asked Jeremy to take a walk with him along the riverbank to see some of the preparations for the defence of the town against a violent and murderous aggressor; one intent on the destruction of the Catholic Church and the elimination of its clergy. He immediately hated himself for saying this when Jeremy's eyes filled with tears and the man just stood staring at the lines of men clogging up his beloved King's River with sharpened stakes and a cocktail of devious death-traps.

"But maybe it won't happen", he muttered, following Malcolm to the riverbank. Ignoring this remark, Malcolm urged him forward, "Let's have a closer look, shall we?"

Malcolm waited on him to catch up. As they drew nearer, a soldier ran towards them. "I'm afraid I'm going to have to ask you not to get too near the riverbank, Fathers. If you happened to stumble and fall in you'd be impaled on a stake, or seriously hurt. Sorry about that."

But they stood close enough to see. Malcolm felt weak at the sight of the river being turned into a hellish stream that would take away life instead of sustaining it. Water was a precious gift from God. It shouldn't be used to kill or bring suffering. But the friars had no say in this: the town rulers had sanctioned these desperate measures.

Jeremy indicated the Blessed Well, located halfway between the abbey and the river. Malcolm too needed to quench his thirst. They took turns cupping the crystal clear water into their hands and drinking deep. The friars had availed of it since the abbey's foundation in the 15th century and many townspeople relied on it too. Jeremy closed his eyes and muttered "holy bubbles come up to me." An age-old tradition.

He rose and sat on the stone casing around the well. Malcolm sat beside him and placed a hand on his shoulder. The old man seemed to be in a trance. "You see Jeremy how unwise it would be for you to stay when we leave the abbey, if we do have to leave...this is the beginning of the preparation for what may befall us. You're not... you're not still intent on staying, are you?"

Jeremy's gloomy expression vanished as if he'd heard the best possible news. "Now I'm more determined than ever not to abandon my holy vocation. And I hope the rest of you will reconsider. We belong here, Malcolm, come what may.

"If we must die, let us die here, our true home... faithful to our God, and not run like rabbits to be hounded by heathens. You know that God tests his people, Malcolm. Well, this is our test. We fail it if we leave. I'm sure of it. Stay, Malcolm."

He turned away, looked back at Malcolm and shrugged. "And anyway, those Cromwellians may not be half as bad as we imagine.

When they see that our presence here has no military purpose they'll just...make fun of us, probably...give us a tongue lashing and then skedaddle!"

Malcolm's heart sank. Where was God, now that he needed him?

*

Marianne and Mark strolled arm-in-arm down the quiet boreen that ran through Harkin's Wood. It was muddy and wet after late night showers, but a welcome change from being cooped up in the castle all morning, where Mark had spent three hours listening to war news from Sergeant Lynch, who'd been sent by the Governor to brief him.

Mark wore his military uniform of brown and dark green for the walk, a lighter green sash denoting his rank and his tricorn hat sporting a peacock feather and harp emblem.

She suspected he'd donned his formal attire to show he wasn't ashamed to be seen with her after what he'd said about her boyish haircut. He always tried to make up for things in that roundabout way.

Inhaling the pleasant country air, she was untroubled apart from a twinge of guilt that prickled in her head. She wanted to be straight and honest, but she couldn't very well tell Mark the full truth about her work on the wall.

He had mumbled approval when she told him that she'd been assisting the women who laboured alongside the workmen.

Fetching water was a womanly enough activity that he approved of, whether it was drawn from the castle courtyard, or wells on the town outskirts to serve other sections of the wall.

But she had to withhold the details of her other work, knowing what Mark's reaction would be.

They'd walked for two miles or more. Mark had said they needed to after feasting on bacon and white cabbage washed down with punch and buttermilk, followed by plates of apple pie.

She liked woodland walks, but missed the warbling of blackbirds and the alluring notes of the lark that flew high above the human sphere. Winter robbed the countryside of its lustre. The landscape cast its bleakness on everything.

It wasn't without its charm, though. She spotted a robin redbreast on the emaciated branch of an ash tree, seemingly nibbling at a seed pod. Earlier, after they'd stepped outside the town barrier, a flock of starlings had swarmed overhead. Rooks swooped and traced intricate patterns in the sky.

True; flowers had shrivelled up or disappeared, and most trees had shrunk to skeletal hulks, but to compensate for that her heart lightened when they passed a holly tree... berries aglow, heralding the approach of Christmas and what in other years would be a time of celebration. Not this year, she presumed...

A cackle of voices distracted her. Mark was reaching for his pistol. She knew it wasn't loaded, but a robber or enemy spy wouldn't know that. From around the bend of the boreen three mantled and hooded figures came skipping. The women stopped and stared, frosty breaths trailing; then broke into hearty grins. Two of them waved.

"Do you know them, Marianne?"

She recognised the work volunteers. She prayed they'd have the sense not to...

"Marianne, hello. And is this your husband, the Captain we've all heard of? Hello Captain Gegan!"

The three of them curtsied. The middle one, tall, freckled and evincing a mischievous glint, blurted out what Marianne desperately wanted her to keep quiet: "The girls and I were just talking about that session yesterday. It was great. I never thought I could throw a stone that far, or lift one so heavy off the ground...I..."

"Lovely to see you Sheila, but we must be going. I'll see you again tomorrow..."

"Oh, yes...by God we'll be ready for them I'll tell ye that. Good day Captain, see you Marianne..."

The three of them scampered past jauntily, leaving Mark looking decidedly suspicious.

"And what was that about? Stones, she said?"

Marianne avoided eye contact, giggling. "Stones? Oh yes. Once the water was delivered to the lads at the wall, some of us offered to hand them the bricks and stones. Might as well make ourselves useful, Mark...."

"Mmm, I see, but she said something about throwing a stone. Why would you be doing that? You don't throw stones at a wall you're trying to build or repair..."

She resumed walking and he had to accelerate his pace to keep up.

"Oh that was just Sheila expressing herself awkwardly...anyway, do you think the wall will be strong enough to withstand...whatever's coming?"

He shook his head. She'd deflected him. "Nothing is certain. I don't even know if the Governor will opt to fight. He may run up the white flag. Nobody knows what he's thinking."

The words stung Marianne. Not that she wanted a fight, with all the risk and possible disaster it could entail. But she didn't wish her efforts, humble though they were, to be for nothing. Her mind strayed to that unofficial training session.

When building work had finished, she'd invited a dozen of the women into a pre-arranged venue, an empty field outside the town, to demonstrate a few battle tactics that might, she surmised, come in handy if things turned nasty for Callan.

In her tomboy days as a child she'd twice won the Mullingar stone-throwing contest in both categories: She threw stones the farthest and managed to lift the heaviest one.

Because only men and boys were eligible to participate in the show, she'd disguised herself as a boy- her father encouraged her - a habit she reverted to on her coach trip from Westmeath.

Within twenty minutes she had the Callan women pelting stones at agreed targets, and trying out heavier stones and rocks to hone their newly acquired skills. Harmless fun it seemed to them. It was good exercise if nothing else, but since the women wouldn't be trained in the use of firearms they should at least have this primitive act of defiance to fall back on.

They loved it, and they'd warmed towards her, oblivious of possible dangers ahead. They might soon be throwing stones for Ireland, with or without Mark's blessing.

***

16

Early December, 1649

Marianne couldn't sleep, which surprised her because she was certain she'd expended all her energy reserves that day, tutoring the women on how best to throw stones.

She craved a mug of buttermilk and that meant a trip to the kitchen on the bottom floor. Since she initiated the training sessions, the numbers of female volunteers anxious to learn how they might assist in defending their native town had quadrupled.

She now had more than fifty belligerent ladies to instruct. Not that she'd complain. She'd specifically asked them to spread the word with a view to building up a solid band of resistance fighters.

Keeping Mark in the dark about the stone-throwing wasn't helped by having so many women freely chatting in the streets, fields, and cookhouses ...good-humouredly reviewing their progress, but that wasn't a risk that bothered her. It wouldn't be the end of the world if he heard...just another silly argument after which she'd gleefully carry on. Also, Mark had enough on his plate, preparing for the arrival of soldiers from Butler Castle to take up residence at Skerry's.

She only wished she could share her firearms expertise with the women too, but even if she could it would serve no purpose since they wouldn't be given any weapons. So, stone-throwing it had to be.

Careful not to disturb Mark, who was snoring gently, his face a vision of untroubled ease, she pulled off the straw-padded coverlet and slipped into her house sandals. Taking the candle that was ensconced outside the chamber at the top of the stone staircase, she tiptoed down, her soft footfalls barely audible to her own ears, and therefore, she knew, not likely to wake Mark...or Cathy, for that matter, who she hoped was sleeping soundly.

She was worried about Cathy. For seven nights running her sleep had been interrupted by nightmares, and the night before she had issued a blood-curdling screech that drew Marianne to her side. Sitting up, Cathy remembered vaguely having dreamt of death raining from the sky, and gory men hacking at each other. She'd spoken rapidly, shaking all over, sweat dripping from her chin. Tonight, she was quiet thus far, so hopefully no bad dreams or crying out.

With each step she took down the narrow stone passage she feared she'd hear either Cathy screeching or Mark calling her back. But, reaching the kitchen, she relaxed and went to fill the mug from the jug. Not waiting to return to the room upstairs, she drank a third of the buttermilk, imagining it replaced her depleted vigour.

Mark would have swigged a tankard of ale or something stronger. She found that buttermilk always gave her a lift, and it didn't leave her with a mighty headache like ale, wine, or brandy often did.

Ascending the stairway, with candle in one hand and buttermilk in the other, her nightdress brushed off the walls. The passage was so constrictive that even a slightly-built person like herself felt hemmed in by it, but that was necessary to thwart intruders. She wondered how effective it would be if...

She noticed one pleasant change since earlier in the week: Cathy had attacked the cobwebs and mopped every inch of stonework, so at least her shift wouldn't be covered in dust when she got back up.

Stepping away from the stairs unto the top floor, she stopped abruptly. Was that Cathy again? She listened, her own beating heart the only sound...but there: a moaning, perhaps.

She entered the chamber, saw that Mark was fast asleep, and pushed back the curtain dividing their sleeping quarters from Cathy's small room.

She cupped the candle to avoid dazzling Cathy. *Asleep, thank God*, and not showing any signs of distress...

She moved closer to the bed and peered at the calm, unruffled face of her friend. *How tranquil she looks, and how...beautiful.*

How on earth had Cathy got this far unwed? Had men been struck blind back in Westmeath that none of them had got a ring around her finger?

Stepping closer, she allowed the candlelight to illuminate from a distance the woman's dainty eyelids, those rosy quivering lips, her snow-white forehead, and the slightly blushing cheeks. She left the mug of buttermilk on the floor and, holding the candle far off; she stooped and kissed her left cheek. *Sleep on, dear Cathy.*

A strange feeling surged through her: Of tenderness and compassion, tinged with an unfathomable angst. Though she loved Mark deeply, she loved Cathy too, in a different way. She wanted desperately to keep her safe, and being in this place built for war wasn't conducive to that aspiration, but she'd do her best...

She turned away to rejoin her sleeping husband.

Both of them happily dreaming...tonight anyway. In a world of troubles even an hour or two of care-free-rest is a little miracle...

*

Mathias Blunt's diary: Second week of December, 1649

I'm wondering again if the Lord wishes to spare me the hazards of battle. Not that I should complain. I have no desire to die if I can avoid it, having so much to live for: my forthcoming wedding to Meg, the many years of married bliss, and my status as a landlord of considerable means that I trust will follow on from my service here.

But I feel obliged to do my bit for England, to share in the struggles and sacrifices that my countrymen are making for this great cause.

The news this morning elicited prolonged bouts of applause. The Commander has decreed that our army will retire into winter quarters, the resumption date for hostilities to be announced in the coming weeks, presumably when this foul Irish weather gives way to conditions favourable to a spring offensive. So, I'm safe for another while, though I take no solace from that.

When the festive air abated and we'd time to consider the bigger military picture the mood at the encampment changed. On the positive side we have much to be grateful for: More enemy towns have capitulated without a shot being fired: Cork...Bandon...Kinsale...Youghal; the list lengthening by the day. And it is to Youghal, a pleasant coastal town, to which we are heading for what our officers deem a well-earned break.

But a shadow hangs over these bloodless triumphs. The vital port city of Waterford remains in enemy hands. And our failure to capture it can only be attributed to the fork-tongued deceit of the Irish.

Taking Waterford is important to us because ships of our glorious Commonwealth navy rest patiently off the coast, waiting to transport supplies to us including additional top-of-the-range siege artillery. These can't be landed while the enemy holds the port.

The Commander, in his customary Christ-like application of mercy and heavenly compassion gave the City Mayor five days to consider his surrender terms. An essential condition was that no further reinforcements would enter the City to bolster its defence.

The Mayor, a sly operator, accepted this condition and so the Commander took him at his word. Though not doubting the Commander's reputation as a man of unparalleled political and military genius, I and many others here in the camp believe that he ought not to have put his trust in those papists, who we know to be league with the Antichrist.

While we sat back on a hill overlooking the city, cleaning our muskets, praying, or reading our pocket bibles...naively waiting for Waterford to surrender, the City was accepting hundreds of extra soldiers, anything up to two thousand veteran Ulster troops.

A spy informed us of this characteristically Irish gambit, but too late. By the time the information filtered through to us Waterford teemed with defenders. The Mayor had deceived us and through our telescopes we could see the Irish laughing and jeering, carousing in the streets in their usual beer and whiskey-swilling fashion.

We hear too that the Mayor has been replaced by a papist military governor who could prove even less amenable to our entreaties than his conniving predecessor.

Added to this setback in the field is the accursed Irish weather. You'd think the Pope himself was directing it. Days of torrential rain have succeeded where no human foe could, in stalling our advance. And disease spawned by the fetid Irish terrain has beset our army. I know from my own relatively mild experience how debilitating it can be, but others have not been as fortunate as I was.

Hundreds are succumbing. I've seen bodies abandoned where they fell. Malaria and dysentery are the prime culprits I'm told, but the plague is reported in some counties.

That's the worst of all and I heard today that it's spread to Galway city, which we've yet to liberate from the foe. On a positive note, I hear that Kilkenny's Royalist/papist defence has also been weakened by it, for which we thank God.

But the gravest news of all, received just as I began to inscribe these words, has been that our Commander, the one chosen by the Most High to lead this campaign, has fallen ill.

We don't know how serious it is, or the nature of the illness, but the chaplain and our officers exhort us to pray fervently for his revival.

*

Mark felt better as he surveyed the repairs to the Western Wall. It hadn't exactly been rebuilt but the crumbling sections and outright gaps in the wall were being replaced by palisades. The stakes forming these were so sharp that the merest contact with the point ensured injury, a zealous worker assured him.

The PP's pulpit appeal for volunteers to help shore up the town's defences had elicited an uplifting response. Hundreds of men aged from eighteen to seventy were on the job, all doing their bit; some of them obviously seasoned labourers, but all fired up with eagerness.

Turning to the Mayor, whom he'd requested to join him on the inspection, Mark voiced his misgivings about suggestions from aldermen that the stakes be tipped with poison. That could prompt a massacre of civilians by Cromwell in the event of Callan's losing, he warned, though it was possible the Roundhead leader would do that anyway.

Mark cast an eye over the lines of men making adjustments to the wall. They toiled with shovels, hammers, chisels and wooden barrows, sweating despite the December freeze that sent shivers through the Captain's body. A thin layer of frost still carpeted the ground.

The Mayor's icy breaths and trembling frame as he strode alongside Mark also contrasted sharply with the moist brows of the workers, most of them stripped to the waist, mud and clay changing their light pinkish skin to a greyish brown.

"The West Gate castle itself hasn't been touched yet Captain. Do you think that can be...improved?"

"Might be better to demolish it and turn the ruin into an obstacle than expect men to defend it in its present condition. But I think we have time on our side to do that, and a lot more of it, if what I heard earlier is correct..."

The Mayor's eyebrows rose prominently. His ears pricked up.

Walking on, Mark savoured the other man's anticipation.

"Apart from this inspection, I asked you to accompany me today because I have some good news, Edward. A messenger to Butler Castle informed the Governor this morning that Cromwell has called a halt to hostilities...he's retiring into winter quarters for at least a month, maybe longer. The war it seems hasn't been going entirely his way. Remember that alarming report about Waterford last week? The City was on the brink of capitulation. Last thing I'd heard was that surrender was imminent.

"But Cromwell has been forced to back off. The Waterford Governor used prolonged surrender talks to buy valuable time. While Cromwell's parley officers were listening to a lot of prevaricating twaddle from the Waterford lads, Ormonde managed to reinforce the garrison with another fifteen hundred soldiers. Cromwell, furious I imagine; withdrew his forces encircling Waterford to Dungarvan, and his whole regicide army into hibernation. Apart from that setback I hear that his army has been weakened by disease and lack of food provisions. It may be that Colonel Hunger and Major Sickness could upset his plans for us!"

The Mayor gasped. "Thank God. Could this be a sign? Maybe the prayers of the people will turn the tide, as Fr. Brannigan has been telling mass-goers for the past month."

Mark regarded him awkwardly. "No disrespect to the good priest, but I suspect Cromwell won't have taken that trick played on him by Waterford nicely. The same tactic won't work in Callan, if he comes here. He'll use the winter respite to build up his forces.

"We have to make it clear from the start that Callan won't be yielding. And I'll be pressing the Governor to ask the Supreme Commander to come to Callan's aid, if necessary in the same way that he bolstered the Waterford defences."

The Mayor's little bout of euphoria abated, but still he beamed, raising his tricorn hat to a group of workers laying stakes as he pondered the news.

Mark continued: "That lull in hostilities gives our side an opportunity to recover from the setbacks we've suffered, and here in Callan more time to prepare. We have to assume Cromwell will head for Kilkenny when he kicks off again in the late winter or early spring. And he'll expect to plough through here as if the town were a chunk of melting butter. Hopefully we can dent his optimism."

The Mayor's expression switched to gloominess as they passed by another work team. Further in from the wall these men were building what looked like a second wall running parallel to it. The Mayor queried this.

Mark acknowledged waves from the workers. Morale ran high amongst them, a welcome sign.

"It's a tactic I saw put to good effect in Austria. I want a thirty foot wall of mud and brick erected behind as much of the Town Wall as we can manage in the time left to us. It mightn't seem as sturdy as solid stone but in some respects in can be more effective. You see, a single cannon ball is absorbed by such a messy clogging surface in ways that doesn't happen with stone, lessening the ball's impact and causing it to fall to the ground."

"Impressive, and with a few weeks to construct this defensive barrier we'll hopefully have completed it before an attack..."

"Yes, of course a sustained bombardment would still punch a hole in any wall or barrier; whatever its composition, but a mud and brick construction is easier to repair too, even under fire, than a stone wall."

As they approached the South Gate, Mark shouted at a gang of boys who were sitting on the wall on either side of the guarded entrance to get down. They responded instantly, disappearing over the top.

The Mayor hadn't said anything for a minute. He looked immersed in thought. Now he spoke, "Captain, do you think we have a chance...really...at beating off an attack? An honest opinion please! The Governor is still reputed to be mulling the idea of not fighting, unless this news of the enemy taking a winter break has changed his mind, which I doubt. The majority in the Corporation favouring resistance is smaller than it was three months ago. It may yet be overturned. If the Corporation as much as hints at surrender, Sir Robert will have the white flag flying before Cromwell even gets here..."

"The honest answer, sir, is that I don't know what the outcome will be. On the continent, I would have given you the same answer in almost every tight spot I've been in. What I can say is that I'm

175

more confident today, seeing the progress on the defences, than I was when I arrived in Callan..."

"And the river? That takes up our defensive curtain from where the wall stops. You think the traps and barriers will be effective?"

"Work started on it weeks ago but stalled. I deliberately delayed re-commencement because the river is such a vital resource for the people. I've seen the stalls weighed down with fish on market days, and all that bathing and swimming at weekends. Fishing will be restricted if not halted along whole stretches of the river once we spike it. I don't want to see locals impaled on stakes."

"What about the town armoury? The Governor is adamant that it shouldn't be thrown open until the last possible minute....he fears the result of so many weapons being distributed randomly. The notion of what he calls an armed rabble roaming the streets bothers him. He opined that he himself might become a victim of newly armed citizens running amok...."

"He has a point. But there's a case to be made for releasing the weapons sooner. Firstly, many of the muskets and pistols in there might not be in working order, or might need repairs, oiling, or whatever. Swords may need sharpening. Secondly, handing out weapons freely to people who have no training in using them won't help the town's defence.

"I'll see the Governor and urge him to open the armoury this week, but with our soldiers present to supervise the procedure, and with the proviso that anyone who accepts a weapon must agree to a training session. I'll ask Corporal Molloy to instruct them. It won't turn them into first-class soldiers but it's better than setting them up as easy prey for the Roundheads..."

They passed through the South Gate and continued their walk, marvelling at the energy and diligence of the men who toiled as if their lives depended on it, which they well might.

Would their efforts save them, and the town, Mark wondered, or just delay its destruction by a few hours, days, or weeks?

Either way, those who dwell within its walls will have done their duty before God and Ireland. That's as much as any of us can do...

***

17

Tom Brennan was serving his usual Tuesday night customers when the alehouse door swung open to reveal two self-assured forms, one tall and the other of below average height. They didn't look like drinkers, not with their formal, overtly disciplined deportments.

The low-sized man stepped in front of the other. Tom had seen him at some point in the previous month, riding past on the street with other soldiers or officers. Probably based at Butler Castle. He hadn't ever called for a drink and Tom suspected that it wasn't for a tipple he'd dropped in tonight.

A sudden dread seized him. He'd heard that the authorities were clamping down on alehouses whose licenses had expired. He'd forgotten to check his own. Several Callan taverns had been fined.

Then he spotted the second man. Master Counihan! He'd only ever once visited his establishment, and that was maybe five years ago.

Had he reported him? And now the straight-laced old fellow was guiding the military folk to him. *What a treacherous...*

"Hello gentlemen, and what can I do for you?"

The officer was elegantly uniformed, with his long dark green coat, lighter green jacket and shining brown rawhide boots that reached up to his thighs. Removing his tricorn hat with its peacock feather he introduced himself as Sergeant Philly Lynch of the Callan military garrison.

His completely bald head displayed a garish birthmark that resembled, aptly enough, a rough map of Ireland.

"And this, as I'm sure you know, Mr Brennan, is the town's great repository of knowledge, Master Counihan."

The Master removed his broad-brimmed hat and bowed. His headgear lacked plumage but had a silver harp broach proudly attached to the hatband. He made the Sergeant look diminutive, towering over him while trying, Tom thought, to make himself smaller to avoid upstaging the officer.

The Sergeant adjusted his hat and raised his voice, sounding more officious. "We'd like to have a word with the patrons, Mr. Brennan, if that's alright with you? It's about the civilian defence force we're putting together to assist the garrison if and when Mr

Cromwell is foolish enough to mount an attack on Callan. You've probably heard the appeal that went out at the Sunday masses or seen the parish news sheet?"

"Ah yes...I did...and I think it's a great idea. I know a lot of the lads that come in here would be more than willing to...help out if they could. Do you want to speak to them yourself...or will I ask them for you?"

Looking around him at the twenty or so men hunched over their drinks at the tables, and standing along the walls, the Sergeant nodded: "I'll l have a quick word...if you might get their attention for..."

Tom banged on the counter with an empty tankard. ""Quiet, lads...for a minute...listen up everyone...this man has an important message for you!"

"Thank you." The Sergeant cleared his throat, his hands clasped firmly behind his back. "Gentlemen, I am Sergeant Lynch and I'm here to invite you to join the newly formed Callan Defence Militia, the purpose of which will be to act in a supporting role to the troops assigned by our Supreme Commander, the Marquis of Ormond, to protect this town from the Regicide army.

"As you know, the enemy has retired into winter quarters, as have our forces in the parts of Ireland where we hold the line against the invader. But here in Callan we hope to avail of the respite in hostilities to better prepare the town for what may come.

"Already, repairs to the Town Wall have enhanced its defensive potential and palisades have been added to further thwart the enemy."

He paused, scrutinising the drinkers closely as if seeking to resolve if they understood him. Some sat listening respectfully, some with tired or indifferent looks, and others rudely chatted as if the Sergeant weren't there at all.

He continued: "As I said, we in the garrison would appreciate any help you gentlemen could offer. It's your town, after all, and I'm sure you care about its future. So...if any man present wishes to join the militia, and fight for his town, his family, and his country, kindly give your name to Master Counihan here. The town armoury will be opened tomorrow and weapons training will commence on Friday at noon on the Motte field..."

The Master stepped forward, a long sheet of parchment in one hand and a quill in the other. He had just placed a pot of ink on the bar counter behind him, which Tom had gently pushed away from a mug of ale he'd just filled for a customer.

The mention of weapons seemed to strike a chord. Several hands went up. Others rose from their tables and the Master was soon busily recording names and addresses. Tom was taken aback by the reaction. He counted eighteen of the twenty-three customers joining up, and the five opting not to volunteer were decidedly unfit. One had a wooden leg, another was deaf, and the remaining three were crippled with an illness of the joints that restricted movement, apart from being obviously too old to fight.

The names all recorded, the Sergeant thanked the customers, and shook Tom's hand. The Master also bowed with gratitude. Tom beamed, relieved that the whole episode had gone so smoothly. "Will ye have something to drink while ye're here? It's on the house."

Both accepted the offer and Tom handed them a whiskey each. At the tables the drinkers seemed uplifted by the commitment they'd given. He wondered about the sincerity of two men who he knew to be inebriated to an inordinate degree. Would they regret their decisions later?

As the Sergeant and the Master sipped away at the counter, Tom felt something stirring within him, a peculiar unease, mixed with an inexplicable feeling that he was missing out on a big adventure, a unique once-in-a-lifetime opportunity that the others had grasped without hesitation.

His heart thumping, he quickly poured himself a whiskey. He felt the reassuring sting of it at the back of his throat as he downed the fiery amber liquid in one go.

He didn't normally drink while serving but these weren't normal times. He felt a little light-headed; squeezing the pewter mug in his hand so tightly he thought it might crack.

While he was still sizing up the pros and cons, calculating whether it would be wise to make such a gargantuan life- changing move, or the height of lunacy; his lips had formed the words and his mouth had uttered them: "Sergeant...Master Counihan. Add my name to that list. It's the least I can do. The town has served me

179

well. I can't pretend this doesn't concern me. That's Tom Brennan, *The Fiery Spirit*, Upper South Street, Callan..."

*

Shane's heart raced as he accompanied Luke into the bowels of the big forge. He'd been here before but not in the attached ramshackle shed where, today, Luke had told him, he'd show him something more exciting than normal smithy work. Luke had gushed with zeal when he told him of the new job his father had, with the war getting closer.

Soldiers had come to the forge to make ammunition for muskets. Edging in the creaky tin door, which smelt of rust and damp moss, Luke entered the shed. Following him Shane felt a blast of heat that almost knocked him to the ground. But instead of the hammers and anvils he'd expected, he saw six men at work, leaning over three different tables.

Luke explained. "I was here yesterday... see that man...with the ladle? The stuff he's pouring is molten lead. The square block he's pouring it into is called a mould, and each groove in it has a circular shape..."

Shane watched wonderstruck. The bearded man with his long canvass apron was slowly pouring the red hot smoky liquid into one groove after another. When he had all of them filled, another man stepped in beside him wearing heavy gloves and took the block out of his way, replacing it with another one.

He saw other men also filling moulds; and one chap was making adjustments of some kind to lead that Shane presumed had cooled, because otherwise he wouldn't be able to touch it. Luke cautioned Shane not to get too near any of the men pouring lead.

"Each groove will yield a musket ball for the army. That's what they told me. That man over there is chipping off any rough bits from bullets to make sure they're perfectly round. They have to be just right to be used in a musket."

Luke ushered Shane to a corner where stood a growing pile of blocks, all containing cooled lead balls.

"Father says all these will be delivered to soldiers in Butler Castle tomorrow. And they'll want hundreds or even thousands more by the end of the week. Must be a lot of enemy soldiers heading for Callan!"

"Lads, out of here, you could get badly burned. On with ye now. Play outside!"

The gruff bellow from a man holding a ladle dripping with fiery lead sent the two of them scurrying. Standing outside the forge, Shane quipped "Wonder what it's like to be shot with one of those. Would you be dead fast, or later, do you think?"

Luke stared at him. "Depends where it hits you. If you get it between the eyes or through the heart I think you'd be safely dead. But if it doesn't kill you...well, I suppose you'd recover. Father says it's better if you didn't die straight away, because then you wouldn't get a chance to say an act of contrition and you might go to hell, with your sins unforgiven. He says he'd want that few minutes to make his peace with God. Wouldn't care to be shot though. It must hurt a lot."

The clip-clop of hooves on the pebbly lane leading up to the forge distracted Shane. Approaching them was an irritable unshaved man in a long shabby coat and mud-caked boots who was pulling a horse along behind him, spitting and grumbling to himself. The horse seemed reluctant to follow but it didn't have a choice. It had a halter attached to a thick rope that the man had curled around his arm.

Whenever his horse slowed or hesitated, he gave the rope an abrupt yank and the animal tossed its head, neighing, its eyes rolling about. What a lovely horse, Shane thought. He'd seen many horses in Callan, towing wagons and coaches or being ridden by people who could afford them, mostly merchants and wealthy farmers.

But this one stood out owing to its shining chestnut brown coat and a dash of white over its forehead like spilt milk; but also because it looked half-starved, with bones threatening to break through its skin, and specks of foam dripping from its mouth. The man called out to the blacksmith. Luke stepped back inside the forge to call his father. While he was inside Shane moved tentatively towards the horse, then regarded its owner. "Can I talk to her, Mister?"

"Talk to her? Talk to the bloody horse? Oh well, if you want to. Huh! She might need a good talking to where she's going."

Shane felt a stab of pity for the animal. "You mean she's going to be slaughtered?"

The man shook his head, "No, but you mightn't be far off. " He laughed, but without a smile. His eyes had no jollity in them. "She's joining the cavalry, that feisty young mare is, boy. She'll be earning her keep, let me let you. And she might wish I did send her to the knackery by the time she's finished fighting for Ireland."

Shane moved closer to the mare. He whispered: "You'll be alright..." He patted her on the head and neck and ruffled her mane, then tickled one of her ears. The foam on her mouth repelled him a little, and he noticed a dried bloodstain behind an ear but said nothing. Something told him this man wouldn't take kindly...

The man scoffed. "You like horses?"

"Haven't thought about it, but she's a grand animal, Mister..."

Before he could respond the blacksmith was standing there. "You want her shoed, Patsy?"

"Yeah, the military want horses and they can have this one if the price is right. I need her done inside half an hour."

"I'll do that Patsy, but if you don't mind me saying so, she could do with something to eat by the looks of her. Luke...Get some oats and a bucket of water."

Patsy didn't argue.

Shane wondered what kind of man he was...not bothering to feed his horse. When Luke returned with the oats and water, he and Shane scampered off down the lane and back into town. Thoughts of a stunningly beautiful but undernourished horse competed in Shane's mind with images of molten metal and newly moulded bullets.

*

Captain Mark Gegan was impressed with the choice of the Motte Field as a training venue. Though outside the Town Wall, the vast stretch occupied what locals deemed to be the "ancient heart" of Callan. The name derived from the huge Motte and Bailey castle that the Norman conquerors had built in the field in the 1200s.

The mighty Motte remained as a treasured landmark. Even if the fifty-foot high flat-topped mound was stripped of its medieval glory. A canopy of Scotch Pines and beeches around the summit enhanced its visual appeal in all seasons. Not that Mark had the time or inclination to admire the scenery.

What he most liked about the Motte was its effect of partially dividing the field containing it into two swathes, which suited him today as the volunteers had been split up into several groups, each of which would be instructed by a different soldier or someone with a reasonable knowledge of firearms. It might be useful to keep the groups separate to avoid unnecessary confusion and distractions.

To his left as he entered the field from Lower North Street he noted lines of fishermen on the bank of the King's River, which marked the field's southern boundary. They'd have to find another occupation soon. Already, large swathes of the river had been spiked.

When he'd viewed the field from the bridge in North Street a week earlier it had looked calm, almost serene; an eye-catching picture that would inspire a poet.

Today its frosty green surface was discoloured by the greys, blacks and browns of male apparel. Men aged between eighteen and seventy stood, sat, strutted about, or were sprinting. Shrill commands pierced the chill winter air from trainers who sought to turn these befuddled bands of non-combatants into fighting men.

Surveying a bedraggled cluster of trainee shooters, and their exasperated tutor, he doubted he'd ever be in a position to call them musketeers. But then, they'd only arrived on the field two hours earlier, and most of them had never held a gun of any sort before today. An obvious drawback in training them in basic marksmanship, and there wasn't much time for them to learn.

The need not to waste precious ammunition constrained him to withhold bullets from them until he was satisfied they could handle the weapons.

The lads posed and postured, some guffawing as they fumbled with the muskets. They'd been asked to put away their clay pipes while training, but they casually resumed puffing after a minute or two of brooding abstinence.

This was all new to them. Hence the anomaly that the only smoke arising from this first training session with muskets on the Motte Field issued from their pipes.

Mark had hoped the muskets in the armoury would all be of the same type. Consistency would have made tutoring easier. But, as he'd suspected, they were a disparate collection. More than half of the seventy men he despaired of coaching to bear arms struggled with ancient imported Dutch muskets, heavy contraptions that required ground rests because only strong men could hold or carry them.

The remainder were more modern, lighter, and didn't require rests; and all but three of the armoury muskets were matchlocks.

The matchlock, even in the hands of a highly skilled musketeer, could take several minutes to load. And each musketeer needed to have a length of matchcord ready to apply to the powder in the weapon's priming pan to ignite the powder that he'd shoved down into the barrel, thus propelling the ball. No wonder Marianne scoffed at the concept, preferring her crossbow, though an arrow wouldn't penetrate light armour or buff-coats.

Thinking of Marianne, he wondered where she was. He hadn't seen her since she rose early that morning. Probably taking walks around the town and district with her friend.

He passed more volunteers puzzling over muskets that they held in a variety of oddball and dangerous ways. One man, squatting in the grass, sat staring into the barrel of his weapon as if intent on self-harm. Just as well he hadn't given out ammunition today. He wondered how many shots any of these fellows would get off before being shot themselves or run through with a pike or sword.

But he wouldn't as much as hint at the dangers. He wanted these men to participate, to whatever extent possible, in the defence, not plant doubts in their heads, however well-founded they might be.

He approached a man he thought a bit too old to be a fighter. His blackthorn walking stick resting on the grass beside him, and he was aiming a heavy musket, wobbling on its metallic rest, at the Motte hill, with one eye closed. A dozen lads had gathered around him, sitting in the grass, all puffing furiously on their pipes.

After a few tense seconds, he mimed a loud bang, spitting as he did so, to the smokers' amusement. Mark complimented him on striking his imaginary target.

"You have the right idea, but look...and listen here, you men...you hold this particular weapon to the right breast, not to the shoulder...and keep your legs apart. Yes...like that..."

One of the sitters spat a mouthful of chewed tobacco and asked: "Can we not use bullets, Captain. How do we know how good we are, if not?"

"In the later stages maybe...we can't afford to squander ammunition...we need everything we have to throw at those Roundheads if they come..."

He walked past a man who swore as the matchcord he was attempting to light wouldn't catch fire, a breeze blowing it out. "Cup your hand around it" Mark advised.

In another part of the field men strutted about with pikes, charging at each other in a way that Mark would have found hilarious if this were a comedy sketch and not part of a supposed rehearsal for the defence of Callan.

He got them to form up properly and soon had them following, albeit in slightly shambolic fashion, his instructions on how to use a pike in battle. None of these had the appropriate clothing- just their normal working clothes. Some wore little more than soiled rags, but they'd have to manage without the fancy trimmings. The time-honoured dress code of war would have to take a back seat in Callan.

Along the riverbank to his left men lay on the ground, aiming pistols at oncoming phantasms, or possibly at the fish. Further in from the river, Idiotic sword fights drew howls of derision from onlookers, to which the amateur fenc ers responded by daring them to do better.

Oh God, please let them learn...if old Cromwell could see this he'd die laughing.

It wasn't all amateurish though. He saw Corporal Molloy further down the field, emerging from behind the old Norman mound, leading about thirty men who marched three abreast, holding sticks for muskets.

Drilling them. Good. No harm instilling a little discipline in this sorry excuse for a militia-in-the-making. In his foreign exploits he'd found that rampant ill-discipline doomed any fighting force. Discipline could prove as crucial as weapons training.

Leaving the disparate scattering of trainees and hangers-on he went to meet the Corporal, who had spotted him and was calling out: "Captain, a word with you!" Molloy signalled the civilian troops to take a break, and they instantly broke up into pipe-

185

smoking and brandy drinking groups. Some ran about erratically, others exercised or tumbled in the grass. Regular soldiers wouldn't be allowed to behave thus, Mark reflected, but these fellows weren't obliged to follow orders.

The Corporal waited until he was out of earshot of his trainees before whispering to Mark: "I'm sorry to bother you with this, sir....but, well... It's your wife..."

"What? Marianne. What about her?"

Pointing to the Norman Mound, he rasped: "She's on the other side of the hill there...and I think she's going a bit hard on the lads. I mean...I've been putting fellows through their paces too, but I don't push them too far, sir. They're volunteers after all!"

Mark stepped back from him, aghast. "Are you saying that Marianne is attempting to...give instruction in the use of weapons? My God, come along. She's gone too far this time. It's one thing to want to join me here in Callan at my post, but...Jesus!"

They quickstepped around to the other side of the mound, and Mark's heart missed a beat at what he saw: Thirty or more men, of varying ages, all armed with muskets, pistols, or swords...standing to attention, and there was his wife shouting at them, scarcely recognisable in a quasi-military outfit of leather coat, riding boots and a tricorn hat that shadowed her eyes...and, *my God...is that a horse whip?*

Her back turned to him she didn't see him approach.

Drawing nearer he heard words of encouragement mingled with dire threats from his wife as she addressed the volunteers lined up before her.

The Corporal pulled at his sleeve. "They think she's a man, you see, Captain. I didn't know her myself until she told me. She reckons they wouldn't pay her any heed if they knew..."

Mark had stopped listening. He swished through the grass and tapped her on the shoulder, causing her to stop in mid- sentence. She relaxed her grip on the horsewhip, now taking it in both hands and holding it like a floppy rhubarb stalk.

"Marianne", he whispered, "What in the name of Jesus, Mary and St. Joseph are you doing here?"

Raising her tricorn a fraction she whispered back: "Oh Mark, darling...I'm just preparing these fine men for the big showdown. You wouldn't want them to face old Cromwell with just a faint notion about how to fire a musket or wield a sword, now would you? Yes, I know...I've had to disguise myself a little...but that's a pretty minor offence, is it not, dearest, considering what we're up against?"

Mark glanced at the formation of volunteers and scowled, then forced a thin smile. He rasped through his teeth: "I'll speak to you later..." wincing to see the trainees staring at him, some nosily trying to make out what he was saying.

"Carry on!" he said aloud, turning around to leave Marianne to her militaristic capers.

The Corporal nudged him as they walked away, the voice of his warrior wife ringing in his ears. She was shouting something about practice making perfect when it came to loading a matchlock. Reasonable advice, if only it came from a real soldier.

The Corporal's expression had changed. Now he looked cheery. "I know it's highly irregular sir, but you have to admit she's got their attention, even if she had them all running and jumping and doing tortuous press-ups earlier, and cracking that whip of hers!"

Now the silly man was smirking. Mark would be having a word with him too. But not today. This rabble would have to be whipped into some kind of fighting-fit shape to have the slightest bearing on the outcome of any battle.

And now Marianne is meddling...

*

Tom Brennan held his musket with one hand while using the other to pour imaginary powder from a slightly misshaped ox-horn down the barrel. He then pushed wadding after it with the rod.

"Right" said the Sergeant, "now you add a smaller powder charge to the priming pan..." He pointed to the relevant part of the weapon, motioning the group of ten men to gather closer to observe the preparation of a musket for firing.

For about the twentieth time that day, the Sergeant demonstrated how to bring a burning length of matchcord into contact with the priming pan. If the trigger of the musket didn't work, you just pushed the burning cord in manually and it ignited the charge, causing the weapon in turn to fire. Each demonstration elicited a spate of questions from baffled men who'd never discharged a gun. Tom was one of them, but he felt he was getting the hang of it.

On the final day of training, a few weeks hence, they might be allowed to fire real bullets, subject to availability. The Sergeant thanked the men and declared a fifteen-minute break. Tom fetched his satchel and removed the wrapped-up pieces of cold beef and the flagon of whiskey he'd brought. Knowing he'd be expected to have alcohol with him he'd taken a large bottle. He offered the bottle to the other men sitting in the grass. Some gratefully accepted, and he filled their pewter mugs.

"That's great stuff Tom, thanks!" It was Peter the Atheist. Tom hadn't noticed him until now. He had that same perpetual look of surprise.

"Peter, why are you here? You've only been in Callan a few months, why would you want to fight our battles?"

Peter sat hunched, elbows on his knees and hands under his chin. He was looking blankly at the Norman Mound, with its skeletal Scotch Pines standing like grim sentinels, scraping at the sky.

His voice was soothing but also, Tom thought, a tad cranky. "It's not just your battle Tom. Or Ireland's for that matter. The people who drove me into exile are coming here to make slaves out of you: In this town, yes, but elsewhere too. They'll be on the lookout for me, and others who defied their precious New Order. Your fight is very much mine.

"Do you not yearn, Tom, for a world where true liberty is granted to all people, not just to certain categories? And, though I don't subscribe to any religious belief, I do believe in freedom of conscience, freedom to worship any God, pursue any dream or fantasy or delusion so long as it doesn't entail killing people who don't agree with you..."

"Hold on there now Peter, that's a real mouthful. Beating Cromwell is one thing, but you can't go around saying that one religion is as good as another. We're almost a hundred percent Catholic in Callan, and anyone saying our church isn't the one the good Lord himself created...is asking for trouble..."

Heads nodded, some men peering suspiciously at Peter, who seemed unaware of their presence.

"No Tom, I think one religion is as BAD as another, as I've said to you before. But I'd give them a license to say and pray and preach any old nonsense that takes their fancy, short of drawing blood from critics...that's the part I object to. Of course we all have the right to defend ourselves from enemies who take it upon themselves to attack us...to steal our land, or enslave us. Whether it's a thief in the night, an assailant who strikes you for no reason; or a tyrant like Cromwell..."

Unsympathetic looks gave way to relaxed deportments and nonchalant shrugs.

Tom took a slug from his mug. "I have to say, we got a good laugh in the alehouse, especially McDonagh, when you told us about how some crazy group in England wanted to grant equal rights to women, put them on a par with men..."

A man tittered, followed by a rising chortle of derision from the others.

Peter smiled weakly, his typical perplexity giving way to embarrassment. "Yes, I know that's a movement that didn't stand a chance. It lasted less tha a month. It disbanded when its leaders were arrested. Some of them got off with a flogging or ear-clipping; others went missing and a co-founder was spotted floating in the Thames. He had a placard attached to him that nobody could read because the water had washed off the message. A warning, presumably..."

Tom shook his head."But they must have been mad, I mean...no country anywhere would allow women to behave like men..."

Peter lowered his voice, and plucked a blade of grass. He examined it as if it held the answer to a riddle. "They mistook the public mood, with so many groups calling for change, an end to the tyranny of kingship; calling for liberties of all sorts. They judged the time had come to give women a political voice...to let them be heard and respected. Naive I know, but other groups too sprang up that got a bit carried away in the euphoria that attended the King's downfall..."

Peter sounded less passionate on this topic but still forceful enough to provoke. A man who'd not shown any interest in the conversation suddenly jumped to his feet, his mug spilling into the grass. "By Jesus, if my Geraldine game me any guff I'd smack her in the gob. Tis no wonder you were turfed out of England; saying them things. The world is bad enough as it is. Political voice me arse!"

"Everything alright, gentlemen?"

It was the other training instructor, the one who'd been drilling the lads behind the mound. A strange little man, with his oversized clothes: Almost comical. And that scar...*he's likely a smallpox survivor.*

Tom laughed. "Oh it is, sir. We were just talking about a strange group beyond in England that wanted women to have the same rights as men...Peter here met some of them before he skedaddled from Cromwell' s bloodhounds."

The trainer said nothing, just turned away and headed at a brisk pace towards the Motte Field entrance, tapping a horsewhip against his right leg. Though a tricorn hat partly concealed his eyes, Tom spied what he took to be a tear rolling down the man's cheek.

An optical illusion, he supposed, as military folk didn't cry.

*

Marianne felt relieved, but deflated too. She'd steeled herself for a ferocious telling-off from Mark after that episode on the Motte field. He'd caught her red-handed posing as a male officer and putting men though their paces.

Though she knew he disapproved of her militaristic tendencies, she feared she'd gone too far this time. She awaited his return to their living quarters at the castle, having prepared a special meal in a half-hearted bid to sweeten him up a bit, or at least dilute his inevitable anger.

But then, just as she braced herself for a blistering row that neighbours might hear even through the thick castle walls, he pushed in the big wooden door and kissed her sensuously on the forehead. Removing his tricorn he slumped into his chair by the turf fire. She'd stoked it into a steady blaze, mindful of the winter chill. She'd seen patches of frost on the stony stairway that morning, glistening in the shadows.

She waited for the expected storm to break, careful not to provoke him in the slightest. "I've got a nice plate of pigs' cheeks and onions, dear. And fresh buttermilk delivered here this morning...."

"Thank you Marianne." He sounded curt and tense. *Here it comes...*

"About that caper today, Marianne: The lads are none the wiser. They were properly fooled by your crazy outfit and believe you were just another trainer struggling to teach them how to shoot and run about and use a sword..."

"Oh, so then..."

"So then, thank God, I'm in the clear and will be spared an embarrassment and an indignity that would have surpassed the pain of any wound I've ever received on a field of battle. Imagine: a Captain's wife goes off when he's not looking and pretends to be an officer...a man...and gets away with it. I'd be the laughing stock of the entire Confederate/Royalist Alliance. But since nobody knows, apart from Corporal Molloy and you and me..."

"Mark, I'm sorry if you felt offended...you know my views on women not being able to play their part in this great patriotic war of ours. I won't pose as a man again...but I'll do anything I can, within the unfair strictures imposed on me, to help defend this town. I've seen the women in action. They can throw stones better than most men I've seen do it. If only they could get their hands on more lethal weapons."

"No, Marianne!" he leapt to his feet, but not in anger... more in shock, she thought. "Oh please, don't give them any ideas about using muskets or pistols. Even stones...well, let them throw stones. Actually, there may be another way the women might help, if they insist on meddling in men's affairs..."

"And how would that be?" Marianne was aghast. Was he coming around to her thinking?

He had poured himself a large mug of ale and was relaxing by the fire. Little sparks flew at his boots. He stubbed them out. "In a siege of a town in Austria I was surprised when, at a crucial phase of the battle when it could have gone either way, dozens of women hurled pots of scalding water and burning pitch from the battlements of two castles and over the town walls. It mightn't have been the decisive factor in repelling the enemy assault, but it did slow them down and gave the men time to re-load their muskets and cannon..."

Emboldened by his temperance, Marianne couldn't help herself. Her arms folded, she reminisced: "I didn't just decide on the spur of the moment to don that military costume, Mark. As I told you many times, I saw my father drilling soldiers when I was seven years old. For several weeks running he brought me along to watch him in action...shouting orders, inspecting weapons to ensure they were properly looked after, showing men how to prime and load muskets, offering advice on sword-fighting techniques, battlefield tactics of every sort. I saw them practising, blowing dummy soldiers to smithereens on the target range. I wanted desperately to get my hands on a gun to produce the same effect...

"I don't recall the minute details...I was only a child for Heaven's sake, but I think I got the gist of the thing. I really believe I have a flair for this military business, Mark, whatever you say. And how did the women's intervention in that Austrian town play out? Did the men accuse them of getting in their way...were they maybe a little jealous that the weaker sex proved they weren't so weak after all?"

"No...No, Marianne. We won that day, and those women did their bit...and yes...every act of resistance, if carried out efficiently, can contribute to overcoming a foe. But that doesn't mean the same tactics will work in Callan. In that Austrian town, there was a gargantuan effort by every citizen and the garrison, a Town Governor who fought with his men, and a fierce resolve not to let the walls be breached. In Callan, we don't know what exactly we'll be up against...yet...or what the Governor will decide. The uncertainty doesn't help. Anyway, where are those pigs' cheeks and onions...I'm famished."

That went rather well, she thought, heading for the table. Mark was stifling a yawn and refilling his mug. Now her mind wandered to an earlier development: Cathy had got herself a cleaning and barmaid job at a local tavern. She'd also be sleeping on the premises.

Marianne would miss her, not only because she was so diligent with her duster and mop in the castle, but she needed Cathy to confide in. Lately they'd been discussing issues that she wouldn't dream of broaching with Mark.

Never mind. Cathy would probably call around on her time-off or they could meet at one of the local coffee or cookhouses.

***

192

18

Shane recited back to Mother the list of items she wanted from the apothecary: Something for head- pains, an ear scoop and toothpick to replace the ones she'd lost while gathering firewood in the fields, and a cure for constipation if the shop had such a medicine. Shane's recitation pleased her. "Off you go, and I'll have a nice griddle cake baked when you get back."

Opening the door Shane felt the street vibrate under him and heard the pounding of feet on the cobblestones. He pressed against the wall to let the soldiers pass. Hundreds of them, it seemed, all marching in perfect rhythm, kicking up dust that made Shane want to sneeze. *Better not, might give offence.* They all shouldered muskets, looking straight ahead as they tramped past him down South Street.

Other householders had opened their front doors, some to wave at these brave men who would, Shane presumed, be fighting to save Callan. When the last of them had turned into East Street, neighbours started to re-enter their homes, but one shouted: "Wait, the cavalry are coming next...."

Not wishing to be delayed further, Shane sprinted in the wake of the soldiers, dust clouds making him cough as he headed to the Upper North Street apothecary.

Bracing himself he pushed open the door of the premises, causing a little bell to jingle. He hated this place. The smell of assorted cures and medicines made him queasy, and one day he vomited after a visit. The shop was busy today, with men and women hunched together examining displays or waiting to be served.

The shelves abounded with glass jars and bottles, crammed with revolting concoctions and gory slivers of animal or bird carcasses. Some of these containers didn't have lids and it was from these, Shane knew, that the stink emanated. Not one bad smell, but several, each competing with the other to get up your nose and make you feel awful.

Shane prayed the other customers would hurry so he could be served and get out. Minutes passed, and the shop mercifully emptied, leaving him free to approach the counter, where Dr. Murray had a big grin ready for him.

"Well, young Dennehy, what can I do for you? Do you need any leeches to draw blood, by any chance? I have some fresh ones, delivered this morning…"

"No thanks Dr. Murray, I need an ear scoop, a toothpick, and something for head pains and bowel movements. They're for my mother, not me…"

The doctor rubbed his hands together. "I have a cure for every conceivable aliment. Now let me see…" He stepped from behind the counter, across which was stretched a disemboweled wolf and two dissected dogs, and ascended a little ladder.

Shane winced at the sight of jars listed as containing swallows' brains, fresh live worms, fox's lung, and discarded nail clippings. Thankfully the doctor didn't pick any of those. He reached for a small phial labeled "buckthorn syrup" and another of "herb winter green."

Returning to the counter, he placed the two cures side by side. "The syrup will clear the bowels, young man, and the winter green should banish pain from your good mother's head. She'll need to pray too. That increases the efficacy…"

Bending he retrieved from under the counter a toothpick that he tested on his mouth before adding it to the items.

"Afraid I have only one ear scoop left…slightly used…there's been a run on them lately. Must be a lot of wax getting into people's ears in Callan, though I think half of them imagine it…"

The ear scoop worried Shane. It looked far more expensive than the old wooden one his mother had used for years and that his grandparents had used before her. To his eyes, the shining copper implement resembled a piece of priceless jewelry.

The doctor seemed to read his mind. "Don't worry, young man, it won't cost the earth. Two pennies to you, I know your mother and she's a great customer. That's five pennies for the lot. No Confederate coinage if you don't mind…"

Relieved, Shane handed him the amount and watched as the doctor dropped the messages into a cloth bag for him. He almost ran from the shop to escape the overpowering stench. Outside the air cleansed his lungs and filled his head with a welcome giddiness.

Approaching the end of North Street he saw a throng assembled around the Cross in the Town Square, spilling into the four streets. He'd be delayed again, but Mother wasn't in that much of a hurry.

He heard loud cheering and hand-clapping. Mingling with the onlookers he beheld the long lines of brightly-dressed men on horses coming down South Street towards the Cross.

The horses trotted along in step with each other, their florally ornamented heads upraised proudly. Shane heard they'd been trained to do that. The riders sported green jackets, long fancy riding boots and tricorn hats with dappled feathers fluttering from them.

Shane hardly recognized the Cross, with long green banners and flags bearing harp symbols wrapped around it from top to bottom. He reckoned that a visitor to town wouldn't know it was made of wood.

The crowd parted to make way for the riders. Shane wished they'd hurry so he could get the cures home to his mother. His heart leapt as the last of the horses began to enter East Street.

That one... with its tail happily swishing as the rider gently spurred her along. It was the emaciated animal he'd seen at the blacksmith's... but healthier now... no bones sticking through: Definitely the same horse. *There's that splash of milk across her head.*

Shane ran towards the horse, cries of "come back here", and "what are you at?" ringing in his ears. He didn't care.

The rider slowed and glanced back at him. Shane ran alongside, patting the animal. "I know this horse", he shouted, "Will she be fighting for Ireland?"

"Oh, she won't be doing any fighting, young lad. That's not her job. That's mine. But this here girl will help us to win, won't you?" He tapped the horse, causing it to shake its head approvingly.

Shane stayed watching until the cavalry had disappeared from view around a corner. He surmised they were heading for the Butler Castle stables at the end of East Street.

He felt the sting of tears, thinking about the chestnut brown beauty that faced danger and maybe death.

Clinging to his bag of cures, he headed home, hoping the war wouldn't come to Callan.

*

Marianne looked forward to meeting Cathy at the cookhouse in East Street. Her friend had started two days earlier in her new job as a barmaid and cleaner at a local tavern. She'd been thrilled to be offered employment but Marianne wondered if she'd find it suitable, given that Cathy had only ever worked in her own home back in Westmeath tending to her invalid brother, apart from a brief stint on the Gegan farm: A relatively sheltered existence.

Now she'd face the rough and tumble of dealing with carousing men in search of love, or brooding over their woes; that'd be attracted to her like bees to a honey pot.

East Street was quieter today; with the traders, peddlers and fish-mongers absent.... just the usual steady flow of riders, coaches, and wagons, and the chattering townsfolk. Smoke hung in cloudlets above them. Some of it issued from clay pipes, with houses adding to the fumes. Some homes didn't even have holes in their roofs, never mind chimneys, and a few front doors in East Street had been opened to release thick billowing smoke into the atmosphere. Thank God the castle had a proper chimney.

She caught the fragrant aromas from *Andy's Fancy Cookhouse* before she'd gotten within fifty yards of it, but...*what's this?*

She saw the platform sandwiched between the cookhouse and an apothecary with a long wooden sign overhead: "Callan Stocks and Pillories." The platform exhibited, side by side, four sets of stocks and three pillories.

Three shabbily dressed undernourished young men occupied the stocks. They lay back in relaxed postures, seemingly unworried, their half-shredded boots protruding from the iron foot-restraints. They were engaged in casual low-toned conversation. Passers-by paid them no heed.

Two of the pillories lay idle but Marianne recoiled at the sight of the woman whose head and hands were displayed in the third. Her face was almost completely covered in smudged fruit and ordure, her hair was tossed and standing on end, one eye had an ugly bluish-black bruise, and her lips trembled. She looked ready to collapse.

Marianne had seen similar punishments in Mullingar and had learned it was often better not to interfere with the ways of justice. But she felt drawn to the woman's pitiable state.

"Hello, are you here long?" she asked weakly, the stench of punishment almost overpowering her. The woman's head moved, her eyes rising to meet Marianne's.

She spoke haltingly, managing a faint smile: "I'm alright. Another short while and I'll be off...can't be much more than a quarter of an hour, I'd say..."

The men in the stocks had suddenly turned their attention to Marianne. Open-mouthed they stared; then one of them jeered. "She's the new woman in town, the Captain's missus, doesn't know the set-up here."

Ignoring the quip, she asked the woman why she was in the pillory.

She turned her eyes from Marianne's inquiring gaze: "I hit my husband over the head with a poker" she stated tersely.

The three men moaned, as if in sympathy with the stricken husband.

"I see, and would I be right in saying that he provoked you in some way...you were angry?"

"Angry? I was. I lost control. Not like me to do that. I never did that before when he..."

"He irritated you?"

"Yes...irritated me...when he battered me with his fists and kicked me until I bled, and used his belt to whip me. I'm not a great cook, see, and he said I should have told him before we wed. He always used to beat me for my failings but this time...something took hold of me. I might have done him real harm. I expected the worse beating of my life, but he didn't touch me.

"Next day he took me to the Court of Justice and here I am...sentenced to five hours in the pillory. The Judge, Mr Comerford, said he'd go easy on me but if I appeared before him again on the same charge he'd have to impose a more severe punishment, as striking a husband with a poker or any such implement he said is a heinous offence...that undermines the sacrament of marriage..."

Marianne felt her own anger rising. She looked around. No sign of the bailiff or the locksmith. She reached for a handkerchief and gently rubbed away the coating of rotten fruit and faeces. When she cleaned the woman's lips she saw they were parched.

"I'll be back in a minute", she whispered, conscious of the three men in the stocks still eyeing her closely.

Entering the cookhouse, she saw Cathy waiting at a table, nursing a mug. She waved at Cathy but headed straight for the counter and asked for a cup of water, saying it was for somebody outside who was thirsty but that she'd be back to meet her friend momentarily.

The server gave her water and she brought it out to the woman, holding it to her lips. She drank it quickly, spilling some.

Guffaws from the three men: "Nothing for us?" one hollered. Another jeered: "I'll have a mug of ale and a leg of lamb, Madam!" They broke into a fit of laughter.

Leaving the woman, Marianne joined Cathy inside, happy to meet her friend but stung by the thought that Mark might be right: *a man's world.*

Half an hour later when she emerged with Cathy from the Cookhouse, the stocks were empty and the woman had been released from the pillory.

*

Mark shivered as he mounted the steps to his quarters in Skerry's Castle, carrying a small candle to illuminate the dark stairway. The cold of an Irish winter almost banished thoughts of war. The dust and cobwebs had reappeared in the stony passage since Cathy's departure but it heartened him to see sprigs of holly, interspersed with ivy and mistletoe, on the walls, a reminder that Christmas was just days away.

Marianne had thoughtfully fastened the glossy green leaves with their bright red berries along the entire stairway, the first sign of cheeriness he'd felt or seen since moving into this shadowy and somewhat oppressive abode.

It would be livelier but also more congested when the soldiers moved in. The berries traditionally symbolized drops of blood that fell from Christ on the Cross, but nobody let that solemn image detract from the holly's perennial air of optimism.

Pushing in the heavy door, he felt the warmth of the blazing log fire that Marianne had prepared. Wall lamps guttered lazily, casting grey shadows across the room. She was standing at the table; her back turned, laying the platters. That lovely smell of roast beef augured well for a hearty meal.

She turned around, smiling, and went to kiss him. Taking his seat, he commended her on having his meal prepared with such perfect timing, as if she knew the precise moment he'd return.

"Any news from the war front, dearest?" she chirped.

"Nothing… I don't expect to hear anything… until Cromwell decides he's had a long enough winter break."

She added potatoes to the beef on his platter and then some cabbage. Not waiting for him to pour his buttermilk she filled his mug.

"It's too kind you are Marianne", he lisped, reaching for the mug to quench his thirst. The dust on East Street after he'd left Butler Castle had sent him into spasms of coughing and wheezing.

Marianne was quiet today, he thought. She was nibbling at the smaller than usual portion she'd taken.

"And did you meet Cathy as planned. Is she settling into that job…where is it…in The *Sign of the Helmet* in North Street?"

"She's only started, but she thinks it'll be fine."

She said this curtly, without looking at him.

"Everything alright Marianne?" He knew her moods, or supposed he did.

"Can I ask you a question, Mark?"

"Of course, what about?"

"Would you ever beat me?"

He almost choked on a morsel of beef. "What? God, Marianne, what kind of question is that? Why would I beat you?"

"I don't know, maybe because of something I did, or said, or failed to do?"

He chewed and swallowed the beef and left down his fork and knife, a mild worry forming. "Why are you asking me this, Marianne? Has something happened?"

She pushed aside her platter and clasped her hands on the table. "In East Street earlier, when I went to meet Cathy I happened to pass the stocks and pillories. There was a woman in the pillory, covered in slime and shit. She'd struck her husband with a poker."

"A poker? Ah well, she deserved to be pilloried for that. Oh Marianne, don't tell l me you're saying a woman is entitled to beat her husband?"

"She had suffered many beatings from him before she finally hit back…and for that she was punished."

"I see…and how do you know all this. Surely you didn't speak to her?"

Marianne sprang to her feet, pushing her chair to the wall behind her. "And why shouldn't I speak to her? A woman viciously abused because…because she didn't cook as well as her husband felt he had a right to expect."

"You shouldn't interfere in that way Marianne. She was placed in the pillory for a reason. The judge who imposed the sentence had his reasons. It's not for us to speculate on the factors that may have influenced his decision."

"Like, you mean, the fact that she had refused to be beaten, day after day, by the man who pledged in his marriage vows to care for her in sickness and health…that she'd refused to let him become her jailer and deadliest enemy in their own house…"

"Marianne, you know I'd never beat you. I don't believe in beating a woman. To me you are so dear, so precious. The thought of hurting you…of anyone, let alone me, causing you pain, abhors me. But you know how it is. A husband is permitted… within reason…to chastise his wife. Moderate correction is allowed to restrain or control…"

"Like whipping her, kicking her in the ribs as she lay on the kitchen floor, punching her in the face…"

"I didn't say that. Oh God, Marianne, you can't change the facts of domestic life. What matters, surely, is that I don't beat you. We can't trouble ourselves with how other husbands and wives handle their disagreements and misunderstandings…"

She glared at him. "Thank you Mark…I appreciate very much that you've opted not to beat me. I'm so grateful. Just to let you know, and please don't take this the wrong way… If you ever do beat me or even look as if you're thinking about doing it, I won't hit you with a poker. I'll blow your head clean off your manly shoulders. That's if I decide to be merciful and quick. I just might deprive you of your manhood. But that's not going to happen, dearest; because I know you won't beat me…"

It took him a second or two to get over the shock of her directness. He sighed deeply. "There's something I must tell you, Marianne. I know we both promised not to keep secrets from each other, but I made one exception. This is it. A day before our wedding your father took me aside and said: If you hurt a single hair on my daughter's head I'll rip out your gizzards and feed your head to a pack of ravenous wolves."

Marianne looked aghast. She tittered. "Then he'd have saved me the trouble…"

Mark returned to his meal, encouraging Marianne to finish hers. "If your cooking was terrible, which it isn't, or even if you didn't cook anything for me, I wouldn't dream of hurting you, dearest. Men who do that are at fault, I agree, but Marianne…please be careful about who you talk to in this town. You can't change how people behave.

"The world will change in its own good time. Back in ancient Rome women were boiled in oil, or thrown into volcanoes, and more recently women were burned at the stake. We're making progress, but some men will beat their wives, and some won't. Oh…I almost forgot. That's a lovely job you did on the stairway. The holly and the ivy…Joy to the world is just what we need right now..."

***

19

Stepping down from the stool, Malcolm faced the stone wall of the eastern wing of the Augustinian abbey church. Looking up, he felt pleased with his decorative work. Sprigs of holly glistened in the frosty sunlight.

Yesterday they'd decorated the church interior. The Prior had prefaced his instructions by referring to the already ornate features of the walls and ceiling, which would be enhanced by the addition of seasonal gilding.

The High Altar could have doubled as the entrance gate to Heaven; such was the loving attention that the friars, helped by lay volunteers and schoolchildren, had lavished upon it. Intricate latticework woven from holly, ivy and evergreen leaves depicted charmingly sculpted Seraphim and Cherubim fluttering around the throne of God.

A Confederate banner; displaying the symbols of Irish Catholic resistance and supremacy was draped across the front of the altar. Red ribbons bedecked the nave and chancel and the three seating spaces of the sedilia, where visiting bishops had often sat in their finery. Each space had statues of the Holy Family, the whole forming a three-sectioned crib.

The passage up to the bell tower had twirling strings of holly and ivy and the battlements on top now projected gaiety instead of their customary somewhat forbidding ambience.

The Priory had likewise been attended to, taking on a happier aura. The kitchen, refectory and even the dormitories twinkled in the midst of monastic discipline and austerity.

Malcolm preferred working outside, despite the winter cold. He'd found that being cooped up inside for too long had a suffocating effect on the mind that no amount of self-denial or prayers for strength could assuage. On either side of him along the grey wall his colleagues were fixated on their festive beautification, perched on stools or ladders to festoon the centuries-old building.

They hadn't made such a supreme effort for years, but this Christmas had a special significance. A temporary peace reigned in Ireland, albeit at the whim of the invader who had retired to winter quarters. He could resume his orgy of conquest at any time.

Locals, loyal as ever to the Augustinians, had gathered the holly over previous days, arriving in the meadow with armfuls and barrows of it.

Malcolm went to get a ladder to reach a high arched window. He noticed that others were not keen about climbing up the walls. Fr. Ambrose in particular avoided ladders since a rung broke under him a month earlier when he was painting over a crack in the refectory ceiling. His weight wasn't conducive to standing on creaky wooden steps.

The Prior had left his office to participate in the adornment. He'd mentioned at breakfast that a large wreath in the shape of a star, signifying the one that guided the Magi to Bethlehem, might be appropriate this year, to be suspended over the main entrance to the church.

As Malcolm fixed the ladder in place and prepared to ascend he saw Timothy, the joker, swishing across the grass to him, gasping from the effort. He removed his foot from the bottom rung, wishing Timothy would let him get on with it. Timothy, hands on hips, blurted "I can't wait for the turkey, or is it a goose this year?"

He nudged Malcolm, his eyes narrowing, and whispered conspiratorially: "With Cromwell waiting to pounce after Christmas maybe we should avoid that particular bird...I'd prefer not to be able to say, as we sit down to indulge, that...our goose is cooked!"

He maintained a stoical expression for a few seconds and then laughed loudly, bending over and clapping Malcolm on the back.

"I think we'd be better served praying for victory, or to be spared the fate of Wexford and Drogheda, than tempting providence by jesting about it." Malcolm said tersely.

Ambrose guffawed. "Ah, you need to appreciate the humorous...even amid the worst of what life throws at us. I pray as much as you, but I believe God would have us laugh too. I'm sure he had a good laugh with the apostles when he wasn't preaching or healing the sick, why wouldn't he? And hey, it's Christmas!"

Malcolm felt chastened. "You're right; it's a great feast, regardless of what lies ahead."

The friars had been working on their happy assignment since early morning and now, close to noon, the church had taken on a joyful facade, in keeping with the spirit of the season if not with Malcolm's own fears and anxieties about the future.

And there was old Jeremy, helping another friar to turn the Priory cloister into a circle of heavenly delight. Their holly was interwoven with brightly coloured pennons and flags.

The church and Priory basked in festive hues, exuding a cheeriness that Malcolm didn't feel. But it still gladdened his heart to see it after they concluded their yuletide abbey makeover. Perhaps a little of its glory, its optimism, had rubbed off on him.

Timothy was right. Bleakness and cynicism held you back. *There's always hope.*

*

Tom Brennan braced himself for the usual Christmas Eve throng. It was only eight o' clock and already the house was half-full. Mags wasn't under too much pressure yet, apart from sporadic groping and spontaneous declarations of love from tipsy customers.

The door swung open, eliciting curses from the drinkers as a blustery wind blew in a sprinkling of the hail that was falling outside, strewing icy pebbles across the floor. *Must get Mags to sweep that away before somebody skids.*

Sparks flew from the big open turf and log fire, mingling glitteringly with the smoke that rose from twenty or more clay pipes.

The Mayor, Edward Comerford, stood framed in the frizzled whitened dark of the doorway. He pulled the door shut behind him. For once he wasn't dressed too formally, sporting a common green workman's coat and jacket and baggy breeches, an outfit that served more to keep out the cold than to impress. Likewise his sturdy leather boots that would keep feet warm in the severest of winters.

He cleaned his soles vigorously in the already soggy doormat, shaking off slush and muck. Then he let down the cowl that protected his cerulean periwig from the elements. Oddly, he was unshaved. At least a day's growth of beard darkened his customary lily-white visage.

Tom quickly averted his gaze when he caught the Mayor eyeing him. *Probably a worried man, like us all.*

The Mayor headed straight for his favourite spot by the fire, which nobody else had coveted, despite the weather: Too busy bantering at their tables or building up to a carousing midnight climax.

Mags went straight to the Mayor as the valued customer readjusted his slightly dislodged periwig and removed his velvet gloves, placing them on the rickety little oak table in front of him.

"Whiskey, Make it a large one, please" he ordered. She promptly obliged.

Tom crossed over to greet him. "Happy Christmas, Edward. I hope the good wife and the family are keeping well." He noticed that the Mayor's right hand was trembling. *Maybe the cold.*

"As well as anyone can expect, given the times we're in...God, what a night...I mean it's a great occasion...but that storm. I almost got blown away getting on the coach at Westcourt. And the hail stones...but I won't dwell on that. Ah, a lovely fire Tom."

Tom sat down opposite him. "Mind me asking, Edward...have you any notion of what's going to happen, you know, when this war kicks off again...I mean here in Callan. You know I joined the militia? We've been training. Not that I'd call myself anything remotely resembling a soldier. Learning how to fire those matchlock muskets and to hold a sword, and all that. But nobody seems to know if there's really going to be a battle, or what our chances might be if there is.

"I heard about those towns surrendering after the fall of Wexford, right up to before the cessation two weeks ago. Callan wasn't one of them. That makes me proud, Edward, that we haven't caved in to...to the foe...so easily. But...do we have what it takes to hold out against them if they take us on...I mean, if Drogheda and Wexford couldn't contain them then what chance have we got...I don't mean to sound defeatist. I'm just trying to reason it out..."

Tom feared he'd said too much, and braced himself for a harsh riposte. Instead the Mayor yawned and massaged his periwig. His eyes were bloodshot, evidence maybe of sleepless nights.

Mags arrived with the drink, which Edward took graciously, complimenting the barmaid on her prompt and professional service.

He sipped the whiskey, winced a little, and left the pewter cup on the table. "I'm as much in the dark as you are, Tom...or anyone else in this town or district. It's down to the Governor. He alone can decide how we'll respond if the Roundhead army turns up outside our walls. We've repaired and reinforced the walls...not to the

205

standard that I'd liked to have seen, but they're in better condition than they were three months ago.

"The garrison is a substantial one: It's now at thirteen hundred, and there 's the militia as you mentioned. A reasonable supply of weapons...for the soldiers, whatever about the civilian volunteers. A shortage of ammunition that we may have to get around in the New Year by begging for, or confiscating, as much lead as we can extract from this unfortunate town. How will our lads fare in a showdown? I honesty don't know. Neither does the Governor or so he tells me, and he's the one who'll decide if resistance is the correct response..."

Tom felt deflated. "You mean he might...surrender?"

The Mayor rubbed at his stubble, as if suddenly discovering it. "He's not a very militaristic man, and I can't see him fighting if he believes that there's little or no chance of winning..."

Tom gasped. He was about to probe further into the Mayor's authoritative mind but held back, in deference to the season that was in it. "Look, it's Christmas, I'll leave all that heavy decision-making to...the higher-ups; your good self included, Edward. Whatever's decided, I'll do my bit. I can just about shoot straight now, I think, though we haven't used any live bullets yet."

The Mayor smiled and shook his head. Raising his pewter cup in mock approval he drained it in one gulp.

The door burst open and another blast of icy wind fanned the drinkers, prompting a string of curses.

Tom beheld the shivering form of Peter the Atheist, flanked by two notorious drinkers that Tom had barred at some point and then reinstated following passionate pleas from their buddies.

Peter untied his cloak and ordered a tankard of ale at the counter from Mags.

"Well Peter" Tom hollered, "have you decided to drink a toast to the Savior's birth? Good man. Maybe having second thoughts about God not being up there?"

Peter turned around, still standing at the counter, his face as usual morphing into a fleshy questioning pose.

"Hello Tom. No, but I have no objection to anyone else observing religious rites or occasions...as I told you before. I do enjoy the festive spirit though and I certainly wouldn't go as far as Mr. Cromwell who, I understand, would like to abolish the celebratory aspects of the season. I hear that plum pudding is condemned by the Puritans as popish pottage, and to be seen eating it is to become a crime. There's talk of floggings and worse for offenders. But that's only in England. He hasn't conquered your neck of the woods yet."

Stunned silence in the alehouse followed d his remarks. Dozens of heads faced him. Then someone laughed and others joined in. Tom saw the funny side of it too, but wondered what restrictions he'd have to contend with if the same Mr. Cromwell's writ were to run in Callan.

He'd heard that the Puritans weren't too fond of alcohol either and they'd imposed heavy taxes on England's alehouses to help fund their war effort. Returning to join Mags at the counter, he tried to banish from his mind the prospect of closure, penury, or banishment. The distracting revelry partly softened his cares but still they lingered, hovering before him like that phantom dagger in the play.

The music had started, and a fiddler was being called upon to play an air to cheer them up. The man put down his tankard, fetched his instrument and began a rousing tune that soon had everyone singing and stamping their feet.

Mags dashed about, weaving in and out between the thickening throng, responding to simultaneous demands for more beer and whiskey from a dozen different directions at once. She somehow managed to see who was ordering through the curtains of smoke and dust forming from the pipes and the perpetual sneezing of snuff-takers.

From a cloudlet of pipe smoke around the fire a voice called his name. The Mayor was almost invisible behind the foggy veil. Coughing and fanning as he went to take his order, Tom was startled to see coins from the Mayor's purse spilling unto the table, a gold sovereign among them that shone through the billowing fumes.

"A drink for everyone here", Edward announced, and though he hadn't raised his voice above a whisper he'd captured the attention of men to all sides of him, including lads who hadn't noticed his presence. He quickly became the subject of an affectionate scrum.Tom had to break it up to prevent unintended injury.

Mags accelerated the tempo of her already rapid service, displaying an uncanny knack for remembering every drink requested and who'd ordered it.

Tom felt better. He found the strength and motivation to attend to his customers, and as the clock ticked to midnight he had a tipple himself and joined in the celebration of "peace to all men."

*

Shane and Luke relished having being called to serve First Mass on Christmas Day. Dozens of altar boys had vied for the honour, knowing that this was the only time of year when they'd receive money for their service, and maybe a surprise gift also. In the ice-cold sacristy Father Brannigan finished his wine and handed the empty glass to Luke.

Attired in a thin white under-garb, he shivered and began rubbing his hands together. "Now lads", he hooted, a note of joy in his tone, "dress me up properly, mind. This is an extra special day, more so this year with all that's happening. Alb first…"

Shane instantly took the long-sleeved white linen tunic from the neat pile of sacred vestments on the consecrated table nearby and handed one end of it to Luke. They carefully eased his head through the orifice intended for that purpose.

It reached past the PP's knees. The alb, they knew, symbolized the purity without which a priest would be just a common man, as distinct from God's anointed. It added another layer of high dignity to Fr. Brannigan.

The sweet smell of incense wafted from behind as a third server fidgeted with a smoking censor. Shane heard that some boys got dizzy from it, but he liked it, especially after stepping in from the stench of sewerage and rotten fish on South Street.

Next came the cincture, which Shane had always thought of as a rope until the PP scolded him and whispered reverently of its hallowed nature. When the boys had pulled it around his waist he waved them off and fastened it into place.

Over the alb they draped the PP with a lavishly bright silk stole. The additional colours celebrated the descent of Jesus into the mortal world, he informed them. Shane was dazzled by the bands of red, yellow, and blue, and the glittering streaks of gold and silver.

He wondered if these would somehow bring warmth to the PP on this freezing day, for, though it was Jesus's birthday, there wouldn't be a fire burning in the church to ward off the chill. Townsfolk would be dressed for the weather, but the priest had just these thin fabrics that wouldn't stop him getting a bad cough. Unless he'd worked out a mysterious deal with God to stay warm.

Shane thought of his mother down there somewhere in the pews. She'd exulted in the news that he'd be serving Mass for Christmas, and he knew she'd be hoping for a gift. Last year he'd received one even though he'd only served the Christmas Eve mass, which didn't have the same divine significance.

Fully dressed, the PP rose slowly and dusted down his vestments. "That's fine lads. Let's go out there and, lads, do the town proud..."

His voice cracked and Shane swore he detected a tear streaking along his cheek. A quick brush of his hand banished whatever it was and the PP added, sadly Shane thought, "it might be my last time saying Christmas Mass, the way things are going..."

The lads followed him out of the sacristy and unto the platform behind the altar. The devout flock, male on one side and female on the other, rose noisily to its feet, beads dangling from entwined fingers. Intersecting multihued rays from the stained glass spotlighted the front rows.

This was supposed to be a happy occasion, but you wouldn't think it by the blocks of worried faces Shane saw when he took his place to the right of the PP. Not a smile among them. Just a palpable edginess and every eye fixed on the celebrant. As if he might announce a miracle. maybe the invaders had packed up and left. The prayers might have worked.

The PP had promised that if God heard enough prayers and if they were offered to him with pure hearts and minds, he might decide to put manners on Cromwell...stop him in his tracks. Shane had prayed for that intention, though not as fervently as Mother who said numerous rosaries.

The PP began the Mass. At the first uttering of that awful foreign language Shane thought again of Master Counihan flogging him for failures in grammar. Did the PP ever get a beating for not learning his Latin? Hardly, judging by the way he rattled it off every day in church. *Never gets a word wrong. I'll never be a priest. Not with all that Latin to learn.*

Soothing images of gifts and a hearty dinner following the Mass crept alluringly into his head as the ritual continued. His taste buds already exulted in the scrumptious juicy mutton being chewed and munched and swallowed. He mustn't dwell too much on that. *It's a sin to let the mind wander at Mass.*

He loved Christmas: From the sound of the bells tolling, to the trimming of the Town Cross with holly, ivy and evergreen, and the festive decorations in all the front windows, whether real glass or pretend.

The music in the taverns and alehouses were for the grown-ups, but he loved the sound of it and the seasonal kindliness that embraced every household. It spread through the town like a non-lethal plague that brought happiness and laughter instead of sickness and misery.

If only every day could be Christmas. That remark from the PP about it possibly being his last Christmas Mass bothered him. *God, please don't let that be....*

But Fr. Brannigan hadn't reckoned on the garrison... or the mighty walls, or the castles...

***

20

Mark Gegan surveyed the festive New Year's Eve spread on the flat Motte summit. Doors resting on logs served as a long makeshift table that almost bisected the hilltop, stretching from where a climber came to rest upon ascending the Motte to the rear of the summit where trees formed a natural barrier. Rush-lights mounted on stakes encircled the merrymakers, guttering in the thankfully light breezes that fanned the old Norman site.

The "table" was laid with wooden platters to which volunteer caterers intermittently added hunks of steaming meat and vegetables. As quickly as the victuals were deposited hungry revellers grabbed the platters and headed off to their chosen patches of ground. Everyone, male and female alike, young and old, seemed to have a mug or tankard in his hand and swigging happily.

The annual event was bigger than on any previous year, the Mayor had told him, due to the "exceptional circumstances."

A tactful way of saying that none of them might be around for a 1650 New Year's Eve celebration, assuming that such events would even be permitted under a Cromwellian regime.

Stars glittered in the freezing sky, obscured only by the wisps of smoke that billowed heavenward from two enormous cooking fires, over which oxen, hogs, and sheep roasted. Sweating men with sooty faces and rolled-up sleeves rotated the carcasses on spits, longing in their eyes for the upcoming fare.

Men held out speckled trout and eels on metal rods at three smaller fires, cursing when their fingers got scorched. Sparks fizzled out upon reaching the emaciated branches of the beech and Scotch pine trees that fringed the summit on three sides.

Dampness from earlier rain showers ensured that no tree would ignite, as had happened one year, according to the Mayor.

To the rear of the summit doors lent by locals for the occasion were being positioned in readiness for the dancing later. That would follow the alfresco dining and drinking. Mark hadn't seen so much wine, whiskey and ale since his days fighting other nations' wars on the continent.

Marianne, instead of remaining by his side for the night as he'd requested had insisted on helping with preparations. There she was, filling tankards. She'd made a point of not covering her smallpox scar, a tactic she often employed to make herself less attractive to men, a way of thwarting unwanted advances.

He disapproved of it, but it was better than the alternative: Marianne throwing punches; or, God forbid, shooting them. She'd wounded a Westmeath lad who tried to rip her clothes off. It probably came as surprise to the man that a woman would be carrying a loaded pistol while strolling through a forest. He lived, but minus his manhood, the poor chap.

Mark had got Marianne to swear she wouldn't sink so low again. She asked him if he meant "aim so low", and he laughed along with her. He'd long since resigned himself to her idiosyncrasies, or at least to those he knew about. God only knew what else she got up to when out of his sight; the training episode being a case in point.

He looked around. He recognised several innkeepers and alehouse owners. Tom Brennan of the *Fiery Spirit* was both drinking and serving beer: A decent fellow. Men sat in groups on the cold ground, singing and joking, swigging from mugs, tankards and jugs.

He heard the rumble of more barrels being rolled up the hill to the summit before he saw them. The line of barrel pushers was flanked by torch bearers whose lights danced in the darkness. Men carrying kegs followed them, their arrival cheered by throngs of revellers.

The fiddlers and the harpists would join them later when the feasting and boozing reached a crescendo. Hearing a voice he thought he knew he turned around to spot the PP Father Branngian, a tankard swaying in his hand, chatting to three nodding lads whose demeanours indicated compliance...probably taking orders. He'd smiled to himself when Fr. Brannigan had appealed for sturdy doors at Mass and stressed that all doors would be returned after the big shindy on the Motte.

No sign of the Governor. He and his wife had been invited, but nobody seriously believed he'd come, due to his obsession with catching the plague. The fact that no one in Callan had been infected didn't seem to assuage his concern.

The Governor's obsession with staying alive bothered Mark. While he wanted to live too- didn't everybody?- there was a point at which any true man must be prepared to put his life on the line for what he believed in.

But what does Sir Robert believe in? If he'll do anything to avoid the plague, will he think likewise of an enemy that can be avoided...rather than fought?

Mustn't be unfair to the man, though: He hasn't been tested yet...

*

Tom Brennan filled a tankard for a man who he suspected had imbibed far too much already. But tonight was the exception as far as the usual reprimands or cautions were concerned. Callan abandoned the normal conventions and alehouse etiquette for the New Year's Eve bash and the unwritten rulebook had been discarded altogether this year as a gesture towards people who might not be alive a few months, or weeks, hence.

The grateful tippler took off with his drink, leaving Tom to warm his hands at the little fire that leapt up from an iron griddle. Its purpose was to cook some fish concoction that a pair of lads had prepared and asked him to watch lest it burn to a cinder. That was half an hour earlier and they still hadn't returned.

He'd serve the revellers for another while before taking a break: *Can't be working always.* The other two alehouse owners who'd agreed to donate the drink this year had already taken a break and were letting people "fill at will" as they called it, trusting the locals not to overdo it, which was a bit on the optimistic side. An apt gesture though for the season of peace and goodwill.

The celebrations were heating up. Soon the music and dancing would begin. Allowing for rainfall, which seemed unlikely given the clear night sky- a canvass covering had been erected above the wooden platform that consisted of all those doors he'd seen being conveyed to the summit.

The procession to the hilltop had reminded him of the Pharaoh's slaves building a pyramid, except that this was a voluntary exercise and there wasn't a whip to be seen.

He noticed that some starry-eyed youngsters had opted to celebrate in their own way, disappearing into the maze of bushes and trees along the sides of the Motte. From the hidden dark depths of the foliage moans and shrieks of passion could be heard, and the odd curse.

Carousing was always a bit unrestrained on festival night, and even the presence of Fr. Brannigan didn't dampen the ardour of love-hungry couples. He'd warned against it in previous years, but possibly he was more lenient now with the drums of war beating.

A woman attired in a blue brocade frock and black hooded cape crept up from the shadows beyond the griddle fire. "I'd forget about that", she said, pointing at the cooking pot. Her voice was alluring and commanding at the same time. Something in her tone prompted an instant response.

He took the pot from the fire, inadvertently knocking the griddle off the circle of stones holding it.

"The lads who own it are over at other side of the hilltop munching beef and singing."

"Thanks Madam...I'm obliged."

"Yes...I came over to you because I've run out of whisky in my corner of this open-air banqueting hall...could you spare some?"

"Of course...do you wish me to carry the keg for you?"

"No, I'll take it."

For a slightly built woman she lifted the full keg off the ground with remarkable ease, but no sooner had she begun to move away when another man practically grabbed it from her.

"I can't allow a lady to be carrying heavy weights, and such an elegant one at that. Where to, dear lady?"

"You", chirped Tom, startled at the sight and sound of the tall man in his silken tunic, velvet breeches and feathered cap.

"Martin Conway, the highwayman. Last time I saw you was on the road to Kilkenny in August..."

The highwayman laughed, touching his thin wispy moustache in a mockingly affected manner. "The same Conway..."

The woman broke into a smile. "Highwayman...you're not here to rob us, are you? I presume that's a costume for tonight."

"No...I'm not here to rob anyone but I am who Tom says...and you are?"

"Marianne Gegan, the Captain's wife. I presume you've met the Captain."

"No, I haven't but I've heard he's a capable fellow, assigned to save the good folk in these parts from the tyrant that's about to pounce on us..."

Tom felt his anger rising. "You should be ashamed of yourself, Martin, robbing and terrorising people at a time like this...when Irish men and women need protecting, not to be preyed upon by their own kind..."

Conway put down the keg, and raised both hands in a gesture of appeasement. "That's all behind me, Tom. The gang broke up last month. With war ripping the country apart we decided our profession was getting a tad too hazardous: Too many soldiers patrolling...on the move everywhere...roadblocks where we never encountered them, on lanes and back-roads. There were seven of us. Four of them joined the defenders in Kilkenny. The City needs every man who can use a weapon, they said. Two are still on the road, and, well, I'm here tonight to join in the festivities...though, if I'm not welcome..."

The Captain's wife, who had her arms folded, suddenly pulled the black hood down to reveal a mannish haircut, a pair of fiery eyes, bared teeth, and quivering lips. Her whole face was a study in anger. Tom recoiled at a smallpox scar that stood out even in the sporadic light from the fires. But he quickly forgot about it when she let loose on the highwayman.

"You ought to be in chains, locked up until the town decides what to do with you. Since arriving in Callan I've seen poor women in the stocks, crying with shame...and for far less than what you do for a so-called living. Instead of skulking around making life miserable for people you should be a soldier, or in the militia. You can rob unarmed merchants, can you? Enrich yourself on other people's earnings. Can you fight an invader?"

Conway looked subdued. Adopting an exaggerated look of hurt pride, he blurted "Are these the thanks I get for offering to help you with that keg? As I told Tom, I've turned my back on thieving. But I'm not going to throw my life away uselessly. Sure, I took risks every day I held up a coach or waylaid a rich merchant, but those were calculated risks. A hangman's rope was a possibility but only if I was stupid enough to get caught. I accepted the risk.

"But standing in front of an attacking band of hostile men, knowing that I can fire just one shot, two if I'm lucky, before I feel a ball ripping into me is not just taking a risk... It's *asking* to be killed. I admire men who are brave enough to take that risk, but not enough to want to join them in an early grave. I'm sorry if that doesn't chime with your high ethical standards Mrs. Gegan but I never claimed, or pretended to be, a patriot..."

"You're a blackguard and nothing else if you won't join us at the walls," Tom fumed. He wanted to hit him, but held back.

Mrs. Gegan, still seething, picked up the keg and headed off to the other side of the summit, leaving Conway facing Tom like a scolded child.

He removed his cap, smoothing its feather lovingly and slumped down in the cold grass beside Tom. Grabbing an empty tankard he filled it with ale from a large jug, heedless of Tom's function in dispensing it.

Sipping it, he soothed "Don't be annoyed with me Tom. I'm not a soldier. But look here... we don't know how this battle for Callan is going to pan out...if there is a battle. I haven't dumped my pistol, my musket or my sword. I'll use them if my own life is threatened. I live these days in a mountain hideout in Tipperary. Only came here tonight for the old shindig. I'll be gone before the sun rises. Isn't it great...a real party in a world gone mad?"

Tom poured him another drink and helped himself to one. Above the rhythmic babble of merrymaking he heard fiddles being tuned up and the tentative plucking of a harp. He took a long swallow and gasped. "Whatever happens, life won't be the same again... for any of us."

*

Marianne's anger abated. Maybe she was too hard on the reformed highwayman, given that he'd packed in the vile profession, even if for self-serving reasons. She ended her catering duties, passing stewardship of the whiskey and ale in her care to a swaggering man who was keen to "serve", he explained, in words that she barely understood. She suspected he just wanted to get control of the drink, but who cared? It was a free-for-all anyway, and it seemed prudent to defer to the locals. She'd been in Callan for only a few weeks.

Where was Mark? *Ah, there he is, talking to those important looking fellows at the dancing platform.* She dusted soot and ashes from her frock and tried to rub off the ale stains- she must have spilled some earlier when pouring- and headed over to join him.

Before she reached him a voice from somewhere behind distracted her.

"Cathy!"

She embraced her friend, who had donned a red damask gown for the occasion; a fashionable golden harp broach pinned to it, but hadn't bothered to cover her head. She looked radiant, black hair flowing around her shoulders, lips pouting. She'd have men drooling over her.

"I got here later than I planned-the tavern keeper needed me. I wouldn't have got time off at all but for the fact that he knew there would be fewer customers tonight because of...this here."

"And how's work at *The Sign of the Helmet*? Not pushing you too hard I hope. I miss you at the castle. I have to do all the house chores now. "

"I know...you'd rather be showing women how to shoot or throw stones!"

Marianne laughed.

Cathy blushed, her cheeks flickering in the rush-light. "The hours are long at the tavern, lots of washing and cleaning, but I'm getting used to it. I get on well with customers. That's something he likes..."

"Come on. Mark will be glad be see you. He misses you too. But to the table first...I fancy a bite. Have you ever seen so much food? Enough to feed a multitude!"

*

Mark sat on a stool provided for the "dignitaries", as he and a few of the more influential guests were designated. Everyone else stood about on the summit or sat in the grass, or on lengths of cloth they'd brought with them, drinking and devouring meat.

Another man meriting a stool was the PP, and he'd perched himself alongside Mark, a pewter cup of whisky clutched tightly. He wasn't in clerical garb, but dressed like the common folk: plain woollen cap, workman's dirt-stained shirt, a sleeveless jacket and knee-length breeches.

The reason being, he explained to Mark, that one must not get above oneself. He was especially wary of the sin of pride, he confided, slurring his words slightly.

217

Mark felt the whiskey go to his own head too, and had slowed his drinking a bit. It might be a no-holds- barred-party, but it was never wise, he believed, to let one's guard down completely. Life was replete with nasty and occasionally catastrophic surprises.

The PP had to raise his voice to be heard as the fiddling had started, drawing dozens of athletic couples onto the platform. Feet clattered and jangled on the doors amid roars of elation from the whirling and whooping dancers. They'd obviously done it before. The hilltop erupted in a chorus of applause as the dancers lost themselves in a musical whirligig.

The PP's face lit up with delight. "It's all about the leg action, you see...listen to that rhythm, and look at those feet. By God there's life in Callan yet, whatever ever about the lads who'd like to snuff it out on us!"

Mark took heart too from the sparkle of the young dancers. What an abundance of energy and spirit.

He'd seen it too in the training sessions...people who knew nothing about weapons of war eager to learn so they could defend their native town.

Fr. Brannigan tapped his own feet in time to the music, swinging his cup back and forth but without spilling a drop of the precious "water of life."

When the dancers had exhausted themselves they left the platform, dispersing into the half-light to rest. Others quickly replaced them but had to make do with a slower dance as a piper played a soulful air and somebody stepped up beside him to sing of Ireland's hapless plight. He evoked centuries of wrongdoing and laid it all at England's doorstep.

The harper then joined in, eliciting cheers from the throng that Mark noticed had swollen considerably since the dancing began. Old folk sat on the ground, smoking their clay pipes, and reminiscing, the PP quipped, about how their dancing was way better than what passed for dancing nowadays.

There was a lull in the musical session to allow for the refilling of mugs, tankards and hungry bellies.

Mark wondered where so many carcasses had been acquired. The PP informed him that farmers had donated, as had the vintners, so that a proper celebration could proceed.

Before the resumption of dancing, a fiddler announced, a local comedian wished to tell a few jokes. Mark listened with barely concealed annoyance to the awful excuse for comedy that ensued, and he noticed that nobody seemed to be listening to the man, let alone bothering to heckle him.

The PP nudged Mark. "The poor lad is doing his best. It's not easy to get a laugh standing on a stage. People laugh more at misfortune or, generally, at things they really shouldn't find amusing...at other people's woes. You've been here a few weeks but I don't suppose you've heard the story of the three jesters who plied their trade on this very hilltop?"

Mark shook his head, evincing an insincere eagerness to hear the story.

"Back when this Motte was a Norman fortress, the lords and ladies here employed three jesters to entertain them. The funny men worked every day but they dreaded Monday mornings because that's when their masters would be in a foul mood after a night of heavy drinking and carousing.

"To encourage the jesters to provide top-class comedy the lofty lords of the fortress decreed that the jester who told the least funny jokes on Monday morning would be tossed down the hillside. You can imagine the pressure the poor lads were under to amuse. Some jesters broke their necks and had to be replaced. And the really funny thing, in a way, is that there was never a shortage of aspiring funny men to take the places of jesters who came to grief on the hillside. They honestly believed they could do better than the failed jesters..."

Mark smiled. He wondered how he'd fare in telling a humorous tale, not that he felt like cracking jokes in his present predicament. The comedian left the platform and the music kicked off again: Jigs and hornpipes in quick succession. Chaotic but jubilant scenes unfolded as competent dancers struggled to step it out in the midst of drunken amateurs who tripped over them and rolled off the platform.

The PP sighed. "Those jesters had a difficult calling in life to be sure. I'm glad I'm not held to that impossibly high standard...I try to the best of my ability to lighten a sermon with witticisms now and again to drive home a point, and always they chuckle...but only because they feel obliged to. Ah yes, if I were a jester back then I reckon I'd have taken a few tumbles..."

The wild dancing fizzled out. Now a more sober group had formed a circle around a singer who was crooning a sonorous dirge. As he sang they hummed along and rotated slowly, arms linked, in a trance-like ritual. Mark wondered if they'd abstained from drink to be able to move so gracefully.

"It's a version of an old Norman dance. It was performed in all the towns they conquered...but our lads have adapted it to their own beliefs..."

The encircling dancers echoed the melodious notes of the singer, creating a pleasant harmony.

When Mark reached for the jug of whiskey to refill his mug he saw Marianne heading towards him, her friend Cathy in tow, both of them holding platters of beef and mutton. Marianne had her hood up. *Good.* That boyish haircut embarrassed him.

He introduced them to the PP, who rose from his stool and bowed graciously. Leaving down his cup, he blessed the women. "Is this the lady I've heard referred to as the Captain's fair warrior? I hope you've found Callan to your liking, Madam, allowing for the unfortunate circumstances that brought you here..."

Mark gritted his teeth. He prayed Marianne wouldn't say anything to inflame the PP. She looked at him, then at the priest, and thanked Fr. Brannigan for his good wishes.

Thank God. She hadn't mentioned anything about women taking up arms...yet...or about women being equal to men any day of the week; as she'd said to him so often, without a trace of anger and while managing to keep a straight face.

Saying it to a priest might be pushing her luck.

21

Marianne was sweating all over in the field at the rear of the castle. From every pore it oozed, and this made her happy. It meant that she'd put in a sufficient effort and deserved a rest.

But she pushed herself a little more prior to putting away the sword and getting back to the castle in time for the midday meal before the soldiers had theirs. She walked twenty paces, turned abruptly, and sprinted towards the wooden stake upon which she'd placed an apple.

The stake was higher than her. That made the challenge trickier but in keeping with what she reckoned she might expect in real combat. Without stopping she drew the sword, and using both hands, swung from right to left, slicing the apple in two. She had the sword back in its scabbard as the split pieces hit the ground.

Faster than last time, she thought. Speed could be vital, but it was wasn't everything. An opponent could shoot her dead as she fumbled with her sword, but if he missed she'd reach him while he rushed to reload. She was fortunate in having a sword that might be described as all-purpose.

Mark spoke of the differences between swords used for cutting, thrusting and hacking...but hers could perform the three functions reasonably well, maybe not as efficiently as the ones designed specifically for each purpose but it was better than lugging three swords around. A strong man would find that onerous enough, but she was slightly built and must allow for her physiological make-up.

That completed her sword exercise for the day. She deemed continuous practice essential to honing her skills...but no point in overdoing it.

She picked up the crossbow. She'd practiced with it earlier and she remembered that she left a bolt embedded in a tree in the adjoining field that extended down to the river. She went to retrieve it. In normal circumstances s she'd forget about it, but ammunition of any sort , including bolts for her crossbow, were in short supply and she wouldn't get a sympathetic hearing from Mark if she ran out of bolts since he didn't care for crossbows anyway.

The bolt had lodged in a branch, exactly where she'd aimed at. Nice shooting, but this wasn't a battlefield. Trees didn't return fire or come running at you. She had to break off a piece of the branch to remove the bolt. She'd never seen what a bolt would do to human flesh but if it sliced through wood like that…

She stood for a moment looking at the river and, beyond it, the field that had served for militia training and that contained the Norman Motte which had hosted the New Year's Eve festivities. Not a soul in the field now, and the Motte had a ghostly ambience, rising out of the earth like an explosive eruption frozen in time.

The river flowed unruffled, unaffected by flooding for a while now. No heavy rain for weeks. But she knew that its tranquil waters concealed deadly man-traps that awaited any enemy intent on crossing it.

She turned around and headed back to the castle. She narrowly avoided stepping into the shitty patch close to the rear wall of the building, where the waste deposited down the chute ended up. A lot more of it since the soldiers moved in a few days before, naturally.

The patch should be signposted, she felt, as it encompassed a hole more than twelve feet deep. Legend had it that a man once fell into it and was never seen again, lost forever in its stinking depths.

She made her way back and re-entered Skerry's via a rarely used metallic door located in the rear of the castle, giving unto the field and river beyond.

Inside, soldiers stood about on the ground floor... smoking, drinking or playing cards. She laid asde her sword and crossbow, opting to take a walk in town to escape the increasingly cramped conditions in the castle occasioned by its newly arrived garrison.

They made way for her, nodding respectfully as she passed through to the street entrance door, which was swinging ajar, letting in thedaylight. Soldiers standing about on the street shouted greetings to her. Dozens more squatted on the footpath, some nursing muskets and pikes, others swigging ale merrily. Others again looked nervous or unsure: Understandable, given what might be in store for them. Having strolled to as far as the wooden cross she returned. She felt restless today.

Collecting her sword and crossbow she climbed the stairway to the top floor. The living quartes had been transformed into a miniature army barracks. Mark, already sitting at the head of the table, had a dozen soldiers with him, drinking ale from mugs and tankards.

222

A young soldier; thumbing a thin wispy beard, stood and whistled admiringly. "That's a nice crossbow ma'am" he crooned, "I heard about them things. The auld fellas had them way back."

She hung it on a nail above the fireplace. Another soldier said he'd never seen a real crossbow, just etchings depicting archers in ancient wars. A third said, half sneeringly, "My grand folk had one...an old antique it was, an ornament to gawk at. We youngsters loved to imagine those bygone times when men had no guns and had to..." he stopped, thinking that maybe he'd gone too far, Marianne guessed. He resumed swigging his ale.

Mark cleared his throat, motioned the men to be quiet. "Ah Marianne, sit down dearest...more bad news I'm afraid."

She pulled out a chair near the blazing log fire, all the soldiers tensing as Mark prepared to enlighten her.

"So...what's happened now?" she asked.

He raised the tankard to his lips, drinking deeply. Wiping ale from his lips he let out a wheezy sigh. "Corporal Molloy here just told me...the Governor's heard from spies that Cromwell has left his winter quarters and is heading straight this way...should be here within four or five days, maybe sooner."

"Well, that can't come as any great surprise surely...it's what we've been preparing for, isn't it?"

"Yes...of course...but now that we know where we stand, I'm imploring you dearest. Once the enemy arrives at the gates it'll be too late to leave...with possibly every exit point blocked to us. So Marianne, while there's still a chance, will you consider leaving Callan? There's a family that lives halfway between here and Kilkenny, a remote location, off the beaten track...where you'll be safe until..."

"Until you and the others have fought for Ireland's freedom while I skulk in hiding. Forget it, Mark, I've already made my decision. I'm not stirring from here until the battle is over. My place is by your side...whether you want me here or not!"

A deathly silence followed, broken only by the ticking of the wall clock.

Then, a soldier clapped. His colleagues, a little taken aback at first, tapped their own hands together. They stood, beaming at her and applauding- all except Mark.

He shook his head piteously and reached for the ale jug.

*

Malcolm assisted in the unloading and packing, despite his decision to remain with Jeremy at the abbey. From the moment he woke that morning an atmosphere of muddled unreality prevailed. The day started like any other. They rose at midnight for Divine Office. At dawn they recited the special prayers designated for that hour. More prayer followed, and a period of quiet reflection on the mysteries of life.

The Mass had a desolate, almost funereal tone. Fr. Kearney performed his priestly duties perfunctorily, and, for the first time ever in Malcolm's recollection, he skipped the customary sermon.

Not a word from the Prior as they breakfasted in silence and, Malcolm thought, an all-pervasive awkwardness, in the refectory. None of the others, apart from Jeremy, made eye contact with Malcolm. Were they feeling just a little guilty about him staying while they were readying to leave?

He didn't begrudge them. He wanted to go too, but it made him wonder at his own motives in showing solidarity with Jeremy. He believed Jeremy was being silly and stubborn, and not in any way contributing to the overall purpose or declared Christian mission of the Augustinians. And he didn't remotely share his colleague's reckless attitude to death.

It was fine for an old man in the winter of his years to be so sanguine and dismissive on the subject. Jeremy was eighty-seven. But Malcolm hadn't yet celebrated his twenty-seventh birthday. Jeremy was being doubly irresponsible given the sacrifice that he knew another friar was making for him.

But he mustn't allow such thoughts to obtrude. The responsibility to a fellow friar was his. Jeremy's motives were a matter for Jeremy.

A cold sun shone down on the meadow. Rooks perched on skeletal yew tree branches observed the friars and sympathetic locals busily moving property from the abbey church and the Priory to be loaded unto wagons, carts and pack-horses.

Malcolm felt a twinge of sorrow when he saw two burley men pulling swollen hessian sacks across the grass to the meadow exit. It seemed incongruous to him that the books he'd grown to know and love should be unceremoniously dragged away by people who probably couldn't read.

He'd had to leave the library earlier, so hurtful was the sight of his old friends, as he thought of them, disappearing one by one from the shelves: The works of Horace, Plato, Livy, Cicero, and Aristotle, among scores of others... all dropping into sacks like spuds uprooted from the Priory garden.

Joining the classical authors in this exodus of literature from Callan would be, he knew, the priceless manuscripts and the books that had been personally handwritten by scribes two centuries before.

The same tomes had survived King Henry's move against the monasteries, only to be once again departing.

Of course he accepted the necessity of safeguarding these treasures from the Cromwellians. But that didn't make it any easier to behold the stripping away of a library that had kept him sane, he believed, as well as informed and spiritually enriched, since the day he'd started in Callan.

Malcolm had also been stung by the Prior's decision not to conceal the sacred vessels of the abbey as the Augustinians had in 1540 to thwart King Henry's clampdown.

Back then, the friars hid the precious receptacles and utensils used in the celebration of the Mass at carefully chosen locations in the parish, retrieving them only when the danger had passed, or at least abated, after Henry's death.

The Prior's logic in not following that procedure- which was a fondly recounted tradition among the friars and the locals- was that this time a captured friar might reveal the whereabouts of the vessels. He also ruled out adding them to the other property being loaded for the flight from Callan. They would then be at risk from highwaymen, in addition to enemy troops that might intercept the friars.

Having prayed for guidance, the Prior had announced his intention to hand over all the vessels to a trusted officer of the garrison, Captain Gegan, for concealment at a location known only to that officer and to the Prior of an Augustinian abbey in France. This removed the risk of any Callan friar breaking under torture, as Fr. Kearney warned could happen to the best and toughest of men, including God's anointed.

Malcolm had helped convey the extra large chalice, the top half of which was solid gold, to the army cart, along with two silver plates upon which the sacred hosts were laid at Mass, recalling the Last Supper, and a Monstrance that was three-quarters gold. Dozens of smaller vessels equally relevant to the time-honoured rituals of the Catholic Church were carried to the cart, which was guarded by five musketeers and two pike-men.

As the morning progressed Malcolm had revised his initial objection to the removal. The invaders had no respect for any of the sacred paraphernalia of a Church they believed to be false and worthy of destruction, but they'd be as liable as any den of thieves to seize an alluring treasure trove.

On reflection, although he appreciated the value, both spiritual and temporal, of the vessels, he knew he'd miss the books more. He observed with a heavy heart an enormous prized collection on the move, the works of the greatest minds on the planet leaving the abbey via a train of swinging sacks.

A book fell into the grass from a large sack two workmen were pulling. They were the last in the line and neither of them noticed it. Malcolm waited until they'd loaded the sack into a wagon outside the abbey grounds, before retrieving the book.

The other friars were too busy to notice. He set off to return to it to the sack, but stopped when he saw the title: *The stars and the planets in God's universe*. He pushed in inside his garb. It wouldn't kill his departing colleagues, or the Augustinian Order, if he kept this book to read while he awaited the foe's arrival.

The Priory was being emptied of anything that could be moved or salvaged, and Malcolm wondered if the Prior had allowed for the needs of Jeremy and himself. He hoped so and offered a quick prayer to that effect.

Answering his prayer, the Prior crept up behind him. Malcolm scarcely recognised him in his disguise. Gone was the familiar grey habit of the Order. Fr. Kearney was attired in the garb of a common labourer: a mud-stained tight-fitting jacket, loosely buttoned; over a soiled and ragged linen shirt. His knee-length breeches were, it seemed, deliberately dirtied for effect. To keep out the cold he had a homespun cloak with shaggy borders wrapped around him that reached to his ankles.

The Prior's yellowish threadbare woollen cap could be the weak point of his masquerade, Malcolm feared, as if an enemy soldier asked him to remove it the tonsure would be a dead giveaway. Non clerical-folk didn't clip their hair in that fashion. It was a mark of special devotion and humility associated with religious orders. The Prior would need to let his hair grow and hope he could keep his cap on till then. Otherwise the tonsure could cost him his head

"I asked the workmen to leave a few loaves of bread, Malcolm, and you can still cook over a fire if you wish. Look, I won't try to pressurise you, but if you can somehow devise a way to change Jeremy's mind, then I encourage you to do it...without hesitation. I've arranged for two horses to be provided so that, if you both opt to leave, even at the eleventh hour, you can make good your escape..."

"Thank you, Fr. Kearney, but I think the only way to make Jeremy leave is to knock him on the head and carry him off in one of those sacks..."

The Prior laughed, and clapped Malcolm on the back. Malcolm found it strange that the Prior didn't seem fazed by having to wear non-clerical attire that divested him, at least to outward appearance, of his true status.

Then again, clothing was just a human convention. The Prior would probably argue that his service to God didn't depend on the clothes he wore. Still, despite his dismay over having to stay to face a grim future, Malcolm felt a sense of relief at not having denied his own true calling by concealing his identity like that.

The evacuation of friars and property was nearing completion...just a few smaller crates and sacks to transfer to the transport outside on Goose Lane. But then came what Malcolm knew would be the hard part for the friars: The farewells.

As the locals conveyed the remaining chattels to the wagons, each of the friars approached Malcolm who stood just inside the meadow gateway. They'd earlier said goodbye to Jeremy, who was now back tending to the garden as though this was a day like any other.

Unlike the Prior, they were still in their habits, seeming in no hurry to conceal their identities. They formed a single file, and Malcolm felt a sudden coldness when the first of them, Fr. Ambrose, made eye contact with him for the first time in days.

227

Ambrose had lost the weight he'd gained in the previous months. It must have been the shock of the war news and the need to abandon Callan. "Malcolm...I can't say how much I regret, but also admire, your decision to remain here. Needless to say I'll remember you, and Jeremy of course; in my prayers. It was great knowing you. God bless you..."

He squeezed Malcolm's hand tightly, then turned away and exited the meadow without a backward glance.

Fr. William, who'd been visibly terrified of the prospect of awaiting his doom in Callan, had relief stamped on his face. The colour had come back into his cheeks. For weeks after hearing of the landing of Cromwell's forces at Ringsend he had taken on the pallor of a living ghost.

"I'd love to be able to say that I wish I could stay with you Malcolm, but that would be a lie. I can't wait to put some distance between myself and this death trap...not wishing to upset you or anything. Maybe Jeremy will have a re-think and you'll be able to...anyway..."

He embraced Malcolm and left the meadow with head bowed.

Fr. Michael, deemed the most prayerful of them all, had a pained expression. His face was drawn up into a knot of wrinkles, and his eyes had depths of anguish that made Malcolm feel uneasier, an extra burden he could do without.

Closing his eyes, he placed hands on Malcolm's shoulders. "No greater love hath he than one who lays down his life for another...that's what the good book says about people who put their fellow men before themselves in the manner that you contemplate, Malcolm."

Opening his eyes, he stood back and shook his head sadly. "I have prayed with an intensity that surprised me, and that almost unhinged my mind...yes...I implored God to resolve this pickle that Jeremy has got you into, though I can see his point too. My dreams these past three weeks have been replete with visitations... from long departed friars....from saints and angels, all assuring me they had you in their thoughts. But you see..."

He leaned close and whispered "you see, Malcolm their hands are tied. The old free will, you know? Not even the supreme Archangels, nor Christ himself, can compel a human being to take a certain course. But as far as I could I have implored the heavenly hosts to try and knock some sense into Jeremy. That's as much I could do, Malcolm."

He stepped back and tut-tutted volubly. "Ah, Malcolm. I hope your tenure on this earth is not coming to an end (pointing aloft) but God always takes the best. If your time has come you'll be directed straight to the loveliest seat in Heaven, I'm sure of it. Goodbye Malcolm!"

Fr. Joseph had been voicing doubts about his vocation in recent months, and the war hadn't helped to allay his growing scepticism about aspects of Church teaching. The Prior had urged him to pray harder for guidance and not to allow doubt to break through the gateways of his upright Christian head. Joseph had opted to stay in the Order, but he'd told Malcolm that if the Prior had instructed him to stay in Callan and face the music he'd have disobeyed. He'd have sold his habit at the town rag-market and headed for the hills.

He fixed Malcolm with a look of high regard. "You're a brave man, Malcolm, but as to whether you're a foolish one too I'm not sure. You know the struggles I've been having with...this whole priestly business...I've decided to stick with it...for a while anyway. But I can tell you that if God himself and the Blessed Virgin descended from the sky and ordered me to hang around for those Roundhead blood-suckers I still wouldn't oblige. Put it there...!

He shook his hand and walked away, turning once to wave smilingly.

Fr. Timothy, the last to say goodbye, was in high spirits. This gladdened Malcolm, because the abbey jester hadn't cracked a joke since Christmas.

Malcolm punched him playfully in the chest. "Great to see you've regained your optimism and your sense of fun, Timothy. It was awful too see you there, moping about...a man of frowns and furrows, you who you kept us all smiling, and sometimes laughing out loud. You were the cause of adding to my list of sins at confession more than once...I nearly died of embarrassment that morning when I thought of some crazy joke you told. It was in the middle of receiving Communion. Fr. Kearney wondered if I'd had too much wine..."

"Ah, we had some good times Malcolm." Timothy peered at the abbey and Malcolm followed his gaze. Its oblong form glistened in heat-deprived sunlight, and its battlements, crowning the bell tower, seemed to touch the floor of Heaven.

"I hate to leave all this behind. I really thought I'd end my days here. It turns out I won't. When I take my leave of this Vale of Tears it'll be from another point of the compass. But exile is better than a premature death any day...begging your pardon. Oh God, I'm sorry Malcolm. It's easy for me to be smug and relieved, because I'm not the one about to become...well...a martyr, I suppose...

"You know, I always wondered what that would be like, Malcolm...remember that saint who was stripped bare and riddled with little arrows, and those poor Christians who wouldn't yield to the Romans and got dipped into big pots of boiling oil. That was some dose. I'll tell you something...I'd want to be in a completely different frame of mind to my usual carefree disposition before I'd consider offering up my miserable carcass just to make a point. I'm afraid I wouldn't die a martyr. I'd rather die laughing...Eh, Malcolm?"

Timothy clapped Malcolm on the back so hard he almost keeled over; then exited the meadow jauntily, whistling a line from a bawdy street ballad.

Fr. Kearney emerged from inside the abbey church, carrying a small bag. He looked so shabby in that disguise. Passing Malcolm, he turned around: "Ah yes, Malcolm. It slipped my mind earlier...Corporal Molloy from the garrison called yesterday and told me that he and a few soldiers will be calling this evening. They're desperately short of lead for ammunition. I told them to take any they can find from the Priory and the church. In normal circumstances I'd not have countenanced such a move, but...better that our side avails of this precious resource than the enemy. You'll give them some ale and bread when they arrive, won't you?"

Malcolm nodded blankly.

"Good man." And the Prior quickly joined his fleeing brethren on Goose Lane.

So, Malcolm thought, the abbey's complement of lead would be joining its gold and silver in exile.

He stood, frozen to the spot, as the men he'd lived, worked, and prayed with departed in a dust cloud raised by the trundling of wagons and the clip-clopping of heavily laden pack horses.

He was left alone, apart from Jeremy, in the vast rolling meadow with its now abandoned masterpiece of godly architecture, and a cloistered Priory stripped to its essentials.

When the friars disappeared from sight and the rattling crunch of their departure had faded, he expected to feel distraught and overwhelmed. Instead there was just numbness and a vague feeling of being a puppet...manipulated by forces beyond his control.

But were the strings in the hands of God? Perhaps this wasn't about Jeremy. Was God testing him, to see if he'd buckle under this herculean challenge...giving Jeremy the go-ahead to create this dilemma for him?

He'd consult some books on this ethical conundrum. That's if the library hadn't been completely cleaned out.

*

"But why won't you come with me? If you stay...Heaven knows what horrors await you."

Edward Comerford sank back in his padded oakwood chair at the ornate dining table in his Westcourt Mansion. He'd already explained why Callan would be too dangerous for his wife if the town were attacked and occupied.

She'd argued with him about that, speculating that things might settle down and the Roundheads might leave them in peace. He'd pointed out, as tactfully as he could, that Cromwell had already shown exactly how he intended to treat the natives, though he spared her the details of events at Drogheda and Wexford.

But his attempts at persuading her to leave, along with their three sons and two daughters, were made more difficult by his insistence on remaining in Callan himself.

If Callan wouldn't be safe for the rest of the family, how could he justify staying on, abandoning them in such a reckless fashion?

The arguments had gone back and forth for more than an hour, and now the room had taken on the feeling of a tension-racked interrogation chamber.

She faced him across the dining table, and although it wasn't as long as that ceremonial monstrosity in Butler Castle where the Governor held forth, it might as well have been a mile long, and his wife far out of hearing distance, for all the impact his words were having.

He repeated, for possibly the seventh time (he'd lost count): "Dearest Juliet, I know how harsh it sounds, and I don't expect you to understand the time-honoured responsibilities and nuances of my position as Callan's sovereign...its Mayor to whom locals look to with reverence, but my position here is very different from yours or that of any common citizen.

"I represent the people, and they have put their trust in me through the esteemed aldermen of the Corporation. I have sworn to promote the interests of this town; its physical wellbeing, just as, you might say, the parish priest looks after its spiritual welfare. Yesterday I even walked the streets to personally assure the locals that I haven't forgotten them.

"You know how easy it is to become estranged from the day-to-day affairs of one's town, especially out here in the comfort and delights of this palatial mansion. Westcourt, I think, darling, has a soporific effect on men. It's not far in terms of physical distance from any part of Callan, but there's a world of detachment socially from all those trusting people out there and...myself.

"This damnable war has at least done that...reminded me of who, and what, I am... or supposed to be. I am privileged to serve the people, and I must stand by that sacred trust accorded to me. Not just in good times, mind, such as we've enjoyed since the great Confederation was formed in 1642, but also in times of great peril when people turn to each other for comfort and turn to me, their Sovereign, for solace, inspiration...leadership. What kind of leader abandons his people in their darkest hour?"

Juliet had shrunken into a deep sulk, the likes of which Edward had never seen her exhibit. But she forced a smile, motioned for him to pass the solid silver butter dish, and said, without looking at him:

"Even if I accepted your decision to stay, I cannot simply pack up and leave. Wait a moment, Edward...you say you feel an obligation to your people to remain. Am I not entitled to take a similar stand on behalf of one I hold dear, you, darling...my nearest and dearest?

"I would be guilty of a betrayal far greater than yours, I suggest; if I left you here alone to face...whatever's coming. You remember our marriage vows? For better or worse...for richer or poorer... till death do us part? We have lived here in comfort and security, and, with God's blessing, have grown richer by the day. How far removed is our status from that of the man or woman barely existing in some smoke-filled hovel, with scarps for food and sleeping on filthy floors? I'll not run from Callan like a frightened maid! "

"Stop dear, please stop... I told you I've been endeavouring to reach out to the people, to...yes...get to know them better...in recent weeks. And yes, I admit there's a divide of sorts between those of us who rule, or thrive, or move in influential circles and the...ah...lower classes and the peasantry.

"I'm addressing that, darling. But nothing I do to change my own life or behaviour, here in this house or elsewhere, will make a blind bit of difference if the Regicides conquer Ireland...whether I stay here or leave...nothing. What does matter to me is that I do my duty and not forsake the people. I owe them that. And I owe myself that too..."

His wife shrieked. "And you owe me nothing then, just a curt goodbye Juliet, there's the door."

"Look Juliet. I owe you my love, that's why I beg you to listen to me. Please. I'll be taking a big risk. But you don't need to share that risk...or the children. It's my marriage vow, dearest, to love and honour you; that is uppermost in my mind when I ask you to leave..."

Edward let it go. What was the point? She'd see reason hopefully when the day of reckoning drew nearer. Gazing over her shoulder, he took in the embroidered Confederate infantry flag on the wall. It hung above the sun-filled frosted bay window: A white cross in red circle against a background of emerald green, and over this central motif rested a crown.

So much for the protection supposedly offered by the monarchy to the fledgling New Ireland that emerged from the 1641 uprising: The new King was without a throne, skulking in fear of his life somewhere on the continent.

And the Green? It was being painted over by the day, washed away by the invaders' all-conquering Venetian Red.

He'd listened to a lovely air plucked from a harp the week before, played by a blind man whose face showed no signs of anguish, just peace and contentment. Love of one's country had that effect, he supposed.

Would the harp again be suppressed, trampled into the ground? A clash of cultures was underway and his side was losing.

He wrenched the napkin from his neck, thew it on the table and rose. Instantly regretting his gesture, he cast a pitying glance at his wife, nodded to her and left the dining room. Reaching for his coat, for it was chilly outside; he opted to take a walk around his beloved Motte Field. Clear his head.

God save Ireland, he thought, and God give me the strength to make that woman see sense.

*

It suited Malcolm to have to have the soldiers and local militia at the abbey, even if they'd come to engage in a mild form of desecration. The other friars may have left but this was still consecrated ground, as were the parts of the church and Priory from which the men had extracted lead for their muskets.

But he welcomed the company. To have the place buzzing with activity just hours after the dusty exodus of his former colleagues was a blessing of sorts.

He was now catering for the lead extractors in the refectory. All were in bubbling humour, despite the approaching storm. The soldiers shared witticisms or sang snatches of ballads; the civilian volunteers huddled together separately, more subdued, but showing no visible signs of fear or foreboding.

Corporal Molloy had a knack for motivating both soldiers and volunteers, Malcolm noticed, when they'd set about hammering, tearing, scratching and lifting to maximise the yield of that normally not very valuable base metal that was suddenly in high demand.

The Corporal, munching at a half-loaf of buttered bread, rose from his chair and mooched over to Malcolm's position at the head of the table, a place normally reserved for the Prior. Pulling out a chair he sat beside him, pouring himself another mug of ale and thanking Malcolm.

"What I don't understand, Father, is why you two men were left behind...the abbey is outside the town walls, so there won't be any of us here to defend it when the fighting starts. And you know what our enemies are capable of, I take it...I mean in relation to clergy?"

Malcolm was about to explain his predicament but a peculiar weariness held him back. "Friar Jeremy and I opted to stay. We've heard the rumours, yes, but we cherish the hope that, if we show these Roundheads that we mean them no harm, they'll leave us in peace."

Even as he spoke he knew the Corporal wouldn't accept his rationale, any more than he did himself. Molloy washed down the last of his bread and asked if he might refill the mugs of the other men. Malcolm waved him on. Jeremy entered the refectory with a large jug of ale and a smaller one of wine. He jovially offered it to the men, some of whom stood to accept his invitation.

The Corporal returned to Malcolm but before he could respond with an expected (and to Malcolm at this point tiresome) appeal to follow the others into exile, another man interjected: "Excuse me Friar...I don't mean to intrude, but could I have a word?"

The Corporal stood up to give way to the civilian. The man had a peculiar questioning expression, as if he was waiting for an answer to some great riddle that nobody had yet been able to solve for him. And was that an *English* accent?

"My name is Peter, and I have a problem that you might be able to help with me. You see, I've decided to stay on in Callan to defend the town. But last night I got thrown out of my lodgings after a blazing row with the landlady. She disapproved of my beliefs and so, well, I have nowhere to go. I could leave Callan. Wagons are preparing to take at least a hundred people out tomorrow, to somewhere safer, but I...I was wondering...with your friends, I mean, the friars...all gone from here...would you maybe have room for me...just sleeping quarters...for a few nights?"

Malcolm chuckled. "A few nights or a few days... that's about as long as I and my colleague may have to live in this world, let alone at the abbey..."

Peter sighed. "Yes, and of course I'll be joining the soldiers and militia inside the Town Wall when I hear the signal to be at my post. I'm told the bells of St. Mary's will ring non-stop for ten minutes. So it's just till then....three or four days I imagine... maybe a week. We're not sure how long it will take the enemy to reach Callan. Cromwell has been known to force-march his troops to achieve an objective quicker than one might allow for..."

Malcolm laid a hand on Peter's shoulder. "You are most welcome to stay here. Would you mind helping us with the water collection from the well...baking maybe...and other little tasks...Do you wish to join us in prayer at dawn?"

Peter shied away. "Prayer...at dawn. Not that I'm afraid. You see, this is what angered the landlady. I'm an atheist. It's why I left England. I faced a flogging or the scaffold for my belief...or non-belief. Yes, I know it's maybe a bit cheeky asking a religious man like you to take pity on me. I'll understand if you refuse..."

Malcolm took a few seconds to register this rare phenomenon. He'd never met an atheist. This merited further analysis.

Haltingly, he replied: "Your beliefs are irrelevant to me, Peter. Needless to say I don't share the view that there's no God. I wouldn't be wearing this habit or sitting here in this Priory if I did. But I see you as a fellow human being in need, and as such deserving of help. Christ said: come to me all you who are heavy-laden and in distress and I will give you rest...You mightn't be a believer, but right now you're about to benefit from another man's belief...if you don't mind me putting it like that."

Peter seemed nonplussed, but then broke into a hesitant smile. "Thank you, Friar..."

"Malcolm. Call me Malcolm."

*

Malcolm stretched and rose, yawning, in his cell. He washed and said a quick prayer before proceeding straight to the refectory for breakfast. Jeremy had called him. Only two days had passed since the others left and already the daily routine had been broken.

They'd skipped dawn prayers and Divine Office, and couldn't celebrate Mass without the sacred vessels. The priestly vestments had also been taken, he discovered. He thought they'd be left alone. Jeremy and himself would attend Mass at St. Mary's Parish Church later. No doubt Fr. Brannigan would be surprised to see them, but he'd surely appreciate the changed circumstances.

Their guest was proving a godsend despite being an unbeliever. He'd cleaned and dusted, and cooked to earn his keep, and he was a genial conversationalist

Listening to the man's extraordinary tale Malcolm had developed a bond of friendship and mutual respect with him. Apart from his atheism, which was an abhorrent deviation in any human being, Peter's other ideas and beliefs were not far removed from his own.

He espoused a universal brotherhood of man, an abandonment of the kind of self-seeking attitude that led to wars and civic upheavals, and the pursuit of wisdom and study, which was lamentably restricted at the abbey by the absence of its beloved library. He emphasised too the value of service to one's fellow man and the need to listen to other people's ideas and be receptive to them within reason.

These could have come straight out of the Augustinian Order's own handbook. He wondered what plan God could have for Peter, given his atheism. Was he testing him? Or had he sent Peter to test their own faith at this fraught and deadly phase of their life-mission?

Peter was in the refectory when Malcolm and Jeremy entered. He had laid the table and prepared their meal for them. Upon seeing them he pulled out chairs, and invited them to sit. The large oatmeal loaf had been sliced into three precisely equal parts and laid out on the wooden platters.

When they sat he poured water for Malcolm and ale for Jeremy.

"Enough Peter...you're spoiling us" Malcolm soothed. Peter sat at right angles to Malcolm, who had Jeremy sitting to the other side of him.

"Well, did you sleep well in our humble place of refuge?"

"Better than I have for months...since leaving England I'd safely say. So...did you, ah...say all the prayers this morning?"

Malcolm shrugged. He used the seconds required to chew his bread to think of an answer. He felt cornered, his mouth a rictus of unease: "Less praying than usual, I'm afraid. We're running a severely truncated version of what we normally do here. We don't have a choice. The Prior granted us special dispensation to skip some of the more formal observances for the duration of this emergency. Except that I don't see us ever getting back to normal..."

Jeremy spoke after mopping away an ale spill from the table: "The Prior arranged for horses to take us to safety if...if we change our minds and decide to scarper. We won't be dong that of course but you, Peter...you feel free to avail of that opportunity. You can be far away from here before those devils arrive..."

"Thank you Jeremy. That's very considerate of you. I might take you up on that. I'll wait until I hear the signal. I'm more inclined to stay and fight, as I've promised the other volunteers, but the allure of escape looms large in my self-serving little head I'm afraid...at least right now when I think of it."

Malcolm rejoined: "We won't think any less of you. It wouldn't be desertion. You're not a soldier. You can leave Callan any time you wish..."

Peter was helping himself to a slice of griddle cake. Malcolm reached for another hunk of bread. He didn't want to press Peter on his beliefs but felt impelled to broach the subject.

"I was thinking of what you told me. You've been through a ghastly ordeal...but, if you don't mind me asking...do you ever have even the slightest...scintilla... of a doubt about your belief that God doesn't exist?"

Peter's questioning demeanour tensed; his eyebrows rising further and his lips quivering. Malcolm presumed that his mind was preparing a finely-tuned response.

"Not any serious doubts, but...in recent weeks, I've had vague feelings of...disquiet, you might say. Not a suspicion that there might be something out there, a creator or divine authority, but a sense of bafflement. I can't give credence to this simplistic notion of a Supreme Being overseeing everything, but I can't get my head around just how everything came into existence. I mean...at the very beginning...way back, when it all started..."

Malcolm saw a clear opening. "Surely that points to an agency or mind that was responsible for everything coming into being?"

Peter sat back, smirking. "But not necessarily a fatherly figure, a man who instructs a band of mere mortals to write all his great wisdom in a book that must then be taken as the absolute truth..."

Malcolm digested his comments, mulling them over. "When you put it like that it does become less easy to accept...for a layman unfamiliar with scripture and church teaching...but words can be deceptive..."

Jeremy broke the two minute silence at the table that followed. "Well, we'll find out soon whether God exits and there's an afterlife when those former friends of yours come calling, Peter. Eh?" He clapped his belly and laughed wheezily.

"Speak for yourself...I might not be here to receive the answer to the greatest questions of all if I take a fancy to that spare horse you mentioned...unless my curiosity wins out and I decide I need to know. If you don't mind my asking, do either of you men ever have a doubt...about your God?"

Malcolm had to be honest, or risk breaching his binding Augustinian vows: "Sadly, yes...not serious ones, but no matter how long we pray and toil and meditate and reason things out those little arrows of uncertainty, whether they originate in Hell or elsewhere, occasionally hit their target and disrupt our innermost cogitations. One of our own members in Callan had been having a vocational crisis. He left with the others, but I suspect he may quit the Order itself soon judging by his persistent questioning of his faith, his unrelenting scepticism..."

Peter wiped his lips and stood, taking the empty platters from the others. Malcolm admired his selfless service and honesty and prayed quietly that the man might find God... before it was too late.

***

22

Shane couldn't contain his joy. He and Luke had been granted permission to see the stables at Butler Castle where cavalry horses were quartered.

In normal times, he learned, only a few horses would ever be stabled there. But now, with the war drawing closer to Callan, more than fifty of these magnificent creatures were being groomed, fed and generally looked after as part of the town's militarisation. Luke's father had connections at the castle, having shoed several horses for the cavalry.

The stable yard at the castle wasn't as large as the general courtyard but it still drew a gasp from Shane. He beheld line upon line of half-doors, with horses leaning over some of them. Soldiers in the middle of the yard warmed themselves at a fire in a rusty barrel that blazed and belched thick smoke into the air. A squally breeze fanned it across the yard. Shane coughed after inhaling a smudge of soot.

Other soldiers stood about chatting or cleaning their guns. A group sat hunched around a map spread on the ground. Were they planning for the war?

Five men were passing from one stable to another with buckets of water and sacks of fodder. Some stable doors had been opened, and men wielding brooms and shovels stood poised to enter, presumably to clean up.

The boys followed slowly in the wake of the feeding men, not wishing to distract them from their work. As they passed each stable, Shane eagerly sought out his beloved friend, as he now thought of the horse with the milk spill on her forehead. If a horse hadn't its head protruding over a half-door, he stood on tiptoes to inspect, squinting to make out its form in the shadowy cubicle.

Fifteen stables he passed. He counted them frantically, disheartened each time his friend wasn't there. He asked Luke to check the twenty-five stables at the opposite side of the yard. Peering into the last of the stables on his side, he ran to Luke, who had got through a third of his quota.

Luke cast him a sombre look. "Maybe she's not here any more. Horses get sick, like us.She might be dead for all we know"

Shane felt a surge of anger. "I'll hit you; I swear I will, if you say that again!"

He left Luke standing, and half-walked, half-ran in search of the horse. Then, three stables from the end of the line, he caught the unmistakable sight of his friend, and the horse knew him too.

Shane rushed to the half-door, pungent whiffs of straw and oats greeting him. The horse, seemingly aware that Shane couldn't reach high enough, bowed its head to meet him halfway. Tears of relief welled up... he wanted to kiss the animal. A silly emotion, he realised quickly. He was content to tickle her behind the ears and stroke its neck. The mane felt fluffy to the touch, like the fur of an extra large cat.

The horse whistled softly. Shane gaped into her chestnut eyes, soulful penetrating orbs that strove to say what words couldn't. Was she trying to tell him something...bridge the gulf between human and animal as no horse had ever done?

Another silly thought that he banished instantly.

Making sure nobody was close by to hear, he whispered: "I hope you're not too lonely in there. Don't worry. Once you've helped the cavalry you'll be back in a lovely field, grazing and running. And I'll be looking out for you."

He heard Luke's footfalls on the cobbles. Stepping back from the half-door, he straightened and tried clumsily to hide his affection.

"We'd better go" Luke said, "The yard is to be closed to outsiders shortly. A fellow just told me. Is that the horse you took a fancy to?"

Shane avoided his gaze. "Fancy to? What do you mean? I just wanted to have a look."

They exited the yard and left Butler Castle behind them, trudging in silence towards the Cross. Shane whimpered: "Sorry. I didn't really mean I'd hit you. Only I thought you wouldn't stay long enough to..."

"To let you find the horse?"

Shane nodded curtly.

Luke turned away as he spoke, kicking pebbles in front of him: "Dad says it's best not to get too fond of a horse that's going to war. Says that makes it easier if the horse...you know...doesn't survive..."

Shane stopped on the footpath. "Don't say that. He'll be okay. I'll ask Father Brannigan to pray for her. That's if it's alright to pray for a horse. I'm not sure..."

"Dad says Father Brannigan will pray for anyone if you give him enough money. Says he'll pray without money too but he puts a bigger effort into it if you pay him. Not sure about horses though."

*

Malcolm led the way to the battlements on the bell tower of the abbey church. It would be a pity, he thought, not to avail of such a calm cloudless sky.

Peter followed on; both of them treading carefully up the ancient stairway to the highest point on the old church. Malcolm carried a storm lantern and his portable telescope. Peter brought the bottle of wine and the cakes. Their footfalls echoed along the passage in the stillness of the night.

Malcolm shivered despite the extra clothing, and the woolen cap wrapped around his ears. He envied Jeremy who they'd left sleeping in his Priory cell. But freezing air was a small price to pay for a clear view of the heavens.

Even in his childhood Malcolm had little interest in recreational outdoor indulgence of the culinary or imbibing sort. Now he fancied a rare treat. Having given so much of his life to the Order he felt entitled to enjoy a brief sampling of worldly leisure, a break from the seemingly endless routine of prayer and devotion.

On the flat roof Malcolm placed the lantern aloft on a crenellation and uncovered the stools that he'd taken up when the Prior insisted on viewing the cosmos last month. Then he mounted the telescope and adjusted the focus to allow for distance. He noticed it was still set for shorter range since his bird-watching stint.

The handgrip was ice-cold to the touch, its gold and silver bands twinkling in a moonbeam. He fixed the telescope on its tripod and pressed his eye to the ocular lens. The immensity of the universe again struck him as a humbling vista, beyond human understanding.

Accustomed to the relative positions of night sky attractions he swept across the firmament to find Mars. There it was: a bright reddish disc. He diverted to mighty Saturn, with that strange ring around it that many a stargazer mistook for a handle.

He saw Jupiter in its awesome glory, but without those four moons that a noted astronomer had seen orbiting it. This telescope obviously didn't have the same magnification. He stood up from his stool and invited Peter to have a look.

"Thanks. I've never seen the sky through one of these..."

Peter fiddled with the telescope for a few second before his eyes adjusted to the lens. "Ah, the moon. Wow. Could those really be mountains and seas? I've heard scholars argue about that. So many stars... No end to them. Is that dust scattered across the space between them..."

Malcolm, glad to see his friend intrigued, answered: "Possibly more stars, but so far away that they look like a dust cloud. That's according to this book I rescued from the library."

He opened a page and read. The author theorized that there were thousands of galaxies, and maybe even other universes apart from our own...

Peter was still engrossed. "I've got a dazzlingly bright one here..."

"Could be Venus. It's referred to the first star to appear in the sky after the sun sets and the last to disappear before sunrise...except it's not a star. It's a planet."

Peter observed in silence for more than a minute. Rising from the stool he said "Astonishing... such complexity and vastness. It makes me feel even less significant than I did five minutes ago. What is man when viewed in the context of...that?"

Malcolm saw his chance. "It doesn't make you any less inclined to dismiss the concept of a creator? I mean... when you see what a mind-boggling spectrum of worlds, objects, and vastnesses...does it not arouse your curiosity as to how all that came into being?"

"How? Yes. But I didn't see God when I looked up there. Have you seen him?"

"Through the telescope? No, but I believe I've seen evidence of his creation, of his existence. If God didn't bring this about, then who, or what, did?"

Peter sat on the other stool. "I'll have another look later, but let's have a drop of that wine. I think I need a drink after feasting my eyes on such..."

"Miracles?"

"Mysteries... anomalies. A lot out there to be explained."

"And are you open to the explanation that I alluded to, and that, when you think of it, solves a lot of those mysteries?"

Peter had uncorked the wine and was greedily devouring a cherry cake. Malcolm produced two goblets and poured for Peter.

Taking time to finish the cake, Peter rubbed the crumbs from his lips and answered. "I'll put it this way. In terms of percentages, I'd reckon there's a one percent chance that your God exists. A year ago I'd have said no percent."

Elated, Malcolm filled his own goblet. "That's progress, my friend."

"It's just being rational. I recognize that there's a tiny chance that something extraordinary is going on. That's all. It's prudent to do so. Life is full of surprises."

"There's hope for you yet, Peter. A little chink of light. God allows us free will, but I think he also drops the odd hint to help us work things out…"

Peter stood up, knocking over his stool, but holding firmly to his goblet of wine. The storm lantern caught his familiar questioning mode, though his face, usually pale, had a rush of blood to it. He reminded Malcolm of a stage actor whose big moment had come.

"Hope?" he rasped, emotion cracking his voice, "I lost that back in England when I put my trust in the likes of Cromwell to reform an unjust society. Instead, they took despotism to new levels. And then my dear friends and colleagues in the reformist movement were hounded like vermin. And hanged. Hope? I've lost all faith in humanity, never mind God, and hope… It might as well be one of those stars up there: Something for us to admire, or feel good about."

*

Sir Robert Talbot settled himself at the table in his newly renovated private dining room at Butler Castle. He hated having to confront his wife, Harriet, with the unpleasant reality but he didn't have a choice.

He'd gone out of his way to protect her from the horrors that had engulfed other parts of Ireland in recent weeks, knowing how feeble a disposition she had. She'd faint at the mention of violence, never mind the sight of a brawl or a bloodied corpse.

244

He rearranged the plates and cutlery. Not that they needed adjusting but nervousness gripped him. The room was a little stuffy, but comfortable and large enough for the two of them. He had opted to eschew the grandeur of the official dining room that hosted lavish banquets prior to his anti-plague crackdown.

Dr. Walsh had strongly advised him to keep contact with anyone who might have visited Kilkenny to a minimum. The disease had killed off a third of the City's military garrison. Being unable to divine who had or hadn't called to the Confederate Capital, as it was still called despite the dissolution of the Confederacy, he deemed it wise to keep everyone out of the capacious hall apart from trusted servants and his wife Harriet.

The days of big feasts to which one could invite friends and assorted pillars of society were on hold until the deadly epidemic had passed, as it would.

Everything eventually got sorted out. The plague ravaged KIlkenny and one or two other towns. But he'd read about similar bouts of that malady sweeping the land in centuries past. It came and went, taking humans who'd got infected and sparing those who had the good sense to avoid it.

The same with this present military quagmire: It all looked dreadful, and of course it was a severe blow to hopes of a united Catholic Ireland under the protection of His Majesty.

That setback, if the war did indeed go against his side, would also pass into the cold pages of history.

But what of his own place in the unfolding drama? He had no desire to give up his life just yet. At forty he had, he presumed, many years remaining to him; to be savoured, to achieve fulfillment as a lawyer, a landlord, and a merchant. The Governorship was just another milestone on life's journey. It certainly didn't need to be his last.

The trick was not to become ensnared in events beyond one's control through misjudgment, which was always possible when either of a set of alternative courses of action seemed equally tenable.

Misjudgment wasn't a concern for Sir Robert: On the basis of the evidence before him, surrender was the only viable option, there being no chance of beating an enemy so numerous and well-equipped, spurred on by fanatical leaders; and armed with the most powerful artillery train in Europe, possibly the world.

But the Corporation wanted him to lead a suicidal defence of Callan, as did the cavalry, the militia, and that insubordinate Captain whose wife strutted about the town teaching silly women how to throw rocks.

He had yet to respond to Cromwell's summons or to inform the Corporation and the other war-mongers of his unwillingness to stage a pointless defence. Donning his lawyer's hat, he didn't wish to give the No Surrender faction any time to thwart his plan to survive this madness.

Before responding to either his underlings or the Roundhead leader, he must be upfront with Harriet. He inspected his image in the wall mirror. He'd chosen his freshly laundered lavender periwig, the one she liked, and dabbed his body with a fresh arrangement of scents imported from France.

She'd appreciate these new aromas all the more, he suspected, if she knew that the ship that conveyed the perfumes to Ireland had barely avoided being sunk by the Regicide Navy. If that vessel had gone to the bottom of the Irish Sea he'd not now smell of those exotic French flowers and spices. He sniffed under an arm, inhaling the essences that were to die for, as those sailors almost did, God bless them.

A scratching on the door, and in she came, with Jackie Doodle in her arms, struggling to break free in search of scraps from the table. She dropped the snow-white poodle, his tongue lolling from meagre exertions, ears flopping and his docked pompom tail wagging gaily.

That fur needed brushing. It flapped in rope-like cords, showing signs of mild neglect, but then Harriet had more than her dog to be thinking about these days. The animal darted around the room chaotically.

"Jackie Doodle!" Harriet's voice had a noticeable starkness to it, or did he imagine that because of what he had to say to her?

The dog stopped, a front paw suspended in air, turning to heed its mistress. Taking his eyes off the frisky poodle Sir Robert took in his wife's magnificence. What a sight she presented today: A different dress, or two dresses rather, one more delectable than the other, with their bright contrasting fabrics and floral embroidery.

And her hair? My God, she had the sense to get rid of that big blob that resembled an enormous jelly about to topple. The style replacing it made her look positively ravishing: It hung in loose waves, flowing over her shoulders, and braded into a lovely high bun at the back; and around her creamy white neck hung a string of gleaming pearls.

"Oh Harriet, you've outdone yourself. What a picture of...of pristine beauty and elegance."

She blushed slightly, performing a quick twirl that caused her dresses to rotate and make a swish that sounded like a gust of wind.

"When you told me last night that you wished to speak to me of something rather important dear, I thought I should look my best, so I hope it's delightful news I'm about to hear, or at least a pleasant surprise."

Opening his mouth to speak, he was struck speechless. *God, she has it all wrong...I knew I should have told her before now....damn.* "Well, dear, as I said, it's an important matter, but sit down...the cook will be here in a minute or two."

He steeled himself as best he could as she poured herself a goblet of wine from the decanter. He filled his own silver chalice and suddenly felt as if this might be his proverbial Last Supper and he The Christ about to share grim tidings.

"Excellent vintage" she crooned, after downing half the measure. "Do you propose to tell me now, or wait until we have finished our meal, dearest?"

He hesitated, at first glad of another excuse to delay, but tightening his fists under the table and taking a deep breath he let the words form on his lips:

"I may as well tell you, Harriet. You know how I've tried my damndest to avoid any mention of the...ah...military affairs...the war, the awfully complicated and ever-changing political crisis. I know you abhor such talk and you don't care to discuss such things...but we have to face up to some sober facts because, my dear, the war is getting dangerously closer and within the space of a week, maybe less, it will be, I'm afraid, upon us..."

"What? I thought you said that awful business would be disposed of and you'd be moving to an even better position in another town?"

"I did, and I was unfortunately mistaken in my analysis. But as for moving...that's something we might be doing. You see, dear, this town hasn't a hope of fending off an enemy attack…an enemy who's drawing nearer to us by the day…by the hour. Mr. Cromwell has offered me the opportunity to surrender and I believe I ought to accept his offer. I…I mean, you see… all of us will be allowed to leave Callan unmolested. If, on the other hand, I were to refuse this offer, the full might of the enemy will be unleashed, and I'm sure that even you, dear, would appreciate the implications of such a calamity…"

Brooding, he continued: "Frankly I don't wish to end up like poor Sir Arthur Aston, the garrison commander at Drogheda. He dillydallied too much when asked to surrender…and paid the price. Can you believe: he was beaten to death with his own wooden leg?"

She shot him a quizzical glance. "But you don't have a wooden leg, dear!"

"No, thankfully, but I'm sure they'd find to something to beat me with!"

Harriet had paled. She stared open-mouthed. On the floor, nibbling at her ankle, Jackie Doodle whined pathetically as if acknowledging the hopelessness of Callan's position.

Her gaze focused between the correctly positioned knife and fork in front of her, she said in a low monotone: "So you'll be leaving soon then. I won't be prevented from accompanying you, will I?

"Oh course not."

"And Jackie Doodle…I know he's only a dog, but I think the world of him…"

"Yes, Jackie Doodle can come too. Look Harriet, I'd love to be able say that as Governor I'll be leading a fierce defence of this town; like those dashing melodramatic fellows you see depicted in tapestries…but the situation is hopeless."

"Oh I don't think any less of you…So when do we leave?"

God, she was taking it rather well. "I can't name the day …yet. When the Roundhead army arrives on the outskirts I expect a second summons will be issued. I'll arrange a parley to let them know that the town is surrendering…and then…we leave."

She looked distracted, biting her lower lip, Maybe it was getting to her now.

"I know it's a lot to digest, dearest, but…"

Suddenly she giggled "I'm alright, I'm just thinking: what should I wear on the day? I mean, what would be most apt in the circumstances. It won't be a celebratory occasion, so something I think more subdued than…this." She pointed disdainfully at her luscious multihued garb.

Sir Robert sighed. He felt a surge of relief, now that he'd found the courage tell Harriet. But he wouldn't share his decision with the Corporation- or anyone else- until the last possible moment.

A cocktail of conflicting emotions stirred inside him as the cook and two servants entered the room and began serving. It wouldn't be his Last Supper, but not the most enjoyable meal either.

Jackie Doodle yelped as Sir Robert threw down a morsel of quail to him. As the dog nibbled, the Governor caught the whiff of a scent he couldn't place from the animal. Harriet powdered and perfumed him each morning before taking him for walkies.

The poodle would soon join Harriet and himself in exile. Not elsewhere in Ireland if he could help it, but as far removed from this benighted country as he could manage: France or Spain would be nice…Austria maybe.

*

Mathias Blunt's diary: Last week of January 1650

On the move again after six weeks of hanging about in this stinking Irish weather. I'm relieved to be leaving this soggy, rain saturated weed-infested valley we've been camping in for the past three days. We'll put it behind us later today, but first we can lounge about, smoking, chatting, playing dice, or in my case, inscribing my thoughts in this diary.

Good to be outside again in the sunshine, week and heatless though it is, after listening to the ferocious pelting of the rain on the canvass. If I had to stare at the walls of that greasy tent for much longer I'd have gone slightly mad I believe.

Now I can breathe the country air again, apart from fanning away the fumes from the dozens of campfires over some of which carcasses are roasting: Livestock given or seized, depending on the owners' loyalty to our cause or lack of it. Mind you, meat from papist pigs or sheep isn't any less succulent.

Soldiers are splashing through puddles, cursing when the water gets into their boots or mud spatters their eyes. Some men sharpen their swords, wisely because the enemy is likely to offer tougher resistance once we draw nearer to his dark papist lair.

Scores of horses are being hitched up to wagons or artillery in readiness for our next big push. We need to allow for delays, with all the potholes in what the Irish think of as roads; and the marshy ground that abounds in this devilish terrain doesn't help. Whatever about the challenges it might pose to marching troops and cavalry, the land truly conspires against our artillery. Those big iron wheels sink with a sickening squelch, as if underground fiends are dragging them down, and it can take ages to free them.

Of course we get rain back home too, but not every second day. This could be God's punishment on the Irish for their sedition, for forcing us to cross the sea to restore this wilderness of forests, savagery, and backward agricultural practises to some semblance of a civilised land worthy of being part of our Commonwealth.

I shouldn't complain, but it's unfortunate that God's punishment has to rain on us with equal vigour owing to our proximity to the foe.

Our objective is Kilkenny, seat of the most evil conspiracy to raise its foul head since Herod's plot to kill the infant Jesus. The way to this City of the Antichrist lies open to us, apart from a few towns in our path that we expect will quickly buckle when they perceive our numerical and technical superiority.

Preliminary summonses have been issued to them, and to assorted castles and makeshift fortifications, and already most of them have either wisely surrendered or indicated a willingness to consider terms.

My elation upon learning of our progress, however, quickly turned to melancholy. Our godly Commander Cromwell has decided to split his army in two and to advance on Kilkenny from different directions. A perfectly logical and strategically laudable decision and I don't question the ways of our leaders, but I've been told that the Commander will not be heading the force to which I have been assigned.

This will be commanded by Colonel Reynolds. He's an officer of unimpeachable quality but I'd much prefer to be led by God's own Leader of Men.

Most of the lads I've come to know and trust over the past four-and-a-half months are now marching towards Mallow behind

Cromwell's banner, and will soon be crossing the Blackwater River, heading from there through Counties Limerick and Tipperary and then into the heart of enemy territory. How I envy them, with Christ himself via Cromwell shining his light on their cause.

Our force under Reynolds is moving in the direction of Carrick-on-Suir, in County Tipperary, and the aim, I understand, is to link up with the Commander's force, hopefully close to Kilkenny.

The Sergeant struts about here in the camp, somewhere in County Cork close to the Tipperary border, reminding us that our meal-break ends in twenty minutes and that we have a long march ahead of us. It's back to the war for us, he hollers. He casts a disdainful glance at me, possibly not approving of me scribbling in the middle of our glorious campaign. I'd better finish writing.

I notice that some men who had given up beer are freely swilling it, forsaking their pledge of abstinence. I'm tempted to have a mug myself. After all, God changed water into wine, so what can the objection be to drinking? Still, I'll check with the chaplain before indulging. This is no time to be imperilling my immortal soul.

I must write to Meg. It's been weeks since I shared my thoughts, and I must reveal some changes to my original proposition to her.

I've abandoned my dewy-eyed notion of retiring and living here in on land granted for my service to England. Talking to some of the men I've seen the error of my judgement. Nigel from Sussex, a straight-talking no-nonsense soldier recently converted to Puritanism, looked me at me as if I'd grown horns when I told him of my vision of married bliss on a bucolic Irish farmstead.

"Have you learned nothing from your stint here?" he asked, incredulous, "How long do you think you'd be living your life of quiet retirement before an Irish savage crept up behind you one night and ripped your soppy heart out? There's bound to be a few of the vermin left after we've done our job!"

So what would he do with his land allotment, I asked him. Smugly, he informed me that he'd sell it first chance he got, and live off the money.

Another man, whose name I've forgotten, had another idea, and it's the one that appeals to me: Keep the land but don't stay in Ireland, he suggested. "You can absent yourself from this hellish place and rent the land...from your cosy home back in England.

That way you make money without the risk of having your throat cut or your house torched...! "

That clinched it for me. How could I even think of compromising Meg's safety by inveigling her into a country crawling with savages and papists? She wouldn't sleep a wink from worrying in this accursed place.

I hate having to tell her of my change of plan. Mind-changing is a womanly weakness, and I hope she doesn't interpret this as a flaw in my character. God forbid that she'll still want to settle in Ireland. I have only myself to blame if she insists on sticking to my original suggestion.

Here comes the Sergeant again. I'd better put away my quill.

*

Roused from his daydreaming by the master's raucous yelp, Shane surveyed the little spread of rushes on his school desk. "Now boys go to it and please… do justice to our dear Saint Brigid. She's our great protector and we're going to need all the protection we can get in the coming days and weeks!"

Shane and his classmates had pulled the rushes from the King's River that morning when the Master marched them all down. He felt like a trooper as they trudged in pairs to the riverbank. It felt good, even with squally rain smattering their faces and dampening their clothes. Anything was better than lessons.

Following the instructions that the Master had repeated several days running, Shane took a length of soft rush and folded it carefully over another length. He'd forgotten exactly what came next so he sneaked a peek at the desk beside him. Yes, that was it. The centre had to be a woven square. It began to take shape. Rather slowly but it looked okay.

He stole another glance at the star pupil whose cross was completed. He was standing and proudly showing it off to the Master. Counihan nodded at him to sit down and began a walk around the classroom to see how the others were doing. Taking Shane's effort in his hands, he frowned, but gave it back, saying: "It's bigger than it ought to be, but that's fine. Hurry up, and get started on another."

Shane completed his task, laid the cross to his left and began weaving the next one. He wondered if the cross-making would continue all day. The Master had stressed the urgency of the exercise: He wanted crosses for every household within the walls of Callan.

The ones outside the walls would have to make their own. They wouldn't be in such need of protection; he'd said, as the invaders, if and when they came, would be concentrating on the walled town. The supposedly best protected part of town could turn out to be the least safe; he'd explained.

An extra-large cross was to be fashioned, he added, for display in St. Mary's parish church in South Street. Fr. Brannigan expected to have it later that day. It would adorn the wall behind the altar for a special Saint Brigid's Day Mass. The gifted pupils would be assigned to make that cross.

Shane assumed he wouldn't be one of them, given that he was way behind the rest of the class who'd produced half-a-dozen in the time he'd taken to weave two. The stacks of crosses grew higher as the day progressed, with not a sound in the room apart from the swishing and scratching of interweaving rushes.

During the midday break, the lads ran wild around the playground. What a relief to be able to breathe the fresh air again after hours of weaving.

Some played soldiers. Shane didn't join them. The chatter he'd heard in the streets and shops about the war soon coming to town partly frightened, partly elated him. But he wasn't in the mood to make light of what his mother had warned "might be the end for all of us."

He lisped that prayer to Saint Brigid. She'd never answered before, but maybe this time was different. This was a big emergency and she'd have to take notice, no matter how busy she was in Heaven.

A loud bang jolted him. The other boys fell silent as though struck dumb. The noise came from the castle that overlooked the school. Shane followed a group of boys to the wall separating the school from the castle. More loud bangs, and sharp popping sounds.

"They're practicing with their weapons", one boy shouted. "Can we see them?" another asked.

They climbed the wall, Shane helped up by a boy taller and stronger than himself. He saw the lines of uniformed men with pikes, all facing straw dummies tied to posts. Suddenly they rushed at the dummies, running them through with the pikes and screeching as they did so.

In another section of the courtyard soldiers were loading muskets. Others sat on the ground, pushing rods down the barrels of the guns or lighting what looked like thin lengths of rope attached to the muskets.

Somebody spotted the boys and came trotting over to the wall "Hey, get down off there, lads. Do you want to get hit by a ball? Ye'll see trouble soon enough. Off ye go. Scat!"

Shane was shaken by the urgency and anger in the soldier's voice...a red-faced bearded man in a dark green uniform, cowhide boots, and a funny looking three-sided hat. He glared up at them, waving a sabre above his head.

"Sorry Mister" a boy yelped, and they all fell back into the schoolyard.

The bell rang. They shuffled into the schoolhouse, agog with excitement at having caught sight of the brave soldiers who'd defend the town.

"Do you think our side will win?" a pupil asked a classmate nervously.

The Master had heard. Rapping the desk with his long blackthorn stick, he called for silence. "That boy has asked the question everyone in Callan wants answered", he said, slowly and with a hint of sadness. "And there's only one answer. It's not as easy as solving a mathematical problem or giving the correct answer to a question in your Latin exam.

"The answer is this: It all depends on our faith in the Lord God Almighty and his Church. If all of you pray with your hearts set on victory, then our lads may carry the day. Only God knows what's going to happen, but be sure to pray for Callan's salvation, and then it'll be in his hands, apart of course from the men of the garrison, and the volunteers who have taken up arms."

Shane thought he detected a tear in the master's eye. That couldn't be right. Masters never cried, and they'd beat you senseless if you cried yourself, but it definitely *looked like* a tear.

The Master arose and walked out to stand in front of his desk. He shook his head gravely. "I have to tell ye lads…this will be your last day in school, for…for I don't know long. It depends on how long it takes to win this terrible war. So, ye won't be hearing from me again…for a while. No point in giving ye homework, but I'm asking ye…again…to pray for our soldiers, and listen…If any of ye has a father who can hold a pike, use a sword, or fire a musket, remind him of his duty. You can tell him I asked you to."

He looked around, stopping to face each pupil. Shane felt that commanding gaze pierce his soul. It sent a tingling through his whole body. The Master's voice sounded different now, not as confident or superior as usual. "Ask him, on bended knee, if you have to…to join in the defence of Callan. Every man must play his part.

"Right lads, the remainder of this class will consist of you all leaving this room…no messing…and taking those Saint Brigid's Crosses to the homes of Callan. Divide into four groups, and do each of the streets. Podge, you're in charge of the East Street group…Malachai, take South Street. Malone…Malone! Asleep again are you? Only for the day that's in it, I'd have your hide. You lead the lads to the homes of West Street."

He stopped suddenly. Those *were* tears…streaming down his cheeks from both eyes. Shane was stunned and the whole class shared his feelings of disbelief and awkwardness. Jimmy Malone, rubbing his own tired eyes, rose from his desk and offered the Master his handkerchief. It wasn't in great condition, Shane thought. Would he get a beating?

Instead the Master nodded his thanks to Jimmy, took the cloth and wiped his face. Blowing his nose loudly, he pointed to the door. "Collect the crosses on the way out and get cracking before it's dark. A cross to every house, mind!"

"Yes Master!" they answered as one. Shane was baffled by the Master's show of what looked like weakness. But he didn't feel sorry for him. Not after the beatings he'd received. He still hated the sight of him. But he'd help to distribute the crosses as instructed.

What happened to the town was up to Saint Brigid now. He hoped she'd appreciate the effort they'd put into the crosses.

If she didn't, Callan could be in for its own Judgment Day, like the one foretold in the Book of Revelation.

23

Edward Comerford released his grip on the ceremonial mace that lay before him. He wasn't aware that he'd been clutching it so tightly until the clerk tactfully nudged him, whispering a reminder that protocol required that the official solid silver staff of office, upon which his initials EC were etched, should remain untouched while it rested on the meeting table.

Irked slightly by this overzealous attention to etiquette, Edward thanked the clerk and dismissed him. This wasn't a time for quibbling over formal niceties.

The eighteen aldermen sat at both sides of the table, all of them ill-at-ease. Some looked fierce and determined, with arms folded and bodies tensed; others subdued and downcast; others still exhibited a restless panicky demeanour. Leaning forward on the table, they frowned and fidgeted, their lower lips quivering: A reflection of their respective positions on the worsening military situation.

The clerk called the meeting to order. The Mayor curtly announced that all considerations of humdrum local administration and court fixtures could await another day, and that day could, he added ominously; be far in the future.

"Gentlemen, we have only one topic to consider today, and it is this!" He held up a parchment that displayed the hated enemy seal.

"Yesterday, the Governor received this summons from Oliver Cromwell, whose forces are advancing up through Munster. Already several towns have fallen to him without a shot being fired, after receiving similar demands to the one I have here. Such is the fear he instils, and given his record to date such fear is understandable. I will read the summons:

"...I should like to inform you that the Commonwealth force will, by the grace of God, be soon be arriving at the gates of your town. Kindly instruct your troops to lay down their arms and accept our unopposed entry into Callan and your lives will be spared. If, however, you opt to resist you will have only yourselves to blame for what follows. Expecting a favourable reply from you. Your Servant, Oliver Cromwell..."

There was stunned silenece, broken after a few seconds by Alderman Crotty who leapt to his feet. Edward expected a fiery reaction from him. Crotty, decked out in green jacket and sporting an extra large harp broach (presumably to appear more patriotic than the others, Edward thought), was shaking with anger; his face flushed, his teeth chattering. Edward feared he'd have a seizure.

Instead he let out a long sigh, intermixed with a low whine. "I say we tell this English upstart that if he attacks Callan it'll be him who'll have cause to be worried about what will happen. How dare he threaten us! And here...You say the Governor passed that letter to you. What does he think? Does he want to hold out, or what?"

Edward asked Crotty to be calm; getting excited wouldn't help, he soothed. The alderman grumpily sat down.

The Mayor sought to calm nerves. "To answer Alderman Crotty's question, the Governor specifically asked me to assure the Corporation that he will reflect carefully, having regard to all relevant civic, military and ethical factors, in deciding on a response to the surrender demand... and among the criteria underpinning his decision will be the stance adopted at this meeting of Callan Corporation. As you know, he is not bound by anything we say, but this firm pledge to take our views into account, I think you'll agree, is to be welcomed.

"Another development I must bring to your attention is that the Governor's decided, and I can see his logic, that in view of the grave situation facing the town, all meetings of Callan Corporation are henceforth suspended until further notice. In fairness, Sir Robert could have dissolved the Corporation on the day he assumed his position here, but he didn't, recognising, as he said to me, the importance of having a local voice to guide him in his deliberations..."

Alderman Clancy rose to his feet. He raised his hands in despair, his face a pale knot of anguish. "Gentlemen, we need to think very carefully about what response we send to the Governor in relation to this summons. The Roundheads are unstoppable! Haven't you heard of their successes? And of what they do to people who dare to stand in their way, let alone actively resist them?"

Crotty was up again. "Outrageous! Defeatist talk... you ought to be hanged as a traitor...or at the very least clapped into the stocks down in East Street... for ruffians and mad bitches to throw fruit at you, or empty pisspots on your treasonous carcass! Haven't you seen the job those lads did on the wall? It's better now than any town wall in Ireland, with the palisades, and earthworks added. And...and..what has all the preparation been for... all the drilling and practising with guns and pikes and swords on the fairground and the abbey meadow and the Motte Field if we're just going to roll over for this...priest killer?"

Alderman Brennan shouted "I support Alderman Clancy. We haven't a chace against the powerful army heading our way. If the choice is surrender or be butchered surely there's only one option open to us?"

"Treachery!" shouted aldermen Crotty, McCormack, and Lynch in unison.

"We'll fight till we drop. Lock up the traitors!" howled Alderman O' Brien as another member catcalled and frothed at the mouth behind him.

"We have to surrender, to save innocent lives", a feeble voice mumbled at the opposite end of the table from the Mayor. "It's not treasonous to act sensibly..." It was the voice of the eldest alderman, Mikey "The Dove" Hennessy, so-called due to his steadfast disapproval of armed action except to repel house breakers and highwaymen.

Crotty roared "No surrender, never, never! We have what it takes to win. The attackers will drown or be impaled on the stakes in the King's River. Our muskets will deal with the rest...And you, Mayor, you should lead us into battle. Will you do that? Will you?"

Before he could answer, Clancy was on his feet again, glaring at Crotty: "And tell me...what would that achieve, will he beat Cromwell over the head with the Callan Mace?"

Crotty began to lunge at Clancy but was restrained by two members who pulled him to the floor. The Mayor called for order, tapping the Mace on the table, though he knew it was not intended for that purpose. The clerk had a worried look, again eyeing a possible a breach of protocol, Edward assumed.

"I have already decided to remain in Callan, at my Westcourt residence. If robbed of my estates, as seems likely to happen, I will have to accept that punishment. My wife and children are leaving this evening for Galway. Not that anywhere in Ireland will necessarily be safe in the coming weeks and months, but I'm informed that conquering the barren land of Connaught appears not to be a priority for the invaders."

Mutterings of approval from the members; even Crotty pursed his lips with admiration. Then, after a moment's grace in response to the Mayor's declaration of intent, argument resumed and verbal jousts continued for over an hour, with heated exchanges on the issue of whether Callan should yield or fight.

Edward sat back, his hands clasped behind his head, allowing free rein to ferocious outpourings of emotion, pleading, and anger in the chamber.

Then, deciding it was time for the Corporation to adopt a position, he pressed for a vote: "All in favour of calling on the Governor to accept the enemy's surrender terms raise your hands."

Not a hand moved for several seconds. Eighteen pairs of eyes fixed on him. His heart thumped. He heard it above the ticking of the wall clock behind him and the rustling of feet under the table. Opinion was about evenly divided, he felt, so this could go either way.

Then a hand went up, and another. A pause followed. Aldermen looked at each other as if waiting to see how their colleagues voted. Eight hands were up: A longer pause.

Edward allowed almost half a minute to elapse before asking "And those against?"

Ten hands arose, all but Crotty's slowly and hesitantly. Three men had their heads bowed as they voted, possibly doubtful of their stance, the Mayor suspected.

Edward relaxed a little, his heart still pounding. He felt a cold sweat on his forehead; his mouth tasted of raw meat. He caught the whiff of ordure from further down the table.

He struggled to avoid showing emotion, or betraying the slightest hint of his own feelings, as he spoke: "It's settled then. The Corporation rejects the summons to surrender Callan to the Commonwealth army. I'll inform the Governor of this decision..."

The aldermen, sombre and muted, began filing out of the chamber, all but Jack Ryan, who Edward thought hadn't looked well earlier: Or at the last meeting either come to think of it. If he lost any more weight he'd be a walking skeleton.

Crotty was helping Ryan to his feet after he apparently swooned following the vote. The pressure had probably gotten to him. He seemed fine now, apart from bulging eyes and his tussled hair standing on end, being helped out by his like-minded anti-surrender colleague. *He'll be lucky if fainting is all he has to endure.*

In accordance with tradition, the Mayor was last to leave the chamber. The clerk, tearful and disconsolate, waited for him to rise and when he made toward the exit, handed him the Mace. Edward thanked him, suddenly overcome with emotion himself.

"Ah, Shawn, will this be the last time I'll sit in this chamber as Town Sovereign?"

As the clerk prepared to seal the entrance, Edward surveyed the empty room where so many voices had been raised, that evening and at hundreds of others since the day he'd first donned the Mayoral robes a decade before.

Sunbeams filtering across the table and chairs, two of which had been knocked over, were weaker than earlier, but starkly illuminated the dust particle spears that ran from floor to ceiling. A deathly quiet had replaced the riotous assembly, though its voices still babbled inside his head.

The clerk gently ushered him out of the way so he could close the door. Then he locked and bolted it. He offered his hand to the Sovereign and Edward shook it heartily.

"Go to your home, Shawn, to your wife and family. They'll need you now more than ever. We must all be strong. I'll be saying goodbye to my dear ones. They must flee. I suggest that you do likewise. As Mayor I must stay, but your work here is done. I fear Callan won't be safe for man or beast before long."

Shawn Holden wiped his cheeks with a sleeve and departed, quickening his pace without a backward glance as he headed off down South Street.

Standing on the footpath outside the Town Hall Edward held the Mace in both hands, its polished silver gleaming in the twilight. An icy breeze rattled his bones.

I'll possibly conceal it; store it away until the invasion is repelled.

Rooks squeaked from their rooftop perches opposite. *Mocking me.* Women passed by on their way to evening devotions at the church, some greeting him, others staring at the treasure he held as he boarded the waiting coach. The driver addressed him reverently, raising his hat. Edward envied him.

Why did I ever go into politics?
He felt shabby and deflated as the coach took him to Westcourt.

*

Shane felt angry with his mother, but admired her too as she repeated for the seventh time that she wouldn't leave her house and join her sister, Shane's Aunt Kathleen, at a farmstead two miles from Callan.

Aunt Kathleen and Mother sipped apple juice at the table, while Shane poked at the fire to stoke it back to life. It had fizzled out in the absence of Mother's usual attention to keeping it aglow.

"I'm grateful to you Kathleen, and you're surely right that it'll be safer at your place, but this is my home. When Jake was away fighting in that other war I waited here for him to return. I lit candles in the church every day for him. I said rosaries every evening.

"He did return to me, minus a leg, but we managed. Then when he died I got along too...with Shane here to help me. He's a good lad. Food has gotten scare in the past weeks because of this new war, but we cope. We always do..."

Kathleen frowned. "I know it's your home, Maura, and it means the world to you, but haven't you heard about these people...they're not like our soldiers. They're devils in human form. And it's this town they're after, so they can go on to ransack Kilkenny and make slaves of anyone living there. Paddy says they'll be here any day now. They've started marching from Cork...thousands of them, he says, and they have weapons that were never heard of in this country. They won't bother us out in Moonarch. There's nothing there to interest them, that's what Paddy says..."

Mother let the words bounce off her, as if the advice was meaningless. "You're so kind Kathleen, but I'm staying put. I'll take my chances. Sure, what would this Mr. Cromwell have against me, a poor woman living in a little house that doesn't even have real glass windows, and barely enough to eat and drink with the food shortage...?"

Shane blushed when Aunt Kathleen turned her head to glare at him. He fiddled with the poker, pretending not to notice her.

"What do you think, young Shane? Wouldn't you be happier, not to mention safer, at Moonarch with us. Will you tell your mother to have sense?"

Shane looked at Mother, searching her face for a hint of what he should say. He knew what she wanted, but would she wish him to give his own opinion or just support her in her resolve to stay in Callan? He slumped forward, facing the fire and staring into it. Poking at the dying embers, he felt a tug-of-war inside his head. "I think I'd like to be with you, Aunt Kathleen, and uncle Paddy in Moonarch...but if Mother stays here then I'll not be leaving either. I couldn't do that. Besides, Master Counihan says we must all play our part in fighting the invaders...we can't run away, he says. And Father Brannigan said we're to be brave..."

Aunt Kathleen finished her cup of apple juice and stood up, wrapping her woolen winter shawl around her and reaching for the empty basket that she'd used to bring eggs and meat to the house.

"If you change your mind Maura, and you can find a coach to take you to Moonarch you'll be welcome. I can't do more than invite you...I'll pray for you and Shane, but please, do reconsider..."

She looked sad and beaten as she opened the door to leave. "God keep you safe Maura" she lisped, and closed the door slowly behind her.

Mother rose and went to Shane. She put an arm around him. She didn't do that often. And she was crying.

Shane dropped the poker and stood, removing his mother's arm gently. "I'll boil the kettle Mother, and the eggs...and cut some bread..."

He left her at the fireside and went to prepare supper. He shivered as he poured water into the kettle from the wooden pail. Somehow the house felt different...less safe...as if an invisible protective canopy had been pulled away.

He'd have preferred to leave, but what if Mother was gone when he returned? That would be worse than death itself, he thought.

*

The clatter of buckets outside distracted Malcolm. He put down the book he was reading.

He surveyed the twenty-five books resting on the otherwise empty shelves that lined three of the four walls. All that remained of the once lavishly stocked library: cheap printed copies of classics, some essential prayer books, and works devoted to the Augustinian way of life. The Prior certainly hadn't been over-generous in considering the intellectual needs or tastes of those choosing to stay at the abbey.

Then again, Fr. Kearney deemed the decision not to leave so unwise and baffling that his attitude to the books was understandable, especially given that a library wouldn't be safe from invaders intent on destroying anything that offended their beliefs.

The book he'd been reading wasn't among those included in the literary exodus. It was the work on astronomy that he'd picked up when a removal man dropped it…and how glad he was that he retrieved it.

It dealt with the great unfathomable cosmos that his telescope could only peep at: with its untold billions of stars, planets, comets and only God knew what other objects out there beyond our own embattled planet.

It was a recent publication as evidenced by the fact that it made no attempt to deny that the earth rotated around the sun, as older books did. Peter, in full atheistic flow, had made much of the Church's insistence on teachings that had since been discredited or at least had doubt cast upon them by scientific discovery.

Malcolm placed the book on a shelf that held three missals and a bible and went to see which of his colleagues had inadvertently distracted him. He'd been reading for hours and the sun seared into his skull when he exited the library. He stepped back into the shade of the cloister.

It was Peter lumbering through the grass, back from the well, a full bucket swinging in each hand and water spilling over the rims.

"No need to overdo it Peter. That'll keep us going for today."

Peter proceeded towards the refectory. "I'll join you shortly, Malcolm. I saw Jeremy in the garden on my way to the well. He seemed, ah…a bit lost. I'll see if he's alright."

Malcolm went back inside and sat in the library chair, one of just two in the large stone chamber with its sturdy wooden floor and ornate religious tapestries. He wouldn't resume reading. He didn't feel like it.

A bit lost Peter had said. That summed up how Jeremy had been acting these past few days. But maybe it went back further than that. He hadn't paid much attention to him when all the friars were at the abbey, but since the evacuation he'd had more time and opportunity to observe his devout colleague.

Jeremy loved gardening; he was the friar that the others had always deferred to on the subject of flowers or vegetables. He knew every plant by its common English and Irish names but also their Latin equivalents. There wasn't a plant that sprouted from God's fertile earth that Jeremy couldn't name and he'd tell you everything that could possibly be known about it, without once having to refer to a book or parchment.

That was what struck Malcolm the most about Jeremy when he arrived at the abbey and was introduced to the eldest member of Callan's Augustinian community. But in the past week, and now that he thought of it, for weeks before then, he'd noticed Jeremy getting strangely befuddled about things.

He struggled to recall the names of plants that he understood better than any other friar. After a few attempts the name would come to him. Malcolm hadn't paid any heed to that. Jeremy was of an age when, surely, a little forgetfulness could be forgiven. He remembered his own father getting a bit absent- minded, and his mother too; and neither of them was as ancient as Jeremy: thirty years younger possibly.

But he'd never heard of a problem such as the one that arose from Jeremy's apparent inability, as of two days ago, to recall any of the names of the friars who had departed… not even that of the Prior, despite having lived in the abbey with them for years, or decades in some instances.

Could that also be ascribed to the ageing process? He wasn't sure. It wasn't a subject on which he fancied himself as an expert. A physician would be better qualified to unravel how the human brain is affected by ageing.

"Malcolm!" Peter was calling outside.

He closed the library door and stepped out of the cloister. Peter was standing in the grass, looking downcast.

"Well Peter, how's Jeremy? You said he was a bit…"

264

"The poor man, yes…he was sitting on the ground, the rake beside him, with a withered leaf in his hands. He was pulling pieces off it and muttering to himself, as if talking to the leaf. I greeted him, but he just had this blank expression. Then, I couldn't believe this…he asked me who I was. I mean, he knows me because we've had meals together for the past three days…"

Malcolm took Peter by the arm and walked towards the garden. He'd look further into this, even if he didn't understand what exactly he was dealing with.

They walked slowly, Malcolm trying to think of what to say to the old friar.

Peter sighed. "Does it matter what state his head's in…if both of you are determined to wait here for the Roundheads? No offence…"

"I made my decision not to leave…because I couldn't abandon Jeremy, and because I respected his principled position. Remaining at his post, you might call it, like a captain going down with his ship…or one of the Christian martyrs upholding the faith…"

"And you still feel the same way about it…"

Malcolm stopped, a giddy sensation taking hold of him. "Questions arise…If Jeremy wasn't in possession of his faculties when he declared his intention to stay at the abbey, then I believe we'd all have responded differently to his announcement. Oh God, we joked that Jeremy would have to be forcibly removed to safety, kidnapped in effect. Now I'm beginning to wonder if we should have pursued that very course. My decision to stay was made without my being aware that this man might be suffering an illness of the mind. That would have rendered his apparent desire to put himself in harm's way in a completely different light…."

"So, are you going to… you know…get him out of here before it's too late?"

"I don't know. It's a predicament I didn't expect…And I can't think of anything in the teachings of my Order that would help me to decide which course…"

"Didn't you say that the locals are providing two horses at the eleventh hour in case you change your minds about staying?"

"Yes, I'd almost forgotten that, speaking of forgetfulness. But then…perhaps Jeremy, whatever about his condition right now, was in a sufficiently rational state of mind when he decided…apart from his forgetfulness…"

Peter's face had screwed itself into that comical questioning mode of his. "I'm afraid I can't help you there, Malcolm. I know that if I knew I was listening to a man whose mind was out of kilter I'd think twice before going along with any proposition from him, let alone one that clearly put my life in extreme, and, as in your case, completely unnecessary danger."

Malcolm was deep in thought. "Then again...I have to take account of God's potential role in all of this. Would the creator have allowed me to be persuaded to stay with Jeremy if it were not the ethically correct option? I must pray for his guidance."

Peter shrugged. "As you wish. Ah, here's our friend. He seems to recognize us as his mates at any rate, even if he forgets my name. He's waving at us."

Malcolm's initial gladness at seeing Jeremy changed to sorrow and despair as he drew closer to the garden. Jeremy's face was blackened with clay, as was his grey habit. Plant fragments rubbed into the clay were dropping to the ground.

He returned Jeremy's wave.

Am I laying down my life to accommodate the irrational whims of a lunatic? And, if so, am I not also irrational, I that ought to know the difference between reason and outright absurdity?

***

24

Sir Robert took another look at himself in the gilded mirror before leaving his quarters for the dining-cum-conference room at the castle. He hoped the extra layer of face-powder would help conceal the mounting anger and frustration he felt at the Corporation's response to the surrender demand.

Those idiots had lost touch with reality. That was clear. The aldermen still reveled in the grandeur of the Confederation, when the country had got a delicious taste of what Irish freedom might be like. But that hopeless quest for an independent Ireland was over. It evaporated the moment the first Roundhead soldier disembarked at Ringsend. There was no excuse at this point for the aldermen's romantic flights of fancy.

They knew what had befallen towns across Ireland that resisted. He'd offered silent prayers to his bedroom statue of the Angel Gabriel, beseeching the seraphic being to knock some sense into those blockheads. The angel wasn't, it seemed, inclined to oblige. Or maybe he hadn't heard his prayers. Would the endless masses and rosaries calling for the town's salvation fall on equally deaf or unsympathetic heavenly ears? He hoped not.

Outside the room his servant Gleeson waited. "Have they arrived?"

"Yes, Sir Robert...the newly appointed leader of the civilian militia, Eddie Morrissey, and Sergeant Darby Dingle, who heads the cavalry troop assigned to Callan...ah... following the unexpected departure of his superior, the renegade Captain Pratt, two nights ago. You'll recall that Pratt left a note apologizing and claiming to be motivated by concern for his family that has moved to Connaught."

"Pratt? Oh yes. He did tell me that things were getting a tad too hot in these parts for his liking..." Sir Robert didn't say the rest of what crossed his mind...that Pratt possibly had the right idea, in the circumstances.

Gleeson opened the door to the dining room; where at the end of its long table sat the two men who he hoped would not prove averse to the notion of avoiding unnecessary bloodshed, unlike the Corporation, or indeed the fiery Captain Gegan who, he'd been warned, was intent on defying any order to surrender. Gleeson asked if Sir Robert wished to be provided with his customary two loaded pistols for the meeting.

He waved Gleeson aside. He wanted to win them over, not get off on the wrong foot if he could avoid it.

"Ah gentlemen...no...Don't approach me... just resume your seats. Plague is still an issue, you understand?"

The two men mumbled assent and sat, settling their arms on the table. Sir Robert straightened his periwig. He'd chosen pink today for a change, the colour of joy and hope, both of which were in short supply these days.

The deportments of the men unnerved him. They were grim-faced and, he thought, suspicious. Their eyes betrayed a mistrust and dislike of him. *Never mind. I'm not a damned politician craving sympathy.* Dingle was even more flamboyantly attired than himself, his war-coat edged with silver lace. Under it he wore a standard cavalry buff jacket. An elegant green sash enfolded his waist, and a silk scarf was knotted around his neck. His hat, resting on the table, had the longest peacock feather Sir Robert had ever seen and the hatband held sprigs of oak, symbolic of battle- readiness.

Morrissey obviously hadn't bothered to dress for the visit. Sir Robert had noticed his rough blackened brown breeches and muddy boots when the militia leader stood. And he reckoned that the man's linen shirt hadn't been washed for a decade.

The scar under a cheekbone could have resulted from a brawl or a swordfight. Gegan had been schooling those volunteers in a form of amateur militarism: A loathsome practice that risked ceding power to the rabble. Morrissey had his woolen cap clasped so tightly on the table you'd think it was a pearl or a pouch of gold.

Sir Robert sat and extended his hands gracefully. "Gentlemen, I have summoned you here because, as you know, the military situation is changing by the day...by the hour. You've probably heard that Callan Corporation has rejected the enemy's surrender offer. I had passed the proposal to those esteemed gentlemen to elicit their ...opinion...of how to proceed.

"I am not, as you know, bound by the Corporation's votes or rulings, and indeed that body has since been dissolved pending the outcome of the war...but I thought it wise and proper to hear its voice. Be assured that I'm giving due consideration to its views, and that these will inform my own response to the growing military threat.

"I now seek your opinions gentlemen as to whether we...ah...should accept the surrender terms or...well...mount a spirited defence of Callan. Ah...before you speak, I should like to update you on the military position. I have this morning received information which, had it been available to the aldermen when they deliberated on this issue, might have prompted an altogether different, and I'm sure, less belligerent stance."

He paused to scrutinize his notes.

"The reports delivered to me- and I have no reason to doubt their provenance or accuracy- state that Cromwell, upon leaving his winter quarters in Cork, split his forces into two commands. One, under Colonel Reynolds, is heading this way to capture Kilkenny, with orders to secure any towns he encounters along the route. Callan is directly in his path. And the strength of this force? Upwards of two thousand infantry, fourteen hundred cavalry, plus an unknown number of dragoons.

"Gentlemen, Callan is defended by a total of thirteen hundred soldiers...most of them garrisoned here at Butler Castle. I'm sure you'll agree that the odds are far from favourable to us. And that's not all. As I've said, Cromwell divided his command. The second prong of this enormous push towards Kilkenny is led by the Lord General himself. It numbers, I'm told, about a thousand horsemen, three hundred dragoons, and between three and four hundred infantry. You can add or subtract a little from these figures, but I'm sure they're reasonably close to what's coming at us."

He paused to sip water and re-check his notes. After a deep breath, he resumed. "As I've told you, I asked the Corporation for its opinion, but those well-meaning patriotic men lacked the crucial and sobering information I now share with you. Before continuing, I would welcome your...evaluation...of the crisis we face, and how best to respond to it."

The men stared at each other. Morrissey had begun to squeeze his cap again and Dingle was pawing the peacock feather in his hat. Their grim flushed visages had turned pale; then reverted to grimness while retaining that deathly pallor...one that Sir Robert expected would blanch many a man's countenance in the coming days and weeks.

The Governor nodded charitably as Morrissey opened his mouth to speak, barely concealing his distaste for this citizen soldier who probably hadn't a clue about military etiquette or the stark nature of the threat Callan faced.

"Begging yer pardon Governor", he said, wiping his nose with a sleeve and rubbing it across his shirt.

Is he doing that to annoy me?

His voice was gruff and lacked respect, let alone decorum. "You said...what was it...two thousand soldiers...several troops of horse and dragoons...and another force under Cromwell that'll hit us from a different angle or on a different day. That's a mighty opposition, I agree, but I have to disagree with your estimate of our own strength. Thirteen hundred soldiers...yeah...but you didn't mention the militia.

"We count, too, Sir Robert, even if some army folk won't give us the time of day. Have you heard of the training? There are men out there today who, ten weeks ago, had never held a gun or a sword or pike. Now they can shoot straight and cut or hack as well as any soldier. There are maybe two hundred of us...and I know… this might sound daft, but their womenfolk want to help too...Captain Gegan's wife has been showing them how to fight, allowing for their weaker bodies of course.

"The Captain has changed his mind about the militia. He didn't think much of us to begin with, but now he tells me we'll do Callan proud. And we will, Sir Robert. We'll be waiting for them, however many of them Roundheads Cromwell sends skulking towards us. That's my answer to you, sir. Even if the enemy had been ten times stronger I'd still say: No Surrender!"

Morrissey sat back, arms folded, defiant... beads of sweat dappling his cheeks.

Sir Robert suppressed a sigh and tried to keep his composure. "And you, Darby?"

Darby Dingle shook his head. Leaning forward, he let out a gasp that broke the momentary silence. "Like my colleague here, Sir Robert, I and the men under my command have no appetite for surrender. The prevailing sentiment is that we must not yield an inch to the foe. We're proud of our military heritage and, speaking for myself I wouldn't dream of breaching a tradition stretching back centuries. My father, grandfather, and great-grandfather all fought bravely...never surrendering. It wasn't an option for them. Ever.

"I don't propose to be the first in my family to play the coward. No, not even, with the greatest respect to you, sir, if you were to issue a binding order to me to turn and run. Yes, I appreciative that your updated information on the strength of the forces confronting us does put a different complexion on things, but I'd also remind you, as my colleague already has, that our defence will be augmented by civilian fighters.

"The enemy cavalry does vastly outnumber my own sixty horsemen, and our highly prized mounts, but you know, Sir Robert, numbers aren't everything. A besieged force can repel a numerically superior enemy by sheer dogged determination. Tactics play a big part too, as you know. So, in spite of the direful scenario you've presented, all in good faith, I concede...I too adhere to the position that surrender must be ruled out completely...whatever the odds..."

Sir Robert felt like he'd just been kicked, however politely or obliquely, in the ribs...told to stuff himself. These men were hell-bent on insubordination, if not outright mutiny.

He wanted to let fly at these two cretins: One, a glory-seeking traditionalist obsessed by ideas of military honour and posthumous adulation; the other full of tavern-fuelled delusions of his home town winning against every outside challenge. *Probably thinks a battle is akin to a hurling match.*

He steeled himself, gently pushing aside his notes. "Very well gentlemen, I still have to have to make a decision as to whether this town will fight...or surrender. I've received the Corporation's opinion, and now you have added your voices to those advocating resistance. Captain Gegan shares your...ah...perspective.

"While I admire your devotion to duty, however, and your patriotism, I must take all relevant factors into account when deciding...including the likely, indeed inevitable consequences of losing to the enemy after refusing to surrender. I'm sure you both know what will happen...?"

They nodded, seemingly resigned to the worst. It was a crushing blow to his hopes for a bloodless outcome, but he'd allowed for it. He could simply overrule them and order a general surrender of the town, but that might provoke a wholesale mutiny and maybe cost him his life.

There was another option- not his preferred one- but that offered him, literally, a way out of Callan. It would also have the merit of avoiding carnage. Whatever the hotheads claimed, resistance would scarcely make a dent in the advancing juggernaut.

*

Mathias Blunt's diary

It has been a day of blessings and misgivings. The blessing came in the form of a messenger with news to warm our hearts, but that was later in the day. The misgivings, for me and I suspect for some of my fellow warriors, arise from an atypical assignment undertaken in good faith that may or may not have been warranted.

That's putting it diplomatically. I'd planned not to record the episode at all but now when I sit down to write I feel impelled to set forth what happened, if only to help cleanse it from my memory. I find sometimes that writing about something allows me to shed an unpleasant or distracting recollection, as though my quill could erase it.

We were roused early, just after dawn, to continue our march to Callan, the town we are ordered to capture and that we'd been warned might offer us resistance. The freezing air provides us with an incentive to keep moving. Exercise wards off the merciless cold that has replaced the weeks of lashing rain and slouching mud.

The countryside we're passing through is much the same as the terrain we've encountered elsewhere since we landed in Ireland, apart from different dialects among the speakers of both English and that damnable native tongue.

Half an hour into our march we found ourselves on the outskirts of a small village. It was unlike any village in England that I've seen in its primitive rawness. It had just one street along both sides of which stood the shabbiest excuse for housing.

All the dwellings were low-sized crude huts or cabins, fashioned I understand from a mixture of mud, wattles and sticks. From some of these smoke blew in thick wisps. Not just from the open doors but through the roofs that were thatched roughly with an entanglement of grass and God knows what other weeds or foliage. If viewed from a distance you'd think the houses spewing all that blue, white and black smoke were on fire.

The street itself was a dusty stripe in the earth smeared with animal dung. Our boots squelched in it, releasing the softer messes once the dry scabs were punctured. Emaciated mongrels lurked outside a few of the hovels. Seeing us approach they sat up and growled, ears stiffening: Vicious things.

Two soldiers cocked their pistols, expecting the dogs to attack. But the animals relented, perhaps realizing, as somebody jested, that it wasn't wise to defy the Commonwealth.

We had sufficient provisions so we didn't intend to bother the savages. As we passed along the street I saw their eyes peering out at us, some through layers of turf or tobacco smoke. They were circumspect enough not to draw punishment.

But as I stepped past the last of the cabins I was startled by a man who emerged abruptly from its pokey doorway in a puff of smoke... like a genie. He was low-sized, with blackened face, from the smoke probably, and huge probing eyes that rolled in their sockets like marbles.

He pulled off his soiled woolen cap and bowed reverently to us. How he survived inside that miserable hut I'll never know. I could see into its dark hellish interior, where five or six children and two adults, all dressed in rags, huddled together, staring at us.

Hundreds of soldiers had already exited the village, so I wondered if God might have intended this man to appear for my benefit.

The soldiers behind me, and to my left and right, were grumbling audibly, asking what the delay was. The Irishman was blabbering frantically in Gaelic to the soldier on my left, his woolen cap squeezed in his hands.

I thought he was begging, or pleading about something. The Sergeant came down the lines, shouting "what's the matter with you men; I didn't give orders to stop?"

We indicated the man and the Sergeant asked him if he spoke English. The man's blank expression indicated otherwise. So the Sergeant called Corporal Jenkins who had learned some Gaelic. Jenkins and the Irishman rambled away for almost a minute, the Corporal nodding impatiently in response to whatever the fellow was telling him.

The Corporal then translated for us. The man claimed he knew a dwelling where three people were assisting priests to escape and had been hiding papist clergy. The man would take us to the house, but only if we paid him three gold sovereigns in advance.

The Sergeant agreed to pay him once the culprits were pointed out, and the man reluctantly accepted that offer. The Sergeant then picked eight men, including myself. He instructed Corporal Jenkins, owing to his linguistic skills, to take charge of our group.

We were to go the house with the man to serve the righteous judgment of our Commonwealth. The location was less than a quarter of a mile on foot so we wouldn't need transport. It wouldn't be viable anyway because we had to negotiate our way through a small wood to reach the house.

The march towards Callan was thus delayed to accommodate this informant who, it seemed to me, was a tad too eager to help us. Given his circumstances I didn't blame him. With three gold sovereigns he'd likely be richer than anyone else in that squalid community of his. But I didn't admire his approach to us.

I didn't know why, but I had qualms from the moment the Sergeant ordered us to locate the alleged priest-helpers. Yes, the penalty for aiding and abetting a Catholic priest was death, and understandably so. But how were we to be sure that this man spoke the truth? That he wasn't motivated by greed, or, equally possible, a desire for revenge against someone, or an entire family, who he believed had wronged him?

As we set off, the informant leading the way, I prayed that he wasn't just using us to line his pockets or settle his private quarrels.

In my youth I'd heard of a man who falsely accused a woman of witchcraft because her husband had beaten him in a card game. Luckily for her, the case fell apart when his dishonesty came to light in court under cross-examination.

This present case was different though. The accuser's honesty wasn't being tested. We were acting on his information as if it were Gospel.

The beech wood was a tangle of weeds and thorn bushes. As with so much of this untamed land no effort had been made to remove these impediments.

The men cursed as thorns ripped the unprotected parts of their bodies, mainly hands and faces, but I noticed a man swearing and holding his crotch. Jenkins advised us to use our swords and unloaded muskets to beat a path through the wood.

274

Could it be, I wondered, that the Irishman had lured us into a trap? What if a band of savages awaited us in the wood? The Sergeant should have given more thought, I felt, to the prattling of this grubby little man before sending us off in search of priest-helpers. The prospect of dealing a blow to the papist cause might blind us to the possibilities of deceit or betrayal.

Thankfully, the wood didn't stretch too far and I felt relief when the sunlight returned after we stepped out into a settlement. This consisted of about a dozen houses, but these were stone and wooden buildings, and all separated from each other.

No smoke issued from the doorways but the houses had chimneys that emitted little puffs. Civilization had arrived in at least a few parts of this benighted island. The Irishman indicated that none of these was the house he had in mind.

He led us across a small field and out over a stile. We faced a two-storey stone house enclosed within a large yard. Farm buildings adjoined the house and turf was stacked high in front of its entrance. Corporal Jenkins reminded the man of his promise, translating for us. He must point out the culprits among those who dwelt in the house. The man nodded. Jenkins went to the door and rapped three times.

We heard the sound of hurried movement inside, clattering on floorboards, furniture shifting, and tableware being knocked over. Someone had a guilty conscience, it seemed.

Jenkins rapped again and shouted: "Open, do you hear...open or we'll have to..."

A latch clicked and the heavy wooden door squeaked open.

A tall well-dressed elderly man, quite unlike the unkempt primitive village folk, stood in the doorway. His closely cropped snow-white hair might possibly have made him look older than his age, and his lean, high cheek-boned face betokened a healthy diet. That white lace collar and spotless linen shirt hadn't been troubled by labour in the recent past, I guessed, nor those suntanned black leather boots.

"And what can I do you for you, gentlemen?" he asked, his voice low-toned and elegant.

Jenkins was taken aback at the man's relaxed demeanor. But maybe it aroused his suspicion too. Did it point to guilt? A man answering his door to armed troops ought to look surprised, if not

275

shocked. But Jenkins seemed relieved that the man could speak English.

The Corporal adopted a formal pose: "We've received a report that enemies of the Commonwealth reside here, specifically individuals who are involved in a conspiracy to help Catholic priests evade justice... and we'd like to have a word, with the...ah...suspects if we may."

The man's face broke into a thin but not disrespectful smile. "And which of us do you propose to...have a word with?" he lisped.

Jenkins sent a soldier outside who promptly came back in with the informant. The grubby chap looked deeply uncomfortable entering the house. Understandably, given that we'd require him to identify the culprits.

Jenkins asked the elderly gentleman to step aside and entered the house, beckoning us to follow him in. He asked the householder to gather all the family and anyone else residing in the house or attached buildings, to assemble in the spacious living room. He sent two soldiers to accompany the man as he went about this task.

Awaiting their return we seated ourselves on the wicker chairs arrayed around the living room. It wasn't a bad house, certainly compared to the multitude of human pigsties we'd seen thus far in Ireland.

This room had neatly kept crockery in a glass cupboard, a table for small meals, shelves of vases and carvings, a brace of stuffed pheasants and, to my disgust, a selection of Catholic plaster statues lined up on a mantelpiece above the embers of a hastily quenched fire. Had they burned incriminating evidence? Above the mantelpiece on the wall a clock encased in varnished ebony ticked quaintly. It reminded me of one in my childhood home.

That display on the mantelpiece had to go, I knew. In the centre a two-foot spotless statue of the Madonna depicted her with hands raised and a foot crushing the serpent; to either side of her crude likenesses of saints and members of the Holy Family barely had standing room, as if jostling for space to stay on the mantelpiece.

The others shared my revulsion. Jenkins was showing his distaste as he played with his cavalier-style moustache. Jenkins I'm told fought for the king before switching to the Parliamentary side; and he retained that twirled relic of his former loyalties.

Knowing that we'd be required to dispose of these idolatrous images I suggested we could dump them outside before we completed whatever business we had there. Another soldier found a cloth sack and we cleared the mantelpiece quickly, scarcely daring to touch the graven images as we dropped them into the sack.

A commotion distracted us. The door burst open and in stepped an attractive young woman of about nineteen or twenty, eyes inquiring and lips aquiver. Golden tresses framed her creamy complexion.

Was her slightly furtive deportment evidence of guilt? I had no idea. It might have indicated culpability-or meant nothing at all.

I'm ashamed to admit that she aroused me. Her red damask gown was a shade too large for her slim sensual form, but I liked the blue satin cloak that hung loosely around her shoulders, and those pleading motions of hers. She wore cherry pink sandals instead of the warmer footwear you'd expect this season. Her toes wiggled alluringly. If I hadn't been a Puritan, and this wasn't Ireland, I might have rushed to kiss her...and maybe, God help me, done more.

After this fine damsel came three curly-headed boys, clad in coarse farm tunics, followed by a portly woman who I took to be a dairymaid or servant because her stained white pinafore smelt of sour milk.

Another two women, possibly in their thirties or forties, stepped in behind these. They were less fashionably attired than the young woman, and may have been servants too. I noticed one of them was minus most of her teeth when she happened to gape at me.

Our men entered next, one nudging the informant in front of him with a pistol. This irked the man, who seemed to resent being treated roughly given his essential role in all of this.

Jenkins rose from his chair and ordered all the suspects to stand side by side in front of the fireplace. They complied, some with hands dangling before them, others posing as if to have their portraits painted.

I saw fear in their eyes. That could betoken guilt, or just a natural response to armed soldiers confronting them.

Jenkins rasped something in Gaelic to the informant. The man rubbed his chin thoughtfully and raised a bony finger to indicate the young woman whose beauty had struck me forcibly. Her jaw dropped, her mouth opened wide. Her tresses shook as she cast a terrified glance across at the old fellow who had admitted us, then at the others.

The informant seemed to be buried in thought, struggling to remember something or someone. T hen he hesitantly pointed at the elderly man, whose initial composure suddenly dropped away. His ruddy cheeks changed to a tomblike pallor.

Almost as an afterthought, he then casually swung his finger in the direction of the eldest of the three boys, whose reaction betrayed knowledge or suspicion of what might await him. He babbled in Gaelic and made wild gestures, directed first at us, then at his fellow suspects.

"Anyone else? Three of them...Is that it?" Jenkins shouted, quickly translating.

The man dithered again. He was clearly unsure of himself. He nodded, now avoiding any eye-contact with the suspects.

Jenkins snapped his fingers. "Right, you three...outside with us. The rest remain here." He didn't have to translate.

A soldier, holding the sack of statues, asked if he should leave them or take them out of the house.

Jenkins spat: "They must be destroyed, take the sack with you."

Jenkins selected five men and left the house with the three unfortunates fingered by the greedy, uncommonly loyal, or vengeful little man- depending on what his motive was.

Watching the three accused ones leave the house, and listening to what were presumably their protestations of innocence, I felt nothing for the boy or the elegant well-spoken Man of the House. I didn't hate them either- I felt complete indifference.

But a pang of deepest regret coursed through my veins and caused my heart to flutter when the young woman glanced back, her face a study in pleading, whether to me personally or to all of us I wasn't sure. Tears traced silvery paths down her cheeks and she'd started to sob. I looked away but her eyes had beguiled me.

The door slammed shut after the three principal suspects- as they'd clearly become- exited under guard. The ones remaining began howling and throwing insults at us in Gaelic. I stood up from my chair and bawled "Quiet...we'll be going soon...have patience!" Pointless of course because only the elegant old man understood English; and he'd gone.

I thanked God that I was among those left in the house to guard the others while justice, as I presumed, was being served on the culprits. I didn't wish to be part of an action about which I had grave doubts. The informant had offered not a whit of proof that those he accused were guilty of anything, let alone the grievous charge of priest-helping. But God's will be done.

The surly group at the fireplace stood, arms folded or hands clasped, occasionally whispering to each other, or looking at the clock behind them. I found myself glaring at it too. Its ticking was the only sound in the house when everyone, us and them, had stopped talking.

Twenty minutes passed. We were getting restless. Then I heard the welcome crunch of boots outside. The door opened and Jenkins stepped in, sombre and a little shaken. "It's done" he murmured, without looking at the trembling group still standing in line under the clock.

Ushering us out, he turned to the group and said, first in English and then in Gaelic "Do not leave this house until one hour has elapsed. Understood?"

Doubtful nods greeted his warning. I thought some of them looked content that their brief house arrest had ended.

Relieved to breathe the invigorating country air again, I shouldered my musket, adjusted my bandolier, and trod behind the others. We'd have to traverse that blasted wood again to get back to the army. It had taken an unscheduled break just to accommodate our quest.

As we drew away from the house and farm the man in front nudged me and pointed: I shuddered, stopping in my tracks. From the sturdy branches of an exceptionally tall oak three corpses swung, dangling gently in the same refreshing winter air I'd just inhaled.

If I hadn't known the purpose of our visit to that house I might have mistaken the three people for scarecrows, so banal and lifeless did they seem, with hands bound and mouths gagged.

Of course...that was why none of us in the house had heard anything of this...execution. Despite myself I had to glare at the doomed trio. The lovely woman's face I couldn't see because her back was turned to me. Her head hung limply, her lovely tresses falling to one side, blowing in the shivery breeze. One foot was

279

missing a sandal. It lay upturned in the grass… beneath her delicate swinging corpse.

The curly-headed boy had a pained look, as if he'd resisted, and the elegant man looked somewhat taller, hanging from a tree that he probably grew up with.

A little further on, I encountered a trail of broken plaster statues. Shards of the Virgin, St. Joseph, the Angel Gabriel and a host of other shattered graven images littered the approach to the farmhouse. I wondered if they'd been disposed of before or after the summary executions.

A third spectacle greeted me: Slumped at the entrance to the wood was the informant, the little man's tattered shirt blackened and blood-spattered, his mouth agape…his eyes frozen in disbelief.

"What happened to him?" I queried, walking on. Jenkins heard me. "He got greedy, said he deserved not three but ten sovereigns, said he'd have to live among hostile folk. When I refused his demand he uttered a foul affront to our leader-unrepeatable - and pronounced the Lord's name in vain. I shot the rascal where he stood. Any objections?"

None of us responded. Halfway through the wood another man alluded to the informant. "The Corporal saved some Irishman the trouble. You know…he could have fooled us about the whole thing. What kind of man would do that?"

I wanted to put the whole episode out of my mind. I asked him not to mention it again.

God be praised I can end my recollection of the day on a positive note. Our hearts leapt for joy when we reached our waiting comrades. Big news from Callan: its Military Governor, a devious fellow and reputedly a lawyer, has pledged to "look favourably" on our surrender terms. So, another bloodless triumph beckons.

I put aside my quill with mixed feelings tonight. Of relief, pride in our army's success, but also doubt, unresolved questions, and maybe a tinkle of shame.

***

25

January 31st 1650

I wish I'd changed into my shoes, Malcolm moaned, as he stepped out of the Priory after evening meal onto to wet frosty grass. It tickled his feet through the sandals. The fog that had shrouded the abbey meadow, reducing visibility to a few yards, had thinned considerably, so he set off to get that niggling chore out of the way before it slipped his mind.

Annoying that he'd left the telescope uncovered on the bell tower. Absorbed in thought and still a little distracted from the wine he'd had last night he'd forgotten that basic precaution of safeguarding the eyeglass against the elements. There hadn't been any rain yet but there might be before the day was over. Darkness would come soon so he'd better get moving.

Entering the church he felt an after-pang from the conversation he'd had with Jeremy at noontide. He'd relayed his final decision on the question of whether he'd stay or leave, which had returned to torment him in the wake of Jeremy's apparently confused mental state.

When Jeremy had handed him the butter across the table, he grasped the old friar's hand tightly and said: "Whatever happens my friend I'll be by your side. Our fate is in God's hands now."

Jeremy smiled and nodded, taking his hand away and proceeding to butter his bread without comment. Peter sipped his coffee and quipped: "I admire your faith and your decency Malcolm, and yours too Jeremy. You'll forgive a stubborn unbeliever for not joining in the rush to martyrdom, though I'll do what I can to defend this old town...even if some of the locals have taken a dislike to me..."

Malcolm gasped at the chill of the tower stairway as he headed up to the battlements. Reaching the top he experienced that mild twinge of euphoria he sometimes felt at this elevation. Closer to God, the Prior had whispered reverently the day he'd accompanied him to stargaze.

The empty wine bottle was there too, alongside the telescope. A sloppy oversight, but in the present circumstances...

He decided to rest for a minute, seating himself on the stool from which he dusted off little frost particles.

The surrounding landscape was almost liberated from the all-encompassing fog, apart from slowly thinning banks of it on the far horizon. Birdsong cheered him, as it always did, and despite a slight headache from the night's immoderation. A single robin landed on a crenellation, turning to face him, its tiny eyes regarding him with mild interest. It chirped merrily and flew off, its day almost over.

He stood to fetch the canvass covering but, as he prepared to throw it over the telescope he stopped. What was that? A faint mumbling, or was it a wind rising...or a storm? To the east, he thought.

 Looking in the direction it seemed to come from he fell back against the wall, shaken by a strange distortion of the landscape. Terrain he knew to be almost unvaryingly green, apart from trees, hedges, and rocks interspersed throughout, had long lines and wide patches of red. Blue, white and grey too...but predominantly red. This alien splash of colour was in continuous motion, like a swarm of multi-hued insects on a stone.

His heart thumping, his hands shaking like the leaves of a wind-blown- tree, he threw down the canvass and reached for the telescope. Settling it on the tripod he felt a rush of urgency.

What are those blobs on the landscape?

Facing it eastward he adjusted the eyepiece, which had been set for faraway stellar objects, rotating and refocusing. The circular field of vision swayed and trembled. He steadied the device, moving it slowly. His heart missed a beat and a deep fear percolated his head, filtering down through his entire body. Sweat banished the winter chill from every pore.

Wagons, carts, and coaches were trundling noiselessly along the roads.

The shape-shifting red blob against the green backdrop resolved itself into soldiers...marching in line, carrying muskets...mostly behind the wagons but some alongside them....others carried long pikes.

Heads bowed, the pike-men appeared to be singing...or praying?

He saw a short man, or was it a boy, banging on a drum.

On either side of the soldiers helmeted horsemen, in leather coats and shining black boots, were riding at a leisurely pace...hundreds of them.

The lines of red seemed to stretch to the far horizon, but how near to Callan were they? Five miles, four possibly. *My God. They must be coming along the roads.* But hundreds of them were crossing fields too and climbing ditches...He saw two men battering down a hedge with...sticks... no, pikes.

To either side of the red column he focused on white, grey and blue uniformed men, also brandishing pikes and muskets. Others appeared to be in civilian clothing, or at least didn't have a distinct military appearance. They carried what looked like pots and flagpoles on their shoulders.

He'd heard of the uniform. *Venetian Red* it was called.

He increased the magnification slightly. More horrors: a cannon being pulled by three horses, and oxen pulling six or seven more artillery pieces behind it. Yet more weaponry was coming into focus beyond these, obscured slightly by the remnants of the dissipating fog.

He saw the lips of men in spirited motion and the strange murmuring sound of the approaching horde had grown louder, though still could only be heard by listening intently. He spied a yellow banner held by two men in black wearing broad-brimmed hats and tawny orange sashes around their waists: "The Lord will smite his enemies!" it proclaimed in block lettering.

A face came into sharp focus. It stared coldly through a grilled helmet. The man's breastplate gleamed in the waning sun. Ranks of similarly clad troops appeared in his field of vision. Others, who lacked helmets or body armour, had eyes of steel. Their stride was choreographed, assured. They seemed driven by an unearthly fervour.

As he looked, he strained to hear their faraway voices, but still just heard that dull murmur, though a little louder now.

In place of pikes or guns some carried long sticks or rods that they gripped tightly and fiercely. Clusters of women attired in that dreary black Puritan garb were on the move too. Some of them carried baskets. Servants? Nurses? Even their lips moved feverishly.

The more he looked and swept the horizon the larger this ghastly blot on the landscape seemed to become. He felt transfixed to the spot, impelled to stand and stare, helplessly... in thrall at the swelling legions.

Their lips never stopped moving as they pounded the earth in their relentless march towards Callan.

He forced himself to pull away. *The bell of St. Mary's was to alert the town...it's not ringing...so nobody else has seen this. Must get the word out. Peter....*

He dropped the telescope. Pulling his habit up around his ankles, he raced down the steps, trying frantically not to trip over his swishing garb.

Running to the Priory he spluttered and roared: "Peter! Peter! They're coming. I've seen them...!"

*

Marianne made way for the soldiers. She was about to descend the stairway of the castle when she heard the thud of footfalls. Since moving in they seemed to have become over-attached to Mark, continuously barging in to him with their complaints and requests.

Some wanted his assurance that the letters they'd sent to their wives would reach them. He couldn't be sure they would. He wasn't sure of anything, with the entire country in turmoil and a battle for Callan possibly hours away. But she'd smiled when she heard him reassure the men that their wives would know that their brave husbands were doing their duty for Ireland. He hadn't answered their question. He couldn't without lying, or shattering morale.

The musty air of the castle had bristled with tension since confirmation came that the invaders had been spotted just a few miles from the town. The church bell had sounded the alarm. Mark didn't seem too fazed by the news. He reckoned that the enemy would have to stay put until the following day at least as it would be unusual for an army to commence a siege at night. And darknbess was only an hour or two away.

Every soldier she saw was on edge. None of them wanted to be here. They'd felt invulnerable in Butler Castle, with its immensely thick walls, abundant provisions, and more than a thousand defenders. They felt out of place and a great deal less secure at Skerry's.

Five of them brushed past her, caps in hands, to see Mark, who was making amendments to his will beside the fire. He'd jested darkly about that earlier, speculating as to whether his wishes

284

concerning the disposal of his lands and estate would be respected by whoever took charge in Westmeath a few weeks hence. He bid the five soldiers sit at the table and went to join them, offering ale and wine to them.

Ear cocked, she couldn't hear any more footsteps so she skipped down before someone else decided to pester or petition her husband. There wasn't room for more than one person to pass another on the stairway, unless both were exceptionally lean.

Passing the second floor the sound of singing and nervous laughter filtered through the half-open door, which creaked on its hinges. On the ground floor women were boiling huge pots of water, assisted by a local timber merchant who'd brought a barrel of pitch to the castle.

The women greeted Marianne cheerily. She had introduced them to basic defensive tactics and they had great faith in her, they'd said, though whether this was justified she had no idea. Throwing stones and heaving rocks about unmolested in the fields was far removed from what they might face in the coming hours or days.

The merchant had supplied the pitch in the understanding that this was a typical weapon used to ward off a siege. Mark had tried to deter him, saying it might be a greater threat to those inside the castle than to any attacker, but several soldiers standing by disagreed. He relented and accepted that they needed everything they could get their hands on to throw at the enemy, if there was a battle.

And it was that big IF that had everyone on tenterhooks because, although the invaders were perilously close to Callan, Mark had yet to receive orders from the Governor.

For a full week rumours had swept the town that he'd surrender, but when Mark queried this just three days ago Sir Robert had dismissed the "very idea" with a snort. That was according to Corporal Molloy, who'd witnessed Sergeant Lynch broaching the subject with the Governor, who appeared to be more fixated on his pinch of snuff than his eagerly awaited make-or-break pronouncement.

The cavalry officer and militia leader had made their views known to the Governor, the Corporal also reported to Mark. They would not, they told him across that abnormally long table of his, contemplate surrender whatever the Governor decided.

That defiant stance could have delayed the Governor's decision, Mark believed. The man didn't want a mutiny on his hands. The Mayor, or ex-Mayor as he was now, and the former Corporation members, had been fluttering about like headless chickens trying to ascertain if Callan was to yield to Cromwell or fight him. They couldn't get an answer either.

Poor old Edward Comerford was a nervous wreck, all authority stripped from him by a military Governor who hadn't the slightest interest in what became of the town or its people.

Marianne stepped out into West Street: Soldiers everywhere...on the street, along the footpaths. A few had climbed unto roofs. Men peered from the top windows of houses, guns at the ready, or resting beside them.

No citizens to be seen, apart from a small band of militia; a motley bunch in their working or Sunday clothes wielding wildfowler guns, and muskets that looked even more cumbersome than the matchlock ones that the soldiers held. They mooched up and down the street as if on sentry duty.

The soldiers were all armed... with muskets, pikes, pistols, or swords. Looking back she saw more of them looking down from the castle battlements, where they stood checking their weapons.

No sign of Cathy. Not that she wanted her here in the castle. Probably with her employer in North Street, hoping their tavern will be left alone if the worst happens. Not a realistic hope, she feared, if a fraction of what Mark had heard of the fate of other resisting towns was to be credited. She prayed her friend would be safe.

How likely was the castle to be able to withstand an attack? Mark said one could never predict the outcome of such a clash, but he'd done everything he could to prepare. Last night the soldiers had tested the openings in the floors and were satisfied that they could with ease either shoot, or pour pitch down on, anyone beneath if the attackers entered the castle and progressed from floor to floor.

Mark hoped that the invaders would be repulsed before they could gain access to the town. Butler Castle with its strong garrison would be difficult to capture. Possibly Skerry's would not even figure in the fighting. And the cavalry was well-equipped, well organized and blessed with high morale. Yes. Callan had a real fighting chance...*if* the Governor opted to let it fight.

Marianne closed her eyes and inhaled the relatively clean air of the street. There was dust, and the stench of a burst drain-not so bad in winter. But it was better than the increasingly stifling atmosphere in the castle.

She walked to the end of the street, eliciting goodwill from the soldiers who knew her as the Captain's wife. Most of the soldiers had greenish uniforms, though of different shades, and a few displayed on their chests or arms the Confederate infantry emblem of a St Patrick's White Cross enclosed by a red circle on a sea-green background. Others wore cloth or bronze harp symbols.

One unusually elegant man with a saintly demeanor, whose uniform was spotless, had a striking cloth or flag draped around his waist like a sash. It depicted the Virgin Mary in purple and red gown clinging to the infant Jesus clad in lily white. She was crushing the serpent under her feet. The pale blue background incorporated an old Irish war cry.

Unlike the other soldiers who wore woolen caps or no head covering, this man sported a feathered tricorn. Though undoubtedly an Irish soldier he resembled one of those Cavalier types that fought for the King against parliament.

The Cross in the Town Square had hundreds of rags and ribbons of every hue tied or pinned to it. Each of them, Marianne knew, represented a plea to the crucified wooden image to protect them from harm. More than a dozen women knelt at the Cross, rosary beads dangling in front of them. They keened as they would at a wake, but their offering, she thought; had an air of hopelessness to it.

She wondered if the people of Wexford and Drogheda had also knelt in prayer.

*

Back inside the castle half an hour later, Marianne was glad of another chance to leave the cramped living quarters. On all three floors troops swore, drank, played dice, or discussed the upcoming challenge in hushed, evasive tones. The general consensus was that the enemy would arrive at the gates shortly, but wouldn't issue a final surrende demand until next morning.

A woman had called, and awaited her at the entrance. Corporal Molloy had helpfully held open the iron door for Marianne. She stepped outside.

"Cathy! What brings you here? Have you finished at the *Sign of the Helmet*? Or did you get time off?"

Cathy stood shivering, a black cloak wrapped tightly around her. She'd lost weight. *Overworked, probably.* But her countenance had changed too. Her eyes seemed to look beyond Marianne and the castle behind her, into some faraway place.

"I've a two-hour break so I thought I'd better come and tell you...I'm leaving Callan tonight and I won't be able to see you again until...until, well...after the battle."

Marianne motioned Molloy to leave them and led Cathy away towards the Cross. "Let's talk about it somewhere quiet...I think *Andy's Fancy Cookhouse* is still open."

They had to swerve in and out between the constant stream of soldiers and militia on West Street. They blocked street and footpaths alike. Some greeted her, doffing their caps with an "afternoon, Mrs. Gegan" or "the Captain's a great man, missus", all of them ignoring Cathy.

Marianne acknowledged each with a thin smile or a nod. She had an overpowering sense of these civic pleasantries and small courtesies fading. They'd been fizzling out as the Day of Reckoning approached.

In the Town Square men perched on ladders were washing the Cross, water splashing from buckets. "Preparing it for Saint Brigid's Day", Marianne noted.

"Oh God, Marianne, I hope the saint will save us!" Cathy lisped; the first words she'd uttered since they left the castle entrance. East Street was less congested but soldiers still managed to obstruct the two women, eyeing them curiously before stepping aside to let them pass. Some of them had muskets slung over their shoulders or swords unsheathed, already fired up for action.

She caught the whiff of whiskey from a group that caroused from one side of the street to the other, humming a patriotic tune.

The East Street Stocks and Pillory were empty. The impending crisis had forced the deferral of punishments, though the district judge had pledged that the backlog, however lengthy, would be cleared once Cromwell had been thrashed.

Marianne felt a tingle of relief to see the cookhouse still open. A door sign declared it would close next day, due to "the uncertain military situation." Marianne thought that a bit of an understatement. Some people in town, she'd heard, treated the upcoming challenge as if it were a shower of rain that they just needed to shelter from for a while before getting on with their lives. War wasn't like that, as Mark never tired of reminding her. The door notice went on to thank "Andy's loyal customers."

All but one of the tables was occupied. They headed straight for it, and Andy shouted from the counter: "What'll ye have, ladies?"

"Two mugs of strong coffee, Andy." Marianne hadn't bothered to ask Cathy what she wanted. It was always coffee. Settling herself at the table Cathy pulled off her cloak. A blazing peat fire had banished the cold and gave her face a gentle luminescence.

People at other tables, mostly men, stared for a few seconds at the newcomers before resuming their confabs.

The steaming mugs arrived and Marianne poured milk into hers. "Well?" she asked, passing the jug to Cathy.

Cathy took a sip and raised her head guiltily. She spoke slowly, hesitantly. "The *Sign of the Helmet,* like a lot of establishments in town, Marianne, will be closing soon...maybe a day or two from now. My boss is packing everything and moving to stay with relatives...in a safer place. It's a farm and he asked me if I'd like to move there too. He says he and his wife will need someone to do housework and some jobs on the farm...."

"So you agreed to go?"

Cathy took a deep breath and bit her lip. "Well...yes...but there's more. You see...Marianne, I've fallen in love!"

Marianne spilled coffee on the table. No need to wipe it off. It disappeared into a splintering crack. The ancient rickety table resembled a map of Ireland with all the rough bits included.

This was unexpected. If Cathy hadn't shown an interest in men back home why did she bother with romance down here?

"It's Charlie, the boss's son. He was friendly from the day I started work at the tavern. But then...he told me one evening as I washed the floor that I was...the loveliest woman he'd ever seen ...since the day he was born."

"Whew...that's a compliment...if somewhat overstated..."

Cathy laughed. "I reddened so much I nearly turned into a strawberry...I felt my insides melting...I never felt anything like it. But that was nothing compared to what happened next. Oh God, Marianne, he knelt down...I was on the floor, shaking like a leaf, with the bucket of mucky water...and he pressed his lips to mine. Not rough or anything. Oh, It felt heavenly...I'd seen people kiss, but I never imagined... it was ...divine."

Marianne stopped her. "And Cathy....have you...gone further? Did you have...what back In Westmeath they call *a joining of giblets*?"

Cathy's mouth dropped open. A mixture of shock and surprise screwed up her face. "No, of course not; Charlie is a devout Catholic. His older brother is a priest somewhere in Cork. Every day after that first kiss he fondled me whenever he saw me scrubbing the floor and his father wasn't present. But he says he can't wait for us to kneel before an altar with rings on our fingers instead of canoodling on the tavern floor..."

Marianne sighed. "So...you're leaving Callan, then..."

"Oh, until this crazy war is over. I'm terribly sorry, Marianne. Of course it's selfish of me in a way. I came here to be with you, just as you wanted to be by Mark's side. And now I'm scarpering .God, I'm sorry Marianne...but... this love thing is like a sickness. I can't shake it off. It's taken me over completely. Now I understand why people do mad things because of it. I even succumbed to jealousy when a man's wife smiled at Charlie the other night. He was serving her in the tavern. Just a silly grin but I hated her...only for an instant, mind...but I swear I could have killed her. I swear I could. I hated her more than...more than I hate Cromwell!"

"But then Cromwell isn't competing with you for Charlie's affections."

Cathy giggled. Marianne took her hand and squeezed it. "Don't think you're letting me down by leaving Callan. I was thinking of your safety when I begged you not to come here in the first place. So...yes... I'm glad you'll be safer."

She paused, looking past Cathy at soldiers drilling outside. They carried pikes and marched in step. Other customers pointed at them.

"Do take care, Cathy. Soon, nowhere in this town will be safe."

***

26

We arrived outside the walls of Callan yesterday evening, having spent several hours hanging about in fields and on roads close to the town. With darkness approaching, we wanted to avoid any contact with the enemy until the following day.

Dawn hadn't yet broken when we started moving again, and the walls were only faintly visible in the gloaming, but Colonel Reynolds lost no time in delivering his ultimatum to the Governor. We already knew what his answer would be but this formal approach was deemed necessary to avoid any misunderstanding.

So a parley was arranged. A low-ranking enemy officer emerged from the stately Butler Castle, hand-held torches flanking him. He spoke flatly: "The garrison will, as you request, depart, having disarmed, taking only baggage and food pouches with them."

The Governor had kept his word. All the soldiers had left the castle within an hour. I was privileged to watch them as they slouched out and down that long street, which was pitch black except in spots brightened by street-lamps. Their flags and ensigns were drained of dye in that dark walk of shame. Not one of them glanced at us. I counted eleven hundred. There can't be many more defenders...

After first light we began to cautiously examine the walls. They appeared to have been patched up from the look of them: different stonework in parts, and big slabs of wood and metal replacing missing stones in places.

No room for complacency though. The walls might still have to be breached if a total surrender of remaining enemy forces in the town isn't confirmed soon. The offer of safe passage out of town for the Butler Castle garrison doesn't apply to anyone within the walls who opts to fight.

With the sun beginining to shine benevolently on us, we could relax a little and get our bearings, without having to watch and listen for the slightest hint of rebels skulking in the night.

We were fortunate to find a large grassy common to encamp on, not far from the town's South Gate. Orders came quickly and we followed the mounted officers and columns of horsemen as they trotted cautiously onto the common, their carbines loaded and ready to fire at the first sign of hostility.

The chaplain on his white mare read aloud from his Bible, adding some words of his own to sacred scripture. He has a voice that travels far, and it pierces your head, filtering its way into your soul: He thundered "we are but ten miles from the lair of the beast, of the papist Antichrist...that seat of deepest treason...the accursed City of Kilkenny. Oh Lord, who smote the vile sinners of Sodom and Gomorrah, let not our brave warriors be thwarted by this town that lies before us. Let victory be ours!"

God seems to have heard him because we proceeded unchallenged. No trace of the enemy here, though that could be because he has concentrated the residue of his depleted strength inside those walls.

As ordered, I had my musket ready. I'd only to attach the lighted match and within seconds I could, God willing, take down any savage I caught sight of. Every other musketeer was similarly on maximum alert. Flanking us the pike-men marched, equally prepared for action. Their eyes darted from side to side, grim determination scrunching their faces. Officers bawled their commands and we went in whichever direction they bid us to go.

For several minutes I had an unpleasant and almost panicky sensation of bedlam...of everything dissolving into chaos. Flags, banners, and drums swished past and around me, helmeted and capped heads appeared and vanished from sight in a flurry of motion...curses and shouts swept the ranks...a drummer was bending to retrieve a shoe that had fallen off. A soldier swore as he dropped a powder bag. Another man was already crunching it into the earth.

Swords rattled in their scabbards, bandoliers clanged off each other, and muskets clattered as men collided in the developing melee. We needed every inch of this spacious common to accommodate our enormous contingent. It was getting crowded, like a busy street on a particularly hectic market day.

But the officers had no intention of letting chaos reign. We, the musketeers and pike-men, gradually settled into place, standing to *attention in groups at one end of the grassy stretch...the cavalry and dragoons were out of sight...but I'd forgotten just how many non-combatants we have with us.*

Wagons and carts laden with pots, pans, and cauldrons rolled along the grass, and lines of men who resembled London street merchants trudged lazily in their wake. Groups of men had already set about pitching tents. Others were busily digging into the cold hard earth with picks and shovels, officers howling at them to work faster. Though not in uniform, these labourers are answerable to the army.

The common had been bare prior to our arrival apart from a few makeshift cattle and sheep pens, and scatterings of feathers. It's a godsend for an encamping army. One end of the vast stretch is partly fringed by a line of ancient leafless trees. We'll have to watch that...enemies familiar with the lay of the land could hide behind that woody screen.

There's a peculiar landmark here that at first sight struck me a possible impediment, though a minor one, to our freedom of movement: A high grassy mound located close to the trees.

But I was quickly reminded that it could in fact be another answer to our prayers: If an artillery bombardment of the town or walls becomes necessary, the mound will provide an excellent elevation for our cannons, increasing their efficacy. Given the weakness of the enemy in this town, few of us expect that'll be necessary, but we have to be prepared...

From where I sit writing this I can see the South Gate's two tall stone towers and the wary sentries watching us. The vast field is filling up quickly...now you'd hardly see the grass with the growing multitude of uniformed men and civilian helpers standing, sitting, crouching, or even lying on it.

The cannons I see are trundling in from the road... light and heavy artillery. Culverins, drakes, semi-culverins, and that ugly squat mortar contraption that I've yet to see used in battle. They say it's deadly at close range but not very accurate. The wagon drivers are flogging the horses to move faster. I hope the ground isn't too muddy or the cannons will get bogged down again like they did near Waterford.

We got permission to rest and I plumped to earth from near-exhaustion, disentangling my heavy-laden bandolier and laying aside my musket. We'd been quick-marching to reach Callan before the enemy had reason to expect us.

I dozed off for what seemed like just a few seconds but was probably longer. The smell of cooking distracted me, and seemed to infuse new life and vitality into all of us, including the near-exhausted and sleeping. It hadn't taken long for the fires to get going and the sheep carcasses seized from a farm outside Callan to be roasted. The farmer wasn't too happy, and even less so when Sergeant Frampton left him hanging from a beech tree; his wife berating us in that frightful language of theirs.

A cook was calling. What a lovely note, sweeter than birdsong. Up rose men who'd been semi-prostrate and snoring loudly; hundreds queued to receive their platters of mutton stew which smelt and tasted delicious to men who hadn't eaten for twelve hours. Only the soldiers guarding the cannons remained at their posts. We're forever on the alert for enemy saboteurs who could emerge from anywhere to waylay us.

A surprise awaited me when my turn came to receive my ration. In addition to the stew I was handed two large biscuits. I hadn't seen or tasted a biscuit for weeks. I devoured them before I sat to eat the meal.

Back in England I took biscuits for granted, like so much else. Not here in this sodden disease-ridden land where I'm told people eat muck and grass for breakfast in the wilder parts. We have a bounden duty to tame these savages.

I heard that a message is to be delivered by us to the enemy at the South Gate. That was two hours ago. We're still waiting for the formal wording of the surrender demand to be agreed upon. I marvel at why it should take so long to put a few words together: The issue is so clear-cut. I pray that Colonel Reynolds will expedite the process.

The prevailing sentiment here is that this town is assuredly about to fall, after the loss of almost its entire garrison. But as the minutes pass some of us are beginning to doubt. Common sense and logic dictate that they'll surrender. They've no choice. But who knows what tricks those papists might be up to?

The chaplain dismounted and traipsed about on the common, reading aloud from his prayerbook. "The Lord will spite down the papist serpent and crush him into the mire!" he shouted, prompting *a chorus of "Amen" and "Halleluiah" , though not from the men who'd dozed off again, some crouching in the grass, clinging tightly to their muskets or pikes, or grasping their sword hilts even in sleep.*

The meal over, my thoughts again turn to this interminable delay: Why are the remaining forces not surrendering? We're prepared for action, as always, but we were assured that resistance was highly unlikely, with the Governor and the bulk of the defenders gone. Now, men are getting edgy, grumbling as they sit or stand in the grass.

I too have a feeling of mild foreboding when I contemplate that wall. The South Gate is still closed to us and those high towers begin to look menacing...

End of Book One

*

The story continues in

Effusion of Blood

Invaders - Book Two

*

Acknowledgments:

I'd like to thank the following people for their encouragement and insights: my brother Nicky, who died in September 2022. He had been helpful and supportive, drawing on his own knowledge of history and literature; Joe Kennedy, of Callan Heritage Society, whose writings on the Cromwellian era proved crucial to me. His map of mid-seventeenth century Callan served as a valuable guide; Frank Geoghegan of Frevanagh, County Westmeath, for information on his heroic ancestor, Mark McGeoghegan; Jim Murray, for advice about medical procedures in mid-17th century Ireland.

I'm grateful to Marianne Lyons-Kelly, of the Kilkenny Heritage Walkers, who has an encyclopedic grasp of everything related to the county's heritage and antiquities; Historian Philip Lynch, for his valuable advice on aspects of mid-17th century Irish history; the Somers family for information on the bridge gate house. Part of it survived as part of Somer's pub; Journalist Jim Rhatigan for publicity in the *Kilkenny Press* online newspaper, and Kilkenny County Library, for its valuable selection of books and documents relating to the Cromwellian era.

I thank the late Tim Kennedy and Eddie Nolan; teachers at the CBS School in Callan that I attended in the 1970s. Tim's approach to teaching history was enlightened and inspirational; while Eddie Nolan did more than any other teacher at the school to highlight aspects of local history. Their positive influence helped to shape the book.

Sean Nikken designed the book cover. It incorporates a detail from the painting *La Défense du château* by Christian Sell.

A lot of research went into the two volumes of *Invaders*. I found the following works especially useful and informative:

Cromwell in Callan: an article by Joe Kennedy in the Old Kilkenny Review (1984)

The History and Antiquities if the Diocese of Ossory: Canon Carrigan. Volume Three.

Exploring Irish Castles: Pat Dargan, Nonsuch Publishing (2009)

Cromwell: An Honourable Enemy, Tom Reilly, Brandon Press (1999)

Cromwell, Our Chief of Men: Antonia Fraser, Weidenfeld & Nicholson; New Edition (2008)

Confederation: Noel Murphy, Togail Press (2021)

The New Model Army-Agent of Revolution: Ian Gentles, Yale University Press (2022)

God's Executioner: Oliver Cromwell and the Conquest of Ireland: Micheál Ó Siochrú, Faber & Faber; (Aug. 2008)

The English Civil War and After, 1642-1658: R. H. Parry (Editor), University of California Press (1970)

The English Civil War: a people's history: Diane Purkiss, Harper Perennial (2007)

Confederate Ireland, 1642–1649: Micheál Ó Siochrú, Four Courts Press

The Bloody Bridge: and Other Papers Relating to the Insurrection of 1641 (Sir Phelim O'Neill's Rebellion): Thomas Fitzpatrick , Sealy, Bryers and Walker

Callan 800, 1207-2007: History and Heritage (companion volume): Callan Heritage Society (2013)

Cavaliers and Roundheads: Bob Moulder, Tarquin Publications (1997)

The Chief Butlers of Ireland and the House of Ormond: An Illustrated Genealogical Guide: John Kirwan, Irish Academic Press (2023)

Warfare in the Seventeenth Century: John Childs, W&N (2001)

***

About the Author

John Fitzgerald is a freelance journalist and writer living in Callan, County Kilkenny, Ireland. He has had hundreds of articles (news reports, opinion pieces, and human interest stories) published in local newspapers in Ireland and in the Irish Examiner's former County Kilkenny supplement.

Apart from his latest publications *Invaders* (Book One) and *Effusion of Blood* (Invaders-Book Two), he is the author of nine books dealing with local history and heritage: *Kilkenny-People Faces Places* (2002), *Callan in the Rare Old Times* (2003), *Callan through the Mists of Time* (2004), *Kilkenny-A Blast from the Past* (2005), *Are We Invaded Yet?* (2008), *The Nore view Folk Museum-a chronicle of real people's lives* (ebook-2015), and *Kilkenny Pubs and Bars* (paperback and ebook), 2015.

His memoir *Bad Hare Days* (paperback and ebook-2009) is s stranger than fiction autobiographical account of his involvement in a wildlife protection campaign.

He has authored two previous novels: *Escape from Grievous Faults* (2016); set in Ireland's grim industrial school era, and *Time to Stop Running* (2018), the fantasy story of an Irish hare who sets out to free his fellow runners from a gang of cruel humans.

***

Printed in Great Britain
by Amazon

28757930R00165